Guardians of Hallowed Ground
═Gettysburg═

Thomas J. Ball

I hope you enjoy my first book.
The journey begins!

Tom Ball

Strategic Book Group

Copyright © 2010
All rights reserved—Thomas J. Ball

No part of this book may be reproduced or transmitted in any form or by any means, graphic, electronic, or mechanical, including photocopying, recording, taping, or by any information storage retrieval system, without the permission, in writing, from the publisher.

Strategic Book Group
P.O. Box 333
Durham, CT 06422
www.StrategicBookClub.com

ISBN: 978-1-60976-560-6

Printed in the United States of America

Book Design: Arlinda Van, Dedicated Business Solutions, Inc.

Dedication

This book is dedicated to all the people out there that have an idea, but no time or resources to put it to paper. I have to thank my wonderful wife Carley, for allowing me to take time from our business to write this novel and for pushing me to get it done. I would also like to thank my great friend Connie Thompson, for helping me with awesome ideas and guidance with the technical writing of the novel.

If you are tired of worn out plots, subject matter that goes nowhere or want to learn something while reading a great novel, I am sure you will enjoy Guardians of Hallowed Ground. There is no sex, murder, zombies or cussing. Only a well known part of American history with a new and innovative twist.

CONTENTS

1. Five Amigos 1
2. All in a day's work..9
3. It'll blow your socks off....................................21
4. Storm clouds ahead..31
5. The other side...39
6. Putting the clues together...............................52
7. Following the dust cloud.................................63
8. Past meets present..73
9. Believe it or not..87
10. A ride into history 94
11. Day 1—Strategy versus might 105
12. The perfect disguises..................................112
13. Battles on two fronts 120
14. Fixing it at all costs.....................................130
15. Wagon train moving out..............................141
16. A peaceful town, for now 147
17. An old friend returns...................................157
18. The story takes a wrong turn......................165
19. Day 2—A regiment of five...........................169
20. Little Big Top 181
21. Unleashing hell 190
22. Hold the line...199

23. Bayonet charge of the 20th Maine..........................206

24. Blood on their hands 216

25. An Omen 223

26. Day 3—Anything goes 233

27. Tompkins to the rescue..244

28. Pickett's Charge..253

29. Protecting the flank 265

30. A glimpse of normality 273

31. Draper's ghost 281

32. The road home..293

Chapter 1

Five Amigos

It was a rare occasion when the five-man team was in the position to relax while on duty. They were more comfortable crouching in fox holes or standing behind 50-caliber machine guns. Each of them had been deployed to hostile areas around the world since they were in their twenties. From the Vietnam War to the Iraqi War, they had seen it all.

Now their expertise would be used to showcase new weapons and battle techniques. Of course there would always be the "special deployment" when the military couldn't accomplish the mission by conventional means. But that was the last thing on their minds as they reclined around the campfire. Tomorrow they would be on their way to an advanced weaponry exhibition at Fort Cox in Ohio.

As the men lay on makeshift beds on the ground, it was eerily quiet—almost as if they were waiting for the next round of artillery to shatter the peaceful June night. Staring up into the sky was Navy Seal Commander Bourque. His steely grey eyes and large square jaw matched his massive physique perfectly.

"What does a night like this remind you guys of most?" asked Bourque, quietly breaking the silence. "It reminds me of my first deployment to Vietnam. The sky at night there was so full of stars and so peaceful, kind of made you forget the hell you were in."

To his right lay Green Beret Specialist Santana. "I think it reminds me of a mission I was on in Nicaragua," he explained. "I was setting up on top of this mountain, for a quick snipe job on a drug lord. He was supposed to be there within a couple hours, but didn't show up for almost twenty four. As I lay there in my Ghillie, I felt like I must've been the only one on the planet to see that many stars from one small mountain. Kinda made me feel real small and insignificant."

If you could see Santana you would not believe this came out of his mouth. He was young, tall and muscular, yet he had the kind of face that told you he was a veteran of many battles. His military haircut and demeanor would lead you to believe he would rather shoot at the stars than look at them.

"Not me," came quickly from Army Ranger Colonel Bates, who was directly across the fire from Santana. "Every time I get the chance to look at the stars, I thank God that I'm alive to see them. After all the near misses I've been in, I know the only reason for the stars is to remind us of our mortality and that the things we were put here to do are not small, but affect a great number of people. Remember the job in Kosovo, boys? We may have only saved that one village, but the families and people in that region will remember what we did forever."

Bates was older than the rest of the men, but did not show his age at all. His short stocky frame and gray hair were giveaways, but the way he carried himself nullified any thought of him being fifty-years-old.

"I don't know if these stars remind me of anything other than being in hot, stinky Tennessee," quipped CIA Special Ops Agent Draper.

Laughter erupted from around the fire as this comment reminded them of where they really were. The pudgy, funny-looking Draper continued.

"I try not to look back at the battles we fought in, but look forward to the battles we will be fighting in. I know that may seem kinda weird, but I've always believed that if you look to the future and think about different scenarios you might encounter, you will be better prepared for anything they might throw at you."

"There's that old CIA brainwashing crap you talk about over and over," sneered Santana.

"It might be crap to you Santana," replied Draper. "But thinking ahead has got me through a lot of tight spots."

The air became quiet once again. Everyone turned their eyes to Weapons Specialist and Battle Historian Tompkins. No one had noticed he had his nose buried in a book the whole time they were talking.

"Tompkins," shouted Draper. Tompkins eyes rose from his book in surprise. "What you guys need?" was his reply.

Draper quickly asked, "What could you be reading that would possibly be more interesting than your four amigos here?"

"Reading tea leaves is more interesting than you four bozos," replied Tompkins with a smirk. "But if you really want to know, I am reading about the most important battle in American History, Gettysburg. We should be passing through there on our way to Virginia, after our demo at Fort Cox. I thought it might be kind of cool to see the reenactment of the battle."

"Hey Bates, didn't you fight in the Civil War?" joked Draper. Laughter once again broke out around the fire. Bates added to the banter as he replied, "The only civil war I ever fought in was my first marriage." This reply even made Bourque laugh a little. "Tompkins, why don't you give us a little info on Gettysburg," asked Bourque. "I was never one for history and I'm sure your voice will help us all go to sleep."

"Sure thing Commander, anything to enlighten you guys' world," replied Tompkins. The men settled back onto their bedrolls waiting for Tompkins to begin.

"The Battle of Gettysburg took place on July 1, 2 and 3 in 1863. Bates—you were there," began Tompkins to a burst of laughter. "The battle was the turning point for the North, as they had been getting beaten up pretty badly up to this point. The South was led by General Robert E. Lee . . . that's not the car in *The Dukes of Hazzard*, Draper. Santana threw a rock at Draper as they all laughed at his expense. Tompkins cleared his voice to gain their attention once again.

"The North was commanded by General George Meade," he began again. "The thing to keep in mind is that the South had 75,000 men and the North had 90,000 men. That's kind of surreal when you think about the number of troops in the battles we've fought," continued Tompkins. "That's a total of 165,000 men. The reason the battle is remembered so well is that it was the bloodiest battle ever fought on American soil. In three days of battle over 50,000 men were killed or were missing. Out of the 50,000 men killed 28,000 were from the South and 23,000 were from the North."

"Hey Tompkins," interrupted Santana. "Was this all just because of slavery?"

"A lot of people think that it was all about slavery," replied Tompkins. "But it was about other things too. People in the South wanted slavery of course. But they felt that the United States Government had no right to take their slave's away. Since the Government was formed after the States, they felt that each State should govern whether or not slavery was legal in their state. Why should a government in Washington tell people in Virginia what to do? They called it States Rights.

The newly formed Government also started taxing trade in the south. So, it brought back a lot of the same feelings as the Revolutionary War, in that why should people in Washington be able to tax people in another State? But I don't want to get into all the reasons why the War started."

As Tompkins began to sound more like a history teacher than the hardened military man he was, Bourque was right. They all began to feel their eyes getting heavy. Tompkins was kind of honored to teach these men about this great battle he knew so well. In truth, this was the fourth time he had read this particular book. He took great pride in knowing the history of America and how it became such a great country. He also thought the old adage of "knowing the blunders of our past, helps us to avoid them in the future," was very appropriate in today's world. So he continued.

"General Lee thought that if he invaded the North he could accomplish two things. One, he could get much needed supplies for his troops from the rich farmlands of Pennsylvania and also bring the armies of the North out into the open so he could destroy them and therefore threaten Washington. He knew General Grant was in Vicksburg, Virginia and would be forced to move to Washington to defend it. As he looked at a map, he found that several main roads converged at Gettysburg, so he thought that would be the best place to gather all of his military might. However, what he didn't know was that a much larger Union force from the North was already moving that way. Lee had three main commanders: General Ewell, General Longstreet and General A.P. Hill. Grant's counter to them was General Hooker and then eventually general Meade. As Lee moved his men North, they had several small skirmishes whenever they met forces from the North. These forces were usually much smaller and therefore no problem to defeat or scatter them. As they encountered these small forces, word eventually got to Hooker. He then began to converge all his forces towards Gettysburg. Back in them days, the eyes and ears of both sides was the cavalry - General Jeb Stuart from the South and General Buford from the North. Stuart's assignment was to move ahead of the main force and report back to Lee any movement of the enemy and their strength. He, however, took it on himself to move too far north and raid some towns and supply trains, which left Lee without proper knowledge of the Union forces or the type of land upon which they were about to begin a battle. The Northern Cavalry, led by General Buford, did what they were supposed to. On June 30, Buford rode into Gettysburg and saw how important the town was because of the intersections of the roads and the many high spots that would offer great defensive positions. Buford had in his charge 2,500 mounted cavalry. They were armed with Spencer Carbines, which were more accurate and could be loaded and fired more quickly than the traditional muzzleloaders of the infantry. Buford had seen Lee's forces moving that way and knew they would be there by morning. He set guards on the roads and in the heights. Then he informed Corp Commander General John Reynolds of the happenings and that he would need infantry support in the morning."

As these last soft words came from Tompkins lips, his eyes closed, his arms relaxed, and the book slipped out of his hands. The only noise around the campfire was the crackle of the fire and some light snoring.

The sound of whizzing shrapnel and explosions brought Tompkins to his feet.

"What the heck was going on?" he thought. He'd obviously slept past sunrise, and where was everyone? Instinctively he dove behind the nearest tree and heard the sounds of beating drums and hundreds of marching feet. The sound of drums baffled him. After a few minutes of listening, he then noticed a battalion of gray shabby soldiers, armed with long muskets, double-timing it down a dirt road towards him. At the end of the road were hundreds of clean blue-clad soldiers awaiting them. Tompkins' mind raced as he tried to comprehend this scene.

"Could I be in the middle of a Civil War reenactment somehow? Or am I dreaming?" As Tompkins tried to make some kind of sense of what he was seeing, three men in gray uniforms approached him from behind.

"Hands in the air friend," shouted one of the men. As Tompkins turned around, he noticed the dirty uniforms and faces. They had no shoes and he thought he heard a southern accent. He calmly felt for his sidearm and realized he was unarmed, so he slowly raised his hands in the air.

"What battalion are you with?" asked one of the men. "We don't recognize your uniform."

As Tompkins looked down at his own uniform, he was glad to see the camo pattern he was so used to. "I'm not in this war," explained Tompkins, "I'm passing through on my way to Washington."

"So you must be a Blue-Belly then," exclaimed another of the men. "And if that is the case, I'm afraid we're gonna havta shoot ya."

"Wait a minute," blasted Tompkins, pushing his hands higher in the air. The battle raging around them was now intensifying. Bullets were whizzing everywhere. Rounds of artillery were exploding and the cries of wounded men filled his ears. "I told you I am not in this war!" Tompkins shouted again.

As the men began to raise their muskets, Tompkins instinctively crouched and did a leg sweep, bringing the three men down on their backs. As quickly as the men were on their backs, Tompkins grabbed one of their muskets and pointed it at the men.

"Leave your weapons and run away," Tompkins loudly commanded.

As the men began to get up to run away, a deafening blast and burning metal rained all around them. Thinking quickly, Tompkins decided to run as fast as he could in the opposite direction of the fighting. As his flight took him further away from the noise, he slowed and turned. Bending over with his hands on his knees, he saw gray-clad men running in his direction. One of them stopped and fired a round towards Tompkins. Mesmerized by the smoke from the musket, he felt a sharp pain in his chest. He looked down and saw blood pouring out of a huge hole in his chest. He fell to the ground on his back, gasping for air. Just then two gray-clad men walked up and looked down at him. One of them took his musket with bayonet fixed and began to push the point of his bayonet into Tompkins' chest. Just as the metal of the bayonet began to penetrate his skin, the world turned black. Then he heard a familiar voice.

"Up and attem boys," shouted Bourque. Tompkins spun his head around as fast as possible to look for something else familiar. He gasped when he saw the other guys rubbing their eyes and stretching their muscles. It was a great feeling when he realized he had been dreaming. He closed his eyes and dropped his head back hard onto his sleeping bag.

Tompkins had always been told as a boy that you cannot die in your dreams, so there was nothing to fear in dreams, and that dreams sometimes are precursors to events that are yet to happen. It took him a few minutes to get his bearings back after this very unusual dream.

"Why did I die in my dream?" he asked himself. "And what could this mean for the future?" Tompkins brought his hands up to his face and rubbed hard. "It was just a dream so suck it up soldier and get moving," he told himself.

The dream was soon forgotten as they got on the road to Fort Cox. As the convoy of two Jeeps, one with a trailer, hit the road, Tompkins was surprised to hear Commander Bourque request more information on Gettysburg. He was actually shocked Bourque remembered anything from the night before. For the next three hours, Tompkins gave Bourque a pretty in-depth lesson on the battle and the area around Gettysburg.

With the other three men in the following Jeep, it was refreshing for both men to talk about something other than what was in the trailers and how the next exhibition was to be laid out. Time flew by as they talked about Gettysburg. Before either of the men knew it, they had reached Fort Cox. They had only forty-five minutes to get their equipment set up and the details of the exhibition worked out, so they began working on the task at hand and all other thoughts were soon forgotten.

Chapter 2

All in a day's work

"Ladies and gentlemen," the Base Commander began. "As you have witnessed from the first half of our Advanced Weaponry Exhibition, conventional arms are very useful and effective in modern warfare. We thought it might shed some light on advanced weaponry by showing you how our forefather's weapons were effective for their times. To demonstrate weapons that helped free our country from the tyranny of England during the Revolutionary War and kept our country from dividing during the Civil War, Weapons Specialist and Military Historian Tompkins will demonstrate and explain a firearm from those eras."

Specialist Tompkins walked across the stage and onto the firing line in front of the large crowd of well dressed men and women. As the eyes of the crowd followed Tompkins across the firing line, it was obvious he had spent a lot of time in the office, or at least reading books. His thin, yet muscular frame and round-wire glasses gave him a kind of "nerdy" look compared to the other soldiers assisting in the demonstration.

As he picked up the first weapon and began to load it, all perceptions of being a nerd were lost. His nimble fingers worked on the weapon as a craftsman works adeptly on a routine project.

"Senators and Ladies and Gentlemen," Tompkins light, yet demanding voice began. "The weapon I am holding before you now was a standard issue 50-caliber smooth-bore flintlock musket during the Revolutionary War and most of the American Civil War. Its effective range is approximately fifty yards. In the hands of a young or scared man, its effective range drops to perhaps thirty yards or less. In the hands of a Veteran soldier it could be fired two or three times in a minute."

Everyone in the audience leaned forward to get a good view of Tompkins as he began to load the musket.

"The first step in loading any flintlock or black powder rifle is to pour a pre-measured amount of black powder into the barrel." Tompkins looked like a modern day Davy Crockett as he reached into an old deerskin bag hanging on his side to retrieve his materials. "Once the powder has been poured into the barrel, you must apply a patch and ball to the end of the barrel." Tompkins reached into his bag and pulled out a white piece of cloth and a lead ball about the size of a marble. "The patch can be any type of cloth or paper. It was usually soaked in animal lard to make an airtight seal and also to make it easier to push the ball down the barrel. The bullet is made of lead." As Tompkins placed the patch and ball onto the end of the barrel, he extracted a wooden rod from under the barrel and with some effort rammed the ball and patch down the barrel and onto the powder. After a couple tamps, he quickly pulled the ram rod out of the barrel. A voice from the crowd interrupted the silence.

"Specialist Tompkins," rang the voice from the crowd. "From what we have just seen, you should be able to reload that weapon more than two or three times a minute." Tompkins eyes strained as he scanned the crowd to see where the question came from.

"Yes Senator, that may appear to be true," replied Tompkins. "But picture a boy of eighteen standing in a line. Bullets whizzing around him. Cannon fire exploding nearby, as men fall on both sides of him with the enemy only thirty yards in front of him. If he does remember to put the powder in before the patch and ball, his shaking hands and tear-filled eyes only hamper his ability to load and fire effectively. But a very good insight ... thank you, Sir," ended Tompkins with a bow of his head.

"Now," he began once again. "You must place a small piece of flint into the flint holder, located under the hammer and then make a small powder trail in the flash pan." He held the long weapon in the air so everyone could see. "When you pull the hammer back into firing position and pull the trigger, the hammer strikes the flint and makes a spark. The spark then rolls down the flash pan and ignites the powder in the pan, which then ignites the powder in the breech and the projectile is pushed out the barrel to the target. Some problems can occur with this type of weapon. First, the flint spark doesn't always ignite the powder, especially in the rain or damp air. That's where we get the expression, a flash in the pan. Next, the flint doesn't always make a spark. And finally, the barrels of these guns don't have rifling or grooves that spin the projectile; therefore, the chance of a true flight path is lessened and the odds of hitting your target are diminished." Tompkins eyes scanned the crowd to get a feel for their understanding of what he was trying to demonstrate. Everyone's face told him they understood the basics of what he was saying.

"This has been a quick overview of this weapon," he began. "As time went on, they did develop rifling for the barrels and used caps to produce the spark, instead of flint. Those were important advancements back then. If there are no questions, I will now fire this weapon at a target fifty yards down the firing range." Since there were no questions, Tompkins shouldered the rifle, aimed for a second and pulled the trigger. As the hammer struck the flint, there was a notable pause as the spark rolled to the powder in the flash pan and ignited it. It then ignited the powder in the breech. The weapon fired with a dull bang and a large cloud of smoke. When the smoke cleared there was a large hole in the target, about one inch outside of the bulls-eye. Tompkins then laid the weapon down and began to speak.

"This shot is effective in killing the enemy in any situation. As time went by, the barrels of these muskets received rifling. Rifling are grooves in the barrel that spin the projectile, giving it a more certain flight path. This gave these muskets an effective range of one hundred yards. The flint was replaced by a small primer cap that produced the spark, making the odds of igniting the powder in the breech much higher." Tompkins smiled as he scanned the crowd and then concluded.

"I hope this demonstration gives each of you a better idea of what advancements in weaponry technology can provide to the Armed Forces." As Tompkins ended his last word, he spun, grabbed an M16 from the table and quickly fired ten shots at the same target. Tompkins then lowered the weapon and dropped out the spent clip. He effortlessly moved down the range to the target, tore it off the holder and returned. "Sorry to startle you with that last burst of gunfire, but I wanted to prove a point," began Tompkins. He then held up the target for all to see. The bulls-eye was completely gone, with only the hole from the musket left.

With a smile on his face Tompkins said, "I was able to fire ten rounds with the M16 into the bulls-eye, run down range fifty yards and retrieve the target, in the same time it would have taken me to fire one round with the musket. Imagine how this weapon would have changed those wars fought on U.S. soil." Tompkins smile turned into a sly sneer as he said, "What we have to show you next will blow your socks off."

Specialist Tompkins quickly turned and walked toward the other four men standing at attention. Compared to Tompkins, the other men were perfect military specimens. Their squared jaws, muscular stature and stoic looks made you feel safe in their presence. As Tompkins fell into line at attention, he once again began to speak.

"The next part of the demonstration will not only persuade you to continue funding the research and testing of advanced weaponry, but will allow you to witness how American lives will be saved in future conflicts. The first advanced weapon in our demonstration is the 10 millimeter sniper rifle with guidance tipped ammunition and micro telescopic optics. I would like to turn the demonstration over to Navy Seal Commander Bourque."

When Tompkins finished speaking, the largest member of the group stepped forward. His stature was more like a professional wrestler than a Navy Seal. His long powerful gait quickly moved him across the range to the front of the audience. In a low, yet smooth, voice he began.

"I am Navy Seal Commander Bourque." As he began to speak it was obvious he was not a man of many words, yet his demeanor commanded your attention. "My service record consists of one tour during Desert Storm, two tours in Afghanistan and three tours in Iraq. I am trained in the use of all military weapons and tactics. I am a Black Belt in Karate and versed in all types of hand-to-hand combat. Today I am going to demonstrate the M10 sniper rifle."

Bourque reached forward and lifted the M10. His forearm muscles rippled with tension as it rose effortlessly off the table. The M10 appeared to be a normal sized rifle, until you took into consideration the massive size of Bourque. In the hands of a average person it would look like a giant caricature of a rifle. Bourque once again began to speak.

"The M10 is a very large and heavy weapon. It needs to be to accomplish its mission. Because of its length and weight, it has very little recoil. The M10 is designed to deliver a very large projectile up to one mile with pinpoint accuracy." He next held up the bullet that was designed to do this. "This is the M10 bullet," he began. "It is much larger than the normal sniper rifle bullet. In each bullet, there is a tiny computer chip that is used to guide the bullet to the locked-on target. This bullet is very similar to the Tomahawk Missile, in that they use the same guidance system."

Bourque then lifted the M10 rifle to his shoulder and peered through the scope. "Once I look through the scope and locate the target, I pull the trigger once. This brings up a guidance grid in the scope. Just like a video game played by your children, the grid locks on to the target. I then fire the weapon. Through the use of the guidance system, the bullet locks on to the target until the target is struck. The target can move in any direction at any speed and still be eliminated. The M10 is capable of firing one round every six seconds. The guidance system will reset itself after six seconds."

As Bourque paused during his descriptions of the rifle, it was most clear he was not comfortable speaking to large groups of people. His short to-the-point descriptions let the crowd know he knew the weapon well, but was not interested in the technology that was used to make it perform.

"The M10 magazine holds 10 rounds," continued Bourque. "This allows the M10 to eliminate ten targets per minute from one magazine." Bourque then lowered the weapon and addressed the audience. "I will now fire the M10 at the flashing light down range approximately one mile away." The audience sat up in their seats and strained to see a barely visible light flashing down the range. "I realize you can't see the target because it is so far away," announced Bourque with a laugh. "We have the light flashing so you have an idea where the target is. I can see the target clearly due to the micro telescopic optics which were designed by NASA. The technology used in this rifle scope is very similar to that used in the Hubble Telescope."

Bourque then shouldered the rifle and peered through the scope. After a brief second you could hear the steely click of the trigger as Bourque pulled the trigger once to lock onto the target, not visible to anyone but him. Next came a surprisingly sharp crack as he fired the weapon. The power of the massive weapon barely moved Bourque's large, thick frame. He then dropped the weapon to his side and began to speak again. "We now will wait for our assistant to bring us the target to see if my shot was accurate." In the distance you could see a camo Jeep speeding towards them. It soon arrived and the assistant stepped out. He methodically walked to Commander Bourque, saluted him and handed him a small object. Bourque then turned and addressed the audience.

"I have in my hand the article that I fired the M10 at. Judge for yourselves the accuracy of this new weapon." He then held up a hockey puck sized object with a large hole directly through the center of it.

"Imagine if I was aiming at an enemy preparing to begin an assault on a U.S. target," Bourque enthusiastically spoke.

As he glanced around the crowd, Bourque could see they were impressed. Good time to end his demonstration.

"If there are no questions," he quickly burst, "I will now turn the next part of our demonstration over to Green Beret Specialist Santana." Bourque quickly glanced around the audience for questions, hoping his part in this uncomfortable situation was over. He noticed one small lonely hand in the air.

"Yes Ma'am?" asked Bourque, his hopes of getting out of the spotlight dashed. "Commander Bourque." A quiet feminine voice began to speak. "What practical use does a weapon like the M10 have in future warfare, where missiles and air attacks seem more practical?"

With a steely glare and a quick smile to mask his unease at an attempt to answer the question, he began.

"The most practical use of this weapon can be traced back through every war ever fought. If you think back to the days of the Revolutionary War, the Civil War or any of the World Wars, the troops were led by Commanders that commanded from the safety of the rear of the battle. Even today, the men making the decisions to fire missiles or order air strikes are usually in a safe area at the rear of the battle. If you could take out the central command, those armies would not be able to function in a manner they need to win the battle."

These were more words than Bourque had spoken at one time in many years. He wasn't even sure if they made sense. He was a man of action, not one of words. He had tried to avoid situations like this all of his life, but to his surprise, he continued.

"There are even more domestic uses for the M10. A weapon like this could be used effectively for surveillance for our President or any world leader. For example, if our President were giving a speech at an outdoor arena such as the Arlington Cemetery, we could station men at distances and vantage points that could offer outstanding views of everyone within the danger area of the President. With the optical advantage of the M10 Scope, our snipers would be able to look closely at any curious situations or out-of-place movements, before any harm could come to the President. And with the guidance projectiles, there would be a very small chance of harming anyone except the targeted hostile."

With a deep breath and another quick smile, Bourque then asked the Senator, "Does this shed some light on the practical use of a weapon like this, Senator?"

"Yes, Commander Bourque, thank you," replied the Senator with a smile. "You're welcome, Ma'am," ended Bourque. He then nodded to the audience and quickly left the firing line, before any other questions could be brought up.

As Bourque turned and stood at attention in line with the others, Green Beret Specialist Santana moved quickly to the front of the audience. His tall, thin, yet muscular frame added credence to the reputation of the Green Berets.

"Good afternoon," began Santana. "I am Green Beret Specialist Santana. I have served two tours of duty in Afghanistan, three tours in Iraq and over eleven special op deployments around the world. My specialties are close range combat tactics and weaponry and hand-to-hand combat." Santana conveniently omitted his special training in advanced sniper tactics and explosives. He never liked to expose all of his talents, since most of his deployments were top secret and in countries that were considered U.S. friendly. Most politicians would not consider a Columbian drug lord a proper military target and would not support their assassination. Santana felt that anyone who contributes to the deterioration of American values is an enemy of the United States. "Today I will demonstrate a new weapon that is perhaps the exact opposite of the M10 Sniper Rifle," Santana continued. "It is a weapon that will be useful in close quarter combat and situations where our personnel may be outnumbered." There was an excited tone in Santana's voice as he continued. "The weapon I will demonstrate today is called the C22 Machine Pistol."

Santana reached to his side and pulled from his holster a unique looking handgun. He held it high so everyone could see it. It was almost the same size as the standard issue 40-caliber semiautomatic pistol issued to most policemen. The distinguishing characteristics that did make it look like a gun from *Star Wars*, were the large clip hanging underneath it and the small scope mounted on top.

"To some of you this might look like a gun from a science fiction movie," continued Santana. "But I assure you it is not a laser gun." There were several chuckles from the audience. "This weapon has several features that make it different from any other handgun used today. The biggest difference from the standard sidearm, is the C22's bullet." Santana lifted the C22 into the air and moved the slide back to eject a small bullet. As the bullet flipped into the air, Santana effortlessly reached out his hand and snatched it from its arc. Holding the small bullet between his thumb and forefinger, he continued.

"This 22-caliber bullet is, in appearance, the same bullet many of you shot out of your 22 rifles as kids. The difference is, this small projectile is not made of lead. It is made of a mercury composite that, upon impact, expands to ten times its current size. Once the target is struck, the properties of the mercury composite change and allow it to expand and actually get heavier. Everyone here has held a small amount of mercury at some time in their life. You probably noticed how heavy it was. The bullet I am holding weighs no more than the average 22 bullet. But upon impact, the molecular structure of the mercury composite reverts back to the weight of the equivalent amount of Mercury." As Santana finished this sentence, he had a confused look on his face, but he continued. "I am by no means a scientist and probably can't explain the process correctly. Let me put it in my own words." Santana took a deep breath and continued. "It's like shooting a 22 rifle but causing the damage of a 50-caliber rifle. Imagine this little bullet hitting the target and ripping a hole the size of an orange." Santana smiled as he thought his explanation was dead on.

"The best way to explain it is to give you a demonstration." As Santana finished speaking, he cocked the gun and spun away from the audience. He aimed the C22 down-range and fired one round at a wooden Silhouette. The sharp crack of the C22 firing was overshadowed by a loud explosion of wood, as the bullet struck the center of the target. From the look of awe on the faces of the Senators, Santana could tell that no one expected the small bullet to create an orange-sized hole in the three-quarter-inch plywood target.

"Imagine if this were the mid section of a human being," began Santana. "But there are a couple more surprises from the C22. The clip for this gun holds 100 rounds and by flipping this switch, the C22 becomes fully automatic. With the use of the red dot optic scope mounted on the C22, what you put the red dot on is utterly destroyed."

Santana held up the C22 and slowly moved it around so the audience might see the red dot in the middle of the scope. He then flipped the fully automatic switch, turned downfield once again, and began to fire the C22. The sharp peal of gunfire was constant for about ten seconds. As the bullets made contact with the target downrange, black wood chunks and splinters exploded in a continuous hellish barrage from the C22. It was as if someone was firing a 50-caliber machine gun from another location.

As Santana stopped firing the C22, he dropped the clip out and made sure the gun was unloaded. He set the small pistol on the table in front of him. It took the audience a minute to comprehend what they had just witnessed. Santana began to speak. "I realize this demonstration takes a few minutes to digest, but are there any questions?" Most of the Senators eyes were still fixed down range with a look of disbelief on the faces. Santana could tell they weren't sure if he really could have done that much damage with such a little weapon. Some heads were turning to the sides, looking to see if there was another gunman firing at the target. As the spectators slowly moved their stares towards Santana, one man's voice broke the silence.

"Specialist Santana," he began. "We all know that mercury is a hazardous heavy metal. Won't the bullets pose a hazard to the people and the environments where they are used?"

"Thank you, Sir," Santana replied with a smile. "The mercury composite in the bullet is only hazardous upon impact. Immediately after contact, the bullet has no inertia. Therefore, the chemical composition of the bullet is changed back to that of the unfired bullet, which is non toxic. I am sure there will be complete studies and reports issued to the Armed Forces Commission sometime in the future," ended Santana.

As soon as Santana stopped speaking, another question arose from the audience. "What type of combat situations would this weapon be best suited for?"

"Thank you for the question, Sir," replied Santana. "The best way to explain the appropriate application for this weapon is to use a personal experience." Santana now stood at ease with his hands behind his back. "One operation I was on in Kosovo will help explain the effectiveness of the C22 in a combat situation," he began. "I was part of a U.N. convoy, moving food and medical supplies to refugees at a camp a few miles out of town. This was supposed to be a peaceful mission, with only humanitarian ambitions. Our intelligence division told us there were no hostiles in the area, so only five of us went as support. We were told the chances of battle situations were nil and that M16s, small arms and limited ammunition were all we were to take. Like a bunch of greenhorns, we followed orders and took the mission. As we passed a palm grove, we heard an explosion near the rear of the convoy. As we quickly came to a stop, the five of us jumped out and took up defensive positions around the convoy. A group of twenty to thirty armed militia began to move on our position. As we returned fire and began to make holes in their lines, we realized we were almost out of M16 ammunition. It wasn't long before we were down to using only our side arms and trying to conserve what little ammo we had." Santana began sweating at the memory of the situation. He reached up and wiped the sweat from his forehead. "The hostiles were within twenty yards of our position and closing in, when a Blackhawk came to our rescue. As the Blackhawk opened fire, we also moved into better firing positions. Within a couple of minutes we were out of ammo. Thank God for the Blackhawk, it took care of the rest of the hostiles for us. If we would have had C22s, and only three clips each, we could have defended our position much more effectively, without the concern of running out of ammo."

As the last words came out of Santana's mouth, there was an eerie silence. It was as if Santana was back in Kosovo for a moment. As he spoke, his mind took him back to that terrifying battle. It was the first of his career and the first time had had taken another life. He didn't realize at the time, but that battle was only a precursor to the next twenty years of his life. As his mind caught up with his speaking, he continued.

"I also feel the kind of destruction the C22 can deliver will repel forces by sheer intimidation. If the man next to you is tore to shreds, you will think twice about moving forward on a position." With this said, Santana scanned the audience for any other questions. Seeing none, he thanked the audience and returned to attention in line with the other demonstrators.

Chapter 3

It'll blow your socks off

As Santana's body went taut at attention, Army Ranger Colonel Bates moved away from the line and into position in front of the audience. To the surprise of the audience, another of the demonstrators walked over to a Jeep parked near the range, got in the passenger side and was driven away. All eyes were fixed on the Jeep as it moved downrange about one hundred yards and stopped. The passenger then exited the Jeep and disappeared behind the vehicle. As quickly as he disappeared, the Jeep pulled away from its stopping point and returned to its original parking spot. Only one man exited the Jeep. Eyes from the audience scanned the vehicle to see where the other demonstrator was, but quickly returned to Colonel Bates as he began to speak.

"Good afternoon, I am Army Ranger Colonel Bates. I have been an Army Ranger for over thirty-two years. My tours of duty have taken me from Vietnam to Grenada and Beirut to Iraq. I have been deployed to every continent and to over fifteen countries. My specialties are in military strategy, all weapons and counter intelligence. Today I am here to demonstrate a weapon that combines two currently used weapons into one very deadly weapon."

As Bates continued to speak, the audience seemed to renew their interest and focus on the new demonstration. Maybe it was Bates' ability to better articulate what he was saying. Maybe it was because he was almost the same age as most of the Senators. Maybe his distinguished military history demanded their attention. Either way, Bates had their attention as he continued.

"The two current weapons that are part of my demonstration are the M16, as previously demonstrated by Specialist Tompkins, and the Rocket Propelled Grenade, or RPG. This demonstration will not be quite as futuristic as the previous two, but the technology involved is still very impressive." Bates reached for the M16 Specialist Tompkins had previously fired and held it at arms length in front of him. "You all remember this weapon, the M16, and it's capabilities from the previous demonstration. This has been the standard issue rifle since the Vietnam War. It is a reliable, accurate weapon that can be used at distances up to six hundred yards or in close combat situations. Its magazine will hold twenty rounds of .223-caliber cartridges." Bates held up the M16 cartridge between his thumb and forefinger. It was easy to see the difference between the huge cartridge of the M10 and the M16. However, they both looked monstrous compared to the C22.

"The M16 can be fired two different ways," Bates began again. "In semi automatic mode, the M16 fires one round each time the trigger is pulled. In fully automatic mode, the M16 will fire rounds continually while the trigger is depressed. It will only stop when it runs out of ammo or the trigger is released." With a grin on his face he added, "This is my weapon of choice in any combat situation." He moved the weapon from side to side in front of him, so all could get a good look at it. After a few seconds he set it back on the table and continued.

"The RPG or Rocket Propelled Grenade should be familiar to all of you. If you watch the news you will undoubtedly see Arabs firing this weapon. It is a lightweight and more mobile version of the old Bazooka." With this said, Bates reached under the table and brought out a long, green weapon with a large projectile on the end. He then moved away from the audience and faced downrange. "I will now show you exactly what this weapon is capable of." He placed the long weapon on his shoulder and aimed it towards an old Jeep about fifty yards downrange. With a loud blast of gas and propellant, the weapon shot the large projectile towards the Jeep. As the audience watched the projectile reach the Jeep, their hands quickly moved up to cover their ears from the blast they all knew was coming. Suddenly, the Jeep exploded with a loud and devastating blast. The Jeep was blown five feet into the air and was being consumed with fire. As the green, twisted body of the Jeep hit the ground, Bates began to speak.

"This is the kind of damage the RPG can inflict on a standard military vehicle. You can see that the Jeep is completely destroyed. Anything or anyone in the Jeep would also be destroyed." Bates then walked back to the audience and set the smoking weapon down on the table. "The main problem with this weapon," Bates began, "Is its size and its inability to be fired rapidly. Also, its projectiles are large and a man can only carry a limited amount of them. What I will demonstrate next is the future of this type of weapon."

Bates then once again reached under the table and retrieved a small satchel. He placed it on the table next to the M16, reached inside it and pulled out what appeared to be a handheld camcorder. The camcorder-looking device appeared to have a large zoom lens fixed to it. Bates lifted the M16 and adeptly attached the device to its underside. Bates then pushed what appeared to be five chicken eggs into the rear of the device. He then raised the newly configured weapon at arms length towards the audience.

"This, ladies and gentlemen," he announced, "is the equivalent of the RPG and the M16, combined into one weapon, plus more. What I have affixed to the M16 is the new micro repeating RPG, or the MR2PG. When I first saw a demonstration of this weapon, I thought they were attaching a camcorder to the M16 for some sort of video exercise. Probably similar to what you all thought when I attached it," smiled Bates. "But what I will show you next will make you look at camcorders in new way."

Bates then walked away from the audience with the new M16 in hand. He faced the still smoking Jeep once again, shouldered the M16 and fired it with several quick bursts. He then reached to the MR2PG and pushed a button with a metallic click. Next he shouldered the gun again and aimed downrange at the Jeep. As his finger depressed the trigger, there was a loud hiss as the projectile hit the Jeep. Once again the Jeep burst into flames as it rose off the ground. Just as the Jeep hit the ground , another shot was heard and the Jeep, or what was left of it, leaped into flames as the deafening explosion tore the metal apart. This was repeated three more times within a few seconds. Finally, the ear-shattering, eye-watering barrage ended. The flaming metal that once was a Jeep now resembled a pile of twisted, smoking metal, with no resemblance to any previously known shape.

Bates then turned toward the table and placed the demonic weapon down. As he slowly eyed the audience, they looked like they had just witnessed the second coming of Christ. Their wide eyes and open mouths brought a shiver to his spine. This was the first time civilians had witnessed this new weapon and the reaction Bates witnessed was humbling. He was used to this type of destruction, as most of his missions were to do just that. But it was now clear to him. What he had been programmed to do for the last thirty years was as alien to the average person as walking on the moon.

For a moment, Bates was back in his home town of Detroit. His platoon had returned from their final deployment in Vietnam and were being bussed to the base from the airport. Worn out from jet lag and twelve months of midnight ambushes, two day fire-fights and sleeping in water-filled foxholes, Bates could no longer keep his eyes open. His mind could not find ease, even when it knew he was in the safety of the States.

As his head bounced off the window, he was awakened to an egg breaking on his window. There were shouts of hatred and people holding signs with anti-American sayings. Hundreds of people lined the road. They were not welcoming home the heroes of the war, but condemning the veterans as killers and racists. This was supposed to be a time to rejoice, and count your blessings. To remember the friends who would not return from that hell. What were these people doing and why were they spitting on the men who fought for their nation? Bates did not understand these people. The hatred towards them grew inside of him.

That actually was why he never got out of the armed forces. He always remembered that day and felt the only people he could understand were his military family. As his mind came back to the present, it all became clear. After this simple display of destruction and the looks on the Senator's faces, he knew the average person could not comprehend this type of destruction. During the Vietnam War, the news agencies reported only the destruction, killing and aftermath. They didn't show the good things the GI's were doing. The people at home only knew of the destruction. Maybe they could not handle the ravages of war and reacted in the only way they could. They held demonstrations and rejected the return of their soldiers. Bates could never forgive those people for what they did, but maybe he could understand a little better. For a quick second Bates could relate to the people he once hated. But all that came to a quick end as a tire on the Jeep exploded with a loud boom.

Bates' mind suddenly came back to the present and the realization of the demonstration's effect on the audience.

"Ladies and gentlemen," Bates began, "I realize this weapon's abilities in warfare are one of a kind. Not only is it designed to kill an enemy, but to destroy it and anything around it. You can see that old and new technologies can combine to create great assets for our armed forces. Are there any questions?"

As Bates suspected, there were no hands in the air, so he thanked the audience and returned to the other demonstrators and came to attention.

As the group of onlookers finally regained their senses, Tompkins took two steps forward and began to speak.

"Ladies and gentlemen, what you have just witnessed are the most advanced weapons the military has to offer. They could be used to save thousands of U.S. Troops as well as thousands of innocent civilians. We do have one more demonstration for you that doesn't entail any gunfire or explosions."

As Tompkins finished this sentence, he could see the eyes of the audience move towards the twisted, burning heap of metal that used to be a Jeep. The thick black smoke towered up towards the sun and gave an eerie feeling of being in a combat zone. All eyes moved back towards Tompkins as he began again.

"As you can see, all of the demonstrators behind me are unarmed and in plain sight. Our next weapon was designed to give us a unique advantage in all types of battlefield situations and recon applications. In a few minutes the demonstration will begin, so all of you should be ready for anything." With that said, Tompkins took two steps backwards and stood at attention with the other three demonstrators. After a few seconds, eyes and heads in the crowd began to move, looking for something to give them the heads up on what was going to happen next. The audience seemed nervous at the uneasy lull in the action. Soon they began whispering among each other and fidgeting in their seats like a bunch of schoolchildren waiting for class to begin.

Just as they seemed to become at ease, an object was tossed into the audience. A nimble, handed Senator caught the object and held it up to see what it was. Much to his dismay, it resembled a hand grenade. With a frightful look on his face, he let out a yelp and threw the grenade out onto the range. As he let the grenade go, his hands, along with everyone else's, were raised to their ears in anticipation of the oncoming blast. Everyone's face was scrunched and their eyes were closed, but nothing happened. Just as the crowd began to lower their hands, a barrage of grenades were thrown into the audience. As the grenades hit the ground, the Senators started to scramble from their seats. Tompkins quickly spoke.

"Don't be alarmed, the grenades are not real. Please remain seated." With the reassurance from Tompkins, they reluctantly took their seats. As everyone got settled, Commander Bourque cleared his throat with a deep, "Ahem." Bourque cleared his voice to draw attention to himself and the other demonstrators. As all eyes drew to them, the demonstration continued. There was a silence for about ten seconds. The silence was suddenly broken with four quick dull thuds as each of the demonstrators were hit in the chest with a bright red paint ball. Everyone in the crowd gasped at the sudden surprise, their heads spinning to see where the shots came from. With no clue as to the origin of the paintballs, the audience once again fixed their eyes on the demonstrators. The only sounds heard were whispers of disbelief at the apparent magical paintballs.

With all the sudden excitement, the expressions of pain on the demonstrators' faces went unnoticed. Even the stoic, hardened face of Commander Bourque showed a hint of displeasure at his part in the demonstration. He calmly pulled his shirt away from his chest to confirm the quarter sized red welt on his sternum. As Commander Bourque raised his head back to attention, he once again cleared his throat. While all eyes were fixed on Bourque, a voice began to speak.

"Ladies and gentlemen, I realize you are all a little bit confused at this point in the demonstration." The muffled voice was unfamiliar to the crowd, but it had their complete attention as it continued. "If you would all center your attention forward, the demonstration will continue."

The eyes of the audience focused to the front once again, most of which were squinting to see where the voice was coming from and what was next. As the quiet calm reached its apex, the eyes of the audience opened wide as a small American flag on a stick appeared to come from thin air. The little flag waived back and forth for a minute, as if held by an invisible hand. What happened next brought the entire group to their feet.

Without any notice, the missing demonstrator jumped up and shouted, "Gottcha." His arms waved in the air as he jumped up, much like a little kid trying to scare a friend.

Everyone in the crowd leaped to their feet in surprise. The only thing the audience could see was the camo-painted face of the man and the flag he held in his hand. Everything else appeared to be a blur of color and light. They were unable to make out any distinguishable features of the person who was standing in front of them.

"Please take your seats," the man asked politely. He began to take off the article of clothing that offered him the ultimate concealment. Within a minute, CIA Special Ops Agent Draper was standing before them, dressed as he was before he disappeared earlier in the demonstration. Once the audience could clearly see his face, the grins on their faces showed they remembered him as the demonstrator that left in the Jeep.

"Sorry for Agent Draper's entrance," spoke Commander Bourque. "He's the funny guy in our group."

With a snotty sneer directed towards Bourque, "Thank you Commander Bourque," replied Draper in a clearly sarcastic voice. "I am sorry for this unique entrance," explained Draper, "The look on people's faces when I do that makes it all worthwhile."

There was a light laughter from most of the crowd at Draper's impish attitude. They seemed happy to see the lighter side of Draper after such an extremely intense day. "Now back to the task at hand," started Draper. "Remember me getting in the Jeep and it stopping downrange? Then it returned back here, with only one person in it. That is where I started my part of the demonstration. I was able to crawl directly in front of you for over one hundred yards, without any detection. I was able to do that because of this."

Draper bent down and picked up the garment at his feet. It was barely visible to anyone in the crowd. He held it at arms length and began to explain.

"This, ladies and gentlemen, is the future of the Ghillie Suit. The old Ghillie Suit was made of different materials of different colors, which helped conceal its wearer. It was very effective in areas that had foliage to hide in. With the new battlefields being desert areas and city settings, we needed more adaptive concealment. Through a joint venture between NASA, the U.S. Marine Corp. and the CIA, they came up with this new suit. The technologies used to develop it are far beyond my comprehension. Heck, I'm just an old CIA man. But I'll do my best to make it all believable."

Draper took a deep breath and continued. "This new Ghillie Suit is made from a light refracting co-polymer material. It will take on the appearance of whatever it is next to." Draper then took the suit from the grassy area of the shooting range, to the gravel driveway only a few yards away. He laid the suit on the gravel, and it disappeared. He then picked the suit up again and walked over to the brick wall of the nearby maintenance shed. He held the suit up against the brick wall and it disappeared once again. The crowd had a look of disbelief on their faces as he stood there holding the suit against the wall.

"The look on your faces tells me you're not quite sure what to think of this suit," Draper had a goofy grin on his face as he continued. "I didn't really believe it at first either. The only way it made sense to me was to actually hold it in my own hands. Draper approached the audience and began to put the suit back on. "I will now give you a close up of what this suit can really do." Draper then walked onto the stage and lay down. He immediately became the same gray color as the wooden floor of the stage. Nobody could tell he was there.

"Go ahead everyone, reach down and touch the suit," Draper said with a playful tone in his voice. "I won't bite." Several of the Senators got up and approached Draper.

"I truly cannot see you," responded one Senator. They then moved closer, reached down and felt the suit. The only response they could muster was a couple of "No Ways" and a few "I can't believe it's."

Draper then stood up and walked off the stage, back to the range in front of them. He removed the suit and laid it on the table, where it disappeared once again.

"There are several other benefits to this suit, besides its concealment capabilities," continued Draper. "This suit is completely waterproof, UV-resistant and very light-weight. It can be an asset in any climate, from deserts to rain forests. However, there are a couple of downfalls with the suit." For the first time during the demonstration, Draper didn't have a smile on his face.

"The first problem," explained Draper, "is the cost. It costs over one million dollars to produce one suit. The second problem is that it takes over six months to produce one suit." With these comments made, there began a lot of whispering among the Senators. But that was understandable. It was their job to appropriate the money for projects like these.

Draper let the Senators whisper for a couple more minutes before he began to speak again.

"This concludes my demonstration. I imagine there are lots of questions, but to explain this technology, well, you better talk to someone a lot smarter than me."

With a smile on his face, Draper thanked the audience and returned to the other demonstrators at attention. With a quick "Hut" from Commander Bourque, the five men spun about-face and walked to the Jeep in which they arrived. They quickly entered the vehicle and drove off the range. Their part in the demonstration was over. Although they had to return later to retrieve their equipment, they were more than happy to remove themselves from the limelight of the demonstrations.

After a quick dinner at the base mess hall, the five returned to the range to retrieve their equipment. They quietly loaded everything into their vehicles and left the base. Normally they would spend the night on the base, but because Tomkins wanted to get to Gettysburg for the reenactment, they thought it best to drive as far as possible through the night.

Chapter 4

Storm clouds ahead

As the five men drove on through the night, there was little interaction between them. Tompkins and Bourque were in the lead Jeep. Draper, Bates and Santana followed in the other Jeep with the trailer full of equipment. Of course there was the light banter over the radio between Draper and Bourque. Draper enjoyed causing Bourque mental anguish. It was like a little brother constantly bugging his older brother. Draper knew Bourque could dismember him at will, so he made sure he never took his banter too far.

Bourque was a giant of a man but had learned at an early age that he needed to restrain from physical confrontation. As a high school freshman wrestler, Bourque once put his opponent in a full nelson and dislocated both of his opponent's shoulders. Later in the same season he slammed an opponent so hard, he broke four vertebrae in the kid's back. After these two displays of brute force and physical domination, Bourque was banned from wrestling in high school in the United States. The next four years of high school he was hounded by almost every college in the country for every sport possible. He however never looked to sports again. He thought his skills could be better used in the military.

As the minds of the guys were relaxing, the silence was broken by the crackle of the CB radio. "Tiger 1, Tiger 1, this is Tiger 2, over." The sound of Draper's goofy call brought a smile to the two men in the lead Jeep. Bourque and Tompkins looked at each other and Tompkins grabbed the mike. "Tiger 2, this is Tiger 1, what can we do for you guys now, Draper," replied Tompkins with a hint of sarcasm.

"I was wondering if you two could help me figure out a little riddle," asked Draper. "Sure Tiger 2, we're listening," replied Tompkins.

"What is man-made, only an inch high, and black and blue? Over," asked Draper. After a minute of thinking between the two men in the lead Jeep, they replied, "We don't know, Tiger 2, what is it? Over."

With a laugh, Draper replied, "The welt on Bourque's sternum after I shot him today!"

The vein in Bourque's forehead immediately popped out as he snatched the handset from Tompkins' hand. "Guess what is five-foot-eleven, black and blue and man-made," asked Bourque in a disturbed tone.

"Gee, I don't know," answered Draper sheepishly.

"You, as soon as we stop!" barked Bourque into the handset.

With a loud laugh, Tompkins grabbed the mike back from Bourque and informed the others, "Hey guys, we're about sixty miles from Gettysburg and it's almost morning. We should come to a place to set up camp soon. We have to go through a tunnel in a small mountain and then we can stop. After some shut-eye we can go through the equipment, and clean and inventory what we're carrying. Then we can take in some of the area attractions and relax for the day. The re-enactment doesn't start 'til July first."

"Sounds good, Tiger 1. We're following your lead. Over."

As the two-vehicle convoy continued down the road, Bates got an eerie gut feeling. He hadn't had this kind of feeling since the Vietnam War. He wiggled in his seat like a little kid getting close to DisneyLand. His uneasiness didn't go unnoticed. "What's wrong, Bates?" asked Santana. "You're squirming around in your seat like a little kid."

Bates gave him a quick look of distress, but kept his focus on the road ahead. "Man, you're really freaking me out!" replied Santana.

Draper, who was in the back seat, also noticed Bates unusual demeanor and calmly asked, "What's going through your head, Bates?"

With a deep breath, Bates answered, "Man, I don't know what's going on. I have this weird gut feeling that I've only had once before in my life."

"What happened the first time you had the feeling?" asked Draper. After clearing his throat, Bates began to speak.

"The first time I had this feeling I was leading a recon unit along the DMZ. We had intel that told us the Vietcong had pulled out of the area we were going to. As we pushed through the thick jungle at ten-meter intervals, I had a gut feeling we would be in a firefight around the next river bend, about five clicks north of our position. As we closed in on the position, I suspected we would encounter the enemy. I had the unit close in and take up flanking positions in a horseshoe-shaped defensive formation. I knew if we were attacked, we would need to cover all sides of our position, but leave a route for escape if needed. I was sure I was going to throw up from the intense feeling, but we then spotted movement ahead in the brush. It seemed like hours before we could determine it was Charlie. As we let them close in on our position, it appeared as if the entire 51st Viet-cong Regiment was closing in on us. Thank God I had three, 30-caliber machine guns stationed at the perfect spots and we were freshly refit with full ammo and grenades.

"I motioned for a full squad grenade toss. All the men in the unit had a grenade in each hand and several at their feet. As the regiment reached about twenty yards, I lobbed a grenade into the middle of them. As I let mine go, thirty-nine others followed. Everyone threw the grenades at their disposal and then hit the dirt. The 30 cals then followed with a mind blowing barrage of fire. What a freaking hell fire mess followed. Explosions and machine gunfire deafened us. For about a minute I couldn't tell what was happening. I gave the signal and everyone unloaded everything they had; rifle fire, handguns, grenades, shotguns. The smoke and noise was unbelievable. When I gave the cease-fire command, everyone's eyes were wide open and focused on the mess that lay in front of us. Not one shot was returned from the enemy, or at least no one in our unit recalls any."

"As we scanned the carnage, I slowly got up and moved forward. I didn't know what to expect, but I knew we had to move forward. Not a single enemy was standing. I ordered a casualty count for our unit and the enemy. To my amazement, not a single man in our unit was injured. The enemy casualties totaled one hundred and forty."

"As the men gathered around me, the unit sergeant walked up and shook my hand. He told me that in his thirty years of service, he had never seen a single command save so many GI lives and work so perfectly. He told me he would follow me into any battle situation, with pleasure. I guess he must have told the commanding General what happened. Before I could file my report on the mission, I was presented with my first Silver Star, by the General himself."

As Bates paused in his story, Draper enthusiastically asked, "Your first Silver Star. How many do you have?"

"Six all together," replied Bates. Santana and Draper looked at each other with amazement.

"What do you think the feeling means now?" asked Santana.

"I'm pretty sure nothing like that is going to happen," replied Bates. "But I'm gonna be on edge until I can figure it out."

As the last word came from Bates' mouth, Draper reached up and grabbed the mike. "Hey guys, I mean, Tiger 1, this is Tiger 2. How about stopping at that store coming up? I think we need to get some fresh air and stretch our legs."

"Everything OK back there, Tiger 2?" replied Bourque.

"Yeah, everything is good. Let's just stop," replied Draper in an unusual serious tone.

Tomkins looked at Bourque. "I don't think I've ever heard Draper sound so serious," mentioned Tompkins.

"Kinda makes you wonder what's up back there," replied Bourque. Bourque raised the mike to his lips, "10-4 Tiger 2, let's take a breather."

As the vehicles turned off the road, the sun was just starting to peek over the mountains. They came to a stop in the tiny parking lot of the little weather-worn general store. Quickly the men were out of the vehicles and stretching their cramped muscles.

Nothing more was said of Bates' gut feeling as they walked up the old creaky wooden stairs of the store.

"Wow," burst Santana. "This is a throwback to the old days. You only see stores like this in old movies."

"Yeah, it's kind of neat isn't it," replied Tompkins.

As the five men walked through the door, they expected to see a modern store stocked with chips, candy bars and refrigerators. As the door shut behind them, they all stopped and looked around in awe. There were animal furs hanging on the walls, tables with bolts of cloth, jars with penny candies, bags of sugar and flour and many other items that made you think you were in an episode of *Little House on the Prairie.*

"Hey, I wonder if Ike Godsey is going to wait on us," laughed Draper.

"Who is that?" asked Bourque.

"You know, the store keeper on the Walton's," bantered Draper.

"Must have missed that show," sneered Bourque.

"Anyway," interjected Bates, "let's get some chow and something to drink and hit the road."

Santana walked up to an old wooden ice box, opened it up and pulled out five bottles of root beer and set them on the counter. Just then an old gray-haired man, dressed in a white apron, appeared from behind a curtain.

"Good day gentlemen," greeted the old storekeep. He slowly looked at each of the men, as if he were studying each of their faces. "How can I help you men?"

"Just need to get these sodas please," replied Santana.

"OK, the opener is over on the ice box," replied the storekeep.

"Wow, I haven't had to use a bottle opener since the 70s," chimed Tompkins. "Who makes these sodas?"

"They are made locally," replied the storekeep. "You boys need any jerky or chewing tobacco?"

"No thanks," replied Santana, "Just the drinks."

"I hope you don't mind me saying so sir," asked Tompkins. "But this is quite a unique store you have here."

"Thank you sir," replied the man. "We try to keep on hand the things the locals might need. If they can get it here, they can save a day's travel to the big city."

"How far is the big city from here?" asked Bourque.

"About twenty-five miles I reckon," answered the man. The guys just looked at each other and shrugged their shoulders. "If that's everything, it'll be fifty cents for the sodas sir," said the man.

"Are you sure sir?" replied Santana. "That's unusually cheap for sodas."

"Well, I can see you boys are military men, so you get a special discount today," smiled the storekeep.

"Thank you," chimed Santana as he handed him a dollar bill. "Keep the change please sir."

The man picked up the bill and looked at it with an odd look on his face. "Thanks," was his reply. The five men nodded their thanks and turned to walk out the door.

"Boys..." burst out the old man. He had a strange, solemn look on his face as the men focused their attention on him. "If you're going through the tunnel, be careful. The road gets a might rough about halfway through or so. Been a lot of strange weather lately."

"Thanks," replied Bates. As the door opened, the storekeeper once again stopped them.

"Uh, boys." They once again turned around and faced the old man. "Thanks for your service to the Union, er, I mean the United States. And for your future help in keeping the balance."

Not knowing what to say next, Tompkins gave the storekeep a quick "Thank you sir," and turned to exit the store.

"Uh, boys," interrupted the old man once again. "Just remember. Parties on both sides of a conflict believe their cause is just. History has shown us which side is to prevail, but there is no true blueprint to achieve its success. If you find yourselves not knowing the correct path to take, just do what you must to preserve the ideals of the whole and the correct path will present itself."

With that said, the storekeeper just raised his hand in a wave and disappeared behind the curtain.

As the door shut behind them, Draper asked the others, "Was that weird or what?" Everyone nodded in agreement and proceeded to their vehicles and drove away. Not much more was said for the next few miles, except how much they liked the root beer and how strange the store experience was.

"Hey Bates," asked Draper, "How's that gut feeling?"

With a look of dismay Bates replied, "Still there."

As the convoy came within sight of the mountain with the tunnel through it, the silence was broken by the crack of the radio. "Tiger 1, this is Tiger 2. Hey, look at those weird clouds at the top of that mountain at twelve o'clock."

"Tiger 2," replied Bourque, "Remember, the old man told us there was a lot of strange weather the last few days."

"Roger that Tiger 1," answered Draper. "I grew up in the heart of Tornado Alley and I ain't seen nothing like that."

"I'm sure once we go through the tunnel the weather will clear up," comforted Tompkins. "It's only sixty-six degrees. It's too cold for any type of tornado or severe storm."

The clouds over the mountain were a very bright white on top, with streaks of purplish gray on the bottom. The motion of the clouds was in no specific direction. They just seemed to be rolling over and over in a stationary position at the top of the mountain.

Soon the clouds were forgotten as a small black hole appeared at the base of the mountain. As the vehicles neared the tunnel, the pavement seemed to disappear into the completely black hole. The taillights on the lead Jeep blinked as it began to slow to a stop. After seeing no other lights in the tunnel and getting one last look at the ominous clouds rolling above them, Tompkins guided the Jeep into the blackness of the tunnel.

The lights of the vehicles seemed useless in the total blackness of the tunnel. As they crept along at a very slow pace, the pavement must have ended as the Jeeps began to bounce through what seemed a gauntlet of giant potholes. Just as they thought the bumps were going to make them sick, a bright light in the distance let them know the end was near.

Bourque's voice broke the silence. "I guess the old man was right about the road being a bit bumpy. The end of the tunnel is in sight though."

"Roger that, I'm starting to taste the root beer again, and it doesn't taste as good this time," answered Santana.

As they drew near the end of the tunnel, the road became smooth once again. They did notice that it was now completely gravel. "They must be tearing up the pavement to replace it," mentioned Tompkins. As they exited the tunnel, they turned down a side road. Tompkins found a good place to camp for the morning and they began to set up camp.

Chapter 5

The other side

Once again the five men found themselves lying around a campfire on military issue sleeping bags. The early morning was extremely hot, humid and uncomfortable. As the sun rose over the horizon, the heat became more unbearable.

"Boy, the weather has really took a crap since we came through that tunnel," whined Draper.

"I told you guys the weather would change once we got through the tunnel," laughed Tompkins.

"Yeah," whined Draper once again, "But I didn't think the tunnel would lead us back to Iraq."

"Seems like that tunnel was almost like a time warp to a different world," joked Bates.

"Hey Bates, this probably reminds you of when you were growing up with the dinosaurs," said Draper, to a group chuckle.

"Well, either way we're here, so let's make the best of it," chimed in Bourque.

As the men's eyes were getting heavy, Santana broke the silence. "Hey Tompkins, what's on the agenda for the rest of today?"

"I figured we rest until 0900 hours," replied Tompkins. "The reenactment doesn't start until tomorrow, so I thought we'd see some of the outlying areas where the troops camped before the actual battle began. It might give us a better understanding of how the troops maneuvered before they got to Gettysburg."

"That sounds good," agreed Draper. "What happened the day before the battle started? Last time you were telling us about it I fell asleep. Not that you're a boring story teller or nothin."

Once again Draper's stupid demeanor and comments brought a group laugh. "Thanks for alerting me to my boring nature," countered Tompkins. "But if everyone was like you, all wars would look like a circus."

Draper took this comment as a good chance to poke some fun at Bourque once again. "Well, if wars were circuses, Bourque would be the bearded lady in the side show." Draper was amazed that all he got out of Bourque was a quick chuckle.

"All right ladies," began Tompkins. "The 30th of June, 1863, was relatively uneventful. The Southern Troops were moving north to draw the Union Troops out of Washington. The Northern Army was moving west to counter any possible advancements of the Confederate Army. What wasn't realized at the time was that the massive forces from both sides were all in relatively close proximity.

The Confederate Armies eyes and ears, the cavalry, was not in the area. So General Lee had no idea of the size of the Union forces, which were already around Gettysburg. The Union cavalry was in a good position, so the North knew what the South was doing and the size of their forces."

Tompkins could see the eyes of the men starting to get very heavy, so he shortened his intended history lesson. "Probably the best way for you dummies to soak all this in, is for me to fill you in as we go. Get some shuteye. I'll wake you up in about three hours, so we can do our inventory and start having fun." Tompkins wasn't sure if they heard all he said, but it was more important they got some rest.

About an hour into their nap, Bates felt the urge to get up. His gut feeling was getting worse as the day went on. As he rose from the camp and walked into the nearby forest, Draper noticed his absence and followed. As Draper parted the brush, he was greeted to the sight of Bates on his knees, throwing up.

"I hope that's not from your gut feeling," asked Draper.

"If it is," replied Bates, "We are in for some real hell. The first time I had the feeling it was more like indigestion. This is definitely more like the flu. Stay sharp and follow my lead, OK Draper?"

"Yeah, sure Bates. Are you going to fill in the other guys?"

"No, let's just see what happens the next few days. I hope it is just the flu."

"Me too," said Draper with a hint of dread. "Let's get back to camp and get some sleep."

As the sun rose ever higher and raised the temperature to stifling levels, Bates' eyes could no longer stay closed. The five men had gotten four hours of sleep. They were used to limited sleep in the field. There were lots of reasons why they might not sleep well in the field: rain, heat, insects, night watch or the anticipation of the upcoming battle. This was different for Bates however. That gut feeling had never really gone away. Even as he slept, the feeling gnawed at his mind. As he lay on the ground staring up at the hazy sky, he went through several scenarios in his mind.

"Why would such an intense feeling be hitting me now? This is a relaxing mission with no pressures at all. What in the world could be coming up that could cause this feeling?" he asked himself.

As Bates' mind raced, a sharp snore brought him back to reality. Bates' eyes moved to where the snore came from. His eyes were met by the still sleepy eyes of Draper.

"You sleeping with your eyes open now or what?" asked Draper.

"No, just thinking," replied Bates.

"Still got that feeling, Bates?" asked Draper.

"Yeah, can't figure out why though," replied Bates. His eyes once again moved to the sky.

"Hey Bates, just try to relax and enjoy this downtime," spoke Draper in a calm voice.

Bates just nodded and continued staring. No matter what Draper or anyone would say to make him feel at ease, he was not going to relax until the reason for the feeling was revealed.

By now, all eyes were opened and limbs were being stretched.

"Boy, it must be at least ninety-five degrees. On a day like this these new fatigues really keep you cool," began Tompkins. "I bet the reenactors will be sweating their butts off tomorrow in their heavy wool uniforms." Everyone nodded in agreement.

"Yeah, but I bet they won't have these huge blisters from their new boots," snickered Santana. As he finished speaking he took his left foot and waved it in the air. Two big red blisters looked neon colored as he peeled off the skin on the biggest one.

"Actually," began Tompkins, "the soldiers on either side of the Civil War would have killed to get your new boots. The Confederates were much worse off than the Union. Could you imagine marching hundreds of miles in your bare feet?" All eyes focused on Tompkins as he continued. "One reason the Confederates moved towards Gettysburg was to get food and clothing. They were a weary Army. The battle actually began when it did because of a rumor that a large cache of boots was in Gettysburg. A small raiding party was moving to Gettysburg when they met the Union Cavalry on July 1st, or tomorrow, one hundred and thirty-six years ago."

"Boy," chimed in Draper, with his usual tone, "traveling with you is like traveling with a living encyclopedia."

"You know they say that when you stop learning, you're dead," seriously added Bourque.

With a sly smile, Draper thought it would appropriate to shoot another jab at Bourque. Since Bourque didn't usually say much, Draper always thought it was appropriate to banter Bourque as much as possible.

"I'm surprised you can still learn anything," jabbed Draper. "Your brain must be crushed under all that muscle."

As usual, that brought a group laugh. Bourque just smiled and kept putting his things in his duffle. Santana then spoke up.

"I don't know what you all think, but I'm getting kind of excited about this trip. I had a dream once that I was in the Civil War, and it seemed interesting. Maybe the reenactment will be cool to see. So let's get our stuff packed and inventoried and start our journey towards the past."

"Said like a true dufus," chimed Draper.

The group seemed to pick up the pace as they policed the camp area and began to inventory their equipment. Within an hour, the equipment was inventoried and vehicles loaded. Once again Bourque and Tompkins took the lead in the single Jeep and Bates, Santana and Draper followed with the trailer of equipment.

As the Jeeps lumbered down the bumpy road, Tompkins began to get edgy. His head moved back and forth from the map to the window to the mirror. Bourque quickly picked up on this and asked, "Is everything alright?"

Tompkins just shrugged his shoulders and replied, "I think so. I studied this map pretty intensely so we could see the countryside on our way to Gettysburg. But this road should be paved."

"Probably just doing some work on it," replied Bourque. "I'm sure we'll hit pavement pretty soon."

Just as they finished talking they came to a crossroad. A small, weathered wooden sign pointed to the right and said, "Gettysburg forty miles." The road sign also told them it was the Chambersburg Pike. As Bourque was looking out the window at the sign, he noticed Tompkins nervously looking at the map again.

"Find out where we are for sure?" Bourque asked.

"Yeah, I think so," replied Tompkins. As he spoke, his eyes never left the map. "Let's get out and talk to the guys for a minute."

"Sure," replied Bourque. "Let's pull into that store parking lot up ahead and you can fill us in on what's up."

"Do it," blasted Tompkins, as if they were in the middle of a battle.

This response left Bourque uneasy. The last time he heard Tompkins say "Do it" in that tone, they were part of a raiding party along the DMZ in South Vietnam. It was a ghostly resemblance since Tompkins was thumbing through Intel maps a mile a minute then, too. The worst part was they were supposed to be two clicks on the friendly side of the DMZ, but were actually two clicks on the hostile side. Bourque was not too concerned though. Tompkins had led them back to the correct position without confrontation back then, so he was sure he could figure out where they were on the Pennsylvania state map. After all, it didn't really matter. There were no hostile forces and no time constraints to their current mission.

"Tiger 2, this is Tiger 1," spoke Bourque into the radio handset.

"Yes, Tiger 1," replied Santana.

"We're going to pull over at the store ahead and look at the map, Over," barked Bourque.

"10-4," replied Santana.

"Wonder what's up?" asked Bates. "Tompkins can read any map ever made." "No biggy," replied Draper. "I could use a cup of coffee."

The Jeeps slowly pulled off the road and came to a stop in the parking lot of the little country store. All of the men quickly got out and came together at the lead Jeep. Tompkins spread the map out on the hot hood of the truck and pointed his finger to a spot on the map.

"This is where we are right now, I think," explained Tompkins. "About forty miles west of Gettysburg."

"So what's the problem?" replied Bates.

"I'm not quite sure what's going on," replied Tompkins. "The map is not completely accurate. According to the map there should be a rest stop right here where we are parked."

"So, big deal, it's not completely accurate," chimed in Draper.

Tompkins eyes never left the map as he continued to explain the situation. "My biggest concern is the Chambersburg Pike is supposed to be a paved main highway to Gettysburg."

As Tompkins finished, the eyes of all the men met.

"Let me get this straight," burst Santana. "This road, which is little more than a cow trail, is supposed to be the main highway to Gettysburg."

"Yep," replied Tompkins.

"What are you talking about?" countered Santana. Bates walked away from the group and looked up and down the road. He bent down and grabbed a handful of gravel, crunched it in his hand and let it fall from his fingers. He quickly turned to the others and said, "This road has never been paved."

"What are you talking about?" quickly countered Draper.

"This road is made of ordinary field dirt and stone. The road base has never been built up with any sand or gravel. When a road is paved, a base of aggregate is always used."

"Hey Bates, you were in the Sea Bee's after Nam weren't you?" asked Bourque.

"Yeah, that's how I know this is all wrong."

"Wonder what the heck is going on," questioned Santana.

"Well, here is what I say we do," began Tompkins. He meticulously folded the maps as he spoke. "It really doesn't matter what is going on. We're in no hurry. We don't have to be at our next demonstration for seven days. We have no immediate objectives, so let's just enjoy the sights and see what happens."

With this said, all the men nodded their heads and shrugged their shoulders in agreement.

"Let's go into the store and get some grub and then hit the road," commanded Bourque.

They all turned and headed up to the store. As they reached the wooden porch Bourque held out his arms to stop everyone. "Doesn't this remind you of the last store we were at on the backside of that mountain?" asked Bourque.

"Yeah, kind of freaky, huh?" replied Draper.

"I don't like it," snapped Bourque.

"Oh just get going, you big girl," replied Draper as he pushed past Bourque's outstretched arms. The others followed

Draper, slapping Bourque on the back as they passed. Bourque slowly followed, even though his mind told him something was wrong. His natural instincts prompted a readiness in his being that could only be described as a hand grenade with the pin pulled.

As Bourque crossed the threshold into the store, he bumped into the four other men standing in the doorway. They were all looking around the store in disbelief. Once again they were standing in an old-time store filled with items that had not been seen in stores for decades. There were furs on the walls, barrels filled with pickles, animal traps stacked on tables, an ice box with actual ice in it, bolts of drab-colored cloth, jars of sugar and an old cast-iron wood stove in the center of it all.

"Wow," burst Santana. "Pennsylvania must be a real backwards place. These last two stops are real throwbacks to the 1800s."

"I'm telling you guys, something isn't right," whispered Bourque.

"I gotta find a bathroom real fast," snapped Bates. His face was pale and his eyes were watery.

"Over in the corner," quickly pointed Tompkins.

Bates quickly ran to the room and slammed the door. The sound of someone throwing up could be heard from behind the door. Everyone just looked at each other for a moment. Soon the door opened and Bates walked out.

As he rejoined the group he said with a hint of disbelief, "That is the first restroom without lights and running water I've been in since Nam."

"Let's just get some supplies and regroup at the Jeeps," commanded Bourque. "That's a big 10-4," replied Draper, "With pleasure. I'm even starting to get a weird feeling from this place."

The five men walked around the store picking up items and quizzically looking at them. They rounded up items they thought they could use from the limited stock and gathered at the register. They placed their items in one group on the counter and waited for someone to assist them. After a minute a young girl appeared from the back room.

As she looked over the group her eyes got wide and her mouth fell open. She slowly proceeded towards them and tried to speak, but only a couple of sputters came out.

"Uh, hello," she finally said. "Can I help you men?"

They stood there staring at her. Bourque was intensely studying the girl. He figured she was in her early twenties. She had long, fine blonde hair with a blue bow tied in the back. She was wearing a blue dress with a white apron tied around her thin waist. The boots she was wearing were worn from use, but still feminine. Her skin was dark from exposure to the sun, yet still gave a youthful glow. Her stature was such that you could tell she worked hard. Her muscles were evident, though small. She was definitely a country girl.

But Bourque couldn't help wonder why was she dressed the way she was and why she was so surprised when she saw them.

The first of the men to speak was Bates. "Yes Ma'am, we would like to purchase these items please."

"Yes Sir, let's add 'em up," was her reply.

She handled each item and wrote down their price on a piece of paper. As she set down the last item, she began to add the numbers up. She was adept at addition, but performed it at an elementary speed.

After a quick minute she looked up with a smile and said, "One dollar and thirty seven cents please."

The guys looked at each other and smiled. Bates stepped up and placed a five dollar bill on the counter and said, "Keep the change." The girl looked at Bates and smiled.

"Thank you, Sir," she replied in a girlish voice. She picked up the five-dollar bill and looked at it closely. She turned it over to look at the back side. "Where you men from?" questioned the girl.

"We travel all over the country," replied Bates.

"I've never seen money like this before," said the girl. "Was this money made up North or in the South?"

"I don't know for sure but I believe it was made up North," replied Tompkins. "If you take it to your local bank they will replace it with whatever currency you would like." "Okay," said the girl. "We have a lot of people from both sides come through here, so I thought I'd ask. Have a good day."

As the girl turned to return to the back room Tompkins asked, "How far is it to Gettysburg, Ma'am?"

The girl spun around and answered with a smile. "About two days ride. It's a good road but awfully hilly. Make sure you rest your horses a lot."

"Thank you," replied Tompkins. A strange smile came over his face as they turned to leave the store.

As the door closed behind them, the first to speak was Draper. "What the heck just happened in there?" There was a hint of excitement and bewilderment in his voice.

"Let's all get in our vehicles and drive for a few minutes," calmly answered Tompkins. "At the next pull off, let's all get out and have a little talk." Everyone noticed the twinkle in his eyes and the half-smile on his face.

"What's going on, Tompkins?" asked Santana. "You have a crap eating grin on your face."

"Just saddle up and we'll all talk in a little while," barked Bourque.

"OK boys, let's get moving," commanded Bates in agreement. The men quickly jumped into their Jeeps and they headed east down the Chambersburg Pike towards Gettysburg.

As soon as they were on the road, Bourque turned his body towards Tompkins and began to speak.

"All right smarty, what's going on? You seem to have an idea of what's up, so let me in on it, will you?" Bourque seemed a little bit upset, as the vein on his forehead was beginning to pop out again.

"Well," began Tompkins, "I've been trying to pay attention to everything that has been happening since our visit at that old store yesterday. I've traveled through this part of the country before and this is the first time I've seen stores like these and met people so, so," there was a pause in his explanation. "So far removed from normality."

"Yeah, I know what you're saying," replied Bourque as he rubbed his forehead. "I've spent some time around the Amish and the Mennonites. They seem uninformed and backwards, but they are well aware of modern technologies and the ways of the rest of the world."

"Exactly," burst Tompkins. "Think about that girl's remark. It's a two day trip to Gettysburg, only forty miles away. And make sure to rest your horses."

Tompkins was starting to talk faster as the pieces of the puzzle seemed to fall into place. "Think about the last two stores," he began again. "And what was on the walls and shelves."

They both took a minute to visualize the two strange stores. Bourque's mind raced over the shelves and all the walls as Tompkins continued to speak. "Remember when we paid for the stuff we got. The storekeeps looked at our money as if they had never seen it before. The maps are not correct. The weather is completely different from what it was on the other side of the mountain."

"All right," laughed Bourque. "Slow down, you're like a little kid in a candy store. What does it all mean?"

With a smile and a quick laugh, Tompkins continued. "Well," he breathed, "the one thing that brought me to the conclusion I am going to tell you is the trees. I've noticed the vegetation and types of trees on our trip today. I have seen at least a thousand elm trees along this road alone.

"Boy, I haven't seen an elm tree in a long time," remarked Bourque.

"Yeah, just what I mean," said Tompkins. "Elm trees were wiped out by Dutch Elm Disease back in the mid 1900s. I've seen lots of young elm trees along this road." Tompkins head was moving back and forth to emphasize his bewilderment.

"I've talked with Bates a little since we left Ohio," began Bourque. "He has been feeling real strange. I've had some feelings that I only get in extreme situations. I've also noticed your demeanor the last day or so is different than usual. I'll admit I'm not the most analytical guy around. Heck, if it isn't military in nature, I usually ignore it. But I know something strange is going on."

The Jeep became silent for the first time since they left the store, Both men's eyes were scanning the countryside as the vehicles slowly traversed the bumpy road.

"And what's up with that goofy smile you've had for the last hour?" Bourque burst out. "I've noticed it several times today. You look like you just seen a dirty magazine for the first time."

Both men burst into laughter. It was a rare occasion when Bourque would attempt humor in a conversation. As the laughter subsided, the radio cracked and Draper's voice interrupted the moment.

"Tiger 1, this is Tiger 2, when are we going to hash out what's going on? Over."

Bourque reached for the handset but Tompkins beat him to it.

"Tiger 2, why don't you pull over up there at that open spot. Bourque and I will go on and see what is up ahead. We'll be back in a few minutes. Over."

"Roger Tiger 1," replied Draper. "But remember you two, the military frowns on gay relationships." You could hear the laughter from the other Jeep and the radio went silent.

"Boy, that guy is a real goof," laughed Bourque.

"Well, he is going to need some humor when I fill them in on what I think is going on." Tompkins voice was excited as he continued. "I wanted to run my idea by you first, before we all talk."

"I'm listening," answered Bourque. "And just get to the point of all this. I'm getting tired of all the details and speculation. I've heard way too much weird stuff today already. I'm starting to get a headache."

"All right," began Tompkins. "Here is what I think is going on." Tompkins took a deep breath and continued. "I don't know how, why or what is up for sure, but when I put all the pieces together, I come up with this conclusion." Once again Tompkins took a deep breath. "I believe we are currently in the 1800s." Bourque looked at Tompkins as if he were speaking gibberish. "From the dress of the people we have encountered and the weather conditions, I'm pretty sure we are back in 1863. June 30th, the day before the battle of Gettysburg."

With a look of dismay, Bourque said, "I'm listening."

"I don't know for sure, but I think it might be best to talk to the other guys about my conclusions. Then we can proceed to Gettysburg. I don't know what they will think of all this, but we must keep open minds."

"Yeah, to think this might be happening you have to keep an open mind," replied Bourque.

Once again the Jeep became silent. Both men were deep in thought about their current situation. "Well, what do you think?" Tompkins finally asked Bourque.

"We have been on a lot of unique missions and seen a lot of strange things," began Bourque, rubbing his chin as if in deep thought. "If this is really happening, I'm glad you're here. You know more about the battle of Gettysburg than anyone I know."

"Thanks, Bourque," replied Tompkins.

It was a good feeling to get a compliment from a war-hardened veteran like Bourque. Tompkins knew he kept his feelings close to himself. Tompkins felt relieved that Bourque's mind was open to his conclusion.

"We need to present a united front to the other guys," began Tompkins. "When we tell them what we think is going on, it will be easier to accept it if both of us believe it."

"I got your back," replied Bourque. "I just wonder what the guys are going to think when we spill this on them."

CHAPTER 6

Putting the clues together

Tompkins did a U-turn and headed back to the rendezvous spot. No more was said as they drove the five minutes back west. As Tompkins and Bourque pulled the Jeep next to the other, they looked at each other and burst into laughter. The only thing Bourque could say was, "Boo Yah hound dog." This made them laugh even harder. As they wiped the tears from their eyes, they exited the vehicle.

As their feet hit the dirt, they saw the other three men were rushing towards them. "Bourque, I better not see any hickeys," laughed Draper as he approached them. Bourque reached out and grabbed him, putting him in a headlock. He slapped Draper sharply on the head and released him. "Don't get jealous now, we have bigger fish to fry," chirped Bourque.

"Let's all sit down and figure this out," commanded Bates.

They all gathered around the equipment trailer and sat on the bumpers of the vehicles. Nothing was said for at least a minute as the men's eyes were focused on Tompkins. Tompkins knew the men were looking to him for answers. He looked at Bourque for some reassurance. Bourque just nodded his head to tell Tompkins to start his almost unbelievable explanation of the day's events and what could lie before them. Just as Tompkins was opening his mouth to start his explanation, Draper burst in.

"We've been talking amongst ourselves and we think we have an idea of what's going on."

"Quiet Draper," yelled Bates. "Let's hear what the brains of the operation has to say."

"Sorry, I'm just a bit excited," explained Draper.

Tompkins took a long breath and began his explanation. "Well boys, this will seem way out in left field but here is what we have come up with."

Tompkins reached into his pocket and pulled out the map he had been studying for the last day. He spread it on the ground and kneeled next to it. He then took out a yellow highlighter and began to speak again.

"We are here." He drew a large X on the map. "According to the map, this should be a paved major highway. It clearly isn't. There also should be a rest stop at this very location. There obviously isn't."

All the men noticed Tompkins unsure demeanor. "In case you didn't notice, the last two stores we stopped at were not the type of stores we are accustomed to. I know you guys have not noticed, but the forest that surrounds us is full of elm trees that should have been wiped out more than fifty years ago."

Tompkins reclined back on his knees and looked at each of the men. They were all at attention like a bunch of school kids waiting to hear the twist in the fairy tale.

Tompkins continued. "Nothing for sure, but from the dress, mannerisms and conversations with the two storekeepers, I would say we are somehow back in the 1800s." Tompkins expected everyone to laugh at his explanation but everyone just kept on staring at him with wide eyed enthusiasm.

"What, no stupid comments, Draper?" asked Bourque.

"I'm just taking it all in," replied Draper.

"How do you think this happened?" asked Santana.

"Well I think it had something to do with that tunnel and storm back at that mountain," continued Tompkins. "Remember how the road got so rough all of a sudden and when we came out the other side of the mountain, the weather was completely different than when we entered? The best I can figure is we somehow went through a time portal or something like that." "Tompkins, you're probably the smartest man I've ever known," interjected Bates. "You really think something like this could happen?"

"I don't know," replied Tompkins as he scratched his head. "I've never really believed in all that sci-fi stuff, but we are in the middle of something strange."

As Tompkins looked around at the men, they all nodded their heads to show him their belief in what he was saying.

"Bates," burst out Draper, "tell them about your feeling."

Bates lifted his head and began to speak. "I don't know if this has anything to do with our situation, but I've had a real bad feeling since our first stop at that old store on the other side of the mountain. I've only had that kind of feeling once before and when I had it, crap hit the fan." Bates stood up and began to walk around the others. "The feeling was going away, so I thought. Then we stopped at that last store and the feeling got so strong, well, you know, I lost my lunch."

"I had a very weird feeling also," added Bourque.

"Well, when I put all these clues together, I come up with the same conclusion," added Tompkins. "We are back in the 1800s."

"What time frame of the 1800s do you think we're in?" asked Santana.

"From the dress of the storekeepers, goods in the stores and the conversations with the storekeepers, I figure we are somewhere in the 1860s during the Civil War."

Tompkins had that silly look on his face again.

"What's up with that smile Tompkins? We all noticed it back at that store," asked Santana. Tompkins looked up at everyone with an almost childish smile on his face.

"I had a feeling a while ago that something strange was going on. At the last store I glanced at a pile of letters on the counter. The postmark on one of the letters was from June 15." There was a pause on his explanation. He slowly looked into the eyes of each of the men before he spit out, "1863." The smile on his face widened as he once again looked at each of the men.

"OK," replied Draper. "What's the significance of that date that would make you so excited?"

"I should have known you goofs wouldn't put it together," replied Tompkins. There was a long pause before Bourque reached over and slapped Draper on the back of the head.

"Think about it, stupid," said Bourque.

The three clueless men looked at each other and just shrugged their shoulders. "All right," finally spoke Tompkins. "We are on the verge of the deadliest battle on American soil. The battle of Gettysburg."

All eyes were wide now as the pieces fell together in their minds. The only sound made was "Crap," uttered by Draper. Tompkins continued his explanation.

"I know just about everything about the battle of Gettysburg. From the weather conditions, I think it may be June 30th, the day before the battle begins. It's June 30th, today, in the real world, so we must be on the same day, just back in 1863. And if that's the case, we will be witness to some real history and some real human devastation."

As Tompkins finished, all faces were fixed on the map now, as if they were ready to continue this unexplainable mission.

"You know guys," began Tompkins. "I really expected you all to tell me I was crazy. What's your take on our situation?"

"I was about to tell you our thoughts on the situation," started Draper. "But Bates told me to shut up." Draper shot a quick smile at Bates. "While you and Bourque were off getting romantic, we came up with pretty much the same conclusion."

"Except without all the specifics," added Santana. "We thought you two would think we were crazy."

"Well at least we're all crazy together," laughed Bourque. This brought a welcome tension breaking laugh to the group of men. Ease seemed to fill the group now as they stood, ready to continue their journey.

"What we need to do now," explained Tompkins. "Is to set up our plan of attack for the next few days. I know the smart thing to do would be to head as far away from this conflict as possible. But for some reason we are here." After a short pause, he continued. "Maybe we are supposed to be here for a reason." He looked at each man in turn and then shrugged his shoulders. "Maybe it is just coincidence."

All the men looked at each other with blank looks on their faces. They were men of action that acted on instinct and reason. They were not used to figuring out why they were in a region or what their objectives were. Being in a situation like this was new to them, but exciting none the less.

"Hey," burst Santana. "Remember when we were at the first store?" There was a sound of true epiphany in his voice. "The old man said 'thanks for your service to the United States and for your future help in keeping the balance'."

"Yeah, I remember that," said Bates. "He then said something I thought was strange." Bates' eyes looked up to the sky as he remembered the old man's words. "He said, '"remember parties on both sides of a conflict believe their cause is just. History has showed us which side is to prevail, but there is no true blueprint to achieve its success'."

As the last words fell from his lips, Bates looked towards Tompkins. Tompkins face was pale and his jaw was hanging open.

"Boys," sputtered Tompkins. All eyes turned to him. "I think we are supposed to be here. But why?"

Once again no one said a word as they all just looked at one another. After a couple of minutes Bourque broke the silence.

"All right men, I think we need to have a game plan. We have enough weapons and ammo to defeat both armies. That's the one good feeling I get from this whole strange mess."

"Yeah, but we can't use them to alter anything that happened during the battle," spoke up Bates. "If we do something to change what happened during the battle, the outcome of the battle and the whole Civil War could be compromised. At least that is what happened in *Back to the Future*." A quick smile came to his face. "I'm surprised Draper didn't say that." Everyone chuckled.

"All right, let's get serious for a minute," began Tompkins. "With all the strange encounters and weird feelings we've had up to this point, I believe we need to cautiously proceed to Gettysburg."

Tompkins picked up the map and spread it on the hood of the Jeep. "Gather round, we need to understand what we're up against and how we should approach the next few days. Whatever we do, we must be very cautious and keep our heads on straight."

After a few minutes of finger pointing and mumbling to himself, Tompkins stood up straight and started to speak.

"On June 30th, today, the Union Armies were camped south and east of Gettysburg. Their main headquarters were located in Taneytown, right here."

Tompkins tapped his thin finger at a spot on the map. The men leaned forward to see where he was pointing. "The Southern Armies were located north and west of Gettysburg along the Chambersburg Pike." Tompkins pointed to another area on the map, causing all eyes to follow his hand.

"Hey this is the Chambersburg Pike, isn't it?" asked Santana.

"Yes it is," replied Bourque.

"Crap," shot Draper. "Are we close to them now?"

"Not that close," replied Tompkins. "We are about forty miles west of Gettysburg and probably about twenty-five miles west of the Confederate main body. This is going to be complicated and confusing, trying to figure out what the heck we are supposed to do."

Tompkins raised his hand to his forehead and began to massage his scalp. "Let me give you guys a little history about tomorrow's events. Maybe we can then figure out our next move."

"We're all ears," responded Bates. Everyone's attention was focused on Tompkins.

"On June 30th," began Tompkins, "Nothing really happened. Confederate troops were moving towards Gettysburg. They thought it would be a good place to be because all the roads in the area converged on the town. So as we speak, they are moving east along this very road. The Northern Army is still well south of Gettysburg but converging fast. General Buford's Union Cavalry will be entering the town today. He sees the importance of the town and the high spots around it. He knows there will be a battle soon and if the South gets to those high spots they will have the advantage in a battle. He has twenty-five hundred mounted cavalry men at his disposal. He will set up defensive positions here." Tompkins points to a spot on the map. "If you guys were awake the other night when I was trying to tell you about the battle, you would already know most of this information."

"Yeah, but who could of known we were about to be thrust back to the 1800s," replied Draper.

"True," said Tompkins with a smile. "I'll let it slide this time."

"The cavalry was the eyes and the ears of the Army," continued Tompkins. "They were always moving forward of the main body of the army scouting for areas of trouble ahead. General Buford spotted the Confederate Army moving towards Gettysburg. That's why he set up his defensive position here."

Tompkins once again pointed his finger to the map. "At this point, Buford dismounted his men and placed cannons at strategic locations here, here and here. He estimated about five-thousand to ten-thousand men would be coming down this road in the morning on July 1st, tomorrow.

"So how did his twenty-five hundred men hold off five to ten-thousand men?" asked Santana.

"Buford was a great strategic thinker and a great leader," Tompkins continued. He knew that if he dismounted his men and spread them along the trees and rock fences, it would appear they were a larger force than they really were. The cavalry was fitted with Spencer Carbines, which could be loaded much faster than the muzzleloaders of the Infantry. They could shoot and reload at a rate of five times faster than their counterparts. They also were much more accurate and could be fired at greater distances than the muskets of the Confederate Infantry. Buford only had to hold off the South for a few hours in the morning while the Union Infantry made their way there. If Buford wouldn't have held that spot, the battle would have turned out much different."

Tompkins went silent for a second. He stared at the map as his mind wandered for a moment, and he thought to himself.

"Wouldn't it be interesting to get into the mind of a man like Buford? He faced a much larger force, but through strategy and leadership he prevailed."

"But anyways," Tompkins continued. "I think our first move will be to figure out where we should be when the battle begins. This map isn't accurate to the terrain and roads back in 1863, but if we set up here..." Tompkins pointed to the map as everyone leaned in to see. "...we should have a good vantage point to observe the battle."

"Let's saddle up," barked Bourque. "Let's keep radios open and keep an eye out for anything. Remember, automobiles haven't been invented yet, so we must use stealth. Draper, how many of those Ghillie suits do you have?"

"Six," replied Draper.

"Could we use them as camo for the Jeeps?" asked Tompkins.

"Sure, if we split the seams they will spread out to about eight-foot square," replied Draper.

"Great," barked Bourque. "You and Santana work on that as fast as possible. We might need them soon."

"Ten Four boss man," replied Draper in a goofy redneck voice.

"Santana, you get out M16s for each of us with three extra mags each," barked Bourque again. "Better safe than sorry."

The men busied themselves getting ready for the unknown that lay before them. Soon all the men were in their Jeeps and were headed slowly down the Chambersburg Pike.

Within a minute of heading towards Gettysburg, the radio broke the silence.

"Hey guys," crackled Tompkins. "Keep an eye out for dust clouds on the horizon. That many men marching will make a pretty good dust cloud."

"Tompkins," replied Santana. "Do we have to keep an eye out for Confederate Cavalry?"

"No," replied Tompkins. "Jeb Stuart leads the Confederate Cavalry during the battle, but he doesn't show up till the end of the second day. He was north of Gettysburg raiding towns for some reason. Our best bet is to proceed cautiously."

The click of the radio ended the brief conversation. Nothing was said by any of the men as they slowly drove down the dirty, dusty road. They were too busy peering out the windows with binoculars, searching for any sign of what was to come next.

The crackle of the radio broke the silence once again.

"I figure we are about ten miles from the rear of the Confederate Corps," excitedly spoke Tompkins. "At our current speed, we should intercept them in about twenty minutes. I'm going to see if there is an alternate route to the north of Gettysburg. We don't want to make any contact if at all possible. Over."

As Tompkins hung the mike back on the hook, he turned to Bourque and asked, "See that haze up there towards the east?"

"Yeah, looks like troop movement, doesn't it," replied Bourque. "We'd better find that alternate route real fast."

"According to the map, there should be a road that will take us north and then east," replied Tompkins. "If we can get ahead of the main body, we should be able to set up camp and be ready for the battle in the morning. About a half-mile ahead there should be a road that heads north."

Tompkins' head was buried in the map again. It was almost as if he were a pirate looking for a buried treasure. His finger was moving all over the parchment, tracing their projected path. Bourque just drove, his keen eyes keeping a close watch for anything out of the ordinary.

"I hope that road comes up quick, that dust cloud is getting thicker," mentioned Bourque. Just then the radio broke in.

"Hey guys." The familiar sound of Santana's voice broke in. "That dust up ahead, is that the Confederate Army? I've seen the same type of cloud in Iraq when the Guard was moving positions."

They all had seen dust trails from troop movements a thousand times. This was different though. It wasn't a huge moving mass of dirt and dust from a battalion of light armament or tanks. This was a thin mass that seemed to hang in the air as if movement was barely happening.

"Yeah, it's the Confederate troops marching," replied Bourque.

"Doesn't seem to be moving very fast," questioned Santana.

"Let me see the handset," spoke Tompkins as he reached towards Bourque. "Remember," he spoke into the handset. "That isn't a convoy of trucks and tanks. What we have making that dust cloud is twenty-thousand men, horses and wagons. I estimate their speed at about two or three miles per hour."

He handed Bourque the handset as his head fell towards the map again. After a short look at the map Tompkins reached for the handset again.

"I figure we can skirt around them to the north and get to Gettysburg before their lead scouting divisions," began Tompkins once again. "Once we get there, we'll set up camp at a safe distance and wait till morning to see the start of the battle. We are only about fifteen miles from Gettysburg. We shouldn't have to worry about the Confederate Army, but we will still have to keep an eye out for the Union Cavalry. They're already in Gettysburg and getting ready for the battle in the morning. Keep a sharp eye out for anything odd, if there could be anything more odd than us."

"10-4, we're right behind you," countered Santana.

There was silence now. The impending unknown hung in the air like the dust trail they were watching. Their minds were locked on the countryside and they were preoccupied with the job of not being detected. The Jeeps lumbered down the bumpy road making slow time towards their future meeting with history.

Chapter 7

Following the dust cloud

The sound of "Whoa" broke through the noise of thundering hooves. The long line of some twenty-five hundred men on horseback slowed and came to a stop on a long ridge outside of Gettysburg. The man at the lead of the column had his arm in the air to signal the stop. As the long line of horses and men came to a stop, he brought up a pair of binoculars and viewed the western skyline.

"Well, what do we have here?" spoke the man in a low, gravely voice. General Buford, Commander of the Union Cavalry peered through his binoculars as several men rode up to his position on horseback. As they stopped, they all saluted. Buford was impervious to their showing of respect as he peered through his binoculars.

"What do you see, General?" spoke one of the newcomers. General Buford dropped the glasses to his saddle and turned towards the men. His thin, weather-worn face had a puzzled look on it. He lifted his hand and stroked his long graying mustache as he began to speak.

"Men, I have been watching the dust cloud of the main body of the Rebel Army for the last hour. It has been moving east towards Gettysburg and our position." He stretched his arm in the direction of the dust cloud and motioned the direction it was moving.

"In the last few minutes, however, I have seen another dust cloud moving north, splintering off the main body." Buford's hand reached up and stroked his horses' head as if not knowing what to say next. "From the speed of it, it has to be cavalry."

"Sir," broke in one of the men. "Our scouts report Jeb Stuart and his cavalry are riding up north about forty miles from Gettysburg. Do you think the Reb's have another cavalry division we are unaware of?"

"Not to my knowledge," replied Buford. "Something is afoot and we need to find out what it is." Once again Buford lifted the binoculars to his face and studied the skyline.

"Major Erickson," began Buford. "Take fifty men and head north to intercept that dust cloud. Keep out of view. If necessary, dismount and proceed on foot until you can get in a position to see what we are up against. Don't engage the unknown force but report back to me what you find. As soon as possible."

"Yes, Sir," replied Erickson with a salute.

"While you are gone," began Buford. "We will set up our defensive positions along the Chambersburg Pike as previously planned." Buford leaned towards the group of men. "Everyone listen," he began with a stern tone to his voice. "We know we will be in a heck of a fight come morning. Make sure your men are rested and well positioned. Put the cannons on the little ridge and use the rock fences for cover. I'll send word to General Reynolds of our situation. Hopefully he can make a forced march and get here in time to help."

General Buford looked into the eyes of each of the men. "Boys, to stand a chance in the morning, we need to know what is moving to the north." The tension in his voice let the men know he was serious. The twenty-five hundred men in his Calvary had followed him into many battles. There was no doubt about his leadership ability.

"God be with you," Buford spoke in a serious voice. "Let's get to it."

As the last word fell from his lips the men saluted, spun their horses and raced back to their positions in line. It was quite a commotion as the huge group of men split up and rode to their postings. The only group not moving were the fifty men designated to scout the new force moving to the north. As Major Erickson gave them their new orders, the men formed a long line by two's and proceeded to move to the north and west.

Buford was the only man not heading towards their new position. He remained seated on his steed, looking up to the sky. He reached up and took off his sweat-stained, off-white, cowboy-style hat and wiped his forehead with the sleeve of his heavy wool coat. From the look on his face you could see he was in a quandary. The silence was broken by the approach of a horse galloping towards him. Buford didn't even turn to see who was riding up.

"Sir," spoke Colonel Brosco. "The men are in place and the cannons have been placed as you directed. Are there any other orders, Sir?" General Buford slowly turned towards Colonel Brosco. He looked him directly in the face.

"Jack," Buford began, "I've been in a lot of tough spots and seen a lot of destruction in my years of service." Buford turned his head and looked towards Gettysburg.

"I know the battle ahead will be a turning point in the war. I can feel it. If my calculations are correct, nearly one hundred and fifty thousand men will converge on this peaceful little town in the next few days." Buford's eyes dropped to the ground as he continued. "I've got a gut feeling that tells me something strange is in the air. It's not the normal pre-battle jitters, but a bigger feeling." Once again he wiped the sweat from his brow with his sleeve.

"Boy, this weather is something else," spoke Brosco.

"Yeah, it sure is nice the rain has stopped though," replied Buford as he looked towards Gettysburg. Brosco could tell he was thinking of other things as he was staring off to the horizon.

"General Buford, sir," said Brosco, "if there is anything on your mind sir, you can run it by me. We have been through many a hard spot and seen a lot of strange things together."

Buford smiled as he looked towards Brosco. He brought his eyes to meet Jack's.

"Jack, my mother told me that once in your life you will be faced with a rare occasion that will define who you are and where your path in the future will take you. She said that everyone has that same chance, but most people won't recognize it." Buford's face was full of tension as he held his fist tightly clinched in front of him. "Keep an open mind she said. Allow all options to guide your actions. If you take care to weigh all the options, doors will be opened and the correct paths will be shown you." Buford slowly put his old hat back on his head. He pulled the sleeves of his coat down his arms and spun his horse around.

"Jack, I believe this will be one of those occasions," Buford shouted over the grunts of his horse. "Remember that and keep a wary eye for anything strange. I have a feeling we have guardian angels around us." With that said, they saluted and rode off towards the other men.

* * *

Through the thick dust the lead Jeep was barely visible. Draper's head popped up between the two men in the front seat like an excited puppy.

"So what's your take on this whole deal?" he asked to either of them.

Raising his hands in the air to show he didn't have a clue, Santana replied, "I'm trying not to think about this whole mess too deeply, at least until we have some proof about where and when we are."

"What about you, Bates?" asked Draper.

Bates let out a deep breath and shook his head. "I don't know what to think about all this. I've always been a hands-on type of guy. I take care of my men and the mission at hand. I've been in a lot of strange situations where I had to think my way out, but I've never been in a situation where I didn't know what my objectives were, or where I was and especially when I was." With a shrug of his shoulders he continued. "I think we should just play along with whatever comes up. Keep our minds open and try to relax a little bit. At least until it's time not to relax."

"I sure am glad we have Tompkins with us on this mission," added Santana. "He seems to have a handle on what's potentially going on."

Bates shot a quick leer at Draper and Santana. "I sure hope he does." His eyes quickly returned to the road. "Let's keep our eyes open and our heads on swivels," concluded Bates. The three men once again returned to watching out the windows as the Jeeps crawled down the road.

Just as silence overtook the three men, the crackle of the radio made them jump.

The familiar sound of Bourque's voice broke over the radio. "Boys, we're about a mile from our campsite. Are the Ghillie suits ready?"

Santana grabbed the handset off the hook. "10-4 chief, we're ready," he replied.

"When we stop, we'll want to get the vehicles covered as quick as possible. We must not be seen," commanded Bourque.

"Gotcha big guy," replied Santana. "Let us know when and where."

"We should be coming up to a good spot to camp for the night," spoke Tompkins to Bourque. "I figure we should be about half a mile from the area the battle begins on July first. If we set up to the north and west of the area, we should remain undetected. We also should be able to get close enough to get a good view of the battle."

"Do you think anyone knows we are here or should we be all right?" asked Bourque.

"Ah, we should be all right," calmly replied Tompkins. "We're ahead of the Confederate main body and scouts and the Union Cavalry should be moving through Gettysburg as we speak."

Bourque set back in his seat at relative ease. He trusted Tompkins completely and knew he had a knack for keeping out of trouble. But something in the back of his head told him not to get too relaxed.

As the Jeeps slowed for a corner, Tompkins pointed out the window and directed the convoy to stop in a small clearing.

"This should be a good spot to camp for the night," shouted Tompkins out the window to the other Jeep. The vehicles pulled up to the clearing and the men jumped out. Bates and Draper were carrying the Ghillie suits that were modified to cover the Jeeps. Bourque was staring at the two men as they made their way to the trailer. He elbowed Tompkins.

"I can't believe those Ghillie suits," spoke Bourque. "You can see them carrying something, but it looks like nothing, or something like that." Tompkins looked towards the two men, and both he and Bourque started to laugh. Both men's arms were stretched out as if carrying something, but the Ghillie suits took the appearance of the grass around them perfectly.

"Yeah it's kind of amazing how those things work that way," replied Tompkins with a laugh. He then returned to unloading their Jeep.

Bates, Draper and Santana spread the first Ghillie suit over the trailer attached to their Jeep. They then scurried around the Jeep, spreading it evenly over its entire body. When they had it just right, they stepped back to see how it looked. They just stood there with their arms at their sides, looking at what used to be their Jeep and trailer. The Ghillie suits covered them perfectly and left them virtually invisible.

"Hey Bourque," yelled Bates. "Come over here and look at this." Bourque dropped the duffle he was unloading and lumbered over to them. He turned and stood in line with the others.

"Unbelievable," was all he could say. Tompkins then walked over and joined the line.

"This is exactly what I hoped they would do," said Tompkins. All of the men stood and admired the work of the Ghillie suits.

The moment was short-lived as Bourque's shout brought them back to reality. "All right girls, the prom dress looks pretty. Now get back to work."

The men began to move, except for Draper. "Hey Bourque," shouted Draper. "I bet your prom date was as big as a Jeep, but not as pretty." As Draper turned to see what type of response he got from Bourque, he was knocked on his back by a duffle that was thrown from fifty feet away. As the laughs started to die down from the other men and Draper picked himself off the ground, Bourque yelled, "I was going to take your mother but I couldn't fit her in the back of my pickup." Once again laughs erupted from everyone.

"Yeah, she is rather large," laughed Draper.

After the moment of levity, it was back to work. They all worked quickly on getting the other Jeep covered. Everyone continued their jobs as the sun began to sink lower in the sky. When they were finished, the only visual evidence of their presence was the open door on the lead Jeep. Tompkins slammed the door shut and all evidence of their presence was gone.

"Let's set up camp over there by those rocks," commanded Bourque. He pointed to a spot about twenty yards from the vehicles along a line of medium sized rocks.

"Let's get some wood for a fire, Draper," said Santana.

"10-4, El Capitan," replied Draper as the two men headed into the woods. "When they return," began Tompkins, "We should talk about our plan for tomorrow."

* * *

The dust trail has stopped," said Major Erickson. "About a mile to the northwest." Erickson dropped the binoculars to his saddle and turned to the other men. "The sun is almost gone and the dust trail has settled. They must have stopped for the night up ahead."

Erickson placed the binoculars in a large leather saddle bag on his horse and wiped the dust from his face. "Let's ride to about half a mile from their camp and proceed on foot. Once we get close, we'll find out the identity of the force and report back to General Buford. Let's proceed slow and keep a wary eye."

Erickson turned his horse towards the northwest, raised his arm and waived it forward. The column of men on horses moved at a trot behind him in a cloud of dust. The last of the horse-backed men disappeared over a small hill as the sun fell behind the horizon.

* * *

"Draper, Santana," shouted Bourque. "Have you found any wood? We need to get a fire going before it gets too dark." Just as Bourque finished yelling, Draper and Santana emerged from the woods with arms full of branches.

"Keep it down King Kong," spoke Draper. "We're back." The two men dropped their load of wood in a pile next to the makeshift fire pit designed by Bates. Santana bent down and neatly stacked the wood in the fire pit. He then grabbed some dry grass to use as kindling, and lit a fire. The flame was small at first but then burst into a true campfire as the wood finally ignited.

"Gather round, meatheads," grumbled Bourque. "Tompkins is going to brief us on tomorrow's plans."

The men grouped around Tompkins as he began to speak. "To begin, we need to determine our position and parameters." Tompkins used his boot to clear the rocks and twigs from a bare spot near the fire. As the firelight shone on the men's faces he continued.

"We are here." He took a stick and marked an X in the dirt. "The battle will begin here. Confederate troops will emerge from this area where they will meet Buford's dismounted cavalry." Tompkins continued drawing lines in the dirt. He glanced around at the men and was happy to see he had their full attention. "Tonight, Buford's men are setting up defensive positions and positioning their artillery. Buford will send word to General Reynolds that he expects a battle in the morning. Reynolds will start a forced march hoping his twenty-thousand men will arrive in time to join the battle. At approximately 7:00am, the battle begins. The fighting is fierce as more than five-thousand Confederate infantrymen come down the Chambersburg Pike. Buford's men hold off the oncoming charge for quite a while."

Tompkins was drawing lines as he spoke, giving the other men a good idea of the direction and location of the fight. All eyes and ears were glued on Tompkins as he was speaking and drawing. The firelight was getting dim, so Bates instinctively grabbed a small log and tossed it on the fire. He barely moved his eyes from Tompkins as he continued. "Man it was a delicate balance between winning and losing the first day's battle."

"What do you mean?" asked Santana. Tompkins raised his eyes from the ground for the first time since he started to speak.

He looked at Santana and smiled. "Well, the battle raged on for hours with the Confederates bringing up reinforcements. The Union's only hope for holding their ground was for Reynolds and his twenty-thousand men to arrive before the Confederate forces broke through. Just as the South was breaking the Union lines, Reynolds showed up. If something would have happened that would have slowed Reynolds arrival, the Union position may have been overtaken and the battle may have turned out different." Tompkins once again dropped his eyes to the dirt and began to draw again. "As it was, the south ended up pushing the Union back through town by the end of the day. The saving grace was that they were pushed back to even better defensive positions. If the south would have continued their assault, instead of stopping for the night, they would have taken the high ground around Gettysburg and may have won the entire battle."

With a big yawn, Tompkins finally relaxed and sat back from his dirt chalkboard. When the men saw Tompkins relax, they, too, for the first time since he started his explanation, relaxed. The warmth of the night and the soft flicker of the firelight eased all their minds. Nothing was said as they stretched their legs and reclined back on their bedrolls.

Through the complete silence and solitude of the ominous night, the loud crack of a branch shattered the moment. Every man instinctively grabbed his M16 and scanned the woods in the direction of the sound. Every one of their senses was pushed to the limit. For what seemed like an eternity, the men quietly waited for any indication of what made the noise. After a minute or two Bourque broke the silence.

"Probably just an animal," he quietly whispered. "Let's just unpucker our sphincters and relax."

"Tompkins," whispered Bates, "Are there any troops in this area?" Tompkins shrugged his shoulders.

"I don't think so," whispered Tompkins. "All the troops should be quite a ways away getting ready for the battle. Bourque's right. It's probably just an animal."

With Tompkins agreement that it probably was just an animal and not trouble, the men once again relaxed. They, however, kept a relatively tight hold on their rifles. It was more of a habit than out of fear. They had found it better to be ready for a fight than to drop your guard completely. It wasn't long before their fingers fell from the triggers and their minds became foggy with sleep.

Chapter 8

Past meets present

Finding their way through the darkness of the woods proved more difficult than they thought. The fifty men slowly creeping through the moonless night, undetected in unfamiliar terrain, was very out of the normal. The men were used to being on horseback, letting the horse traverse the rough terrain. Moving through the darkness was not their forte, as most battles and scouting activities ended at sundown.

"Watch your step men," whispered Erickson. "We don't want to give our location away."

They could see the light from the fire now and hear the men talking. "Stay back and be ready to advance on my signal," whispered Erickson. He slowly crept towards the edge of the woods. His eyes strained to see his path. As he pushed the branches of a bush to the side, he could see five men around the fire. He quickly scanned the entire clearing, expecting to see at least ten times that number of men around many fires. From forty yards, he could not make out their uniforms. There were no horses or flags. No distinguishing marks of any kind to give him an idea of their identity.

Just as Erickson was ready to head back to his men, one of the five stood up and stretched his arms. By the firelight Erickson could see he was wearing an unfamiliar uniform. One he had never seen before. After stretching his arms, the man walked over to a spot and pulled a blanket from what seemed to be thin air. The man then returned to the fire and sat down.

Erickson didn't understand what he just witnessed. His eyes strained to see from where or what he had pulled the blanket. With no idea what was happening, Erickson slowly returned to his men.

"Let's retreat back to our horses and report to General Buford as fast as possible," he whispered to his men.

The fifty men slowly made their way back to their horses and headed for Gettysburg to report their unusual findings.

* * *

"Hey Bates," whispered Bourque. "The hair on my neck is standing up. I feel like we're being watched."

"Me too," whispered Bates.

"I'll get to the bottom of this," whispered Draper. He then reached into his duffle and pulled out a Ghillie suit. He pulled it over himself and disappeared into the night. The other men quietly waited for his return to the campsite.

After fifteen minutes, Draper reappeared at the campsite and sat down. He neatly folded the Ghillie suit and put it into his duffle. "I didn't find anything," spoke Draper, "And nothing found me, so I guess we're all right ."

"Yeah, let's get some sleep," reassured Tompkins. "It's been a long and unusual day. I have a feeling tomorrow is going to be a doozy." Tompkins looked at his watch. "I'll set my alarm for 5:00am. That should give us enough time to figure out what the heck we're going to do."

"Do you think we should have a sentry through the night?" asked Santana.

"Naw, we should be all right," replied Tompkins with a laugh. "Bourque sleeps with one eye open anyways."

As the laughs subsided, the men's minds and bodies were finally at ease. It wasn't long before all eyes were closed. Soft snores were soon in the air as the men drifted into sleep.

* * *

The lights of the Seminary, just outside of Gettysburg, were flickering from the dancing flames of candles as the fifty men on horseback came to a halt outside the front entrance. Being the makeshift headquarters of General Buford, the men were met by several guards as Erickson dismounted.

"Who goes there?" questioned one of the sentries with his side arm drawn.

"Major Erickson reporting to General Buford," replied Erickson. The man quickly came to attention and saluted.

"Sorry, Sir," he quickly replied. "General Buford is awaiting your report inside, sir."

Erickson saluted the soldier and turned to his men still perched on their horses.

"Dismount men and water your horses," ordered Erickson. "Be ready to ride again immediately." His men turned their horses and galloped over to a long watering trough. They dismounted and let their horses drink.

As Erickson entered the Seminary, he was met by Buford. The men saluted each other and walked into the parlor.

"What's your findings Bob?" asked Buford. He then turned and motioned Erickson to sit in a nearby chair. As the men reclined in the plush chairs, Erickson began to speak.

"My report is kind of strange, General Buford." Erickson took off his hat and swatted it on his knee. The dust fell to the floor in a little cloud. He then looked up at Buford and continued. "We located the unknown force about four miles to the northwest of our battle lines. We approached them on foot from about five-hundred yards, so we would not be detected. As we came to within fifty yards, what I saw was rather odd indeed." Erickson rubbed the sweat and dirt from his face with the sleeve of his thick woolen coat. "Boy, it must still be at least ninety degrees out there," remarked Erickson. "Get on with it Bob," commanded Buford with added excitement.

"Yes Sir, sorry Sir," said Erickson. "The force making the dust cloud was not enemy cavalry." Erickson looked Buford right in the eyes and said, "It was only five men."

"Are you sure Major?" questioned Buford.

"Yes, Sir. We combed the woods around them and found no horses or signs of horses. There were just five men sitting around a campfire without a care in the world." Buford then leaned forward and loosened his collar. "What were their uniform markings?" he asked.

"That's another strange thing, General," replied Erickson. "They were wearing uniforms that I have never seen before. Green uniforms with brown and black markings on them. It looked like they wanted to blend into the forest."

"Huh," remarked Buford as he rubbed his chin. "Doesn't sound like anything I've heard of from the Confederate Army." Buford had a puzzled look on his face as he now stood up and began to pace in front of Erickson.

"You said you didn't find any horses?" asked Buford.

"No Sir," replied Erickson. "Not a sign." Erickson then stood up and faced Buford. "Then something even stranger happened," added Erickson. "One of the men stood up and walked away from the fire. From out of the thin air he pulled a blanket. As hard as I could stare, I could not see any type of wagon or case from which he could have pulled the blanket. There must have been something there, but I could not see it." Buford turned towards the window and stared out at the starless night. His mind was cluttered with Erickson's ramblings. He turned to Erickson and placed a hand on his shoulder.

"Bob," he said. "Something strange is afoot. I better have a look for myself." "Yes, Sir," replied Erickson. "The men are waiting outside as we speak. It's about a thirty minute ride from here. I'll have your horse saddled and ready in five minutes."

"Thanks, Bob," replied Buford. "We're gonna have a battle here in the morning. We need to get this settled as fast as possible. I need to be back here to ready our men and prepare our battle plans."

"Yes, Sir," replied Erickson with a smile. "Hopefully we can keep that schedule."

Erickson then turned to leave the building but was stopped by Buford. "Bob," Buford said. Erickson spun around and stood at attention.

"Bob," began Buford. "I've had a strange feeling something odd was afoot. This may be it." With a stern look on his face, he calmly said, "Hopefully it will help us with this monumental battle we have before us. If it is against us, we may be in a world of hurt."

"Yes sir," answered Erickson. "I sure hope General Reynolds can force a march and get here in time tomorrow." Buford then turned back to the window and once again starred out. With his arms behind his back, he took a deep breath. "Me too, Bob, me too."

No more was said as Erickson departed to prepare for their upcoming ride. Buford remained at the window, however, deep in thought.

"What could this mean?" he murmured. "With the impending battle looming large as the cause itself, how can I divert my thoughts towards anything but finding a way to victory?" Buford then turned and walked towards the door, stopping just short of it. "Keep an open mind and work quickly," he told himself. "Maybe these strange events are part of a bigger picture. Trust your feelings and trust the Good Lord and all things will be used for good. Remember what your mother told you when you were young. Eternal vigilance towards the cause will guide you through many a hard circumstance."

As if released from a hypnotic trance, Buford shook his head and left the bright comfort of the Seminary for the dark ominous unknown that lay before him.

As Buford and his scouting party rode through the dark, hot night, Buford could not ignore the feeling that something strange was going to happen.

***

Back at the campsite, Bates was having the same problem. As he lay on his sleeping bag, his stomach was once again flipping over.

"Hey Draper," he whispered. "I'm getting that feeling again except this time it is really bad. I think I'm going to..."

Bates jumped up before he could finish his sentence and ran into the woods. It was evident what he was doing from the gut wrenching sounds he was making. Everyone sat up.

"What's his problem?" asked Bourque.

"It's his gut feeling again," replied Draper.

"Sure hope he figures out what is making him so sick," interjected Santana.

"Wonder if it has anything to do with our present situation?" asked Tompkins.

"You all right?" shouted Draper.

"Yeah, I'm feeling better now," answered Bates. "I'll be there in a couple minutes, just gotta get my head clear."

"Let us know if you need anything," replied Tompkins. "Let's try to get some shuteye. Morning is going to hit us soon."

The four men lay back on their makeshift beds and closed their eyes. Bates, on the other hand, was sitting on a stump with his head in his hands. "I gotta figure this out," he told himself.

He took a deep breath and stood up. As he took a step he heard a twig snap behind him. He quickly turned to see what made the sound. He was met by several blue-clad men with rifles pointed at him. Bates first thought was to pull up his M16 to defend himself, but he quickly realized he had left it at the campsite.

"Hands up partner and don't make a sound," said the closest man. Bates slowly raised his hands and placed them on his head. "Now turn and slowly walk towards the fire," directed the man. "I'll drop you like a rabbit if you try to run."

Bates turned and headed towards the fire with the unknown men close behind him. His mind raced as he slowly made his way through the dark woods. He thought he could use the dark to make an escape, but where would he go? He didn't know how many men were in the woods or where more of them might be. If he ran, the other men might be caught in the crossfire. So he hesitantly decided to obey the man and play it safe.

As Bates stepped out of the woods, no one at the campfire moved. He could tell that they were sleeping from the muffled snores he heard. He slowly made his way towards the fire. Suddenly he caught movement on both sides of him. He slowly moved his head to the left and then the right. He was surprised to see at least twenty or thirty men on either side of him. From their dark uniforms he could tell they were from the Union Army. His mind and body came to a halt as the realization of what was happening hit him like a brick.

"Tompkins was right," he murmured under his breath. He also noticed the knot in his stomach was gone for the first time since they started this trip. "Well at least I know what that gut feeling was about," he thought to himself. "Now we'll see how the rest of our little vacation goes."

As Bates and his captors came within ten yards of the campfire, they were greeted by a large muffled explosion.

"Bourque," yelled Draper. "I hope that doesn't smell as bad as it sounded." As Draper rolled over in his bed, he caught a glimpse of Bates' empty sleeping bag. As it dawned on him that Bates was still in the woods, he raised his head and looked toward the dark forest. His eyes widened as he seen Bates and the other men descending on the camp. Draper's hands moved to his M16. He slowly moved it to his lap and flipped the safety off.

"Wake up," he whispered to the other men. Their eyes opened expecting the light of morning to blind them. Instead they awoke to the distressed look of Draper grasping his M16. They immediately scrambled for their M16s and pulled them to their laps.

"Easy does it guys," whispered Bourque. "There are about forty men in blue uniforms behind Bates. I've been watching them for a while now." As Bates and the men approached the camp, the four men around the fire sprung up and shouldered their rifles.

"Easy guys," screamed Bates, as he froze in his tracks. Being the war hardened leader, Bourque quickly scanned the scene and made a quick decision. He knew they could easily defeat the unknown force, but at what cost? They might get off at least one clip each, but one of them would surely be wounded by the unknown force. And then how many more men are hidden in the woods?

In the split seconds these things ran through Bourque's mind, he quickly and sharply barked, "At ease men. Lower your weapons." As if spoken by God himself, they dropped their M16s.

"Good choice men," spoke one of the Union soldiers. "Everyone put your hands in the air." The four men laid their rifles on the ground and slowly raised their hands in the air. Bourque looked at Tompkins and to his surprise, Tompkins had that funny smirk on his face.

"Better wipe that grin off your face until we find out what is going on, don't ya think," whispered Bourque. Tompkins glanced back at Bourque and the smile dropped from his face.

Bates walked up to the campfire and joined the other four men. The band of mysterious soldiers closed in around them, rifles at their shoulders. As they entered the light from the fire, Tompkins could see they were from the Union Cavalry. They all carried sidearms and were aiming Sharp's Carbines at them. He estimated the size of the group to be about twenty men.

"Easy men," spoke one of the soldiers. "We're here to find out who you are and what your intentions are." He alone dropped his weapon to his side, turned and called out, "General, the site is secured." He then turned and faced the five men once more. The sound of many boot steps echoed through the night. Within a few seconds, the size of the group doubled to about fifty. They surrounded the campfire with rifles shouldered. A small gap opened in the mass of men as General Buford made his way to the campfire. He walked up to the men and eyed them up and down as if he were studying aliens.

As he looked at Tompkins, Tompkins instinctively brought his arm up to a salute. When he realized what he did, he slowly, sheepishly lowered it. The other four men were looking at him with contempt. Buford just stood there and stared. He saw the flag on Tompkins chest and *United States* sewn on his uniform. With a strange look on his face, he saluted Tompkins back.

"General, Sir," broke the silence. "Is it safe to lower our rifles?" As Buford looked at each of the men closely he replied, "I believe it is, Major."

The Major gave the order to lower their weapons and the men slowly lowered their rifles. There was a lull of any action or words for a moment as everyone was trying to figure out who the other was. Buford then walked over to a large rock next to the fire and sat down.

"Sit down men," he ordered. Everyone sat down, except for Tompkins. Buford shot him a quick look and continued to speak. "Listen men." He was leaning forward on the rock, elbows on knees. From the tone of his voice, they could tell he was intense. "Who are you and what is your mission in this area? I don't recognize your uniforms, but I see our flag and *United States* on them." He once again stared at the emblems on their uniforms. "If I were a gambling man, I would have to say you five men are on the Union Side.

As Buford stopped speaking and looked into the eyes of the men, Tompkins turned to the other men. They were all looking at him as if waiting for his reply. Bourque gave Tompkins a nod of reassurance and he began his explanation.

"General Buford, let me introduce us." Tompkins pointed to Draper first. "General Sir, this is CIA Special Operations Agent, Colonel Michael Draper." Draper stood up and saluted Buford out of respect. Buford stood and saluted Draper in return.

Tompkins then pointed at Santana, who immediately stood at attention. "General, this is Green Beret Specialist Major Gregory Santana." Santana then saluted Buford and Buford saluted back.

Tompkins next pointed to Bates. "General Buford, the man you found in the woods is Army Ranger Colonel Matthew

Bates." Tompkins gave Bates a quick look of contempt since he was still seated. Bates slowly stood and gave Buford a weak salute. "Sorry General Buford," Bates spoke. "I'm still a little on edge from our meeting in the woods."

"Understandable, Colonel," replied Buford. "Relax a bit, we have no hostile intentions towards any of you." Buford gave Bates a small smile. Bates then sat down with the other men. Tompkins took a deep breath and pointed towards Bourque. "General Buford, this is our leader. Navy Seal Commander, Brigadier General Thomas Bourque." Bourque stood at attention and saluted Buford. Bourque knew he didn't have to salute his equally commissioned counterpart, but knew it would show respect and assist in this most unusual meeting. As Bourque stood at attention, Tompkins could see everyone's eyes widen as the massive, ogre-like physique of Bourque blocked out most of the light from the fire. Buford stood for the first time, dwarfed by Bourque's gigantic stature, and saluted.

"I definitely would want General Bourque on my side," replied Buford with a laugh. There was a small rumble of laughter throughout the Union troops.

"Thank you, Sir," replied Bourque, as he fell at ease. As the laughter stopped, Tompkins continued.

"My name, General Buford, is Marine Weapons Specialist and Battle Historian, Colonel Frank Tompkins." Tompkins saluted Buford and extended his hand to Buford. "Sir, it is an honor to meet you," excitedly spoke Tompkins. Buford saluted Tompkins and then shook his hand.

"Thank you, Colonel," replied Buford. "Let's all sit down and get to the brass tacks of all this." As everyone once again sat down, the air seemed a bit lighter.

Buford once again leaned forward and began to speak. "Now, we witnessed a large dust cloud from our battle position, yet we see no horses or wagons. How do you explain this?"

The five men looked at each other and smirked. Bourque nodded his head in the direction of the Jeeps, giving Tompkins the go ahead to show Buford and his men their first secret. Tompkins rose from the ground and began his explanation.

"General Buford, I think it would be best to explain our intentions before we go any further." Buford nodded his approval.

"Colonel, that might shed some light on the whole situation," calmly spoke Buford. Tompkins nodded and continued.

"We are on a joint military government training mission. We have weapons that, in the right hands, could change the face of the Civil War. We are traveling across the country giving exhibitions to government and military dignitaries." Tompkins knew he was speaking only partial truths. He knew to expose their hand too quickly might cause problems. He thought it would be best to ease Buford and his men into what is going on.

"We have and have always had the charge to defend the United States of America," he continued. "We did not expect to be in any battle situation during our mission, so this has put us in an unusual situation."

"What are you getting at, Colonel?" asked Buford.

Tompkins' wasn't quite sure where to go next with his explanation. He could see his ramblings weren't getting by Buford. He looked to Bourque for some reassurance. Bourque just gave him a shoulder shrug with a blank look. The other men had the same look on their faces. Tompkins gave them a sneer. Sweat was beading on Tompkins forehead and his stomach was souring. He looked up and down the line of Union Cavalry and ended up at Buford. Buford could see Tompkins was faltering, so he stood up and placed a hand on his shoulder.

"Son," he began, "I can see you're circling the wagons here. We've already established we're on the same side, and I've only got a short time to get to the bottom of all this. We're expecting a battle first thing in the morning, so if you could possibly help me understand this, I would greatly appreciate it."

Buford took his hand from Tompkins shoulder and sat back down on the rock. Tompkins took a minute to collect his thoughts and then continued.

"General, let me show you why you found no horses or wagons, but first let me tell you one thing." Tompkins wiped the sweat from his forehead. "I know you are a great leader and your men are part of an elite Union Corp. I've also heard you are a visionary type of man and open minded." Tompkins looked up and down the line of Union men. "Men, you might not understand all I am going to show and tell you, but please bear with me as I do my best to explain all this." Tompkins then turned and started to walk away. All heads turned to follow him.

"Follow me if you would," Tompkins requested, as he walked towards the Jeeps. Before he reached the first Jeep, he stopped and turned toward the following troops.

Tompkins looked for the familiar faces of his men. They were in the front of the group and gave Tompkins the reassurance he needed to continue.

"I am going to show you the reason you saw a dust cloud without any horses." He slowly turned towards the invisible Jeep and pulled off the Ghillie suit. There was a gasp from the troops as they saw the Jeep appear out of thin air. Tompkins couldn't help but smile when he saw their reaction.

"What in tarnations is this?" asked Buford with a tone of amazement. "It looks like a wagon of sorts, but where are the horses?"

The dim light from the fire gave only a partial view of the Jeep. Tompkins turned towards the Jeep with his back to the troops and Buford. He stood there for a minute as the troops talked wildly amongst themselves. Tompkins knew that he must be cautious in how he presented the equipment to Buford and his men.

As all the options ran through his head, Tompkins walked over to the other hidden Jeep and trailer and pulled off the other Ghillie suit. Once again the troops burst into conversation over what they were viewing. Tompkins, with a wide grin on his face, turned back around and faced the troops. In his hand he held the Ghillie suit he had pulled off the trailer. As his mind once again raced for the right way to proceed, he let the suit drop to his feet as he began to speak.

"General Buford, what I have uncovered before you are called automobiles. To make a long story short, they are basically railroad locomotives that do not need rails." Tompkins knew his time for explanations was short, so he tried to make it as simple and believable as possible.

"These vehicles take the place of many horses and wagons and can be driven for long periods of time at high speeds."

"Hold on a minute," burst out Buford. "How are these vehicles powered? The steam powered locomotives are very large and require wood for heat to make the steam. From the size of these things, it would almost seem impossible." There wasn't time to get into all the dynamics of the combustion engine, so Tompkins offered a quick explanation.

"These vehicles," he began, "are equipped with internal combustion engines. Instead of wood producing heat, they use a liquid fuel source, similar to kerosene, that basically does the same thing as wood."

Buford just stood there with his arms behind him, staring at the Jeep.

"All right," Buford burst. "This is no time to try and understand all this." Buford approached Tompkins and pointed to his feet.

"What kind of material is this, that can totally conceal what is beneath it?" Tompkins took a quick glance at his feet. The Ghillie suit was lying on his feet up to his ankles, giving him the appearance of having no feet. He just laughed, bent down and picked up the Ghillie suit. As he picked up the suit, his hand disappeared underneath it. Buford reached out and grabbed the suit from Tompkins hand. Buford held it out in front of him and examined it on all sides. He slid his arm between the folds and it disappeared. He lifted his eyes from the suit and looked to Tompkins.

"What explanation do you have for this?" asked Buford as he held it out in front of himself.

"This is a new type of camouflage," began Tomkins. "The material refracts light so it takes on the colors of whatever it is next to. We call it a Ghillie suit. It actually is designed to be worn by an individual person, but we needed to conceal the vehicles so we cut the seams to spread them out."

As Tompkins finished his quick explanation, Buford stood there shaking his head in disbelief. He had a smile on his face as he handed it back to Tompkins. He reached up, took off his hat and slapped it on his knee. The dust from the ride hung in the humid air as he began to pace. You could see he was trying to piece all of this together.

He finally turned back towards Tompkins and asked him, "And what explanation do you have for yourselves, Colonel? I'd really like to be able to understand all this."

For the first time, Bourque stepped forward. "General Buford," he began, "I think we should explain ourselves in private. If you would have a couple of your most trusted men gather with us around the fire, we can explain ourselves. I don't think all the men need to be privy to what we have to say."

Buford reached into his pocket and pulled out a pocket watch. He popped the top open and looked to see what time it was. "Two thirty in the morning," he murmured to himself.

"All right," Buford spoke in a stern tone. "I have about an hour before I must leave for camp. Let's start talking."

Chapter 9

Believe it or not

Buford walked towards his men and shouted out two names. The two men emerged from the ranks and followed Buford to the fire. The rest of the troops moved away from the fire and sat on the ground talking quietly amongst themselves. Tompkins and Bourque started towards the other three men and they all walked to the fire.

"So far so good," whispered Bates.

"I think they believe this is really happening," chuckled Draper.

"It is real, you horse's butt," chimed Santana.

Tompkins then stopped their progression towards the fire, turned to them and said, "We only have a short time to explain ourselves. I have an idea what they need to hear and how to make it as simple as possible. Just follow my lead." They then made their way to the fire where they sat and joined Buford and his two men.

"These are my two most trusted Brigade Commanders," explained Buford. "I trust them with my life."

Buford pointed to one of the men and said, "This is Colonel MacDonald." He pointed to the other and introduced him as Colonel Newton. "I figure between the three of us we should be able to make some sort of sense out of all this." Buford looked at his men and smiled. His smile faded as he turned his attention back towards Tompkins.

"All right now," Buford began. "We don't have a lot of time. I've had a feeling that something like this was going to happen." Buford took off his hat and placed it on the ground in front of him. "For some reason I get the feeling our meeting isn't just coincidence. Every ounce of sanity tells me it is fate. I believe our meeting is a necessity to the outcome of the battle before us." Buford's tone and face portrayed a rare intensity. "Somehow or someway we are going to need your assistance and you ours. The good Lord imbedded these thoughts in my subconscious, and I refuse to ignore them."

Buford's men were looking at him as if they were seeing him for the first time. They knew him as an old war horse they trusted to lead them into battle. They had never heard him speak about matters like this before.

"So let's hear it," he calmly spoke. "Our ears and minds are open." Buford extended his arms out as to invite any type of explanation.

Tompkins now felt the heavy weight of responsibility pressing on him. What he said and how he said it would determine their part in this whole sordid mess. He looked once again at his men. They were looking at him, waiting for him to start. He had been told by each of them many times that he was the smartest man any of them knew, and that they were glad he was on this mission. Now was his time to solidify their support. He took a deep breath, turned to Buford and his men and began his explanation.

"We know you are Brigadier General John Buford. You're the commander of two brigades of cavalry for the Union Army. You've set up defensive positions just west of Gettysburg in preparation for the upcoming battle. You've sent word to General Reynolds to bring up reinforcements as quickly as possible."

The four men with Tompkins looked at each other as Tompkins was talking. They had heard Tompkins talk like this many times. He was very good at lecturing people about many topics. They knew if anyone could present their story in the proper way, it was Tompkins. As Bourque looked at Buford during Tompkins' explanation, he could tell Buford was very interested in what he was saying.

"At approximately seven o'clock tomorrow morning, you will encounter Confederate forces totaling five-thousand men. Because of your defensive position and your new carbines, you will hold off the first wave of attacks with relative ease. As the Confederates bring up more reinforcements, your lines will hold, but barely. General Reynolds shows up just in the nick of time with twenty thousand men. Reynolds is then killed by a Confederate sharpshooter as he leads his men into battle."

Buford's stern quizzical look became one of terror after Tompkins revealed Reynolds' demise.

"How can you say that?" interrupted Buford with an indignant tone. For the first time Buford seemed enraged. He was now on his feet and pointing at Tompkins. "How could you know the day's events before they happen? And how could you be so brash as to say General Reynolds is killed!"

Buford and Reynolds had been through many battles together and had become very good friends. Buford was not in the frame of mind to believe one of the Union Army's best commanders and one of his best friends was going to die in this battle.

There was a silent rage on his face and in his eyes. His hands were shaking as he pointed at Tompkins with contempt.

Tompkins saw that Buford was not accepting his explanation as well as he had hoped. He quickly thought about the best direction to go from there.

"Sorry, General Buford," began Tompkins. "Please sit down for a minute and I will explain more."

Buford reluctantly took his seat on the rock and looked down at his feet. As Tompkins took a moment to gather his thoughts, Buford looked him in the face and said, "Colonel, I am running short on patience right now. You best get on with the rest of the story before I completely run out."

"Yes, Sir," replied Tompkins. "This is where the explanation starts to get really strange and hard to believe."

With his glare still intact, Buford responded, "Boy, it can't get much harder to believe than it already is, so get on with it." Tompkins continued.

"I can see you're upset with what I've told you about General Reynolds' death. We know this takes place because ..." There was a long pause as Tompkins stared at Buford.

"We are..." Tompkins began to stutter. Bourque's elbow in his side brought him out of his trance. "We are from the future. The year two-thousand-nine to be exact." Tompkins waited for Buford and his men to start laughing or to call him crazy.

"Go on," was all Buford said. Newton and MacDonald rose to their feet as if to say they didn't believe him. Buford reached out an arm to stop their ascent and motioned for them to sit back down.

"We know the events of the upcoming battle and the ultimate outcome," began Tompkins again. "We know the outcome of the whole Civil War." Tompkins was becoming excited now. It was as if a huge weight was being lifted off his shoulders as his explanation got quicker and his voice became more relaxed. "Heck, we know the outcome of every battle of the war from Antietam, Fredericksburg and Gettysburg, to the surrender of the Confederacy at Appomattox."

When Tompkins blurted out the ultimate ending of the war at Appomattox, his explanation came to a sudden halt. His eyes widened as he turned to Bourque. Tompkins could see Bourque was not happy he had supplied Buford with this information. Tompkins instantly began to think of a way to cover his blunder.

"What do you mean the surrender of the Confederacy at Appomattox?" asked Buford in an excited tone.

Tompkins' mind raced as Buford's question added to the pressure to cover his tracks. Tompkins knew Buford was an open-minded, visionary type leader, but would this new knowledge change Buford's mindset in future battles? Would Tompkins' slip of the tongue change the outcome of the entire war?

For the first time Tompkins realized the delicate balance that needed to be kept in order not to change the past. If Buford entered into a single battle differently than he was supposed to, chain of events would be started that could cause a ripple effect. It could change every aspect of the war and the entire history of the United States.

"Tompkins," said Bates. Tompkins' head jerked towards Bates as if he was startled by a ghost. "Don't you mean the surrender of the South at that particular battle?" Tompkins mind eased at Bates' remark. He now knew that the other men were aware of the balance that must be kept.

"Err, yeah," remarked Tompkins. "It was the first time the South surrendered a battle during the war."

Buford stood up and took off his hat. He paced around the fire for a moment insolence. He was trying to absorb this new information and Tompkins' remarks. He wasn't interested in the fine details. The whole story was hard enough to believe.

"Could they possibly be telling the truth?" he thought to himself. "Did Tompkins divulge the outcome of the war and then try to cover his error? They presented a lot of information that they most likely couldn't have known just out of the blue." Anyhow, his mind told him these men were genuine and potentially useful in the upcoming battle. He didn't know how, but he didn't have time to figure it all out now. He did know he had to trust his instincts.

He turned to Tompkins. He rubbed his chin as he began to speak. "Men, I believe the story you are telling me is true. I would like to sit around the fire here and get into the details, but I do not have the luxury of time. I need to get my thoughts on the battle ahead and my men." Buford once again sat down and placed his hat back on his head. He sternly looked at each of the men in turn. "The one question I need answered is this." He leaned forward on the rock towards them and asked, "Can I trust you to support the Union Army and keep the balance?"

The five men had heard the phrase *keep the balance* before. Now they realized what it meant. They looked at each other and nodded their heads in agreement. Bourque rose to his feet.

"General Buford," he spoke in a commanding voice, "We will serve our country to the best of our abilities. We will do our best to keep the balance in any way possible." The rest of the men then stood up next to Bourque. "I know you realize the predicament we are in. Our intervention in this war, other than to keep the balance, would be treasonous to all we believe in. Not only could it change the face of history, but our own existence." Bourque took a step towards Buford and leaned towards him. He looked Buford right in the eyes and spoke calmly, yet assertively.

"I believe we are all on the same page. Believable or not, this is real. Our hopes are that we can just observe the battle from a safe distance. However, we are at your disposal if needed. Tompkins can fill you in on our abilities to assist you on our way back to Gettysburg." Tompkins stepped up to Bourque's side.

"If you would like to take your first ride in an automobile," asked Tompkins, "we should be heading to Gettysburg."

Buford just stood there looking at Bourque. Finally he moved. He turned his attention towards Newton and MacDonald.

"Get the men back in the saddle and move them to Gettysburg." He moved a step closer to them and motioned them to move closer to him. "Don't say a word about what we have discussed here," he whispered to them. "I'll be riding along with these men."

He quickly saluted his men. "Do you understand what has just taken place?" he asked MacDonald.

"Yes, Sir," MacDonald replied. "I don't know if I like the idea of you riding back with them though."

Buford smiled and placed his hand on his shoulder. "You're a good friend and soldier," Buford exclaimed. "You have to trust me on this. Meet me at the Seminary upon your return, but just the two of you."

The two men saluted, spun and barked the command to saddle up to the other men. The two men disappeared into the darkness and were gone. Within a of couple minutes the fifty men were gone and the sounds of branches cracking in the woods was all that was left of their encounter.

The six remaining men stood around the fire in silence. It was an awkward moment. Buford trusted the men with very little explanation. Tompkins figured he would have to sell the story to him in detail. He had studied the commanders of the Civil War throughout his life in detail. He always assumed they would be extremely hard-nosed and closed-minded. He never thought they might be open to concepts of time travel and futuristic machinery. Tompkins felt that Buford was not the norm. Other commanders might not be so open-minded as Buford, so he thought it might be important to avoid any encounters with them.

"All right men," said Bourque. "Let's get moving. General Buford will ride with Tompkins and I. We'll fill him in on the details once we're on the road."

"Yes, Sir," replied Bates. "We'll have our radio on."

The men headed to the Jeeps. Draper and Santana picked up the Ghillie suits and folded them haphazardly. They jumped into the Jeep with the trailer, along with Bates. "General Buford, you will ride with General Bourque and I in the lead Jeep," spoke Tompkins. Buford had a smile on his face as he unclasped the saber from his side and studied the Jeep. The three men in the second Jeep laughed as Buford tried to figure out how to get into the vehicle for the first time in his life.

Chapter 10

A ride into history

"Boys, this is very strange," said Bates.

"Yeah," replied Santana. "When I joined the armed forces I knew I was in for an adventure. I never imagined this type of adventure though."

"Hey you guys," burst Draper. "You always give me crap about being from the CIA, but now it could help us."

"And how is it going to help us now?" asked Bates.

"I can call in and get intel on the Battle of Gettysburg. They might be able to get us the right intel for the first time in history." The three men laughed as they started the engine.

In the lead Jeep, Bourque turned his head to make sure Buford was ready for his first trip in an automobile. Buford was sitting back in his seat with an anxious look on his face. Bourque smiled and turned back around. He reached down, turned the key and the engine started with a rumble. Bourque turned around again to see the expression on Buford's face. A wide grin was spread across his face. As Bourque turned his attention back to the Jeep's controls, he gave Tompkins a wink. Bourque then put the Jeep in gear and it bucked forward. In the rearview mirror Bourque could see Buford reach out to brace himself. As the Jeep gained speed, Buford looked out the window with a look of amazement.

"How fast can this contraption go?" asked Buford.

"About five times faster than the fastest horse in your brigade," replied Tompkins.

"Well I'll be jiggered," said Buford as he relaxed his grip on the door handles. Feeling more at ease with his new experience, Buford leaned forward. "Now, can I hear your explanation for your presence here?"

Tompkins feverously filled Buford in on the events that led them to their present situation. Tompkins was amazed at Buford's ability to understand and believe their situation. He had a few questions but listened intently to all they had to say. The Jeep became silent as the lights from Gettysburg came into view. The immenseness of the situation hit Tompkins like a freight train.

"This is Gettysburg in 1863," he thought. "This little town is on the verge of being torn apart by the largest and deadliest battle to ever take place on American soil. And we are in the middle of it all. This is real." Tompkins shook his head. He had to focus on the events before them. The other men were counting on him to get them all through this. His attention focused on the lights of the town.

"We'll be coming to the Seminary soon," Tompkins informed the others.

"How did you know where my headquarters was at?" Then Buford laughed. "I should have known you'd know where my headquarters is."

There was a pause before Buford's next question. "What are you carrying in the wagon back there?" Tompkins and Bourque looked at each other. Bourque wrinkled his brow to give Tompkins the go-ahead. Tompkins hesitated for a second and then began. "Remember when I told you we travel around the country giving weapon exhibitions?"

"Yeah I remember," answered Buford.

"The wagon, but we call it a trailer, is full of weapons and ammunition used in those exhibitions," replied Tompkins. Buford became more interested with this new information.

"What types of weapons are you talking about?" asked Buford.

"Besides the Ghillie suits you have already seen," began Tompkins. "We have three unique weapons with three different purposes." Tompkins repositioned himself in his seat to face Buford squarely.

"We have the M10 Sniper Rifle," began Tompkins. "It is equipped with guidance tipped ammunition and micro telescopic optics." Tompkins could tell from Buford's face that he didn't understand a word he said. "The rifle is one-hundred-percent accurate at one mile. It is equipped with a telescope-like device, similar to your binoculars, but much stronger. Through this device, we can see targets at greater distances."

Buford nodded his head to show he understood.

"The hard to believe part," continued Tompkins, "is the bullet. It has a device that locks on to a target and will travel to that target even if it moves."

"Unbelievable," burst Buford. "I'd like to take a look at that."

"You can see them all in time," replied Tompkins. "The next weapon is designed to deliver complete devastation to its target. It is called MR2PG." Tompkins took a second to figure out the best way to describe this weapon. He knew he had to keep it simple if Buford was to get the full effect of its abilities. "Imagine one of your cannons compacted down to fit on a carbine," explained Tompkins. "It is called a Rocket Propelled Grenade or RPG. It can be fired five times in less than one minute, delivering a charge much more destructive than a twenty pound cannon. The really unique aspect of the weapon is that it is mounted to a rifle that can be fired one hundred and fifty times a minute."

Tompkins could see Buford was trying to picture the weapon in his mind. "I can not imagine such a weapon, but go on," said Buford.

"The last weapon is a pistol that can be fired one hundred times in a few seconds," began Tompkins. The bullet is made of a material that..." Tompkins stopped his explanation and smiled. "You'll have to see it to believe it," he smirked.

Buford sat back in the seat and took a deep breath. "I'm trying to understand all this," he breathed. "But like you said, I'll have to see them in action to understand them." Buford now looked out the window at the lights of his encampments. "I think our best move is to conceal these vehicles and get you men some Union uniforms. It will be important for you all to be as inconspicuous as possible. You can hide the vehicles over by that barn."

Buford pointed to a dark building silhouetted in the distance. "Bring in those weapons you were telling me about and I'll get you some uniforms," ended Buford.

The Jeeps came to a stop outside the lights of the encampment, next to the barn. The men busied themselves getting the Jeeps covered with the Ghillie suits. They each grabbed an M16 and one of each of the new weapons. They then made their way through the dark to the Seminary, where they met Buford waiting outside the door. He led them into the light where Newton and MacDonald were waiting.

"General, Sir, can we meet with you in private?" asked MacDonald.

"Yes Colonel," replied Buford. "I'll meet with you in the kitchen in a minute."

"Have a seat men, I'll be with you in a few minutes," said Buford. He extended his arm to show them to the parlor. Bourque and his men sat down on the hard wooden chairs that surrounded a large wooden table. Buford quickly made his way to the kitchen where his two Brigade Commanders awaited him.

"What's on your minds boys?" asked Buford. MacDonald quickly approached Buford.

"John, we've served with you for over ten years. We would follow you into any battle and trust you completely." MacDonald shot a look at Newton and he stepped forward and joined them.

"We were wondering if it is prudent to trust these men," began Newton. "Especially on the eve of such a battle."

Buford looked at each of them straight in the eyes. He then reached out and put hand on each of their shoulders.

"I've never trusted anyone as much as I trust you two," he began in a soft caring voice. "With you two by my side in battle, I feel invincible. Not only are you my most trusted Commanders, but my friends."

Buford then took his hands away from their shoulders and walked to the window. He stood there for a minute, staring our at the blackness of the night.

"For a while now," he began in the same calm voice. "I've had a feeling something strange was about to happen. It's one of those feelings that make you lay awake at night." Buford then turned to face the men. "I don't confess to know how to make sense out of all this. I do know I trust these men." Buford's face took on a serious look. "There's something telling every fiber of my being that these men were sent here for a purpose. God only knows the reason right now and I expect we'll be privy to the answer soon." Buford took a step towards them and placed his hands behind his back. "Let's keep an eye on them for now and see if they can be of service to us in the next few days."

MacDonald walked up to Buford and smiled. "We have never doubted you in the past, we're not about to start now," he reassured Buford. MacDonald saluted Buford. "Let us know what our orders are, Sir." Newton stepped up next to MacDonald and saluted.

"Thanks for your understanding," asserted Buford as he walked towards the door. At the door Buford turned and smiled. "I think you might want to come with me. We all might get a glimpse into the future of warfare."

The two men were at Buford's heels as he walked into the parlor. As the three approached the table, around which sat the five mystery men, they were amazed at the weapons that lay on it. The three men walked up to the table and stared at the blued metal of the weapons of destruction. The men seated around the table looked at each other and smiled. Bates stood up and grabbed the MR2PG. He held it out like a kid at show and tell.

"What in the world is that?" asked Newton, his eyes running up and down the weapon.

Bates took a step back and spoke. "This, men, is the MR2PG." He flipped it over to show all sides of the weapon. "There are two main parts to its usefulness," Bates began again. "It is a rifle and a, er," Bates hesitated a second as he tried to put it into words the three men from the 1800s would understand. "It's a rifle and a cannon all in one compact design," he finally explained.

"What do you mean this is a rifle and a cannon?" asked MacDonald. "I can see it is some type of rifle, but how can it be a cannon?" Bates stood the rifle on its stock on the table and popped out the clip.

"The rifle part of the MR2PG is rather simple," he began. "This is the standard issue rifle in the future." Bates rotated the clip to show the three men the bullets in it. "This clip holds twenty-five rounds," explained Bates. "It can fire the rounds one at a time or automatically fire them in succession. It has an accurate range of four hundred yards."

Bates handed the rifle to Buford. He slowly lifted the gun to his shoulder and peered through the red dot scope.

"This rifle, even with this contraption mounted to it, is not as clumsy as our carbines," noted Buford.

You could see from the look on his face the rifle didn't seem real. Buford handed the rifle to MacDonald, who shouldered it and aimed it out the window. He then handed it to Newton who in turn examined the rifle closely. After a minute he returned it back to Bates. Bates immediately continued his explanation of the weapon.

"The cannon part of the weapon will be hard to believe." Bates then cocked the forearm and a small ball fell out of the gun. Bates held the ball between his fingers and began again. "This little ball will do ten times the damage of one of your sixteen pound cannon charges. This gun will fire this charge accurately at one hundred yards."

Buford and his men just stood in disbelief, staring at the weapon being held on the table. "The usefulness of this weapon is multiplied by its ability to deliver five of these charges, one right after the other, in just a few seconds." Bates then inserted the charge back into the rifle. "And it can be reloaded very quickly," he finished. Bates then laid the rifle back on the table and asked, "Are there any questions?"

"Yeah, lots," answered Buford. "But unfortunately we don't have the time right now." Buford then reached across the table and picked up the small pistol and asked, "What can this little guy do?"

Santana stood up and reached for the pistol. Buford carefully handed the pistol to Santana.

"This is the C22 Automatic Pistol," replied Santana. "It is a compact weapon that delivers the same result as dozens of armed men." Santana pulled the receiver back and popped out a small bullet. He held it between two of his fingers and waved it for the men to see.

"How much damage can that little fella do?" asked Newton with contempt. Santana just smiled and handed the bullet to Newton. The three men examined the bullet and handed it back to Santana.

"All right, go on," said Buford with a half laugh in his tone.

"This bullet," began Santana, "is very small, but when it makes contact with its target, it expands and creates very big holes." Santana put his thumbs and forefingers together to form a large hole. "I would say this little bullet will do five times the damage as one of your 50-caliber mini balls." The three men looked at each other and shrugged their shoulders. "Probably the most unique aspect of this weapon is its clip holds one hundred and fifty rounds." Santana pulled the clip out and showed the three men all the little bullets stuffed inside it. "This little gun can fire all one hundred and fifty rounds in less than one minute. So this gun could take the place of more than one hundred and fifty men or more. The clip can also be changed in a second, so it could actually take the place of more than that."

After a short pause, the only response was "Unbelievable."

The three men once again just stood there staring at the weapon and each other in disbelief.

Buford then reached into his pocket and retrieved his pocket watch. He flipped it open and looked at it closely. He then put it back in his pocket and mumbled, "It's four thirty, we need to get this wrapped up as quick as possible." He then took a step towards the table and pointed at the M10.

"Give me a quick idea what this monstrosity can do," asked Buford as if he were in a hurry.

Bourque stood up and grabbed the rifle with one hand. He handed it to Buford who had to use both hands to hold it.

"The quick overview of the M10 is this," began Bourque. "Give me any target within a couple miles and I'll punch a hole in it every time." Bourque's expression remained the same as he continued. "The rifle has a special bullet that locks onto a target and once fired, tracks the target until it makes contact with it. This scope allows us to see targets that we can't with the naked eye."

Bourque pointed to the scope mounted atop the large rifle. Buford pulled the rifle up to his shoulder and looked through the scope out the window. He looked for a minute and then lowered the weapon.

He turned to MacDonald and asked, "How far away is that stone farmhouse out there?" MacDonald looked out the window and then back at Buford.

"That farmhouse must be at least one and a half miles across that field, sir," replied MacDonald.

Buford then handed the rifle to MacDonald. He struggled to shoulder the rifle and then looked through the scope.

"Well I'll be jiggered," laughed MacDonald. He handed the rifle to Newton who took his turn looking through the scope.

"This is not possible," was all he could say.

He then lowered the rifle and handed it back to Bourque. The three men looked at each other for a moment without saying a word. Buford then turned to the five men and raised his hands to show he was at a loss for words.

"All right," burst Buford. "I have to believe you've been telling me the truth. I don't know how or why, but I believe."

Buford began to pace in front of the table, his hands behind his back and his head down. Once again it was evident he was trying to absorb all of this new information. After a minute, Buford stopped and faced the men seated around the table.

"I believe you five men are here for a reason," he began. "I don't know why, but I know it." He once again began to pace. "I think our next step is to get some quick rest and meet again here at five thirty. Your new uniforms are by the door, I suggest you put them on as soon as possible." Buford then stopped and pointed to Tompkins. "You and I need to talk about all this further. If you could fill me in on some of the battle details, maybe we can figure out your part in this mess."

"Yes, Sir," replied Tompkins, as he stood to his feet. He looked to Bourque and said, "Why don't you guys get a little rest and check on the Jeeps? I'll be here with General Buford."

"10-4," replied Bourque. "We'll be back in an hour."

The four men grabbed their new uniforms and exited the Seminary in the direction of the barn and Jeeps. Buford and Tompkins remained in the parlor with MacDonald and Newton.

"Why don't you two go and check on the troops and get a little rest? Meet back here at five thirty," directed Buford to Newton and MacDonald. The two men saluted and exited the Seminary.

As they passed the parlor window they saw Tompkins and Buford shake hands and sit down. They began to talk and nod their heads as they discussed the upcoming battle. MacDonald and Newton looked at each other but didn't say a word. They disappeared into the darkness to get things in order for the upcoming battle. Neither had any idea of the scope or importance of the battle that lay ahead.

At the barn, behind the Seminary, Bourque and his men checked the Jeeps and the weapons inventory they so easily concealed. After everything was secured, the four men entered the barn through a small wooden door on its back side.

The barn was as pitch black as the night. Bates clicked his flashlight on and broke the endless black. The four men stood there and followed the beam of light as it moved around the barn's walls. To their surprise, the only things in the barn were several piles of hay and some farming implements. As the beam moved around the walls, it stopped on a small kerosene lantern that was hanging on a nail. Draper moved over to it and took it from its perch. He unscrewed the filler cap, looked inside and then replaced it.

"It's full," he said as he dug for a lighter in his pocket. Soon the lantern emitted a soft glow and the men gathered near it.

"Let's get these new uniforms on before someone finds out our identity," commanded Bourque. "Then we can sit down for a few minutes before we have to meet back at the Seminary." The men quickly began to pull off their uniforms and put on the new heavy woolen Union uniforms.

"I wonder how it's going for Tompkins?" said Santana.

"I hope he doesn't give any more information that might screw up the battle," added Draper.

"I think Tompkins is smart enough to realize what he's up against," assured Bourque. "After his mistake earlier, I could see he realized how delicate the balance is. And Tompkins is not the kind of man to make too many mistakes. We all can testify to that."

"Amen to that," added Bates.

All of them knew the kind of man Tompkins was. He had gotten them out of more sticky situations in the past than any of them cared to count. They all had complete confidence in his knowledge of the upcoming battle.

"I wonder what would have happened if Tompkins wasn't with us on this mission?" asked Draper. "I wonder how much crap we would be in right now?"

"I have a feeling we would be in a Union prison right now," replied Santana.

The men finished buttoning up their coats and adjusting their trousers. They all looked at each other in their new threads and began to laugh.

"Gees, Bourque," laughed Draper, "they must have sheared about fifty sheep to make your uniform."

Bourque spun around and took a bow. "I'm just surprised they had a uniform that was big enough," he added. Bourque then walked over to a haystack and plopped down on it.

"Sit down, boys, and close your eyes for a few minutes. I have a feeling we won't be getting much sleep in the next few days."

The other three men plopped down in the nearby haystacks and closed their eyes. Their minds raced about what was going to happen in the next few days.

"I am really surprised," whispered Draper.

"About what?" asked Santana.

"How little commotion there is outside, on the eve of such a huge battle."

"That's true," answered Santana. There was a moment of silence.

Bates' voice broke the silence. "We're the only ones that know how big and deadly this battle is going to be." The men just let out deep breaths as they reclined in the hay in silence.

CHAPTER 11

Day 1—Strategy versus might

The hot night was coming to an end as peeks of light began to show over the horizon. The four men slowly made their way from the barn to the Seminary. They looked like Union soldiers for the most part. Except for the high gloss shine on their boots, they looked like any of the other soldiers.

"Hey guys," blurted Draper. They all stopped and turned towards him. "What is wrong with my appearance?"

They all looked at him and shrugged their shoulders. Then Bates spit out an, "Ah." Draper stood there at attention with his rifle butt in his hand. He looked like a regular Union Colonel.

"You could pass for a Union Colonel except they don't usually carry an M16," blurted Bates. They all laughed as they realized how funny Draper looked with the M16 against his shoulder.

"How are we going to disguise our weapons?" asked Santana.

"I'm not going into any battle situation without my little baby here," added Draper. He slowly stroked the barrel of his rifle as if it were a pet.

"Let's see what Tompkins can come up with," replied Bourque. "Let's get inside before it gets too light out." The men picked up the pace as they walked to the Seminary.

As they passed by the parlor window, they glanced inside to see Tompkins and Buford seated around the table. Tompkins was pointing to a map that was unrolled in front of them. Buford was studying Tompkins' finger as it moved around the map.

"Sure hope Buford and Tompkins are making headway on the plans for today," commented Bates as he looked in the window.

The four men entered the Seminary and made their way to the parlor. The two men seated around the table looked up and sat back in their seats.

"Boy, time sure can go by fast," exclaimed Tompkins. Both Tompkins and Buford were staring at the four new Union recruits.

"You guys need to scuff up your boots," said Buford. "You look like fancy lads going to a dance with those shiny boots. And don't wave those rifles around too much. Most everyone will know they are not normal military issue rifles."

Buford had a smile on his face. He seemed pleased with his own levity. "Other than that, you men look good. Have a seat." As the men sat down, Buford stood up.

"I must see to my men now, Colonel," said Buford. "I believe we know where we stand." He shook Tompkins' hand and exited the room.

Tompkins raised his arms in the air as he yawned. "Man I could use a break from all this thinking," burst out Tompkins after his long yawn.

"How did it go?" asked Bourque.

"Good, I think," replied Tompkins.

"Why don't you go change into your new uniform and take a quick break?" commanded Bourque. "We'll hold down the fort here for a few minutes."

"Good idea," replied Tompkins. "Be back in a minute." Tompkins grabbed his uniform from the table and left the parlor. Bourque immediately turned to the three men seated behind him.

"Today is going to tax our abilities to maintain our composure," he began. "We need to think about everything we do in the next few days. We can't afford to make any mistakes. If you have any questions, make sure you ask."

Bourque's voice changed to a deep serious tone. "Whatever you encounter out there, we must stay together if possible. If we do something to change any event, we will then have to try and correct it. That might not be a pleasant activity depending on what we need to do."

Everyone nodded their heads in agreement. Bourque turned away from the men and looked at the map lying on the table. Soon the other men were standing next to him studying the map.

"We are here," stated Bourque. He pointed to a point on the map. "The battle starts here." He moved his finger to the southwest and stopped. "You guys remember this crossroad on our way here?" asked Bourque.

"Yeah," they all replied.

"The South will be coming in this direction, and Buford's men will be set up along here." Bourque's finger was moving around on the map. Everyone's eyes were following his finger.

"You can actually see that area from the tower of this Seminary," said Tompkins. Everyone's attention shifted to Tompkins as he approached the table.

"Nice digs," spoke Santana. Everyone was looking at Tompkins in his new uniform. Like them, he looked the part.

"Thanks," replied Tompkins. "I see you're familiarizing yourselves with the map. Buford told me he chose this building for his headquarters because he could see the battle from the tower. We decided that would be the best place for us during this part of the battle."

"Sounds good to us," added Bourque. "As far away from any chance of screwing up is a great place for Draper," laughed Bourque. Draper looked at Bourque. Everyone expected a comeback from Draper, but all he said was, "True."

"I do, however, want to have as much firepower up there as possible," commanded Tompkins. "I know what is supposed to happen and if it doesn't, we need to fix it."

"That's a different attitude than I expected," mentioned Bates. "I figured you would just want to watch the battle and not get involved. Why the change of heart?" Everyone's eyes were on Tompkins. He had never mentioned the chance that they would have to get involved in the events of the battle. He had implanted in their heads that it would be best not to get involved. It was odd for Tompkins to change his thought process in such a short period, and they knew it.

"I know it wasn't what I told you we should do when I first figured out what was happening," began Tompkins. "After talking with Buford about his feeling on this matter, I came to a different conclusion."

"What could Buford know about the matter?" interjected Bates.

"It wasn't so much about his knowledge of the situation, but his feelings," replied Tompkins. "Buford told me about some dreams and feelings he had been having for quite a while. He said he knew something strange was going to happen, which is why it was so easy for him to believe our story. I remembered the comments from the old storekeeper about keeping the balance and then Buford's comment about keeping the balance. I don't think it's coincidence they both said the same thing about keeping the balance." Tompkins walked around the table and faced the men. "Remember when we thought maybe we are here for a reason?" he asked the four men.

"Yeah, but isn't it a bit of a stretch to think that?" answered Bates. Tompkins looked at Bates and smiled.

"Isn't it a stretch to think we are here at all?" Tompkins replied.

"But how are we going to know what we are supposed to be here for?" asked Santana.

"We can't know for sure," answered Tompkins.

"But with your knowledge of the battle and the things that are supposed to happen, we should have a pretty good idea if we need to intervene," interjected Bourque. "Exactly what I was thinking," burst out Tompkins.

"Boy, this is really getting complicated," added Draper.

"That is why we need to stay in contact and not get too emotionally involved in the battle," replied Tompkins. "All we can do is to do our best to figure out if we must intervene. If we do something that we shouldn't, we'll have to figure out how to correct it."

Tompkins took a second to look at each of the men's faces to see their reactions to what he was saying. He was surprised to see they looked in agreement with him.

"Look guys," he began again. "I don't know what to expect. I never dreamed we would be in this situation. All I can say is, let's do our best to get through this without getting one of us killed. We just have to trust our feelings and our abilities and we'll get through it. If we run into a situation that we can't figure out on our own, let's put all our heads together and figure it out. I think we can use General Buford as a good buffer also. He seems to have good feelings and instincts for matters like this." Tompkins looked around at the men again. They all nodded their agreement as he looked at each of them.

"All right then, if we are all in agreement, let's get our equipment and meet up in the tower in fifteen minutes," commanded Bourque. "Move quick and don't be conspicuous. Draper bring any extra Ghillie suits you have, and don't be shy with the ammo. We don't know what to expect." Bourque looked at everyone in turn and gave the command, "Let's do it."

"Boo Yah," rang from the group as they headed for the door.

As Buford walked among the hundreds of white tents, his mind was on one objective, the battle that was sure to come in a couple of hours.

The men were beginning to stir as the sun started to break through the dark humid night. Fires were lit in neat rows and rifles were set in tripods outside each tent. The sound of clanking cast-iron fry pans and coffee pots filled the air and the aroma of frying meat filled his nostrils. He had been in this situation dozens of times and each time it was the same. The calm before the storm. It was always hard to believe such a peaceful setting was going to be the place of such massive loss of life. Yet Buford felt comfortable with it. Fighting was in his blood. It was hard for him to imagine a life without cannon fire and blood. He was more comfortable smelling black powder from rifle fire than perfume on a pretty woman.

Buford wondered how the five men were going to fit into the scheme of all this.

He hoped they could watch in safety, but somehow he felt they were to be a more integral part of the battle.

"General Sir," brought Buford from his trancelike state to the task before him. "Yes Colonel, what's up?" replied Buford. Buford was glad to see it was his good friend Colonel MacDonald.

"How did the rest of your meeting with Tompkins go?" MacDonald asked. "Fine, just fine," he replied.

"What are they going to do with the battle on the doorstep?" asked MacDonald. Buford looked at him and noticed for the first time the intensity in his eyes. "We decided they will observe the battle from the Seminary tower," replied Buford.

"Sounds like a good idea."

"Walk with me for a minute, Randall, please," Buford requested.

"Yes, Sir," replied MacDonald.

Buford began walking with MacDonald by his side. Buford walked at a slow pace with his arms behind his back, as he looked back and forth at the commotion that was beginning in the encampment.

"Randall, I have a matter I want to confide in you."

"You know you can trust me in any matter," replied MacDonald.

"These strange happenings with the men from the future," he began. "I believe they will need to be part of this conflict. In the pit of my soul I believe this. How they are to be part of it I can't figure." Buford stopped and turned to face MacDonald. "I need you to watch for anything strange. I need you to be my eyes and ears on the battlefield. If you feel something is out of place or that you need to speak to me, leave and report to me immediately. We need to work together to find out the implications of these men being here, instead of in the future where they belong." Buford turned and started to walk again.

"Sir, you know I am going to do my best in any situation," MacDonald began. "I think I know what you're talking about. There is a mysterious air around this place, I felt it when I first got here. It's almost like there is another objective to be completed, other than the battle."

"Yes, that's the feeling I have," replied Buford. "If something happens and you find yourself fighting or needing the assistance from one of these men, please do so wisely. It's not that I don't trust them, but what they do here needs to be dealt with very delicately. They must not do something that will change the outcome of this battle."

"I understand and will do my best, Sir," answered MacDonald. "I must be getting to my men now. We will be in contact before the battle begins." MacDonald saluted Buford and walked away in the opposite direction they were walking.

Buford's pace quickened as he realized the present situation. He now had the daunting task of bringing his two brigades together to fight a much larger force. It didn't bother him that they would not fight in their usual manner, on horseback. He knew their new carbine rifles and their great defensive positions would equalize these problems. As Buford approached a group of men, they stood at attention and saluted. Buford saluted them back.

"We need to get all commanders together for a strategy meeting as quick as possible, Major," Buford commanded one of the men.

"Yes, Sir," he replied as he spun and left the group. "Get ready for a battle, men," Buford said, as he walked back towards the Seminary.

Chapter 12

The perfect disguises

As Bourque made his way up the steep stairs of the Seminary tower, he was surprised to see Bates, Santana and Tompkins standing at the rail, looking towards the Union defensive positions.

"Where's Draper?" asked Bourque.

"We haven't seen him yet," answered Santana.

"I hope he gets his rear in gear, the battle will be starting in a little bit," said Bourque with a hint of tension in his voice. He set the M10, two M16s and a duffle filled with ammo on the wooden floor.

"I'm here," yelled Draper as he jumped out from beneath one of the Ghillie suits. He was positioned in a corner, completely concealed by the suit.

"Time to get serious, you goofus," shouted Bourque. "Let's get a count on our weapons and ammo," he commanded. Bates went to everyone and took a tally of the weapons and ammo.

"We have three M10's and five C22's," Bates began. "Two MR2PG's and five M16's. We have two Ghillie suits, one has the seams separated, and about one thousand rounds for each gun and fifty grenades for the MR2PG's. Of course we all have our sidearms and five clips for each of them. That ought to do, I would think."

"Thanks Bates," said Bourque. "If we need more ammo or weapons, we can make a quick trip to the Jeeps."

The men busied themselves putting the C22's in their holsters and attaching clips to their belts. The filled their pockets with any extra ammo they could. Once finished, they all looked like ticks ready to pop.

"With these heavy uniforms and all this equipment, I must weigh three hundred pounds," laughed Santana.

"Well we're better safe than sorry," replied Bourque.

"All right, it's time for a quick briefing on the battle," spoke Tompkins as he waved his arm for them to gather round him.

"You can see the Chambersburg Pike right out there." Tompkins pointed out the tower to the northwest. "The Union defensive positions are there and along there."

The other men followed his hand as he pointed in the correct direction. It was fairly easy to see the positions, even though it was quite a distance. Bourque shouldered the M10 he was holding and looked down the scope in the direction Tompkins pointed. With the help of the micro optics, Bourque was able to count the stripes on the soldiers' uniforms at the furthest defensive position.

"Boy this scope really gives you an edge," remarked Bourque. "I can see the Union flagmen very clearly."

"What are Union flagmen?" asked Draper.

"They needed some way to communicate what was happening," answered Bourque. "So they used flagmen to relate information. Kind of like Morse Code, but with flags."

"That reminds me," interjected Tompkins. "They used this very tower as a main observation point and flag relay point. Wonder if we'll have company up here during the battle?" All the men's heads turned to look at Tompkins.

"The main body of the first wave of Confederates will come right down the Pike," began Tompkins again. "Buford placed scouts about three miles down the Pike. They will send word when the Confederates start marching this way. They just come marching up the road, unaware of the Union defensive position. That's when the battle begins. The Confederates are forced to retreat the first time they meet. They, however, come back in larger numbers and with reserves. The Union positions hold for about three hours, until General Reynolds shows up with his infantry. Buford's lines are faltering as Reynolds shows up. The Confederates start converging on the Union positions from three sides. The dismounted cavalry abandon their lines and work their way back to Gettysburg. They know they will be overtaken, so they retreat back to town. Reynolds' division holds the line and forces the Confederates to a slow advance. Only an hour into the battle, Reynolds is shot and killed by a sharpshooter. As the day goes on, the Confederates force the Union troops to retreat through Gettysburg. The Union troops take defensive positions on the east side of town on Culp's Hill."

Tompkins jaw was getting sore from all the talking and his mind was on the upcoming events. He felt he had told the guys enough about what was going to happen.

"Well, that's a quick overview of the day's battle. There are a lot of details, but for our part, that should cover it. If we need to know more, I can fill you in."

"When the Union troops retreat through Gettysburg, should we be ready to retreat also?" asked Santana.

"Yeah, I figured we'd retreat ahead of the Union troops," replied Tompkins. From what I've read, the retreat through town turns into a mess. There were a lot of men running through the narrow streets. It caused bottlenecks and confusion. I don't think we want to be part of that, but we can figure that out when the time comes."

The sounds of footsteps interrupted the men and sent them scurrying to conceal their weapons. Draper held up the Ghillie suit as the other men placed their rifles underneath it. Draper then carefully tucked the Ghillie around the weapons and backed away from the weapons. The door to the tower opened, and Buford walked in.

"Good morning men," he spoke. "I have a companion for you." Another man then walked through the door armed with flags of different colors. The men all turned to Tompkins and smiled. Tompkins nodded and raised his eyebrows to show them he was right about the flagman.

"I have briefed him to our situation," began Buford. "I have his assurance that he understands what is going on."

Buford reached back and grabbed the young man by the arm. He pulled him towards the other men like a father showing his son there was not a monster in his closet. The young soldier reluctantly moved forward.

"This is Corporal McMaken," announced Buford. "You can introduce yourselves. I have to get back to the front lines."

"Yes Sir," answered Bourque. "We'll take care of the details." With a quick salute, Buford hurried out the door and down the steps.

The men introduced themselves to McMaken and turned their attention back to the countryside. McMaken stood behind them with his flags. He studied the men like they were from Mars. He finally got up enough nerve to speak.

"Excuse me Sirs," he sheepishly spoke. "Is it true what the General told me about you?" All five men turned to him and stared.

"Yes son," reassured Bourque. "Whatever General Buford told you is true." McMaken looked at each man and once again in a sheepish voice asked, "can I see them weapons then?"

Bourque walked over to the Ghillie and pulled it back. The weapons they had concealed suddenly appeared. McMaken took a step towards them and smiled.

"Well I'll be dipped," was all he said. The men laughed at his remark.

"Better put your head on straight, Corporal," commanded Bourque. "If we are in your way, just tell us to move."

"Yes, Sir," replied McMaken.

Bourque reached into the pile of weapons and pulled out one of the M10 rifles. He shouldered it and peered through the scope. To his surprise he could see a flagman waving a flag. He quickly turned to Tompkins and asked what time it was. Tompkins replied, "0600 hours." Bourque then looked back through the scope. He could see a large dust trail coming from the west. He dropped the rifle to his waist and turned around.

With a worried look on his face he addressed the others, "Boys, we're about to be a part of history." Tompkins ran to his side and grabbed the M10. He quickly looked through the scope. His body began to shake and his eyes started to water. All he could muster to say was, "Corporal, you better start your job." Tompkins handed the rifle back to Bourque and moved to the other side of the tower. McMaken moved next to Bourque and looked across the field.

"Here we go," he muttered as he began to move his flag in specific patterns. Bourque backed away and walked to Tompkins.

"You all right?" he asked. Tompkins looked at him with a frightened look.

"I've never seen that look on your face before," said Bourque.

Tompkins mustered a small smile and replied, "I've never been this scared before."

Bourque grabbed Tompkins by the shoulders. With a little shake and a smile he replied, "We got this."

Tompkins took a deep breath and smiled. "Yeah I know," he replied. "The huge scope of it all just hit me." Bourque released his shoulders and smiled.

"Let's take a look at history," Bourque calmly said. They moved back to the other men and gazed across the field.

As they all leaned on the tower rail watching the commotion, McMaken was reverently sending signals with his flags. Santana motioned to the others and pointed to three figures on horseback. It was Buford, Newton and MacDonald. Their heads were turned towards the tower watching McMaken's signals. They suddenly spun their horses around and Newton and MacDonald raced towards the front lines of the impending battle. Buford spun back around and looked back towards the tower. He lifted his hand to the brim of his hat in a salute. They saluted back as Buford spun around and raced to catch the other two riders.

Tompkins checked his watch and looked at Bourque. "We should be able to see the Confederates coming up the Pike," he informed Bourque. They both grabbed a M10 and peered through the scope. They carefully scanned the horizon before settling on the large gray mass of men moving in a large dust cloud towards Gettysburg. A man near the front of the line of marching men was unwrapping a flag from its cover. The wind caught the flag, and it began to wave in the air.

"There's Ole Dixie," said Tompkins. Santana ran over to the cache of weapons and grabbed the remaining M10. He joined Tompkins and Bourque at the rail and looked through the scope. He quickly sighted the gray mass and the waving flag.

"Wow, this is really happening," he shouted.

"Let me see," asked Draper like a little kid. Bourque handed him the M10 he was using and backed away. Draper moved in and looked down the scope.

"Un fricken believable," he said in a quiet voice. Bates was the only one not wanting to look at the oncoming mass. Tompkins turned to him and pointed to the M10. Bates just shook his head.

"I'd rather wait till I see the whites of their eyes," he said with a laugh. Draper turned to look at him.

"Hey Bates, you can see the whites of their eyes with this rifle." Draper smiled and turned his attention back to the field.

Bates had noticed that McMaken was no longer waving his flags. He was just standing in the middle of the tower, watching what was happening on the field. His eyes couldn't help but move to the men peering through the scopes of the rifles. Bates could see he wanted to say something.

"What is it Corporal?" asked Bates.

"Well, Sir," said McMaken in a quiet voice. "I was wondering if I might look through one of them rifles there."

Tompkins stood up and moved to the side. He held out the M10 for McMaken to grab. McMaken had a smile on his face as he grabbed the heavy rifle. They could see he was surprised by its weight as he struggled to pull it to his shoulder. He cautiously leaned his face into the scope and closed one eye. He moved the rifle across the horizon and suddenly stopped in the direction of the gray mass. His closed eye suddenly opened wide.

"Oh my goodness," he muttered. "If we had a weapon like this, we could end this war real quick."

Bourque raised his head from his M10 and grabbed the M10 from McMaken's hands.

"That is why you cannot say a word about any of this," Bourque commanded. With a surprised look on his face, McMaken answered, "Yes, Sir, I understand now." He then returned to his flags and stared out at the field.

Tompkins walked away from the rail and looked at his watch.

"Hey guys," he said. The men turned their attention from the field towards him.

"It's about seven o'clock, the battle should be starting." The sound of cannon fire stopped Tompkins from continuing. The men quickly turned their attention back to the field. As Tomkins grabbed the M10 from Bourque, they returned to the rail and the view of the beginning battle. The cannon fire was now becoming more constant. As Draper peered through the M10 at the front line of the Confederate mass, a cannon blast leveled the first two lines of men in gray.

"Wow," yelled Draper, lifting his head from the rifle. "Did you guys see that cannonball blow the first two lines of Confederates to pieces?" He quickly returned his attention back to the battle.

Santana handed his rifle to Bourque, who quickly shouldered the weapon and looked through the scope. He instantly found General Buford on his horse with his saber raised. As he let the sword fall, the first rounds of rifle fire began. Bourque's view moved to the gray mass as the firing continued. Gray-clad bodies were dropping by the dozens. The smoke from the rifle fire showed the long lines of Union soldiers. They were spread out for over a half mile or so. There was quite a gap between the firing soldiers, but with the fast reloading carbines, it appeared as if there were twice as many men as there was. The Confederate mass began to retreat. Buford's strategy had worked. Even though they were outnumbered by more than two to one, the long lines and continuous fire made the Confederate commanders think they were up against a larger force than they were. There was a sudden slowing of gunfire as the Confederate forces retreated back down the Pike.

"Did you guys see that?" asked Santana. Both Tompkins and Draper dropped the rifles from their shoulders and turned towards him.

"That was pretty cool," replied Draper. "Buford's plan really worked." They both then looked to Tompkins.

"That's the way it was supposed to take place," said Tompkins. "In a little while the Confederates will be coming down the Pike in larger numbers. The Confederate commanders heard the battle and will send reinforcements."

Tompkins turned back towards the battlefield and pointed to the main front of the Union lines.

"You can see the Union troops piling up the rocks and reloading right now," he began. "The lines will hold for the next Confederate advance. Buford is going to bring up his men from the areas that weren't attacked, making it look like there are even more troops than there were at the start."

"Buford really is a great General," boasted Bates. "He would make a good addition to our little group."

"I don't think he would make it in our group," replied Draper.

Bates turned to Draper and asked, "Why not?" Draper rolled his eyes and started to laugh.

"If he were in our group, he would be about two hundred years old." Everyone looked at him and began to laugh. Santana thought it was a good time to take a shot at Bates.

"Yeah, Buford and Bates would be about the same age," he shouted. Once again everyone laughed. The laughter was not in the usual tone though. It seemed more of a cover for the tension everyone was trying to hide.

CHAPTER 13

Battles on two fronts

While the others were joking around, McMaken was sitting on the rail looking out across the battlefield. His face showed his distress at the whole situation. Even though the losses for the Union were almost nil, he did know the men who sacrificed their lives for the cause. Tompkins was watching McMaken as he sat in a trance. He quickly elbowed Bourque and nodded his head for the men to move with him to the other side of the tower.

"All right guys," Tompkins began. The men were in a small huddle facing Tompkins. "We've just had our first contact with the problems we are going to face over the next few days."

"What problem did we have contact with?" quickly asked Draper. Tompkins face suddenly became pale. His eyes fell to his feet for a second before he began to speak. "You see McMaken over there," Tompkins whispered. All heads turned towards McMaken but no one spoke. As they quietly watched McMaken sitting on the rail with tears in his eyes, the reality of the situation struck them.

"See what I'm talking about," whispered Tompkins.

"Yeah, I think I know what you're saying," replied Santana.

"Look guys," whispered Tompkins. "Even the things we say in front of these men can affect the battle. While we were making light of the situation and laughing, McMaken was distracted from his job. If our laughing or stupid comments made his mind wander or distracted him and he missed a signal, the battle could be changed."

Everyone nodded in agreement. It was an intense moment for all of them. They now knew how delicate their role in this conflict must be. Every soldier they came into contact with, every word they said, every second they distracted a man from his duty, could be the reason for history to change.

"Let's get our heads on straight and take this serious," commanded Bourque in a stern tone. "Get to the rail and watch the battle. If you must say something, direct it to myself or Tompkins."

"10-4," responded Draper as he picked up the M10 leaning against the rail.

The other two M10's were quickly on the shoulders of Tompkins and Bourque. They peered down the scopes and scanned the battlefield. Union soldiers were working to better their positions, and the cannons were being reloaded and recalibrated.

After a short period of inactivity, Bourque spotted a flagman at the very far edge of the battle line, signaling the troops of the Confederate movement. McMaken began sending signals to Buford and the other commanders instantly. Bates and Santana were watching McMaken as he made the signals. They quickly walked to the other side of the tower and began to speak.

"I see what Tompkins was saying," whispered Bates. "If we were distracting McMaken, he might have missed the signals and not relayed them correctly to Buford." "Yeah, we better start paying attention and keep our wits about us," replied Santana.

They then returned to the others. Bourque instructed the two men to watch the back side of the Seminary for anything out of the normal.

As McMaken continuously signaled the field commanders, Tompkins spotted a dust cloud beginning to form on the horizon. He stared hard through the scope until he saw the first line of Confederates rise over a small hill on the Pike. He quickly nudged Bourque and pointed to the horizon. He let out a small whistle and waved his hand to the others. They immediately came to the rail and watched intently as the dust cloud became visible to the naked eye.

On the battlefield the commanders on horseback rode down the line and gave instructions to their soldiers. It was a strange sight. They were used to relaying information by radio and now understood the difficulty the command had in getting their information to the front lines of a battle. Through the use of flagmen and verbal commands, they did a very efficient job nonetheless.

As the cloud of dust became larger, the sounds of cannon fire began. Once again the accurate Union cannon fire blasted holes in the Confederate ranks. The returning Confederate cannon fire caused havoc on the Union lines and sent men running for cover. It was obvious to the five men that the Confederate command now had an idea what they were up against and retaliated accordingly. The first rounds of rifle fire soon added to the deafening barrage of cannon fire. Confederate ranks were once again dropping by the dozens as the carbines cut into their long lines. There was much confusion on the Confederate side as the Union defended their position brilliantly. Buford's decision to bring all his men to the front line surprised the Confederate command. They now thought they were facing reinforced Union lines. After an hour of fierce fighting, the Confederate lines began to retreat once again.

As Tompkins viewed the carnage from the relative safety of the Seminary, he was befuddled by this style of warfare. He had only read about this type of fighting. To see it in action shocked him. The determination of these soldiers was unbelievable. To march in lines in front of the enemy as they leveled whole brigades was disturbing. Tompkins knew the soldiers were dedicated to their cause, but to walk into a hail of bullets was ludicrous. He watched in horror as the battle raged on. Soon, to his relief, the gunfire subsided as the Confederate ranks retreated. He knew it was only a short reprieve as the larger dust cloud was converging on the battlefield. Tompkins knew this time the Confederates would spread out their lines and attack from two sides.

As the battlefield became quiet for the time being, Tompkins looked at his watch. It was approaching eleven o'clock, the approximate time Reynolds would be bringing up reinforcements. He slowly looked around the tower and saw that all the men were busy watching the events on the battlefield. He took a second to catch his thoughts and then returned to the railing with the other men.

As they all strained their eyes to see as much of the happenings as possible, movement to the west caught Santana's attention.

"Bourque," whispered Santana. "I seen a couple of men moving through the woods over by the barn."

Bourque swung the M10 in the direction of the barn. He slowly moved the gun, scanning the woods some fifty yards from the barn. As the gun swung in a steady line, it suddenly stopped and moved back. Bourque stopped the swing of the gun and calmly called Tompkins over to his position.

"Tompkins," he quietly called. "I have some movement over near the Jeeps and the barn."

Tompkins walked over to Bourque and took the M10 from his grasp. He shouldered the weapon and peered through the scope. He quickly caught the motion in the woods. Two men were slowly making their way through the underbrush. Tompkins reached up and tuned the scope to see them more closely. Using the scope allowed him to even see the color of their eyes. Tompkins raised his head from the gun and turned to Bourque. The look on his face told Bourque that trouble was imminent.

"What's going on?" asked Bourque.

"There are two men sneaking through the woods towards the barn," replied Tompkins.

"Who are they?" asked Bourque.

"From their uniforms, I would say they are Confederate Infantry," replied Tompkins. "They must have made their way around the Union battle lines and are trying to get an idea of the size of the Union forces. I don't think they are any threat to anyone."

Bourque and Tompkins stood there looking at each other as if trying to calculate their next move. Bourque's eye's widened as his mind made the final calculation.

"What if they stumble on the Jeeps?" he excitedly asked Tompkins. "They just might find our weapons."

Tompkins looked at him and rubbed his eyes.

"If they find our weapons, crap could hit the fan." He shouldered the M10 once again and watched the two men for a moment. "Yeah," he murmured, "they're headed straight for the barn." He then dropped the rifle from his shoulder and turned towards the other men.

"Hey guys," he quietly called to the others. They turned their attention to him, and he waved them over. They quickly gathered in a circle around Tompkins and Bourque.

"What's up?" questioned Draper.

"We've spotted two men making their way through the woods towards the barn," answered Bourque. "If they make it to the barn, they may find the Jeeps and our weapons."

"We need to figure out what to do and quick," replied Tompkins. "This will be our first intervention in this battle, so we must be smart about it."

"Who are they?" asked Bates.

"I could see them pretty clearly through the M10," answered Tompkins. "They appear to be Confederate scouts or something." Tompkins turned his attention from the group and pointed towards the barn. "That is going to be our battlefield in the next little while."

"What's the plan?" chimed in Draper. "Couldn't we just drop them in the woods using the M10?" All eyes turned to Draper as Bourque slapped him on the back of the head.

"We can't just go off like loose cannons you idiot," barked Bourque in a quiet forceful voice. "We must keep our heads on straight and think about every little thing we do. Remember our little talk a while ago and how anything, no matter how small, we do could change this battle?"

"Yeah, I do," replied Draper as he rubbed the back of his head. "Every time you smack me in the back of the head you remind me of my dad."

"I'm surprised the back of your head isn't completely flat," chimed in Santana.

"All right, let's figure this out," commanded Tompkins. "We have to stop those guys from getting to the barn and the Jeeps. But we must not change what they are going to do in the battle." Tompkins put his hands on his waist and thought for a moment.

"They are only two men," said Bates. "They're quite far from the battle. Maybe they don't play a big part in the battle. Maybe they get captured or killed anyway." Bates looked at each of the men in turn, looking for their agreement.

"That is probably true," replied Tompkins. "What should we do?" he quietly mumbled to himself.

"I have the answer," commanded Bourque. "I'll take care of this in my own way."

Bourque winked at the four men, spun around and grabbed the Ghillie suit. He instinctively reached down and felt his belt to make sure he had his C22. He then turned to them and said,

"I'll be back in a minute, cover me." He raced to the stairs and disappeared.

"Wonder what he has in mind?" asked Bates. "Hope he knows what he is doing."

The four men raced to the rail of the tower. They grabbed the M10s and watched the barn to see what Bourque was going to do.

"There's Bourque," yelled Draper, the only man without an M10. The others brought their weapons towards Bourque as he ran to the barn. When he reached the barn, he quickly put the Ghillie suit over himself and disappeared.

Once Bourque disappeared from their view, they swung their attention to the woods. The two men in the gray uniforms were crouched down at the edge of the woods. They were talking to each other as if they were trying to figure out their next move. Suddenly they bolted from the woods towards the barn and the Jeeps.

"Oh crap," said Santana. "They're headed right for the Jeeps."

The four held their breaths as the men got closer to the Jeeps. Of course they had no idea they were there, thanks to the Ghillie suits. The two men were now at a full run as they met the Jeeps head on. Both men ran into the side of the lead Jeep and were knocked back as if they ran into a brick wall, their weapons flying through the air. The two men lay on the ground shaking their heads and rubbing their faces. After a few seconds, they rose to their feet and approached the Jeeps. Just as one of the men reached out to touch the Jeep, he disappeared. The other man stepped back as if he had just seen a monster. His eyes were open wide and his jaw dropped as the man reappeared on the ground like an invisible monster had just pooped him out. As the man turned to run back to the woods, he too disappeared.

The men in the tower started to laugh quietly. "Bourque," laughed Tompkins quietly. The men in the tower switched their attention from the happenings near the barn and looked at each other in amazement.

"Now that's a man of action," said Santana. They smiled at each other and returned their attention back to the barnyard. Both Confederate men were gone.

"Bourque must have taken them into the barn," spoke Bates. "Wonder what he plans to do next."

As the men stared out at the barnyard, footsteps turned their heads towards the stairs. The steps became louder but no one appeared. Then, as if from out of thin air, the two gray clad men fell to the floor. Their hands and feet were bound by ropes and their mouths covered with duct tape. Then Bourque took off his Ghillie suit and stood over the two men like a lion over its prey.

"I took care of the problem," smirked Bourque. "The rest is up to you guys." Bourque walked over to the railing and threw the Ghillie suit over the weapons lying on the floor. He then sat on the railing and looked out over the battlefield. He let out a deep breath and relaxed his strained muscles. The other men didn't realize it, but he had just carried the two, two-hundred pound men, one on each shoulder, more than three hundred yards.

As Bourque sat on the railing rubbing his spent biceps, his mind took him back in time to a deployment in Kosovo.

The air had been hot as usual, much like the day in Gettysburg. His platoon was making a sweep through a small village, looking for weapons stashed there by rebel forces. As the men walked through the village, the children ran to them like they were the Easter Bunnies. They laughed and held the men's hands as they walked down the dirt road through the middle of the small huts. Bourque was not a man that took to small children, but the joy of the smiling faces and the appreciation they showed his men kind of choked him up.

As the line of men was overtaken by the hoard of laughing children, an explosion near the rear of the line brought them into action. Mortar fire began to fall like leaves from trees. The men and children scattered.

Bourque found refuge near a stone wall along the road. His rifle was at his shoulder and all his senses were heightened. As he looked to his men's positions, he was horrified at the scene before him. The children were running across the road in confusion. The mortar explosions were leveling them as they ran crying in fear. Bourque knew the best place for him was behind the stone wall, but his instincts took over. He sprang to his feet and raced down the road. As he ran he scooped up as many children as he could and brought them back to the wall. Two at a time, four at a time, he made several trips to try and save as many as possible.

On what he figured was his last trip, he spotted two of his men lying by the side of the road. A blast had left them unconscious and wounded. Without thought, he ran to the men. He knelt down and threw one man over his shoulder. As he stood to take the injured man to the wall, the sounds of vehicles broke into the village. Machine gunfire now replaced the sounds of mortar explosions. Bourque looked to the wall, over one hundred yards away. Out of the corner of his eye he spotted a truck with men shooting the villagers as they drove past. Everything seemed to be in slow motion.

Bourque knew he would not be able to return to get the other man, so he instinctively knelt down and hoisted him onto his free shoulder. The weight of the men, with their forty-pound packs, felt like a ton. He spun and ran towards the wall with his precious cargo. Bullets tumbled through the air all around him as he made tracks to safety. He knew the vehicle was going to overtake him as he weighed his options. The M16 in his hand was his only way out. He stopped, knelt down with a man on each shoulder and fired his M16 from his hand. His wrist felt like it was breaking as the recoil from the automatic rifle strained his grip. To his surprise, his aim was perfect, and the men in the truck fell like scarecrows in a high wind. The truck spun out of control and smashed into one of the huts.

Bourque instinctively rose to his feet and continued down the road. As he reached the wall, he laid the men down on their backs and turned to return more fire. To his pleasure, his men were doing the same thing. After several minutes of firing and grenade explosions, there was a welcome silence. Bourque remained alert as he viewed the carnage. Bodies of men, women and children lay around the village. The sounds of people crying filled his ears. He let out a loud whistle and waived his arm to signal his men to converge on his position. As they ran to his position, Bourque realized all twenty five men were accounted for. They circled him and his human treasures and knelt down. Bourque stood and ordered the medic to see to the two wounded men. As the medic went to work, one of his men walked up to him and saluted.

"Sir," the soldier addressed Bourque. "That was the damdest thing I ever saw."

The rest of the men stood and saluted. "Boo Yah," they said in unison. Bourque returned their salutes. He noticed all the men looking behind him. He turned around to see what they were looking at. Behind him sat sixteen children and the two injured soldiers.

The faces and bodies faded away as Tompkins' voice brought him back to their present situation.

"Bourque, you all right?" asked Tompkins.

"Yeah, just taking a break for a second," he replied.

"I've been talking with the men you captured," Tompkins began. "They are Confederate scouts from the 7th Tennessee. They said they were sent around the battle-lines to get into good sniping positions. They figured the barn would be a good spot. Once they got to the edge of the woods, they found they were too far from the lines to be effective. They were going to go into the barn to look for some food before they headed back."

Tompkins stood with his arms across his chest as he continued. "I can't remember why, but I know the 7th Tennessee was important for some reason. Maybe it will come to me. But anyway, let's leave the men tied up and gagged until we figure out what to do with them. I've been watching a large dust cloud coming down the road, I figure we have about twenty minutes before the battle starts again, and this is where it will get pretty hairy."

Bourque and Tompkins returned alongside the other men on the rail. They were all looking at the battlefield through the M10 scopes. McMaken was sitting on the rail resting on his flags, staring at the men from the 7th Tennessee. You could see he had contempt in his eyes for the men. Even though the men had little part in the battle so far, they were nonetheless the enemy and McMaken had lost several friends to the enemy.

Bourque had been watching McMaken. He knew that McMaken was an integral part of the Union's communications and he must remain sharp.

"Hey McMaken," yelled Bourque. "There's a big dust cloud coming down the road, you better pay attention."

"Yes Sir," replied McMaken. He immediately turned his attention to the battlefield and the task at hand.

As the dust cloud became larger, McMaken caught sight of the flagmen down the Pike waving their flags. He immediately began flagging the commander on the field. Soon after the communication began, the sounds of the first cannon fire began.

Chapter 14

Fixing it at all costs

"All right boys," shouted General Buford with his sword in the air, his horse bouncing nervously at the impending turbulence. There were six other commanders on horseback standing alongside him.

"This is it. We must hold to the very end. General Reynolds and his infantry should be here to assist us very soon. Let the rebels feel the full brunt of our carbines." Buford pointed his saber in the direction of the dust cloud. "The rebels will be attacking on two fronts. Hold them at all cost. If there is a hole in the line, fill it. We must remain steadfast." Buford dropped his sword and put it in its sheath. "God be with you and your men."

The men alongside Buford saluted, turned their horses and rode off down the lines to their respective positions. Buford was carefully watching the flagmen as the cannons continued to fire. As the farthest soldiers down the line began to fire their carbines, Buford turned his horse and headed for the Seminary.

"Hey guys," burst out Draper. "I think General Buford is headed this way." Everyone turned their attention to Buford as he rode towards the Seminary.

"Let's not get in the way," started Tompkins. "This is where he commands the battle from. We must not give him any information or help him in any way."

"Aye Captain," replied Draper, still looking through the M10 scope. "The Confederates are coming in full force now. Wow, there must be ten thousand of them." Draper dropped the rifle from his shoulder and handed it to Bourque. He then shouldered the rifle and said, "We could take em if they came at us in lines like that."

The sound of heavy boots rang up the stairs. Buford appeared from the small doorway almost out of breath. He did not even look at the five men as he ran to the rail and looked through his binoculars. As the battle raged on, Buford became more intense. He was shouting and talking to himself as he paced the tower floor and watched through his binoculars. Finally Buford noticed the two gray-clad men tied up and sitting in the corner of the tower.

"Who in tarnations are these men?" shouted Buford in an agitated tone.

"They were captured on the grounds, sir," replied McMaken.

He looked at Bourque and winked. He had been listening to Tompkins and knew what he was saying was true. He thought that if he took responsibility for the men, Buford might not be too distracted. He was right, Buford just shook his head and said, "Good job." He then returned to the rail and his command.

The battle that was raging in front of the men was becoming more and more intense. The number of gray-clad soldiers coming to the battlefield was overwhelming.

Buford's men were holding their own in the face of these great odds.

The smoke from the cannons and rifle fire made a thick haze around the field. It was getting hard for Buford to see the front lines of the battle. The five men moved to the other side of the tower, trying to stay out of the way. They kept quiet as they watched the battle from the scopes of their weapons.

They had never seen a battle such as this. The lines of Confederates were being ripped apart by the Union cannons as they marched across the unprotected fields and roads. The Confederates were marching in such large masses that the small number of Union soldiers were having trouble holding them off. Just as the Confederates would make a break in the line, cannon fire would back them off just in time.

As the battle raged on, Buford kept mumbling to himself, "Come on Reynolds, where are you?"

Tompkins kept thinking, "Don't worry, he will be here soon."

Buford's lines were falling apart as the mere number of Confederates attacking them was too much to counter. As the lines began to falter, the Union soldiers would quickly reform at points further back on the field. This gave them the time they needed to hold off the enemy surge.

"Hold that line," Buford would shout every few minutes. The sweat ring on his old hat was getting larger as his pacing and shouting became more intense. Buford shouted at Mc-Maken to send a signal, when out of the corner of his eye he spotted a flag coming towards him.

"Thank God, it's Reynolds," Buford shouted. "Corporal, signal reinforcements will be arriving soon."

"Yes, Sir," replied McMaken with a smile. His flags signaled the good news to the field commanders. Within a minute or two, Buford excitedly ran down the tower stairs to meet his old friend Reynolds. He jumped on his waiting horse and rode across the field behind the Seminary.

"Good afternoon John," greeted General Reynolds. The dark-haired, hard faced General smiled as he saluted Buford. "Are your lines holding?" he asked.

"They're holding for now, but there's the devil to pay if we don't get some help soon." Buford took off his sweat covered hat, saluted Reynolds back and then shook Reynolds' hand.

"I have about fifteen-thousand men just down the road," replied Reynolds. "They should be on the field in a short bit. What are we facing here today?"

"The Confederates are attacking with about two corp. I believe," replied Buford. "Looks like about twenty-thousand men. We are holding them for now, but I'm down to about two thousand men."

"Can you hold till I can get my men on line?" asked Reynolds.

"I reckon we can," replied Buford. They saluted each other. Reynolds turned to his horse and started back to his men.

Buford quickly returned to the Seminary tower and his command. As he pulled up his binoculars, he was surprised to see his men following his orders to the tee. As their lines failed, Buford instructed them to fall back to specific lines and take up fighting there. As they fell back, their lines became tighter and, therefore, making it harder for the Confederates to break through. His men were now at the final line and holding their own. With the promise of Reynolds and his fifteen-thousand men, Buford sat down on the rail for the first time. The thundering sound of soldiers double timing across the field eased his stress. He knew they might have a chance now. He looked at Tompkins and smiled.

"What's the verdict so far?" Buford asked.

"Textbook so far," replied Tompkins. He, too, was relieved the battle was proceeding as he knew it was supposed to. The only glitch was the two Confederate soldiers that remained bound on the floor of the tower. He was pretty sure they were inconsequential to the outcome of the battle and, therefore, wrote off any problems from their capture.

Tompkins motioned for the other four men to come closer. They formed a small circle around Tompkins. He wanted them to know what was going to happen in the next little while.

"So far the battle has gone off without a hitch," he began. "The next big event is the arrival of Reynolds' corp. and his eventual death."

"How does he die?" asked Santana. "And when does it happen?"

"Reynolds is shot by a sharpshooter," Tompkins whispered. He was sure to speak low enough so Buford and McMaken could not hear.

"He is killed by a single shot to the back of the head shortly into the battle. He is leading his men in a charge when it happens. I would like to help him out, but it would definitely change the battle."

"I think if we keep our cool and not make any hasty decisions, we should be fine," Bourque reassured them. The men seemed to fall at ease after his statement.

"Yeah, let's play it cool and see what happens next," replied Tompkins. "The only thing we have to be aware of is our time to retreat through town ahead of the Union troops. We will need to reposition the Jeeps, which will be the hard part. I think I know a way around town that will keep us out of the view of the town folk and soldiers."

"All right, let's get to the rail and see what's happening now," commanded Bourque.

They returned to the rail and viewed the battlefield. With the influx of Reynolds infantrymen, the whole battlefield became a big confusing mess. There was smoke and explosions everywhere. Dead bodies and horses lay all over the field. Men scurried everywhere with litters, trying to get the dead and wounded off the field. Men on horses were directing the soldiers as they entered the field of battle.

"How on earth could they make any sense out of all this?" asked Draper. "If it weren't for the different colored uniforms, you wouldn't know who was who." Draper had a real confused look on his face. You would swear he was going to cry if you didn't know him. "Look at all the dead soldiers and horses out there. This is madness." Draper walked away from the rail and stood in silence, staring at the floor.

"That's the way they fought back then," said Tompkins. "They didn't know what we know now or have the weapons we have."

"What do the townspeople do after this mess?" questioned Draper. "Didn't you say fifty thousand people died here and how many horses? What did they do with the bodies? They must have rotted all over town. I can't even think of the smell."

Draper's voice had a hint of confusion and remorse. He had seen a lot of death in his years, but this was more than he could stand.

"Easy soldier," said Tompkins. He reached out and grabbed him by the shoulders. "Get a grip on yourself. This is part of history. It's real. Be thankful we don't have to look forward to this anymore. Sit down and relax."

They all sat on the floor of the tower while Tompkins explained some of the details. "With all the dead bodies and animals around the town," he began, "the townspeople would dip their handkerchiefs in peppermint and place it over their noses as they walked around town. A lot of the time, the soldiers were buried in mass graves. They tried to do it as quickly as possible, but with the heat they were fighting an uphill battle."

Tompkins continued to fill them in on some of the happenings around town. They felt at ease with Tompkins' information. When he was done, they all seemed to be more in touch with what was going on around them. Once again they got to their feet and stood at the rail.

Tompkins stood by himself as the others watched the battle. He was shocked that the war-hardened veterans of dozens of battles could be affected by what they are seeing here. It had not crossed his mind how cruel war in the old days was. Even the World Wars were much more cruel than now. Tompkins was thankful for the technology of the present day. They didn't have to be witness to most of the horrors of war. It could be done from long distance.

"Tompkins," shouted Bourque. "Isn't that Reynolds over there to the east?" Tompkins mind came thundering back to the reality before them. He looked through the M10 and saw General Reynolds and about five thousand men, advancing towards a small woods along a small ridge.

"McPherson's Ridge," mumbled Tompkins.

"Everyone pay attention," he shouted. He leaned over to the four men and whispered, "This is the spot where Reynolds is killed."

They all looked at him in shock. *Was this really going to happen?*, was written all over their faces. They all focused their attention from Tompkins to Reynolds.

Reynolds was on horseback leading the column of soldiers. The Confederates were held up in the small woods. One of the commanders, a short ways from Reynolds, was knocked from his horse by a lead bullet. He landed on the ground and grabbed his arm. Another commander down the line, was shot and killed by the thunderous volley of gunfire from the Confederates in the woods. They all watched Reynolds raise his sword and shout a command to his regiment. With a shout, they all charged for the woods.

"Forward men, forward for God's sake and drive those men out of those woods," murmured Tompkins.

"What was that, Tompkins?" asked Bates.

"That was what Reynolds said just before he was shot and killed." answered Tompkins. "That was the command he just gave, I think."

No one moved their attention from Reynolds as the battle continued. Reynolds remained atop his horse, directing the charge.

"Boys," nervously whispered Tompkins. "Something is not right. It should have happened by now."

Tompkins continued to watch as Reynolds kept pushing his men forward. "The 2nd Wisconsin should be in the front as the 7th Tennessee mows most of them down." After saying this Tompkins raised his head from the rifle and looked at the two men seated on the floor behind them. His eyes got wide as the realization struck him like a kick in the groin. He reached over and grabbed Bourque's arm.

"What is it?" asked Bourque.

"Remember when I said the 7th Tennessee sounded familiar?" whispered Tompkins.

"Yeah," replied Bourque. "Did you figure out what it was?"

"Yeah," replied Tompkins with a look of horror on his face. "Reynolds was killed by a sharpshooter from the 7th Tennessee."

"OK, what does that mean?" asked Bourque in a bothered tone.

Tompkins reached over and turned Bourque's head toward the two captured men. Bourque's eye's opened wide as the realization of his actions hit him.

"You mean..." said Bourque.

"Yep."

"What do we do now?" Tompkins, shrugged.

"Hey guys, listen up," whispered Bourque. "Remember how Reynolds was supposed to be shot? Well he's supposed to be dead right now and he isn't."

"We didn't do anything to change that, did we?" asked Draper.

Bourque just turned his head towards the two men he captured and then looked back at them.

"You mean one of them?" asked Draper.

"Yep," answered Bourque.

"What's the stinking odds of that?" said Santana.

"But now we have to figure out, very quickly, how to fix it," interrupted Tompkins. "If the battle goes on much longer with his lead, things are going to get real messed up, real fast."

"Do you think we need to take care of this ourselves?" asked Bates, like he didn't want any part of it.

Tompkins stood there with a blank look on his face. He knew what had to be done, but how could they do it? Reynolds was one of the greatest generals of the Civil War.

As if in a trance, Tompkins quietly spoke. "I know what we need to do."

Tompkins voice was solemn and his face was white with fear as he continued. "I thought it would be so simple. Maybe we would have to shoot a couple Confederates. Maybe we would need to sabotage a wagon or two. I never thought we would have to kill a Union General."

The sound of Tompkins' voice was like that of a eulogy. No one had seen him in this frame of mind before. He was usually cool and calculated. The water-filled eyes and the soft voice left Bourque no choice.

"I got this. Cover me," he said in a commanding voice, as he slung the M10 over his shoulder and grabbed the Ghillie suit. "I'll be back in a minute." He then ran down the stairs and out the building.

Buford spoke for the first time in an hour. "Where's he going?" he asked.

"He's just checking on the Jeeps," answered Bates. After that statement Bates turned to Tompkins gave him a solemn smile.

"We better watch Bourque's back," commanded Bates. They all peered through their scopes with added enthusiasm.

"This may not be ethically correct, but it's what's going down," added Santana. "Let's make sure our commander is safe."

Tompkins raised his head from the rifle and looked at Santana. Santana looked back and nodded his reassurance that it was the right thing to do. Tompkins smiled and went back to looking through his scope.

Bourque slowly made his way from the Seminary, to a small ridge just to the east. He pulled up the M10 and scoped the distance. He then slung it back over his shoulder and moved further away from the safety of the Seminary grounds. Just as he became completely exposed from all directions, he disappeared. As Draper intensified the magnification of the M10's optics, he noticed the very tip of Bourque's M10 sticking out of the Ghillie suit.

"Hey guys, two o'clock, on the ground in the shadow of that big tree. See it?" whispered Draper.

"Yeah, I see him now," answered Bates.

They all knew what was to happen next, even if they didn't like it. They had faith in Bourque and knew he could shoulder the responsibility. Out of all of them, Bourque was the most experienced in killing. He was used as a killing machine by the government for years. If they had an impossible mission that involved killing, they knew Bourque could do it. Hand to hand or with a weapon, Bourque was lethal.

As the four men watched for any interference with Bourque's mission, Buford took interest in what they were doing. He walked over, just as a very sharp, almost alien peal of gunshot rang across the field. It was a sound that was not to be heard again for over one hundred and forty years.

"What in God's name was that?" questioned Buford.

All heads turned towards Tompkins. The sweat on Tompkins forehead was beading in large drops. Tompkins' mind was elsewhere and he didn't even hear Buford's question. Tompkins was thinking of a quote he read in one of his history books.

"I have seen many men killed in war, but I have never seen a ball do its work so quickly and effectively, as the ball that struck General Reynolds."

This was too surreal for Tompkins. He had studied history with pleasure, but never thought he would have to take part in such a dark deed. A nudge from Draper brought him back to this so-called reality. His head spun to Draper as Draper moved his eyes toward General Buford, who was standing behind him impatiently. Tompkins turned around and faced Buford.

"Yes, general, what do you need?" he nervously asked.

With a look of contempt, Buford said, "I asked what that unusual rifle report was."

Tompkins knew Buford could not handle the truth, so he quickly wove a lie. "That was Bourque, sir," replied Tompkins. "He spied someone around the Jeeps that was from the Confederacy, so he took them out."

As Tompkins wrung his hands in nervous anticipation, Buford replied, "Was that the big rifle with the telescope on it?"

"Yes," replied Tompkins. "It was the M10." Buford looked him hard in the eyes and smiled.

"That rifle sounds like it really packs a punch," he commented. He then spun and returned to his post at the edge of the rail.

Tompkins and the other men knew they had just dodged a major bullet. They all stood there and stared at each other. Tompkins wondered if they realized what had really just happened. As he looked into each of their eyes, for the first time he saw a look of lost abandonment. He felt like a father who didn't have a good explanation for his kid's question.

"Did this really happen?" asked Santana with a sound of dread.

Tompkins had seen Santana kill dozens of men in his service. He never saw or heard him mention any of them with such dread.

"Yeah it really happened," replied Tompkins. "I think we better think about this from a historical perspective." Tompkins always looked at everything from a historical perspective. He found it gave him a basis for all his actions. "We didn't kill a man in cold blood or for no good reason. If we didn't take this action, the whole face of our existence might have been in jeopardy." Tompkins looked at Santana and gave him a quick smile.

"I'm just glad we have Bourque with us," spoke Draper. "He has those big shoulders for a reason I guess."

Draper spoke of the many instances in the past, when Bourque had to step forward and take the responsibility for their actions. During many missions, Bourque stepped forward without a word and performed tasks that no one else wanted to. He was a complete military weapon. Not one of them had ever seen Bourque with remorse on his face or heard him speak of regret for his actions. That is why they followed his lead without question. They knew he would have their backs and do anything to ensure their safety. He was more than a military weapon to them, he was their leader and friend.

As the reality of the events were hitting the men pretty hard, their attention was turned to the battlefield as the gun fire and cannon fire became more intense.

Chapter 15

Wagon train moving out

The waves of gray-clad soldiers were finally gaining ground against the blue. As they watched from the safety of the Seminary tower, they were becoming alarmed at the retreat of the Union forces. The lines of blue uniforms were starting to be pushed farther towards the little town. As the Union soldiers turned to run, they were mowed down by volleys of Confederate fire. The men stood at the rail with wide eyes as the Union forces started to make retreat towards Gettysburg. As they watched in nervous anticipation, the sounds of heavy boot steps came from the tower staircase. Soon Bourque appeared from the doorway with his weapon slung over his shoulder and the Ghillie suit in hand.

"You all right?" asked Bates. Bourque just looked at him with a solemn face. "Yeah, why wouldn't I be?" replied Bourque.

"I don't know, just thought that what you just did might bother you," answered Bates.

Bourque shrugged his shoulders. "I was just keeping the balance like we were told to. The consequences of not keeping it would have been much worse than what I did."

Bourque set the M10 and Ghillie down and sat on the railing.

"Remember you guys, this is just another mission," Bourque began. "We aren't sure what we are supposed to be doing, but we must react with clear minds and decisive actions. I don't know any of these people, but I do know what I have to do. And like always, I do it."

Bourque stood up and looked sternly at the men. "Right now I think we might want to get our crap together and get out of here. They fighting is pushing this way and I don't want to get caught in the middle of it. Don't you agree Tompkins?"

Tompkins was amazed at Bourque's ability to blow all this off. But then, that was Bourque. Action spoke louder than words to him. Tompkins knew Bourque felt something about what he had just done, but he also knew it was not the time to discuss it. Bourque was their leader and had to keep up a positive front.

"Yes, we were just watching the Union lines starting to retreat," answered Tompkins. "I think we need to move the Jeeps to our next position and get set up for the night."

"All right," said Draper, "But what's our plan?"

"Well I have been thinking about our options," answered Tompkins. "I've come up with a pretty cool plan that will allow us to move through town without sticking out too much." Tompkins smiled and grabbed his weapon. He picked up a couple more rifles from the stash and looked up at the others.

"Grab our stuff and let's get to the Jeeps," commanded Tompkins. "I'll fill you in on the rest down there. I do have to talk with Buford for a second, so I'll be right behind you."

The men moved over to the weapons and began to gather them up. With arms full, they proceeded to move down the stairs and out of the tower. Tompkins turned his attention to Buford, who was at the railing watching the battle.

"General Buford," interrupted Tompkins. "We need to move out pretty soon. We will move the Jeeps to a safe place for the night." Buford looked at Tompkins and smiled. "Well, the battle is telling me to do the same," he replied. "What's your plan for retreat?"

"We are going to move through town and set up camp between Culp's Hill and Little Round Top," replied Tompkins. "Most of the fighting will go on to the north and the south of where we will be, so we should be O.K."

"How do you plan to get through town with your vehicles?" asked Buford.

Tompkins smiled and calmly replied. "I was thinking we could cover the Jeeps with the Ghillies and some tarps. We can hook up a couple horses to them and pull them through town like they are supply wagons. With our uniforms and commanding ranks, no one should bother us."

"That's a heck of a plan," enthusiastically replied Buford. "Hope all goes well." Buford took a step back and saluted Tompkins. Tompkins smiled and returned the salute.

"Thanks for your help General Buford," said Tompkins. "We will be in touch later tonight. We may need your help again."

"Well you know where to find me," replied Buford. "I can't help but get the feeling that your part in this conflict is not over." Buford took off his sweat-stained hat and wiped his forehead. "Remember to do your best to keep the balance at all costs. Try not to come into contact with too many people if possible. I'll pray for you and your men." The sound of a nearby explosion took Buford's attention back to the field. "Thank you, General, we'll be seeing you soon," concluded Tompkins as he started to head down the stairs. As he exited the tower, he stopped and turned around. He took one last look at the tower platform and Buford. He felt a twinge of remorse that this part of their adventure was over. He then turned and headed down the stairs.

As Tompkins ran across the Seminary yard towards the barn, the smoke was hanging over the battlefield like smog in Los Angeles. The cannon and rifle fire was starting to calm down, as the Union forces made a hasty retreat to rear defensive positions. Tompkins was happy to see the four men were waiting for him near the barn. As he made it to the others, he bent down and caught his breath.

"What's our plan for retreat?" asked Draper. "We better get moving fast to keep ahead of the Union retreat."

"Let's go inside and I'll explain," answered Tompkins.

The five men quickly made their way into the barn and the muffled quietness of the shelter. They stood in a circle as Tompkins began to reveal his plan for this part of the adventure.

"What I had in mind was an ordinary supply train, making its way through town," explained Tompkins.

"Wait a minute," interrupted Bates. "We have to take the Jeeps when we move, how are we going to get them through town undetected?"

"Hold your horses and listen to the plan," replied Tompkins. "What I think we can do is keep the Ghillie suits on the Jeeps and cover them again with tarps from the barn. We can then hook up a couple of horses to pull them through town. We can just sit on the Jeeps like they were wagons."

With a smile, Tompkins looked at the other men. They had no expressions on their faces. Bourque finally spoke up.

"Sounds like a plan to me. Let's get moving," he commanded. "Draper, you have experience with horses, there are a couple of harnesses up on the wall there. Go to the stable and grab a couple horses and figure a way to hook them up."

"10-4," replied Draper as he grabbed Santana by the arm and pulled him out the door.

"Bates, you round up some tarps and secure them over the Jeeps with that binder twine over there," ordered Bourque.

"Aye Captain," replied Bates as he jumped to his new task.

Bourque then turned to Tompkins and looked at him with a blank expression. Tompkins knew Bourque had something to say, but he didn't know how to say it. He knew the task Bourque just completed didn't really bother him, but he felt he should say something to him about it. Tompkins reached out and slapped Bourque on the shoulder. "What you just did saved us a lot of grief," commented Tompkins with a soft tone. "The objectives of this mission are unknown and may be a bit strange to us. I, well all of us, are glad you're here. You give us all strength and leadership in situations like that."

Bourque finally broke a smile and nodded. "I know I had to do what I had to do," replied Bourque. "But for some reason it felt wrong." Bourque's head dropped, as he continued to speak. "I've killed hundreds of men without any remorse.

I never had to kill one of our own." As the last word dropped from his mouth, his head picked up and he smiled again. "I guess I'm glad I was the one to do it though. One of the other guys might not be able to handle it so well." Tompkins smiled back at him.

"That's just what I said," Tompkins laughed.

"I guess sometimes you just have to talk about it," replied Bourque. "Enough girl talk, let's get in gear and get the heck out of here." Bourque reached out and squeezed Tompkins shoulder. "Thanks," was all he said as he walked towards the door.

Outside, Draper was harnessing two horses to the front of the lead Jeep. Santana was hooking a chain up between the lead Jeep and the Jeep with the trailer. Bates was throwing a tarp over the remaining part of the trailer. It was quite a strange sight to see the tarp thrown over nothing. The Ghillie suits were certainly doing their job.

Bourque and Tompkins jumped in to help the others finish their tasks. After about twenty minutes, they stepped back and looked at their creation. They all shrugged their shoulders and laughed. The two Jeeps and trailer looked pretty good. They agreed that if they didn't know what was under the tarp, they wouldn't even take a second look.

"All right guys," said Tompkins as he fell to his knees in the dirt. "Here's our route."

He started drawing a crude map in the dirt with a stick. His hand was moving as he started explaining the map. "Here is a rough drawing of Gettysburg. If we follow the main road east through town, we should be able to keep ahead of any large troop movements. Once we get through town, we will need to head southeast till we get about halfway between this little hill, called Little Round Top and this ridge just outside of town, called Culp's Hill." Tompkins hand was creating its own little dust cloud as he was scratching in the dirt like a chicken looking for bugs. "If we can make it here," he began again, as he drew a big X in the dirt, "We should be in a good spot to camp for the night."

Tompkins stood up and brushed off his pants. He clapped his hands to get rid of some of the dirt on them. He turned his head quickly and looked at each of the men. He threw up his arms and said, "Ready to go?"

Draper took a step forward and laughed, "Grab a seat, we're going to funky town."

Everyone laughed as they jumped on the hoods of the Jeeps and got comfortable. Draper grabbed the reins and gave the horses a snap on their rears. "Yo," he hollered as he snapped the reins again and the horses bucked forward. They strained at the weight of the vehicles, but soon had them moving.

As the makeshift supply train made its way into town, the men kept an eye out for any problems that might lay ahead. They all made an effort to study the town and the many buildings that lined the road. Tompkins was busy imprinting the unbelievable scene of the historic town in his brain. He never in his wildest dreams thought he would be traveling through Gettysburg in the 1800s. The pictures he had studied all his life gave little trueness to the actual town. They portrayed the era as black and white, dusty and plain. People in the pictures always looked sad and worn out. According to the books, the buildings were supposed to be tattered and colorless. Tompkins found it refreshing to see all the color and life that was the reality of the time. White sheets hung on clotheslines in back yards. Blue drapes hung in windows and flower gardens were full of color and radiance. People smiled at them as they drove past with their load. The sounds of the battle could be heard in town, but the people seemed oblivious to the potential problems that lay ahead.

Tompkins took a deep breath and stretched his cramped legs. It was a relief to him to know that only a couple of the townspeople would be killed during the battle. Their biggest problems would be cleaning up the carnage that would surround the tiny hamlet.

Chapter 16

A peaceful town, for now

The Jeeps bounced along the bumpy road as they made their way through town, without any problems. Just outside of town was a large stone building. It seemed to be a busy place as many uniformed and plain-clothed people were coming and going. As they came up to the road leading to the building, it was clear to them they were at a Union field hospital. Although it was a busy place, very few people on stretchers were being brought in. Most of the people were standing in doors and windows as if waiting for business.

"If they only knew what was coming," murmured Tompkins.

He had read about the ghastly stories of the Civil War field hospitals. The screams of wounded soldiers, either waiting to be worked on or from the operations without anesthetic. Piles of dead bodies outside the back doors and the grass stained red from the blood of the fallen. Tompkins had to shake his head to bring his mind back to the present.

As they made their way to the last buildings, before they were out of town, a young girl stood alongside the road as if waiting for them to come. As they approached her she waved for them to stop. Draper looked to Tompkins for his OK. He thought there could be no harm in stopping to talk to the little girl, so he nodded his head. Draper yelled, "Whoa."

The makeshift wagon train came to a slow stop. The young girl cautiously approached the horses and gently petted one on the nose.

"Where are you men from?" she asked in a soft girlish voice.

Tompkins stood up on the hood of the Jeep and replied, "We are from the Union Army, on our way through town with supplies."

The young girl smiled and approached the men. She had an innocent aura around her. Her bright smile and pleasant demeanor made all the men smile.

"Are you here to protect us?" she asked Tompkins. He smiled and took off his hat. "We sure are Ma'am," he replied.

"We all, I mean the towns people, surely thank you for all your help and support," she spoke as she extended her hand to shake his. "My name is Ginnie," she announced. "Ginnie Wade."

As Tompkins reached out to grasp her hand, he felt a sudden shiver run through him. His reach for her hand suddenly stopped and his face lost all expression. The young girl just kept her arm extended and gave him a smile. Tompkins reluctantly met her hand and gave it a slow shake. The other men were staring at Tompkins, wondering what was going on in his head.

"It is a pleasure to meet you, Ginnie," replied Tompkins. "And it is an honor to protect you and your towns folk from harm." Tompkins just stood there bent over with Ginnie's hand in his. He finally let her hand go and sat back down. His eyes were filled with water as he sniffed hard. He turned his head away from her gaze for a second and wiped his eyes.

"You better get home now, I'm sure your mother needs your help for dinner," he quickly said. Ginnie smiled a big smile and laughed.

"Yeah she probably does," Ginnie giggled at him. "My sister just had a baby and mama is home helping her with the chores and all."

Ginnie smiled once more and gave the men a wave. She turned and headed down the road towards town. All five men gave her a quick wave and said good bye. Once the girl was out of hearing range, Bourque gave Tompkins a slap on the back and said, "What in the world was that all about?"

Tompkins turned his body towards them with his head down. As he lifted his face to meet their eyes, Bourque's suspicions were proved true. Tompkins had a tear in his eye as he looked at the other men. They said nothing as he began to speak.

"That girl, that cute little girl, is one of the most famous figures in the battle of Gettysburg," started Tompkins, with another sniffle.

"What's going on?" asked Draper. "I've never seen you like this before. How could one little girl get to you like this?" Tompkins just looked at Draper for a second with a sad expression on his face.

"Why is that girl so famous?" asked Santana. "She didn't fight in the war, did she?"

With that said, Tompkins thought it best if he explained his sudden emotional breakdown. Tompkins felt like it was an emotional break down, but most people get more emotional during *Bambi*.

"That young girl's last day on this earth is today," began Tompkins. He took a deep breath and gave one last sniffle. "She is the only civilian that is killed during the battle," he explained. "She was standing in the kitchen of her sister's house on the outskirts of town, when a bullet mistakenly was shot through the house, killing her as she was making bread for her family."

The rest of the men's heads dropped. No one moved or said a word for at least a minute. It was a rare thing for this group of men to feel remorse at anything. They had seen so much death and disaster. The reality of life hit each one of them. That innocent smile and pretty face was not going to be there after tomorrow. The sincerity of her words as she thanked the men, would be some of her last to be spoken. The men's heads turned to see her as she hurried down the road back to her family, unaware of the certain demise that awaited her the next day. Bourque was the first to come back to the reality of their predicament.

"What a shame," he said. "But we need to get moving."

The rest of the men looked at him and shook their heads in agreement. The five tough men took deep breaths and cleared their heads as Draper yelled, "Yo." The horses once again jerked the load forward. The men passed the last house on the outskirts of town in silence. As the horses gained momentum and speed, Tompkins pointed his hand to the right. Draper pulled the reins and the horses veered down the right-hand road, heading past Culp's Hill.

As they took the road that led them around the back of Culp's Hill, Tompkins kept an eye to the west. The Union Forces would be retreating to this area during the afternoon and he wanted to stay ahead of the retreat. They made it almost a mile before Tompkins spotted the first wave of the retreating Union army. They were setting up at the base of the hill, digging holes and piling logs up for defensive cover.

They, however, kept moving undetected as the afternoon light began to dim from the lowering sun and the cloud of smoke that hung over the area from the cannon and rifle fire.

"Another mile or so and we should be able to set up camp for the night," shouted Tompkins.

The horses pulled the Jeeps and men slowly down the bumpy two-track. The men kept an eye out for any trouble. All they found, though, was a peaceful and serene trail. The only hint of the battle that was raging to the west was the smell of black powder and the sound of cannon fire and explosions.

Nothing more was said as they made their way into the hills that surrounded Gettysburg. They hadn't forgotten the scenes of the battle earlier in the day and how easily their intervention into the conflict almost cost them their future.

As they drove on, the sun began to sink lower in the sky and the sounds of the battle began to diminish. Tompkins was the only one of them who knew what was happening.

He stared out into the woods as they made their way south. His mind was trying to picture what was happening on the battlefield and throughout the town. He could vividly picture the blue-clad Union soldiers retreating through the narrow streets of the small town. They would only stop to see how far the Confederate troops were behind them.

"Oh what chaos that must have been," he thought. "All that confusion from the troops and the townspeople. None of them knowing what was happening. By now the townspeople were hunkering down and locking their doors. The mothers and fathers gathering their children into one of the rooms of their small houses. The storeowners pulling down their shades and bolting their doors, so no one could see what wares they had inside. All of them scared out of their wits and not a single thing they could do about it."

Tompkins got a shiver as he thought about all the small towns he had made his way through during his military history. How those townspeople must have felt the same as the people of Gettysburg. He felt a shiver run through him again as the realization of what was going on hit him. This was no different than Iraq or Afghanistan. The same things were happening this very moment, back in their time. Tompkins shook his head to clear his thinking. He looked around and saw a small clearing ahead.

"This should be a good spot to camp for the night," he shouted to the other men. They all picked up their heads with excitement, as their uncomfortable journey was coming to an end.

"You think we'll be all right here tonight?" asked Draper.

"Yeah, this spot should be as good as any," replied Tompkins.

Bourque stuck his nose in the air like an old hound dog and took a deep breath. "The sounds of the battle are pretty light and the smell of the black powder is almost gone," he stated. "We should be far enough away from the battle to get a little rest tonight."

"I'll fill you in on the details when we get the camp set up," countered Tompkins. "The battle really gets going tomorrow, and we had better be prepared for anything."

Tompkins pointed to the clearing and Draper steered the horses towards it. As they entered the clearing Draper let out a "Whoa," and the horses came to a sudden stop. The men jumped off their perch and stretched their legs and arms.

"Wow, am I glad we don't have to travel like this very often," announced Santana. "I wonder if there's a chiropractor in town," laughed Bates.

"Quit with all the whining and let's get camp set up," commanded Bourque with a hint of frustration.

"We need to relax and enjoy this whole strange occurrence while we're here," said Draper. "Oh yeah that reminds me, how and when are we ever going to get back to the present, or the future, whichever it is?" He looked at Santana and laughed. Santana didn't return the laugh.

After a minute, Draper turned to Tompkins and asked, "How do you think we're going to get back to the correct time?"

Tompkins just shrugged his shoulders and kept unloading his bags from the Jeep. Everyone looked at each other with unsure expressions.

They had not talked about the subject before. They hadn't even thought about how or when they were going to get back to the correct time. Panic overtook Draper as he thought about it for a second.

"Hey Bourque," he shouted. "We need to figure this all out. It's starting to freak me out."

Bourque pulled his head from inside the Jeep and glared at him. "I have no idea what we are in for or how we are going to get out of this whole mess," shouted Bourque like an upset father. "Let's just get camp set up and we can discuss it, O.K.?"

All eyes turned away from Bourque as they hurried to get their bags out of their Jeeps. They seemed to pick up the pace, as if once they got camp set up, the whole situation was going to be figured out. They made a firepit out of rocks and set up their bedrolls around it. Even though they were in a hurry and in this most uncomfortable situation, the camp was squared away as if they were going to be inspected. The men then sat down on their bedrolls as if they were going to be read a bedtime story. They even looked like little kids waiting for their dad to join them.

Just as they became comfortable, Draper jumped up and ran to the Jeep. He reached inside and pulled out an M16. He spun around and held it out.

"Anyone else need a little security? I'm not letting this little baby leave my hands all night."

Very quickly everyone said "Yeah," and Draper handed everyone a rifle. With their trusted killing apparatus of choice in their hands, they lay back and relaxed for a moment. Even Bourque seemed to let his guard down a little as they sat in silence, looking at each other and the serene scene around them.

"What's going on with the battle now Tompkins?" asked Bates. All eyes turned to Tompkins as he set his M16 next to him on the ground.

"The battle right now is more of a massive retreat by the Union and a chase by the Confederates," began Tompkins. "Remember that little ridge just on the outskirts of town? That is where the Union forces are heading as we speak. The Confederate forces are following them through town with little resistance."

Tompkins looked around at the guys and saw he had their full attention. Their eyes were bright and wide like kids listening to their grandpa tell them a fairy tale.

"Once the Union troops make it to the ridge, they turn and put up a great defensive fight. They knew they had to protect that ridge, as it was the best high ground around. If the Confederates were in control of that ridge, they could use it to set up cannon positions that could reach almost anywhere in town. One of the biggest blunders of the battle was made by one of the Confederate generals. General Ewell was in charge of taking the hill. As the night fell, he didn't feel it was necessary to take the hill right then. He thought the Confederate army could take it in the morning or whenever they wanted to. What he didn't realize was the Union forces spent the entire night building ramparts across the hill. They chopped down trees and piled up rocks. They dug holes and trenches to gain a better defensive advantage. In the morning when the Confederates began their assault, they were met by a well entrenched Union defense and were tore apart. But I'm getting ahead of myself."

Tompkins jumped up and walked to a bare spot in the grass. "Come over here, I'll show you what happens the second day."

As the men gathered around him, Tompkins began to draw in the dirt with a long stick. He quickly drew the town of Gettysburg and the surrounding topography.

"Here is where we are now," Tompkins began. "And here is where the battle was this morning." Tompkins drew X's where he was pointing and continued.

"The Union defensive positions are in the form of a fish hook along these small ridges and hills." Tompkins drew a fish hook in the dirt stretching from the town to two small hills to the southeast. "Most of the fighting that we hear about happens on these two hills here. There were many deadly battles along that ridge just outside of town. You remember Culp's Hill, we drove around it about two hours ago, just after we seen that young girl. It's the ridge I was just talking about."

Tompkins looked around at everyone, to see them all nodding their heads in agreement. "I think we should concentrate our analysis on the two small hills, but I don't want to downplay the battles that happened at Culp's Hill. If the Confederates would have been able to take that hill, they could have swung around behind the Union forces and probably crushed them."

"Do these two small hills have names?" asked Santana.

"Yeah this one is called Little Round Top and this one is called Big Round Top." Tompkins wrote their names in the dirt next to his little round symbols representing the hills. The men watched him intently as his dirt map was becoming larger and larger. Tompkins then drew a little square to the west of Little Round Top.

"This is Devil's Den," he began. "It's a little outcropping of rock that was used by the Confederate sharpshooters to try to take this hill. I will show you the terrain first thing in the morning, hopefully before the fighting begins."

"What kind of fighting can we expect tomorrow?" asked Draper. "Will it be similar to today?" Tompkins turned towards Draper and smiled.

"Most of the fighting is similar to today's," responded Tompkins. "Remember, fighting in the past was more of an honor between the opposing forces. It was a show of power and determination. That's probably why they rarely fought at night and never used camouflage or stealth."

"There had to be some sort of fighting like that," replied Draper. "I can't understand why men would march at each other and just stand there to be killed. When I was watching the battle this morning, I almost got sick watching them stand in front of each other, taking turns shooting each other. And then the Confederates marched across the lines of the Union and just got ripped apart. They never left their ranks or ran or tried to hide. It was ludicrous."

Draper waved his arms wildly as he spoke. When he had finished speaking, he dropped his arms and put his head in his hands as if disturbed.

"Watching the battle this morning really enlightened me to the old styles of warfare," spoke Santana. "I never in my wildest dreams thought they really fought that way and that people would sacrifice their lives so thoughtlessly for a cause." Santana just sat with a blank look on his face.

It was obvious to Bourque, Bates and Tompkins, that this unbelievable experience had taken a toll on the two younger warriors. Sure, they had seen tons of battles and death, but to see such blatant death in this manner was hard for them. Modern warfare teaches to kill from distances with little respect to the opposition. These men that fought today had to stare their enemy in the face before they killed them. Their cause was more important than whether they lived or died. The battles of the World Wars were not as deliberate as the Civil and Revolutionary Wars, but they still had a personal feeling. The thousands of Americans who lost their lives to save Europe were adamant in their beliefs about human life and a cause. Today, killing and warfare are taken lightly and without much thought. If a country could bolster the same sense of commitment for a just cause, as our forefathers had, that country would be unstoppable.

"Hey, guys," spoke Bourque. "Let's keep our focus on this moment and what we need to do here. We can't think too much into this. Remember, we are not sure what we will need to do tomorrow, so we must keep our heads clear."

Everyone's eyes focused on Bourque. His demeanor gave them a sense of safety and seemed to align their thoughts. As Bourque looked at each of the men and saw he had their attention, he said, " Go ahead Tompkins, keep talking."

Tompkins once again began his explanation. "The most famous battle tomorrow happens here." Tompkins pointed to Little Round Top, and everyone leaned in to see. "Although, there were many intense battles all along this side of the line." Everyone's head followed Tompkins' hand like puppies watching a treat being waved in their faces.

"I think we need to focus our attention on Little Round Top though." Tompkins took a step back and let the stick drop from his hand. He looked to the sky and wiped the sweat from his forehead. "It's going to get dark pretty quick. Let's all go back to our campsite and relax. I'll give you the rest of the story in a minute."

Everyone just slowly turned and returned to their spot around the campfire. They all sat down, but they remained tense, as if waiting to hear the ending to a fairy tale.

Chapter 17

An old friend returns

"Relax everyone," ordered Tompkins. "We need to remain at ease. We already know what could happen if we don't think clearly. We almost screwed up big time this morning. Luckily we were able to correct our error."

"It's kind of hard to relax," burst out Draper. "We are in the middle of one of the greatest battles in history, and we aren't even supposed to be here. We don't know what we should or shouldn't do and we don't know how or when we are going to get out of here."

All the men sat there staring at Tompkins. He felt as if the fate of the men and their future was in his hands. Even though he had no sure answers for any of their questions, he knew they needed him to at least give them some sort of direction.

"Listen," he began. "I am not sure how or when we are going to get out of this. I assume we were put here for some reason. I'm hoping we will be put back into our own time, once we complete the mission we are here for."

The tense sound in Tompkins' voice told the men he was starting to get upset. They weren't stupid. They knew he didn't have the answers they were looking for. Bourque knew he needed to step in and help Tompkins.

"There are things we can and cannot control," he interjected. "Unfortunately, this is one we can't control. I usually don't let myself get into these situations, but I had no choice, none of us did. Tompkins can't make this go away. We can't shoot our way out. Nobody's coming to get us out. See this vein in my forehead? When it doesn't stick out anymore, we will know we are back where we belong."

Bourque quickly raised his huge finger and pointed to the large vein that was popping out of his forehead. Everyone knew what it meant when the vein was popping out and no one wanted a piece of what it meant. Draper however felt it was a good time to lighten up the mood.

With a smile on his face Draper replied, "All that vein means is that it's time to change your Depends diaper, you old fart."

As everyone let out a laugh, Bourque's vein stuck out a little further. With a quick pounce, Bourque was sitting on Draper's chest. Draper struggled under his massive weight, but only found himself being more controlled.

All of a sudden Draper remembered Bourque's wrestling stories and quit struggling. Bourque just sat there and then began to smile. He turned to the other guys and smiled.

"See, the vein is gone." Once again he pointed to his forehead. "This must be where I belong," laughed Bourque.

Everyone began to laugh uncontrollably. Bourque jumped up, returned to his bedroll and sat down. Draper just lay there laughing. He lifted his head and looked at everyone.

"Now I have to change my shorts. Thanks a lot Bourque." As the tears ran down everyone's faces, the laughs began to subside. Soon the camp was silent as the tension from their predicament was forgotten for the moment. Everyone was lying back on their beds enjoying the warmth of the setting sun.

"Let's get a small fire going before it gets too dark," said Bates.

"Yeah I could use a hot meal," replied Santana.

The two men jumped up and quickly scooped up some dead branches and leaves. Draper helped by grabbing an armful of branches from a nearby fence row. As Santana was crouching over the small pile of branches with a lighter, Tompkins reminded him not to make it too big.

"We don't need any attention tonight, so keep it as small as possible," ordered Tompkins.

Draper was busy going through the cooler in the rear Jeep. He shut the door and walked to the fire with an armload of Army issue food packages.

"I never thought I would look forward to eating MRE's," laughed Draper. "I'll just pretend it's deep dish pizza from downtown Chicago."

He sat down with a thud and began going through the bags. "We have four choices for dinner tonight boys," he announced. "There's spaghetti, turkey, beef stew and hotdogs and beans."

Draper began throwing the bags of food at the men as they called out their choice. Draper paused as Bourque called out his choice.

"I know I'm not going to give you hotdogs and beans Bourque. We don't need a gas cloud hovering over us tonight." As usual, everyone laughed. Everyone put their full attention into eating while Tompkins began to explain the battle that lay ahead.

"Tomorrow the battles will be very intense," began Tompkins. "The main battles will be fought on the two ends of the Union line. We already discussed the battles at Culp's Hill. The other end of the Union line is Little Round Top." Everyone's eye's were locked on Tompkins while their spoons continued to feed their mouths. "There are a lot of details, but I'll just give you the overview." Tompkins set his dinner down and crossed his legs Indian style. "The Union lines stretched from the town all the way to Little Round Top. The very end of the line was on Little Round Top. The Confederate commanders tried to convince General Lee to let them move their troops around Little Round Top and attack the Union lines from the rear. General Lee didn't think it was necessary for them to do this and, therefore, wouldn't allow it. The Confederates always liked to attack right in front of you, showing their strength and determination. The very end of the Union line was taken by the 20th Maine Regiment. They were led by Colonel Chamberlain. During the battle, the Confederates kept attacking their position. Chamberlain used the fact that the hill the Confederates were trying to come up was very steep. By the time the Confederates made their way up the hill, they would be tired. He had his men pile up the rocks and positioned them behind trees and logs. They had a great defensive position."

Tompkins looked around at everyone around the fire. He expected them to be half asleep again. They however were wide-eyed and paying close attention.

"Wow," exclaimed Tompkins. "I expected you all to be going to sleep by now." Draper sat up and stretched his arms in the air.

"Before when you told us stories," Draper began, "I thought it was just to bore us. Now I am very interested. Knowing as much as possible about this battle may save our butts." Everyone nodded their heads in agreement and turned their attention to Tompkins.

Tompkins looked at his watch and began to speak once again.

"Well, it's getting late and I think we will need all the rest we can get. I'll just give you guys the short version."

"Sounds good," replied Bourque as he lay back on his bedroll.

The sky was black now and the sounds of the battle were gone. It was hard to believe they were in the middle of this great battle. If they weren't careful, they might forget what was going to happen in the morning. Tompkins uncrossed his legs and stretched out across his bedroll.

"The most famous part of the second day's battle was the bayonet charge that Chamberlain ordered," Tompkins began. "His regiment had repelled the Confederate charges all day and were running out of ammo. After a near collapse of his line, Chamberlain's men reported they were out of ammo. As they witnessed the next charge of the Confederates coming up the hill, he knew they would not stand another attack. He knew that the Confederates must be worn out and almost out of ammo also. He then ordered his men to fix bayonets. And on his command, they attacked the oncoming Confederate charge using only bayonets. The unusual and daring maneuver paid off and they captured their attackers, ending the battle on their front."

Tompkins looked around at the men. He saw their eyes getting heavy as they strained to pay attention to his words.

"Well, let's get some rest," ordered Tompkins. "I'll take the first watch. In a couple hours I'll wake you up, Bourque."

"10-4," replied Bourque.

The men all resettled themselves and closed their eyes. They were ready for some down time. Some time when they didn't have to think about anything or worry about what was going on around them. It was only a minute or two before snores could be heard around the campfire.

Tompkins kept a sharp eye and ear for anything out of the ordinary. He felt safe with the steel of the M16 in his hands. As he stared at the small fire, flickering against the blackness surrounding the five men, Tompkins thought hard about the events that would be coming up the next day. He knew the events like the back of his hand, but he couldn't help but think about the events of the that morning.

It was a surprise to him, how easily their actions changed the events of this enormous battle. The men relied on him and his vast knowledge of the battle to guide them through it, without complications. But how could he know their intervention was not going to change the balance. He shook his head to clear out the cobwebs of doubt. "Just keep an open and clear mind," he mumbled to himself.

The quiet of the night eased his mind and the time passed very quickly. Before he knew it, Bourque was tapping him on the shoulder.

"It's my shift. You get some sleep," Bourque whispered.

Tompkins turned his head and smiled. "It's a calm and uneventful night so far," he whispered back. He then lay back on his bedroll and put his hands behind his head. He stared up at the stars without expression.

"I think you need to get some sleep," Bourque once again whispered. "Stop trying to outthink this situation. We can't control any of this until it happens. If you're too tired, you won't be able to think clearly."

Bourque had the stern look of a parent trying to get his kid to go to bed. Tompkins looked at him and winked.

"Ten four boss man," he replied with a southern accent. Soon his mind stopped working overtime, his eyes closed and he drifted off to sleep.

It was Bourque's turn to stare at the darkness and think. His mind raced back to the past day's events. His mind froze. All he could see was the sight of General Reynolds through the tunnel of his scope. The cross hairs locked on the General as he took one last deep breath and let it out. The pressure from his finger increased and the trigger smoothly depressed. There was no flinch or movement as the crack from the M10 sent its projectile to its target. General Reynolds instantly fell from his horse to the ground. The men close by ran to his side and knelt down to assist him. Bourque knew there was nothing they could do. As he had done a hundred times before, his target was eliminated. He felt no remorse at what he did. As the hundred times before, he did what he had to do. Bourque didn't have time to think about what had just transpired, he had to get back to the Seminary tower. His mind ceased to think as he instinctively retreated to safety.

The flickering of the fire and a crack from the red hot wood brought him back to the present. It seemed like only a couple of minutes had passed, but when he looked at his watch, it was only an hour before the sun would be rising. He stretched his arms and stood up. He slung the M16 across his shoulder and headed to the edge of the woods to take a leak.

As he quietly approached the woods, the light of the rising sun made it possible to see shadows against the darkness of the woods. He quickly scanned the horizon and then the woods for any movement. His eyes strained as he cautiously brought his attention to several dark figures that didn't belong there. He unslung his M16 and made his way towards the dark figures. Like a ghost, Bourque made his way through the woods. He made no noise as he moved. He kept his eyes locked on his targets as his feet traversed the brush like they had eyes of their own. He came to a sudden stop as one of the figures began to move. As the lead figure moved, the others moved in turn. It was obvious to Bourque this was military style movement. He bent down to make himself as small as possible. He quickly moved in a direction to intercept the lead figure. As he reached his intended location, he stood behind a large maple tree. Of course it only partially hid his gigantic frame, but to the normal person, he looked like part of the tree.

It was only a minute or two before the lead figure came to the tree and stopped. Bourque reached down and unsheathed his twelve-inch knife. He slowly raised it, knowing the figure would soon be coming around the tree. As he figured, the man slowly moved by the tree. Like a leopard, Bourque moved towards the figure. He grabbed the man from behind and slid the knife up to his throat.

"What can I help you boys with?" whispered Bourque.

The man dropped his pistol and took a deep breath. The other men quickly came to the aid of their leader, but it was too late. Bourque estimated there were at least twelve men with muskets. They circled Bourque as he held the man from behind with his knife against his throat. Bourque looked like a father holding his five year old son, as his massive frame dwarfed the captive man.

"Easy big man," said the man Bourque was holding. "Everyone put your weapons down and back away."

Bourque instantly recognized the voice of the man he held. The raspy voice could have only came from one man. Bourque slowly dropped his knife from the man's throat and released his hold on him. The man took a step and turned to Bourque.

"You got the better of me once," laughed Bourque. "It wasn't going to happen again."

He raised his hand to a salute and then reached out to shake the man's hand. Buford took out a match and struck it on his belt buckle until it lit. The glow of the light showed a smile from the familiar face. Buford raised his hand to a salute and then reached out to shake Bourque's hand. The two men laughed as the tension of the situation eased. The other men quickly closed in on the two. From the small light of the match, Bourque could make out two other familiar faces. MacDonald and Newton stood behind Buford with smiles on their faces.

"I can see you three are inseparable," commented Bourque.

"I never leave home without 'em," laughed Buford.

"Let's move over to the fire and surprise the other men," said Bourque as he pointed to the small fire, almost too small to see.

They all moved to the campsite. Bourque let out a loud "ahem" to wake the sleeping men. Instantly, the men had their M16's in their hands and were on their feet.

All four men had their rifles shouldered and were scanning the group back and forth. "Drop your weapons," shouted all four men in unison.

"Hold on guys," shouted Bourque back. "Keep your fingers off the triggers."

As Bourque spoke, the men raised their heads off their rifles.

"You men wouldn't shoot an old friend would you?" calmly spoke Buford. Tompkins head rose in the air as he heard the familiar voice. "General Buford?" asked Tompkins. Buford stepped forward and entered the soft light of the fire. The four men dropped their rifles and smiled.

"Gosh, we thought we would probably never see you guys again," interjected Draper.

"Well it's hard to get rid of old ghosts like us," laughed Buford.

The four men looked at each other with blank looks. They all thought the same thing at the same time. "I wonder if he realizes he is a ghost in our time," they thought. They all laughed as the tension of the moment was gone. Draper bent down and threw another log on the fire. The light from the little fire soon grew bright enough to see all the men's faces.

Chapter 18

The story takes a wrong turn

"Come on over and sit down," said Tompkins as he motioned Buford and his men to come around the fire. They all moved in around the fire and sat down.

"Well isn't it strange that we should meet again," said Buford in a light tone. "I thought you five might camp in this area."

"To what do we owe this meeting?" asked Tompkins.

Buford stood up and walked to the outside of the circle of men. He walked with his head down and his hands behind his back.

"There really isn't any reason for this meeting," he began. "I know you know what is going to happen tomorrow and it is all inevitable. There is one strange thing that has happened that made me think of you." Buford stopped and took his hat off.

"What is it, General?" asked Tompkins.

Buford looked Tompkins in the face as he began to speak. "Last night I got word that a flash flood kept one of our smaller regiments from making it here today."

"What regiment was it?" asked Tompkins. Buford's eyes narrowed as he said, "The 20th Maine."

Tompkins eyes grew wide as he heard Buford say that the 20th Maine was not going to be at the battle in the morning. Tompkins said nothing, which made Buford concerned. "Is that going to be a problem?" Buford asked. Tompkins looked at him and then at the other men.

"It's all right Colonel," said Buford, "These men are privy to the situation. You can say what needs to be said." Tompkins swallowed hard and began to speak.

"Tomorrow's battle will be long and hard. One major historical part of the battle involves the 20th Maine." Tompkins rose to his feet and walked around the men seated around the fire. The men could tell there was something big about to be revealed. "The 20th Maine Regiment," Tompkins began again, "will be stationed at the extreme left flank of the Union line, on Little Round Top. They have orders to hold that position at all costs. If they allow the Confederate Army to take that position, they could then move behind the Union lines and ultimately destroy the Union Army." Tompkins paused for a moment to collect his thoughts.

"What if we were to station another outfit there?" asked Bates.

"Yes, I'm sure we could have another regiment take their place," assured Buford. Tompkins had an annoyed look on his face as he looked hard into the fire.

"The whole thing about the 20th Maine is this," he began. "The Confederates hit that flank extremely hard all day long. Colonel Chamberlain held his men together against very steep odds. Towards the end of the day his regiment found themselves without ammo and facing another charge by the Confederates. Chamberlain knew the Confederates must have been worn out by now and also low on ammo. With no other choice, Chamberlain ordered his men to fix bayonets and prepare for a charge against the Confederates. He would swing his men down the hill like a door and force the Confederates to retreat into their own ranks. The maneuver worked and secured the Union left flank." Tompkins now looked at Buford. "I don't think many men would have issued a bayonet charge at that point and against those odds." Buford rubbed his chin and stared into the fire. He slowly lifted his head and looked at Tompkins.

"I don't believe many men would either," he calmly agreed.

After a minute of silent thinking, Buford stood up and looked up into the predawn sky. He took a deep breath and let it out as he closed his eyes. Everyone around the fire watched him closely as he stood there looking confused. Finally he sat back down and turned his attention towards Tompkins.

"What do you propose we do about this situation?" Buford asked.

Tompkins stared back at Buford for a moment. He didn't know what to say. Everyone was expecting him to come up with the cure for this situation, but he hadn't had time to think about it, let alone come up with a plausible plan. Bourque could see the dilemma Tompkins was feeling so he spoke up.

"I have an idea how to bring things closer to the way they are supposed to be," he burst out into the tension-filled silence. "If General Buford and his men were to ride to the 20th's position and inform them they are needed at once, they could double-time it here in a couple hours."

Bourque's eyes were wide and he had an excited look on his face. It was almost as if he had just won first prize at a spelling bee. Bourque's head spun from Buford to Tompkins to see what response they had. Tompkins looked at Bourque and smiled.

"That may work," Tompkins said. He now turned his attention to Buford. "If you could get to the 20th as soon as possible and get them to run here as fast as possible, we may have a chance." Buford was still staring at Tompkins as Bourque spoke up again. "Yeah, and if you could bring them around the back side of Little Round Top, they could file into their spots as soon as they get there."

Everyone's eyes were moving from Tompkins to Bourque to Buford as they spoke. They almost looked like they were watching a tennis match.

"But what if they get there and the battle has already began?" asked Buford. Tompkins and Bourque looked at each other for a moment before Tompkins spoke up.

"If you can get them there as soon as possible, we should be able to hold off the Confederates for quite a while." A smile came across Tompkins' face as he looked at Buford.

"I trust you know what you're talking about," responded Buford. "Now we need to saddle up and get moving if this whole plan is to come together."

Buford stood up and saluted Tompkins. Tompkins saluted back as Buford spun to face his men.

"Saddle up men," shouted Buford. He then spun back around to face the five men standing around the fire. He quickly threw his hat on his head and straightened his coat.

"God be with you men," he spoke in a firm voice. "Remember to keep the balance and trust your feelings. A normal person would think we were insane, but I know we are not. This is one of those spots in life that define who a person is. I hope we all come out of this how we would like to."

After another salute, Buford turned and headed for his men. Within a couple minutes they all disappeared into the darkness of the woods. The five men stood there for a minute, staring into the fire.

Chapter 19

Day 2—A regiment of five

"Let's get this camp cleaned up and figure out what we're going to do," commanded Bourque. The men quickly started to get busy. They did their work with vigor now. The excitement of this new part of the adventure seemed to put a jump in their step.

The sun was brightening the surrounding woods as the men pulled the Ghillie suits off the Jeeps. They had loaded their gear and were waiting for direction from Tompkins. No one noticed Tompkins had his map out once again and was studying it intently. As the other men finished their tasks, they gathered around him like a bunch of schoolgirls, trying to hear a secret being told. Tompkins raised his head and glanced around to see that all the men were there.

"All right," he began. "This is where we are now." He pointed to a spot on the map. Everyone stood on his toes to see over Tompkins' shoulders. Draper, the shortest of the group, pushed his way between Bourque and Santana.

"Want a box to stand on shorty?" laughed Bourque.

"Got one," responded Draper. They laughed for a moment and then turned their attention back to Tompkins.

"Are we done being stupid for the moment?" asked Tompkins. Everyone looked at each other and nodded.

"Well Draper is stupid for life," injected Bates. "But let's move forward anyway." Tompkins just shot Bates an impatient look and continued.

"We need to move behind this ridge and come up the back side of this little hill."

Tompkins' finger once again moved across the map as all eyes followed. "The battle takes place right here on the front of the hill."

"How come the Confederates didn't move around the back side of the hill and take the Union from the rear?" asked Santana.

"General Lee didn't think it was necessary," replied Tompkins. "Lee thought his forces were invincible. When several of his brigade commanders brought up the idea, he told them they were not to move around the backside of the hill, but to attack from the front. If the Confederates would have moved around the backside and attacked, the war might have turned out differently."

Tompkins lowered his head back to the map for a moment. "I figure we can make the short jaunt in about a half hour," began Tompkins again. "We should be able to take the Jeeps almost the entire way. Once we get about here, we can conceal the Jeeps and proceed on foot."

Tompkins finger was pointing to a spot about three hundred yards from the backside of Little Round Top. Everyone was still staring at the map as Tompkins continued. "Once we get to our position, we'll have to figure out what we're going to do next."

Tompkins dropped the map to his side for the first time since he began to talk and turned to the other men. "Let's get movin'. We need to be there before everyone else."

"Boo Yah," said Draper.

"Boo Yah," rang from everyone in unison as they moved towards their Jeeps.

The Jeeps pulled out of the meadow and back onto the road. They proceeded very slowly down the dusty road. Tompkins knew they had better not create a dust cloud or rev the engines too loudly. They crept along the road until they reached the first large hill, Big Round Top. There was a narrow trail that led behind the hill, so they proceeded down it. The branches of the trees and the brush scraped down the sides of the Jeeps as they slowly made their way behind the hill.

It wasn't long before the trail closed in on them to the point they could go no farther. The lead Jeep stopped and Tompkins grabbed the radio handset.

"O.K. this is as far as we go," he quietly spoke into the handset. "There was a little slit back about twenty yards, if we need to get out of here in a hurry. Let's get our guns and ammo and cover the Jeeps. Grab as much ammo and all the weapons you can. We don't know what we'll need to do for sure."

"10-4," replied Bates.

The men once again jumped out of the vehicles and proceeded to grab all the weapons and ammo they could carry. Santana and Draper threw the Ghillie suits over the Jeeps. None of the men spoke as they carried out their assignment. The sounds of belts buckling and the clack of steel rang through the woods. The metallic sound of receivers and bolts moving to load their weapons brought the reality of the moment home. They had performed this act hundreds of times before, but not under these strange circumstances.

"Everyone gather here," commanded Bourque.

The men quickly loaded the last of the ammo into their belts and duffels and moved to Bourque. He turned and scanned each man up and down, checking to see what weapons each man was carrying and how much ammo. It was much harder for him to get a good count on the weapons as the Union uniforms hid most of the sidearms and ammo.

"Do we have all the new weapons?" asked Bourque.

"Yes, Sir," replied Bates. "We also have all the ammo for the new weapons. I figure we have about ten thousand rounds between us, not including the hundreds of rounds for our M16s."

"That should cover us," answered Bourque.

"Draper, do you have the extra Ghillie suit on you?" asked Tompkins.

"Sure do," replied Draper. He reached into his duffle bag and his hand disappeared as he pulled out the suit.

"Great, we may need that today," said Tompkins. He took a deep breath and then looked into the woods towards the end of the road. "Well, let's get this part of our adventure under way."

He then started to walk into the woods. The remaining men looked at each other and followed Tompkins into the thick forest.

It was easy for the men to traverse the base of the hill, following the many deer trails that skirted the steep hill. They quickly made their way to the base of Little Round Top. They gathered at the bottom and stared up the long slope that led to the top.

"I'm not looking forward to this part of the trip," remarked Draper.

"Me neither," answered Bourque. "But we better get going anyway."

The men began the slow assent up the rocky, tree-covered hill. Their breathing soon turned to panting. They had to stop to catch their breath.

"Gee, the Confederate Army must have been at a real disadvantage, having to climb up this hill to get to the Union lines," panted Santana. Tompkins laughed as he tried to catch his breath.

"That's funny you said that," remarked Tompkins. "One of the generals from the Confederate brigades told General Lee that they should move around the hill and attack the Union Army from the rear. All the Union forces would have to do is roll rocks down at them."

"I can see what he was talking about," said Bates.

After a minute or two, the men once again started to climb the remaining slope. Once at the top, they found rocks and logs to sit on and relaxed for a minute.

"What's the plan now?" asked Santana.

The men gazed out at the surrounding landscape. The humid haze and the glow of the rising sun made the bright greens of the fields and forests almost black. The browns of the wheat fields broke up the complete green cover that surrounded them. As the men sat in silence, taking in the peaceful setting, they once again felt at ease.

"Wow, this place sure is beautiful," remarked Santana. "It's hard to believe it is going to turn into a bloody mess real soon."

"Yeah it's kind of surreal isn't it?" said Bates.

For a minute the men sat in silence. Tompkins then stood up, walked to a rock and jumped up on it.

"It's about five a.m.," he began. "The Union forces should be moving this way right now." His head turned back and forth as he scanned the horizon, looking for some indication of Union troop movement. Suddenly his head stopped moving and he pointed to the north.

"There are the Union troops now," he calmly indicated. "They will be here in about a half hour. We better plan our next move real quick." Tompkins jumped back off the rock and joined the others.

"I think our best bet is to pretend we are part of the 20th Maine," began Tompkins. "When they set up the lines, we will take the very end of the line. We can tell the commanders that our remaining forces will be here soon."

Tompkins took off his heavy wool coat and squatted down in the dirt. He drew a circle and a line across it. "This is the hill we are on and the position of the Union lines." He then drew a line coming up the hill. "This is where the Confederates will come from."

Tompkins squatted there for a moment staring at the dirt picture he had just drawn. Bourque rose from his rock and squatted down next to him. He reached out and pointed one of his giant fingers at the picture.

"How many men does the 20th Maine have?" he asked Tompkins.

"About three hundred men," he replied.

Bourque brought his hand up to his chin and rubbed it. His mind raced through the options before them. "I've been thinking about how we can make this work," he began. "If four of us take up positions at the end of the Union line armed with C22s and M16s, we should be able to hold the position until the 20th Maine arrives. One of us can take up a position on the higher ground with the M10s and cover us against any possible problems. If things look like they are getting out of hand, we can use the MR2PGs to neutralize the attack."

Bourque and Tompkins stood up and turned to the others. "That sounds like a plan to me," replied Tompkins.

Everyone nodded their heads in agreement. "Now who wants to be on the front line, and who wants to take up the sniper position?" asked Tompkins. Once again everyone looked at each other.

"I think Tompkins should take the sniper position," blurted out Bates. "If something bad were to happen, we need him to be safe. His knowledge of this battle is the only thing that is going to get us through it."

"Yeah, and when the 20th Maine arrives he can figure out what to tell them and how to get them into the battle so history won't be changed," added Draper.

"OK, so it's settled," said Bourque in a commanding voice. "Let's get the M10's to Tompkins and us four need to get the C22's and all the ammo. Make sure it is evenly distributed between us four. Make sure you have your M16's and ammo. Give Tompkins an MR2PG. From the high ground, he can cover us with it also."

The men busied themselves exchanging ammo and weapons. They looked like a bunch of kids trading marbles as they completed their task. Belts were tightened and pockets were packed with ammo.

The sound of marching feet broke the forests silence.

Bourque took a step back and looked at each man. It was always his charge to ensure his men were outfitted correctly for all occasions. As Bourque's eye's scanned the last man he nodded his head and turned to Tompkins.

"Well, I think we're ready," Bourque commented to Tompkins. "Where should we position ourselves?"

Tompkins pointed to an area down the hill about fifty yards. "See that large reddish rock?" Tompkins asked.

"Yeah," replied Bourque.

"Head down to that rock and wait for one of the brigade commanders to give you your orders," commanded Tompkins as he slung one of the M10's over his shoulder. "Remember to play dumb and tell them that your regiment will be there soon." Tompkins pointed to Draper and smiled. "You make sure you let Bourque do the talking and no goofing around. If we don't hold this position, all hell will break lose." "Don't worry about me," replied Draper. "I know the scope of this mission and its importance. Bourque is the commander and I'll let him do the talking."

Draper saluted Tompkins and turned down the hill. He quickly made his way down the slope with his weapons and ammo. Santana and Bates saluted Tompkins and followed Draper. Bourque and Tompkins stood looking at each other in silence. Tompkins reached out towards Bourque. Bourque grasped his hand and firmly shook it.

"Let's do this thing," Bourque said.

Tompkins smiled and released his hand. "This is really important," commented Tompkins with a hint of comprehension in his voice. "If we didn't have the new weapons with us, I don't know what we'd do."

"I feel confident with these new weapons that we can hold this position without any problem," replied Bourque in a calm tone.

"Yeah, but something always gets screwed up," Tompkins calmly said.

"You know," said Bourque, "every man that has ever used a gun has wondered what it would be like to use them in a battle from the past. I always said I could take the place of five hundred Civil War soldiers if I had an M16 and a couple dozen hand grenades. Well now I'll get the chance to see if I really can."

"I sure hope you can," replied Tompkins with a laugh. "Oh yeah, does everyone have their Kevlar vests on?"

"Yeah, everyone is armored," answered Bourque. "With this heat and humidity, I had to order Draper to put his on."

"Well if he gets hit with a 50-caliber lead ball, he'll sure be glad he has it on," said Tompkins with a smile. "Well, you better get going. Remember I have your back. If things go really wrong, haul your butts back up here. When the 20th Maine gets here, I'll toss a smoke grenade down at you guys. As they start to get in line, you four better disappear. Good luck Bourque," ended Tompkins.

"Good luck Tompkins," replied Bourque. They headed their separate ways with no further words.

Tompkins made his way to a small clearing at the top of the hill. He positioned himself behind a large rock with several large oak trees on both sides. From his vantage point, Tompkins could view about forty yards of the Union line. Even without the use of the M10's scope, he could see all four of his comrades with ease. He quickly set a duffle full of ammo on the rock next to him and fished out several clips of ammo. He loaded all of the rifles and leaned them against the rock. He then did the same to the MR2PGs. Tompkins felt sure he could ensure his and his men's safety with these weapons.

He had a strange feeling about this whole mess though. He thought it might just be excitement, but he knew he better keep all of his senses keen. As he watched the other men getting ready for the upcoming battle, he took a minute to relax and survey the surrounding beauty.

Bourque, Santana, Draper and Bates busied themselves piling up rocks and logs about ten yards apart. They figured they could cover at least ten yards of the line each with the C22s and much further with the M16s.

As the men worked on their defensive positions, Bourque took a step back to survey their work. He quickly noticed their rock and log piles offered them no cover from the sides. If the Confederates were able to flank them, they would be susceptible to gunfire from the side.

"Let's make sure we pile some rocks on both sides," commanded Bourque. "If they are able to flank us, we need to have side cover." Everyone's head popped up from their piles, and they looked at Bourque.

"Do you really think they will be able to flank us?" asked Santana.

"I wouldn't think so, but we better take the precaution anyway," replied Bourque.

"We had better pile some rocks up across the entire line also," interjected Draper. "If we need to move, we better have some cover to move to."

"Good thinking, Draper," said Bourque in a surprised tone.

"Hey, I can think when I want to," laughed Draper.

"Yeah, too bad it wasn't more often," added Bates. Everyone chuckled as they continued to improve their positions.

Tompkins was intently watching the men below. He was surprised at how quickly they were working. It was enlightening for Tompkins to know they all took this very seriously. His mind quickly recalled the many missions they had been on in the past. The first thing that came to him was the massive silhouette of Bourque, ordering troops like dogs at obedience training. As he commanded, the men would instantly do it. They were not afraid of Bourque, but just his voice demanded their obedience. Tompkins never knew a more perfect person to command. Not only was his appearance and voice intimidating, but he had an aura of experience and confidence that made men follow him. He was happy to have Bourque in charge of the men below him. He knew Bourque would do what had to be done in any situation.

Tompkins' mind began to wander, but he was suddenly pulled back to reality by a wave of blue-clad men coming over a small ridge to the north.

Tompkins quickly grabbed an M10 and viewed the moving blue wave of men. He then dropped the M10 and stuck two fingers in his mouth. A loud whistle gained the attention of the men below. The eyes of the four men were on him instantly. He waved an arm and pointed in the direction of the coming Union troops. They all turned their heads in the direction Tompkins was pointing. After a minute they were able to see the men moving through the woods.

"Everyone come here," commanded Bourque. The men quickly ran to him. "The troops coming are on our side," said Bourque. "They are unsure what is going to happen and most likely scared out of their minds. We need to blend in as much as possible. Look scared and confused. I will do the talking. I hope they believe what I am going to tell them."

Bourque lifted his head and looked over the top of the other men. He took a deep breath and brought his head back down to the others.

"Get into your positions and ready your weapons. I'm going to talk with the commander of that brigade."

The men trotted to their rock piles and squatted down behind them. Bourque quickly moved along the hill to intercept the oncoming brigade. As he came to the first man in the line, he stopped and saluted the man. The man's eye's got very wide as he looked at the markings on Bourque's uniform. He then lifted his eyes to Bourque's. Bourque stood a good foot and a half taller than the soldier and about three times as wide. The man's hand immediately swept up to his hat in a salute.

"Hello, Sir," said the soldier in a shaky tone. Bourque looked down at the man with a stern look.

"Who is your brigade commander son?" replied Bourque.

The man turned and pointed to a man moving up alongside the column of men. "Colonel Nash is the commander of the 19th Michigan, err, our brigade, Sir," answered the soldier.

Bourque brought his eyes back to the soldier and smiled a little. "Thank you soldier," replied Bourque as he moved to meet the man.

When the two men met, they saluted and shook hands.

"Good morning sir," said Colonel Nash. "I am Colonel Nash, commander of the 19th Michigan Regiment."

"Good morning Colonel Nash," replied Bourque. "I am Colonel Bourque of the 20th Maine."

"It looks like a beautiful day for a battle, doesn't it?" said Nash with a half laugh. "Yes I suppose, if a day was good for a battle, this would be as nice as any," replied Bourque. Nash turned to his men and shouted for them to halt and be at ease.

"What are your orders Colonel Nash?" asked Bourque.

Nash looked up at him and nervously answered, "We have orders to take up a defensive position at the very end of the Union line. We were told the 20th Maine was supposed to, but they were held up somewhere south of Gettysburg."

"We will take up the end of the line, Colonel," commanded Bourque. "We were held up by a flood, but a few of us forged on ahead anyways. The rest of our brigade should be here very soon."

A look of relief came over Nash's face.

"To be honest, I was not looking forward to holding the end of the line," explained Nash. "We were told to hold the end of the line at all costs. We would not be able to retreat and there would be no reinforcements to assist us. If the Rebels were allowed to move around the end of our line, they would then be able to take the rest of the line from the flank. It will be a very important position and well, to tell the truth, we have never been in that position before."

Nash's lips started to curve into a smile at the word of his new assignment. "We will take up positions at the inside of the end of your line, Colonel Bourque. We will do our best to assist you in any way possible."

Bourque smiled back and pointed down the hill towards the other men.

"I will show you where our line will end, Colonel Nash. You can have your men set up from there."

The men turned and walked along the line of men until they got to the end of the Michigan Regiment. Nash gave the order for the men to follow them as they made their way along the hill. As they approached the first rock pile, Bourque stopped about twenty yards short.

"This will be the end of our line," said Bourque. "Have your men pile up rocks and logs to hide behind. We will cover the end of the line from here." Bourque pointed along the hill showing Nash the rock piles they had already built.

"Thank you, Sir," replied Nash. "God be with you and your men. With any luck, we can hold our positions and maybe help end this battle."

Chapter 20

Little Big Top

Nash saluted Bourque and turned to tend to his men. Bourque saluted back and turned to walk back to his men. As he began to walk he suddenly stopped. He had a thought.

"Nash," Bourque hollered. Nash turned and headed back towards Bourque.

"Yes Bourque, what is it?" he replied.

Bourque brought a hand up and placed it on Nash's shoulder. "We are going to be using some new types of weapons," he explained. "It might sound kind of loud down here, but we should be able to hold. Maybe tell the men at this end of the line not to be too surprised at what they hear."

Nash could see that Bourque was completely serious about this and nodded in agreement. "Yes sir," was all Nash said as he spun around and headed for his men. Bourque let out a long breath in relief. He was kind of surprised he had thought of telling Nash that. "Tompkins would be proud of me," he thought as he made his way back to his men.

As Bourque reached the other men, they jumped up and raced to him.

"How'd it go?" asked Bates. "Did they believe you?"

"Did they fall for it?" asked Draper in a impish tone.

"Easy does it guys," replied Bourque. "They believed everything I said. We're set to go."

Everyone seemed to relax at Bourque's report.

"I had better report what happened to Tompkins. He'll be wanting to know how it went," said Bourque. "You guys keep an eye out. The Confederates should be coming pretty soon."

"Sure thing," replied Santana. "We'll let you know if we see anything."

Bourque grabbed his M16 and headed up the hill towards Tompkins. As he was climbing, he spotted Tompkins scoping the woods with one of the M10s. The gun scanned back and forth and then stopped at a point directly over Bourque. Realizing something was up, Bourque double-timed it to get to Tompkins. As Bourque reached the rock that Tompkins was leaning the rifle over, Tompkins reached out and pulled Bourque behind it.

"Look out over your position, down the hill about two hundred and fifty yards," excitedly burst out Tompkins. "It's pretty thick, but you can see movement down there." Bourque grabbed an M10 leaning against the rock and peered through the scope, down the hill. He only saw the green of the trees and brush for the first few seconds, but then he saw a gray figure move from behind a tree. Soon a mass of gray appeared in a long line, moving up the hill with some difficulty.

"We got about ten minutes before they're in range," murmured Bourque.

He dropped the gun from his shoulder and leaned it against the rock. He then slapped Tompkins on the shoulder to get his attention. Tompkins turned his attention away from his M10 scope and looked at Bourque. Once Bourque was sure Tompkins was listening, he began.

"I met with the 19th Michigan commander and filled him in on what we wanted to happen."

"Did he buy what you told him?" asked Tompkins.

"Yeah, he was happy to let us take the end of the line," answered Bourque. "I told him the rest of our brigade would be here soon. The Michigan boys will be forming a line to the north of ours."

"That sounds good," replied Tompkins.

"Oh yeah," blurted Bourque. "I also told him we were going to try some new weapons, so they shouldn't be shocked by the amount of firing we will be doing."

Tompkins looked at him with a quizzical look. "That was good thinking Bourque," he said. "I'm glad you're on board with all of this."

Bourque smiled with a smug look on his face. Tompkins saw it and slapped him on the back.

"You better get back down there and let everyone know what's going on," commanded Tompkins.

"Should I let the Michigan guys know what is going on?" asked Bourque. Tompkins thought for a second and then answered. "Sure, you can let them know the Reb's are coming."

Bourque looked at Tompkins with a strange look. "Boy, you're even starting to sound like a Civil War soldier." They both laughed for a second before things got serious again.

"Good luck down there," said Tompkins.

"You too." Bourque started to head down the hill, but then stopped and turned to Tompkins.

"Let's do this thing right," said Bourque.

"I got your back," replied Tompkins.

"Boo Yah," chimed Bourque, as he turned and hurried down the hill.

Bourque made his way down the hill like a Bigfoot on the run. In a minute he was next to the other men, pointing down the hill towards the ascending Confederate line. Bates, Draper and Santana quickly spotted the gray column and ran to their rock piles.

"I have to let the Michigan guys know they're coming," panted Bourque.

He ran with ease across the hill towards the Michigan line.

"The Reb's are about one hundred yards down the hill and coming this way," shouted Bourque.

Colonel Nash saluted Bourque and shouted a "thank you" from halfway down the line. Nash then pulled out his saber and addressed his line. Bourque didn't move as Nash began to speak.

"The enemy is right in front of us men. We need to hold fast to our positions and pour the lead to them. Don't think about the man next to you, but concentrate on the job at hand. The reason we are here is for the freedom of all Americans. To die for the betterment of all mankind is a noble thing. We need not think of ourselves, but of our nation."

Nash stood there with his saber in the air. As his words stopped, his men gave a round of cheers and then settled into their positions.

Bourque stood there in amazement at the scene. Such a simple speech could raise the morale of those men. He had to remember, these men were not fighting for land or in retaliation. They were fighting for the cause of freedom and the hope of their relatively new nation. Bourque nodded his head and smiled. It was refreshing to see such patriotism from soldiers. It gave Bourque a chill down his spine. He quickly brought himself back to reality and headed back to his rock pile.

When Bourque slid into his position, he put all his attention down the hill. His mind raced as to what to do next. He weighed all the different scenarios in a split second and then addressed his men.

"Let's use our C22s first," he shouted down the line. "Wait for the Michigan boys to shoot first and then time your shots with theirs. Try not to use the full automatic setting if possible. If you see anything you don't like, call out so one of us can help. Remember Tompkins has our backs from up the hill."

Bourque went silent for a moment as he looked down the line at the Michigan men. They were all peering down the barrels of their muskets, concentrating on the targets moving up the hill.

"Can you guys imagine only having one shot at a time?" shouted Draper. "Makes you appreciate our technology." Grunts of agreement rang from everyone.

"It doesn't seem fair," spoke up Santana. "I mean, we have the upper hand and they don't even have a clue what we could do to them. Kind of like shooting bunnies in a pen." Everyone chuckled at his remark.

"That's a real manly way to put it," shouted Bates.

"Let's concentrate boys," commanded Bourque. "Lock and load."

The eyes of the men were concentrated down the hill. The green of the forest and the dim morning light made it much darker than in the open.

As the Confederates made their way up the hill it was obvious they were not used to climbing hills. Normally, they would be looking in front of them for the enemy, but most of their heads were hanging down as they panted their way towards the Union line.

Draper held his C22 loosely in his hand. His M16 leaned against the rocks next to him. A pile of clips lay at his feet, ready to be grabbed. He was totally into what was happening in front of him.

He was amazed at the methods used by the Civil War soldiers. The gray line of men moved directly in front of him. They were not trying to hide or conceal their movement. They did not fire as they moved. It was a scene right out of a movie.

As he watched intently, he heard the cocking of the rifles from the Michigan line. He assumed they would be firing soon. Since he was closest to the Michigan line, he knew the others didn't hear what he heard. He gave Santana a quick whistle and motioned him to be ready. Santana then in turn passed the information on to Bates. Bates turned towards Bourque to let him know, but when he turned his head, Bourque was already aiming his C22.

At the top of the hill, Tompkins was watching all that was happening through one of the M10s. The barrel of the M10 was slowly scanning the gray line of the Confederate wave. He figured the line was at least a quarter mile long and two men deep. All in all, he figured the number of Confederates to be around sixteen hundred. He estimated the number of men coming up on his four friends positions to be around two hundred and fifty. Bourque was at the very end of the line and was positioned perfectly. The end of the Confederate line was to the inside of his position about five yards. This meant he would not have to worry about his flank, but could concentrate on keeping the other men safe. As he watched Bourque behind his rock pile, he could see the tension on his face. To his surprise Bourque set the C22 down next to him and picked up his M16. This made sense to Tompkins. Since he was at the end of the line, no one would see him firing. At least not until it was too late. Tompkins swung the M10 towards the other three men. They looked calm and focused.

As the Confederates moved closer, they all kept glancing to the Michigan line. They waited for them to fire, starting their part of this chapter in history.

Tompkins was starting to become tense as he once again concentrated on the moving gray line. As he scanned over the positions of his men, something caught his eye. He slowly brought the scope back to where the odd movement was. As his eyes focused on any movement, he found it. Draper was turned around towards him and waving like a little girl. He then blew Tompkins a kiss and turned back around. Tompkins had no choice but to lower the M10 and laugh out loud. Only Draper could bring levity in a situation like this.

Draper quickly regained his composure and brought his rifle back up to his shoulder. Just as he found the Confederate line, some forty yards downhill of the Union line, a horrendous thunder of black powder rifles erupted. The smoke from the slow burning powder filled the forest. The front line of Confederate soldiers fell to the ground as the Union lead balls tore through their ranks. The loud sound of the Rebel yells filled the woods as thick as the smoke.

Tompkins had always heard the expression "Rebel Yell", but had no real idea what it truly meant. He knew the Confederates would hoop and holler as they attacked, giving them the appearance of larger numbers and confusing their opposition. He never thought the tactic would work. The sounds of the attackers was loud and obnoxious. It was a bothersome noise and kind of made you mad. He now saw why they did this and that it really did work.

He quickly brought his attention to his men. They brought a new sound to the battle. Their nitro powder ammunition made sharp cracks as they fired in rapid succession.

To the far right, Draper was firing his C22 as fast as it would fire, without being in automatic mode. The men in front of him were falling like they were being struck by lightning bolts from God. He had no problem holding his part of the line.

Next to Draper was Santana. He was also firing his C22 in rapid succession. The gray men in his line of fire were falling into lifeless heaps as he continued his defensive onslaught.

Bates was next in line and bore the largest brunt of the attack. The Confederate line was heavily reinforced directly in front of him. As his C22 spewed death to the attackers, they filled the holes and kept on coming. Bourque was firing his M16 into the holes, which gave Bates the reprieve he needed to regain his advantage, to the advancement of the Rebels. As the attacking Confederate soldiers slowly moved up the hill, they stopped only to fire quick shots at the Union line. They were probably pretty good shots, but the thick cloud of lead the Union line was delivering to their ranks must have shaken them enough for their shots to be ineffective. The Union line suffered only minor losses.

As the carnage became more evident to the advancing Rebels, their movement forward came to a halt. The Confederate soldiers were looking around them and slowly retreating back down the hill. Their yells stopped as they turned to retreat. Their yells were replaced by the hoorays of the Union troops up and down the line.

Tompkins brought his attention from the Union line back to his men. They were still concentrating on the retreating Confederates. Their weapons were still in firing position and their fingers were still on the triggers. As the danger was minimal, Bourque brought his hand up in a tight fist and twisted it back and forth. The other men looked to him and brought the weapons they were holding to their sides. Tompkins knew this was the signal to cease firing and relax your weapons. He was amazed how quickly the other three men saw the signal. It was almost as if they had one eye on the Confederates and one eye on their commander. If he didn't know better, he would almost think there was an umbilical cord linking the four of them. There was no doubt in Tompkins' mind they were a true fighting machine. Whichever side of the battle they were on, that side definitely had the advantage.

As the retreating Confederates moved out of sight, the four men came together at the center of their line. The smell of black powder filled their nostrils and almost made them choke.

"I can't recall ever smelling this smell or seeing this much smoke during a firefight," commented Bates.

"Thank God we've came a long way from here in weaponry," replied Santana.

"My dad used to hunt with a muzzle loader when I was little," began Bourque. "The funniest parts of his stories were how his rifle misfired and that was the reason he never brought a deer home. I used to think he made the stories up so he wouldn't have to gut a deer, but now I can see what he was saying. I must have seen at least fifty men pull their triggers and nothing happened."

"There were a couple times when I thought the Rebels were going to break through the Michigan line," commented Draper. "But then the Rebels would have a round of misfires and the Union would regain the advantage."

"It's kind of funny," replied Bates. "When I was young, my family visited a Civil War battlefield somewhere in Tennessee. One of the things that stuck with me from the tour was just that. They said the South was at a disadvantage because they used inferior weapons. The guide said they sometimes had no choice but to use thinned down powder because they were running so low. Most of the artillery and weapons manufacturing companies were in the north. They even had to use weapons that came from England or France.

I can imagine powder, traveling months across the ocean is going to collect some moisture."

Everyone nodded as they listened intently to Bates. He was usually not a man of words. The men held him in high regards. They knew he had seen more action then most of them combined. Usually when he spoke, they all listened.

"I had better run up to Tompkins and see what he thinks is going to happen next," shouted Bourque. "Bates, why don't you run over to the Michigan guys and see how they fared. Draper and Santana, you take up defensive positions and watch for any Confederate movement. I don't think they'll wait long to attack again. Now that they know what they're up against, their next attack will be better planned and more intense." Bourque looked around at the men. They seemed relaxed and in tune with what was going on. Bourque was impressed that they were taking this as seriously as they were.

"Let's be quick," commanded Bourque. The men split up and took to their tasks.

Chapter 21

Unleashing hell

With the excitement of the battle, Bourque's adrenaline peaked. He ran up the hill like a grizzly bear chasing a meal. In only a minute he was standing next to Tompkins.

"What do you think?" calmly asked Bourque.

Tompkins looked at Bourque and smiled. "Looks like everything went well."

"Everyone did exactly like they were supposed to," replied Bourque. "I am really proud of those three. They are really into this battle."

Tompkins once again smiled, but this time it was more of a sneer.

"That's a good thing," said Tompkins. "The next Confederate charge will be much more intense."

"Yeah, I told them it probably would be," countered Bourque.

As Bourque was speaking, Tompkins lifted the heavy M10 and peered through the scope. He slowly scanned down the hill as if he were looking for something.

"What's up now?" asked Bourque. Tompkins lowered the rifle and looked at Bourque.

"It won't be long before the Reb's make their next charge," he explained. "This time they will precede it with cannon fire. The first charge was just to feel out the Union strength. This time they know what they're up against. They will try to move around our flank and take us from the rear. You must be ready to defend the flank." Tompkins set the rifle down and wiped the sweat from his brow.

"Boy, it sure is humid today," he said.

"That should work to our benefit," replied Bourque. "I noticed they had a real hard time coming up the hill. Most of them had their heads down and struggled to climb the steep part of the hill. And I also noticed they had a lot of misfires. The humidity will definitely cause them problems." Tompkins turned to Bourque with a quizzical look.

"Good observations," replied Tompkins with a real smile this time.

"See that gap to the left of your position?" asked Tompkins. He lifted a hand and pointed to a small gap in the trees where the hill became less steep.

"Yeah, I see it," responded Bourque.

"That is where they will try to flank you," replied Tompkins. "Tell the other guys to cover the front of the line with the C22s on full auto. Tell them to make sure they have clips ready to replace spent ones. You also make sure they don't turn the flank on us. I will support you from up here with the M10 and the MR2PG. We should be able to hold it, I think."

Tompkins now looked to be in deep thought. "You said they had their heads down as they came up the hill," he asked Bourque.

"Yeah they were pretty tired coming up the hill," replied Bourque.

Tompkins once again looked to be in deep thought. "Let's do this," Tompkins said with added vigor. "As they come up the hill, I will start to pick them off with the M10 way before they get to the gap. You also start shooting early with the M16. If we can make them think our line is longer than reported, maybe we can get them to turn into the main line before they want to." Bourque just stared at him.

"Great idea," burst out Bourque. "If you lay some MR2PG blasts to the left of them, maybe we can turn them like a herd of cattle. Once they start coming directly at me, I can mow them down easily."

The two men stood looking at each other like they just discovered a new planet. Smug looks of content fell over them as they thought.

"Let's not get too cocky though," broke in Bourque, shattering the self fulfilling moment. "We both know that plans don't usually work like we think they will. Remember Panama. We almost lost our platoon by thinking we were smarter than we were."

Tompkins' head dropped as he recalled Panama. He lost one of his best friends when a plan went really wrong. Bourque knew he hit a sore spot.

"Sorry I had to bring that up, but it was the first thing that came to me," responded Bourque.

"Aw, that's O.K.," replied Tompkins. "That was a long time ago. But it is true." Tompkins took a deep breath and lifted the M10 up again.

"Let's get our plan rolling," he said. Bourque nodded his head in agreement and turned to leave. After a couple steps, he spun around and asked, "When should the 20th Maine be here?"

Tompkins shrugged his shoulders. "Hopefully soon," he replied. "We need to get out of here before something weird happens."

Bourque turned and headed down the hill again. Tompkins could hear him as he ran down the hill in giant bounds. His laughter seemed to echo through the whole forest.

"This whole thing is pretty weird if you ask me," he shouted. His laughter faded as he disappeared down the hill.

Bates quickly made his way across the hill to the Michigan line. He asked the first man in the line where his commanding officer was located. The man looked at Bates with a grim look and told him he had been killed during the charge. Bates placed a hand on his shoulder and told him to hold fast.

"Who is the next in charge?" asked Bates in a comforting voice.

"I believe it to be Major Roo, he is right there." The man slowly lifted his hand and pointed to a young man standing near the rear of the line.

Bates walked over to him and saluted. Major Roo saluted Bates back. Roo had a scared look on his face. "What can I do for you, Major?" asked Roo.

Bates smiled. "I am with the 20th Maine," Bates explained. "We are stationed next to you at the end of the line. I just came over to see how you fared from the first charge."

The young soldier looked at him with a solemn face. "We only lost a couple men. One of them was Colonel Nash, our commanding officer. I guess I am in charge now." Bates knew this was a delicate situation. He knew he had to offer some type of support to the young man.

"Well, you look like a capable man," Bates replied. "Make sure your men are fully behind you. If they sense you are unsure of yourself, they will falter. Give them a figure of strength to rally around. Bark out your commands and show no fear. I know you can do it. You must know you can do it."

Bates smiled and offered his hand to the man. Roo reached out and shook his hand with a stern look on his face.

"Thank you, Major," he responded with sincerity. "I will take your advice and apply it. I must be strong for my men." Bates smiled.

"That's the attitude of a leader," Bates replied with a salute. "If you need anything, we will be right over there." Bates pointed towards the end of the line.

"Thank you for your kind and encouraging words," Roo said.

"You're very welcome. This next charge is likely to be more intense," Bates spoke as he turned to return to his position. "Make sure you have enough reserves to fill any holes. We'll keep an eye on you from our position."

Bates kept walking as he spoke his last words. As he came to the man he first met, he placed his hand on his shoulder. "Have faith in Major Roo," Bates spoke in a reassuring voice. "He is a very able commander."

The man just looked up at Bates and smiled. "Thank you, Sir."

As Bates walked past the man, the man called to him. "Sir." Bates stopped and faced the man. "We were told you were trying out some new weapons."

"Yes we are." Bates' mind raced as he thought of explanations to give the man. "They seem to be working very well," the man replied. "If you see us in need of assistance, please feel free to help us out."

Bates smiled at the man. "Don't worry son. We'll keep an eye on you." Bates turned once again and walked toward the other men. For the first time since he became part of this incident, he saw the human side of the war. He thought it was interesting that people have the same reactions to war, whether now or in the past. He had seen the same reaction time and again from young recruits. All he could hope from these young men was that they perform when they were counted on. In his present day situation or in this situation, he needed that young man to fight and fight with every part of his soul.

He soon made his way back to his position. Draper and Santana ran over to see what was up.

"So how did the Michigan boys fare?" asked Draper.

"Pretty good," replied Bates. "They lost their commander and a couple men, but nothing too major."

"Who's in charge over there now?" asked Santana.

"Oh, some young major named Roo. I think we better keep an eye on them. They seem to be unsure about his leadership ability and a bit downhearted."

"I should be able to help them out if they need it," answered Draper in a serious tone.

"Hey guys," shouted Bourque, as he slid down the last few feet of the hill. "Tompkins says it won't be long before the Confederates make their next charge." Bourque put his hands on his knees and bent over as he tried to catch his breath. "Man, that hill is a pain in the butt."

"What did Tompkins say?" asked Bates.

Bourque straightened up and stood tall. He took a couple deep breaths and let the last one out slowly.

"Tompkins said this charge will be more intense than the last. He said they will be firing cannons and much more ready for the fight this time. The first charge was just to feel us out. Now that they know what they're up against, they will be much more prepared."

"Is anything different going to happen?" asked Draper.

"Yeah, Tompkins said they are going to try to flank us. See that gap in the trees over there?" Bourque pointed a finger towards the small gap in the trees. "They are going to try and come through there, where the slope is less steep. They think they can use the gap in the trees to move around behind us."

"Do you have any ideas what we should do?" asked Santana.

"Of course we came up with something," replied Bourque as he rolled his eyes. "I am going to concentrate my efforts on that gap and keeping them from flanking us. Tompkins will assist me from above. You will have to spread out your coverage to include my part of the line. Put your C22s and your M16s on full auto and let them have everything you got. Don't give in for a second. If you need to use grenades, use them. If you need help, just holler."

"Hey Bourque," burst out Bates. "What about the Michigan boys? They seem pretty susceptible to defeat right now. Should we try to help them if they need it?"

Bourque just stood there looking down the hill. The others could see he was trying to figure out what to do about this new problem.

"We are only supposed to take the place of the 20th Maine. If we interact too much with the Michigan Boys, we might end up screwing up history. Remember, they only had one shot per thirty seconds. We have thirty shots per thirty seconds. If you do feel the need to help them, do it sparingly, if at all." Bourque became quiet again. He opened his mouth to speak, but then closed it as if he was afraid he might say the wrong thing.

"Remember, if one person lives that is supposed to die, the whole face of the future could change." He then brought his hand up to his head and rubbed his neck. "I guess just use your best judgment, but be prepared to fix what you mess up. I'm not going to do it for you."

With that said, Bourque walked down to his position and began piling rocks up on the outside of his cover. As the other men got behind their own rock piles, the sound of an incoming cannonball broke the relative silence. The cannonball exploded some fifty feet over their heads in the tops of the trees. The sound of falling branches and splintering wood made them all dive into their rock piles on their stomachs. The sound of cannon fire could be heard in the distance. It only took a second for the sound of whizzing cannonballs and explosions to drown out all other sounds in the forest. Most of the cannon fire was overshooting their positions, but was landing short of Tompkins' position.

Bourque stuck his head up over his rock pile and looked down the hill. A solid wave of gray was advancing on their position, with much more energy this time. He quickly motioned for the others to look down the hill. As the other men brought their weapons up to aim, Bourque scanned the extreme left of his position for any Confederates trying to flank them. Just as Tompkins said, there were about fifty gray bodies moving in a line towards the gap. Bourque pulled up his M16 and began to fire into the left side of their line. As the brass casings flew from his rifle, the gray line became shorter and shorter. His accuracy was undisputable. As more men began to fill the holes he was making, a large explosion took the whole left side of the Confederate line out. Tompkins had unleashed hell from the MR2PG.

The other three men began to fire their weapons. There wasn't a second between rounds as the four men fired at will with their fully automatic weapons. The rebels fired back, sending fragments of rock flying everywhere. Their aim was much more accurate this time.

Draper kept an eye on the Michigan line as the fighting intensified. Soon the forest was filled with smoke and dead bodies. The sounds of dying men and gunfire choked out any other sound. Santana was firing his M16 in bursts. He would take down five to ten Confederate soldiers with every burst. Bates was firing one shot at a time, going from one end of the line to the other.

Draper had yet to fire a round to help the Michigan Brigade. They seemed to be holding their own.

Bourque was firing his M16 as if he were in a cartoon. The ground around him was covered with an inch of spent brass casings. You could hear the sharp report of the M10, as Tompkins was firing as fast as possible. About every ten seconds there was an explosion in the Confederate line, as Tompkins would then fire the MR2PG. Their plan was working. The pressure Bourque and Tompkins put on the outside of the Confederate line turned them back to the front of the Union line. As the Rebs swung around in front of Bourque, he dropped them like cardboard silhouettes. It only took them a few minutes to persuade the Confederates to retreat and regroup. The gray line in front of the four men slowly drifted back down the hill. They would only stop to fire a quick shot and then continue to move away.

The Michigan line was not faring as well though. There were dozens of blue clad men slumped lifeless over the logs and rocks, up and down their line. The holes that were made in the Michigan line were instantly filled by reserves. The rifles of the Michigan men continued to spew hot lead at the Confederate line. As more and more gray bodies littered the forest, the heart of the Rebs broke. They too, began to slowly retreat back down the hill, their yells and hollers stopping as they jumped over fallen friends. Once again the Union line erupted in hoorays when they realized their victory in the charge. As quickly as they came, the Confederates were gone. All that remained were the dead and the dying.

The bodies in front of Draper were stacked like cord wood in a long line. The once gray uniforms were covered with dark red blood. All throughout the smoky woods, the moans and cries of the wounded filled the air. Bodies in blood-stained coats clawed at the dirt as they tried to move in any direction. Draper eyed the devastation he and his comrades had evoked. He was amazed at their effectiveness.

He then glanced to his right towards the Michigan line. The bodies of the dead Confederates were spread out evenly among the trees and brush. Though the two hundred men of the 19th Michigan were effectively holding off the Confederate charges, anyone could see the bullets were coming from a long line of fire. In front of the four newcomers, it was much different. Draper scanned to the left, past his piles of dead. He looked to see if the other men had the same results as he. The dead were piled in similar fashion all along the line in front of the other three men. He could see they were also taking time to evaluate the damage their new weapons inflicted on the Confederates. Bates met eyes with Draper as they looked down the line. They needed no words to express what each other was feeling.

"Holy crap," shouted Santana, jumping up from behind his rock pile. "I can't believe they just kept coming in lines like that. Things sure are different nowadays."

CHAPTER 22

Hold the line

Everyone rose from behind their rocks and walked over to Santana. They stood there looking out over the carnage in awe. The sounds of the wounded were waning as they slowly crossed over to death. The Union line to their right was busy tending to their wounded and dead. They made little noise as they performed the horrible task. A few of the Michigan men made their way through the dead bodies scattered over the forest floor. They were gathering needed ammunition before the next Confederate charge. Some of them stood over bodies with heads hung low. Their lips were moving but no words were said.

"Hey Bourque," spoke Draper. "What are those men doing out there?" He pointed towards the men standing over the dead. Bourque stuck his head out around the men and looked where Draper was pointing.

"They look like they are saying prayers over the dead. Back in the old-days, it was considered respectful to pray for all the dead."

The four men stood in silence, watching the men move to as many lifeless bodies as possible.

"Wouldn't take them long to pray over the dead on our line," remarked Bates.

"We piled 'em pretty neatly down here."

"I can't believe how they just kept coming in lines," murmured Santana again.

"That's the way they used to do it," said Bourque. "I'm glad we don't do it that way now."

The men stood looking at the piles of dead men lying in long rows along the line in front of them. They didn't need to say anything. They were used to seeing the dead, but not in this type of circumstance. They were used to sniping at long range, or at least from one hundred yards or more. The men didn't look at each other as they looked over their morning's work. Each one of them had watery eyes, but didn't want to show the others their feelings. Although they appreciated the struggle they were in, they still didn't feel as though there was a true enemy. Their usual foe were the scum of the earth. Men that deserved to die. These men were fighting for a true cause. For their families and a way of life. Even though they didn't agree with their point of view on the war, they still respected them for fighting for what they thought was a great cause. The silence was overwhelming.

Suddenly it was broken by the loud voice of Bourque. "I had better get my butt up to Tompkins and see what we are up against in the next while."

Bourque turned and once again began his assent up the hill. About ten yards up the hill he paused and turned.

"You guys hold down the fort, I'll be back in a minute," yelled Bourque.

He quickly made it up the hill and jumped behind the rock with Tompkins. A smile came to Tompkins' face as the men nodded their heads at each other.

"Looks like you four are holding your own down there," said Tompkins in a light tone.

"Yeah, we seem to be getting the job done," replied Bourque. "What's going to happen next?"

Tompkins thought for a second before he answered. "The next charge is the last charge, before the 20th Maine is supposed to do their bayonet charge."

Tompkins looked over his shoulder towards the woods at the very top of the hill. He squinted his eyes as if he were expecting someone or something to appear from the dark green woods.

"What ya looking for?" asked Bourque.

Tompkins focused his attention on Bourque. "I thought I heard hooves a second ago."

"Maybe the 20th Maine boys are coming," answered Bourque.

"I don't think so, it sounded like a lot of horses. The Maine boys should only have a few."

Then a blue-clad body emerged from the thick undergrowth. To both men's surprise, it was Buford and a small group of his calvary. As the men approached Bourque and Tompkins, smiles came across their faces. They seemed as happy to see them as the two men were to see them. Buford, MacDonald and Newton stepped to the front of the men and saluted. Bourque and Tompkins saluted back and then let out deep breaths of relief.

"Boy, are we glad to see you guys," burst out Tompkins. "We were just talking about our next move."

Buford smiled and moved around the rock. He looked down the hill and viewed the carnage. His head moved up and down the line as he stood with his arms crossed across his chest. After a few moments of staring down the hill, he turned around and faced Bourque and Tompkins.

"It appears your weapons and your men have performed up to expectations. It looks like there were several hundred men holding the end of the line down there." A large smile came across Buford's face as he finished speaking. Newton and MacDonald both moved around the rock and looked down the hill.

"Holy cow," said Newton in disbelief. "You guys are really the only ones holding down the end of the line?" MacDonald then burst in. "And you four killed all them Confederates down there?" He was pointing down the hill. His faced looked like he was standing with God himself.

"Yep, we had to do the devil's work this morning," replied Bourque with a proud tone in his voice.

"We were able to hold the line," replied Tompkins. "We can hold it for as long as needed."

"Well, it shouldn't be for long," said Buford. "The 20th Maine is only about five minutes from here."

Tompkins felt a wave of anticipation roll over him as Buford told them of their relief's approach.

"It's a good thing," replied Tompkins. "The next charge is supposed to have the Maine's bayonet charge in it. I was wondering what we were going to do if they didn't show up." Buford looked at him sternly.

"Well, they'll be here, but there is a small problem."

"What's the problem?" asked Tompkins.

Buford took a deep breath. "When we reached the 20th Maine, they were ready to cross the river. When we told them of the situation, they immediately charged across the river. It wasn't till they reached the other side that they realized almost all of their powder and ammunition was now wet. They will be here, but I don't know what good they will do without the ability to fire their weapons.

The men stood there not knowing what to say. Tompkins turned away and rested his elbows on the big rock. He put his head in his hands and stared out over the forest below. It was only a minute or so before the solution hit him. He lifted his head like he had just been shocked. He spun around with a big smile on his face. The eyebrows of the other men lifted at the sudden motion.

Bourque just smiled and said, "The answer just hit him."

"You're right, I just figured out what to do." The look on Tompkins' face told the other men they needed to pay close attention. "Ride back and give them our position. The Confederates will probably start their next charge soon. We will hold them off until the 20th Maine gets here. By the time they get here, we should have them pretty well beaten down. I will tell the Maine boys we have them where we want them, and they should do a bayonet charge. At that point, we will offer rifle support until the charge is over."

Buford looked at Tompkins with surprise. "If you don't find your way back to your time, I will have a place in my brigade for you."

Everyone smiled and gave a chuckle. Buford then straightened his coat and stood up straight. "I guess we better get this plan under way, don't you think?"

"Sounds good to me," replied Tompkins.

Buford offered his hand to Tompkins and then Bourque. "God be with you two," said Buford as he turned to his men. "Let's get going boys, we don't have much time." The three men in blue turned and walked back into the dense underbrush. Bourque then turned to Tompkins. "Boy, they disappear like ghosts when they leave, don't they?"

Tompkins laughed. "They are ghosts after all." Both men laughed.

"Now get down there and fill the other guys in on the plan," commanded Tompkins. "Tell them to offer support until the charge is over. After you are sure everything is in line, head back up here so we can make a quick exit."

"Should we follow them down the hill if need be?" asked Bourque.

"Sure, if you think you should," replied Tompkins. "Just be careful. I can only support you for a short ways down the hill. I can always come down behind you and offer as much help as I can."

Bourque quickly jumped around the rock and headed down the hill towards the other men. He soon came crashing through the brush just behind the men. They all ran to him to get their orders.

"What do we have to do now?" asked Draper. Bourque was still panting from his run down the hill. He lifted his eyes and met the other three's.

"The 20th Maine boys are only a couple minutes away. When they crossed the river, their powder got wet, so they will not be able to fire when they get here."

The other men's eyebrows raised in surprise. "What good will they be?" asked Santana in a calm voice.

"How can we keep the balance if they can't shoot?" interrupted Draper. "Oh man, we're screwed now." Draper turned a circle as he squirmed before the other men.

"Just relax sissy boy," burst out Bates. "I'm sure Tompkins came up with something." They all looked up at Bourque with hope.

"He did come up with a plan, didn't he?" asked Bates with some hesitation. Bourque laughed. "Oh ye of little faith," he crooned. "Of course, he came up with a plan."

Bourque reached out a huge fist and punched Draper on the shoulder, knocking him two steps back. "Ouch, you big gorilla," whined Draper. "Just tell us the plan. "

"All right, gather round," commanded Bourque. As they formed up in front of him he began. "The Maine boys can't shoot, but they still can do their bayonet charge. We will continue to hold this line when the Rebels make their next charge. We will do just what we did on their last charge. They will probably try to come around the end again, but this time with more energy. Once again, I might need you guys to keep an eye on me. The Rebs should be running on their last cylinder by now. We shouldn't have much problem."

"So when the Maine boys come down the hill, we should just hold until they form up and do their charge?" asked Santana.

"Yeah," replied Bourque. "Once they make their way down the hill a bit, follow them, giving fire support as needed." Bourque turned to Draper. "Don't do anything you don't have to," commanded Bourque in a tone directed towards Draper. He then turned and looked up the hill towards Tompkins. He raised an arm and pointed up the hill.

"Tompkins will give us support from the hill. Once we are out of his range, he will come down the hill and follow us as best he can." Bourque looked at each of the men. "Any questions?" Everyone shook his head no. "Good, I just seen some movement down the hill, the Confederates must be coming up the hill now. Let's lock and load one more time. Good luck and don't take any unnecessary risks."

Before Bourque could finish, the men were heading for their positions. A whistle from Tompkins up the hill let them know something was happening.

Draper dropped behind his pile of rocks, and glanced at the Michigan line. They seemed to have enough men to do the job, but they looked scared as hell. Draper gave a quick loud whistle to get the man on the end of the line's attention. The man looked up from his rifle and turned his head towards Draper. Draper pointed down the hill and mouthed, "Here they come." The man quickly turned his attention down the hill. He squinted to see any movement. After a second his eyes got wide. He quickly motioned to the men down the line to look down the hill. As the word spread, the men hunkered down behind whatever they could and aimed their rifles down the hill. The man on the end of the line turned back to Draper and smiled. He raised his hand to say thanks. Draper smiled back and nodded his head to show he understood.

Chapter 23

Bayonet charge of the 20th Maine

At the top of the hill, Tompkins was peering through the scope on the M10. He scanned the line of Confederates moving slowly up the hill. He noticed they were concentrating more to the end of the line than they had before. He lifted his head from the rifle and looked nervously over his shoulder. He hadn't heard any motion behind him, but he impatiently awaited the Maine regiment. He returned his eye back to the scope of the rifle and looked closely at the gray line moving towards Bourque's position. It looked like at least one hundred men would be converging on Bourque's position in the next few minutes. He moved the scope to Bourque. To his surprise, it looked like Bourque anticipated what was coming. He was placing M16 clips along the base of his rock pile and placing C22 clips on top of the rock pile. To Tompkins it looked like Bourque was getting ready to unleash hell upon the Rebels. Tompkins lowered the rifle and grabbed one of the MR2PGs. He made sure it was fully loaded with RPG rounds and the rifle clip was full. He did this three more times with each of the MR2PGs. He then grabbed the other M10s and repeated the process on them. When he was sure all the weapons around him were ready for the fight, he once again watched the scene below through the scope of the M10.

The Confederates slowly came within shooting range of Bourque. He raised his hand and whistled. He gave the command to fire at will. The four men put their fingers on the triggers of their weapons. Three massive explosions ripped the forest apart to Bourque's left. Tompkins rained three MR2PG rounds down on the end of the Confederate line, hoping to turn them in towards Bourque, as they had the last charge.

The smoke and debris fell from the tree tops as the yells from the attacking Rebels began. Bourque began firing the C22 on full automatic. The little bullets began tearing holes in the bodies of the gray line. He concentrated his efforts on the very end of their line.

Bates was also firing his M16 on full automatic. He was mowing down the Confederate line as they tried to cross the pile of dead already on the field. He was keeping an eye on Bourque's position as he covered his own.

Santana and Draper were holding their positions with ease as they switched between the C22s and the M16s.

The sound of M10 rounds flying overhead gave them all a sense of security. They knew Tompkins had their backs if anything should go wrong. More MR2PG explosions rang over the Rebel yells. The entire end of the Confederate line was now gone. Bourque was concentrating on the center of the line in front of him. They had made their way over his line of dead bodies and were closing in on his position. A quick burst of C22 fire ended their attempt to overtake his position.

Tompkins was firing the M10 as quickly as he could, concentrating on any threats that could harm his men. He was concentrating on a tight line of men who were trying to advance between Bourque and Bates. He fired the M10 and punched coffee can sized holes in his targets. When he was sure the they were secure, he swung his attention back to Bourque.

To Tompkins' horror, two gray-coated men were standing behind Bourque. They were pointing their weapons at his back. He wasn't even aware they were there.

Suddenly, Bourque turned his head and saw the men. His left hand swung behind him and grabbed the barrel of one of the rifles. The other man pulled his trigger. Nothing happened. Bourque sprung to his feet and grabbed both men by the throat. The men had no time to react. They had never encountered a complete killing machine like Bourque. With a man's throat in each hand, he lifted them into the air like he was holding puppies by the napes of their necks. He then glanced up at Tompkins and winked. Tompkins knew what he wanted done. Tompkins squeezed the trigger as the cross hairs of his scope hit the man in Bourque's left hand. The man's mid section exploded as the bullet hit its target. Tompkins then noticed more men coming up the hill directly in front of Bourque. He lifted the scope and locked onto the nearest man. Bourque heard the M10 rounds whizzing over his head. He knew what was happening. He gave the man in his right hand a quick twist. He could feel the man's spine crunch at the force. He then threw both limp bodies to the ground and turned his attention back to the Rebel advance. It only took a minute to push the gray line back as the C22 rounds and the M10 rounds from up the hill did their jobs.

Bates was also firing his M16 into the flank of the group. Santana was covering his line and Bates' center. Draper was covering the rest of the line. If the five men had not served together in so many battles, the results may have been different. It was almost as if they worked with the same brain. They were a force that most conventional armies couldn't deal with, let alone a Civil War army.

As Tompkins took a deep breath of relief, he heard the sound of many boot steps rushing over the top of the hill. He quickly swung around and raised his hand. The forest erupted with blue-coated men racing towards him. The man in the lead ran up to Tompkins and saluted.

"My name is Colonel Chamberlain. I was told by General Buford to double-time it up this hill to your location."

His entire regiment now made a long line across the top of the hill. They were panting from their race up the hill. Tompkins was surprised to see so many older soldiers. He was used to seeing young Confederate men through the scope of his M10. Almost all of them would not have the chance to grow old.

Tompkins returned Colonel Chamberlain's salute. He got the chills as he stood in the presence of the man that was so revered in history. This was the man that gave the Union Army a ray of hope in their darkest moment. The Union Army had never won a large battle up to this point. Command in the Union Army was at a low point. Politics, lack of vision and bravery was the norm throughout the Union command. This one man renewed the vision of bravery and selflessness throughout the Union Army. One man, and a bayonet charge in the face of horrible odds, gave hope to a nation. If Chamberlain hadn't performed his bayonet charge that day, history may have been different. That was why it was so important he do it now.

"Colonel Chamberlain, sir," replied Tompkins. "We have been holding off the Confederates now for several hours. We have cut their numbers by hundreds. Most of our men are almost out of ammunition. We think the Rebels must be in the same condition. If you were to perform a bayonet charge down this hill, with our fire support of course, you could drive the Confederate lines down the hill and take the day."

Tompkins kept a serious look on his face as he explained the situation. Chamberlain and a few of his brigade commanders listened intently as Tompkins spoke. They would look at each other now and then and rub their chins.

"And General Buford thought this to be the correct action?" asked Chamberlain. "Yes, Sir," replied Tompkins. "I believe his words were, 'The Confederates are ripe for the picking and today could be the last day of the harvest.'"

Chamberlain looked hard into his eyes. His dusty face was tired but his eyes were still bright. He stood up straight and saluted Tompkins.

"Thank you, Sir. We will sweep down this hill and end the day's battle now."

He then turned to his men and pulled out his sword. He raised it in the air and shouted at the top of his lungs, "Fix bayonets." His men shouted, "Hooray," and began to attach their long bayonets to the end of their rifles. He gathered his commanders to him and explained their next move. Tompkins had to listen to this.

"We are going to perform a bayonet charge. We will sweep down the hill, swinging towards the center like a door. We will force the Confederates down the hill into their own ranks. Do not stop the charge at any cost. Tompkins is sure the Confederates are almost out of ammo and in desperate shape." He took a second to look at each of his commanders. "Let's do this for our families and our nation. Be strong and quick. Now let's move down that hill and take their spirits. Give quarter to their wounded and those that surrender. God be with you."

Immediately his men ran to their position in the line. They held up their swords, along with Chamberlain.

"Bayonet charge," yelled Chamberlain.

"Bayonet charge," rang from the entire line.

They moved in unison down the hill. They were running as fast as they could on the terrain. As they reached the four men and the Union line, they were moving at a good pace. Bourque and the other men stopped firing as the wave of blue swept by them. Once the blue wave passed by Bourque, he started firing at any soldier who was outside of their line. Draper on the other side of the line started firing at any soldier to the inside of their charge who was fixing to fire at them.

Bates and Santana could not fire as the Maine men blocked their view. Santana jumped over his rock pile and began to follow the Maine boys. Bates saw him do this and immediately abandoned his rock pile. The two men followed the Union line about twenty yards to the rear. As a hole opened up in the Union charge, they would stop and fire at any Confederate they could see. It was quite a mess.

The Confederates were running away from the charge, only stopping to turn and fire their one round. They would then continue running as fast as they could. Dozens of Confederates froze and were taken captive by the Union Army. As the Maine boys swept inward, towards the inside of the line, the Confederates became confused and started to run. Many just stopped and held their hands up in surrender.

Draper and Bourque soon abandoned their positions and took off after the Maine line. They stopped and shot any Rebel who posed a threat to the charge. As they approached the bottom of the hill, things got messy. Once the Confederates reached even ground, which is where their commanders were located, they turned to fight. The sound of sword against sword and bayonet against bayonet filled the forest. The sounds of the wounded and the yells of surrender lifted into the treetops.

The four men following the fight stayed back to offer any support they could. Tompkins joined them about three-quarters of the way down the hill. The five men then came together to watch the ensuing battle. Draper was watching the battle to the center of the line. Blue and gray bodies lay everywhere. He felt he might be able to help some of the wounded, so he headed towards a few men about forty yards away.

"Hey, where are you going?" shouted Bourque.

Draper turned as he walked. "I'm going to see if I can help those men over there."

"Be careful and get back here in five minutes," commanded Bourque.

Draper shook his head and made his way to the three men laying around a large tree. When he finally made it to the men, he immediately began to see if they were alive. The first man lay there lifeless. Draper checked him for vital signs. He soon moved on to the next. He put his fingers on the man's throat. He felt a pulse. He ripped the man's blue coat from his chest and backed away. The man's bloody chest was torn apart by a well placed 50-caliber lead ball. Draper took the coat he tore off him and held it to his chest. He knew even if he stopped the bleeding the man was still going to die. He reached down and grabbed the man's hand and folded it over the coat on his chest. He then moved to the third man. The man, dressed in gray, lifted his head and smiled at Draper with dim eyes. Draper put his hand on the man's head and pushed it back down.

"Just lay still," ordered Draper.

"Am I going to die?" asked the young Confederate soldier.

"I don't think so. Where are you injured?"

The man opened his shirt and showed Draper the hole through his abdomen. There was a thick stream of bright red blood pumping out of the hole. Draper instinctively put his hand over the hole to stop the bleeding. The young man reached up and grabbed his arm.

"Sir," he asked in a low calm voice. "I know you're from the north, but could you say a prayer with me before I pass?"

Draper raised up and stared at the man.

"Of course I will, son." He smiled the best smile he could muster. The man closed his eyes and held onto Draper's arm tightly. Draper bowed his head and said a prayer for the man, just loud enough for the man to hear. When Draper finished with an amen, the man looked at him with watery eyes and asked, "Sir, I'm sorry for this whole mess. I hope God will forgive me and let me into his kingdom. Thank you for your prayer."

He reached into his pocket with a blood covered hand and pulled out a small cross. He reached out and placed it in Draper's hand.

"Take this, so that you will remember this place and the kindness you have shown me. I sure appreciate you being here as I pass."

The man closed his eyes and swallowed hard. He then opened his eyes again and looked at Draper with a smile. "Heck, maybe I can come back and visit you from the other side sometime. God bless you, sir."

He then closed his eyes again and let out his last breath. His tight grip fell limp as the life left his body. Draper sat back on his heels and stared at the young man. He then looked down at the hand-carved cross the man had given him. He slowly put it into his pocket and stood up. He looked over the three men lying there lifeless and said another prayer. He opened his tear-filled eyes and turned to head back to the others. As he moved across the gruesome terrain, he heard someone call for him. He turned to see a gray-clad man aiming a rifle at him. Draper froze. He just stood there, looking at the man. He could see the man's finger tense as he pulled the trigger. A flash of smoke and a loud blast followed. Draper could almost see the large lead ball hurling towards him. He felt the bullet strike him in the chest, knocking him to the ground.

Bourque was watching Draper as he stood there frozen. He instinctively pulled up his M16 and pulled the trigger. The bullet was a perfect shot, hitting the gray-clad man in the forehead. The man flew backward from the bullet strike and landed on his back. Bourque immediately dropped his rifle and ran to Draper's side. Draper's eyes were closed and blood was streaming from the corner of his mouth. Bourque knelt down and pulled Draper to his lap.

"You're always going to be a pain in my butt, aren't you?" laughed Bourque in a frightened voice. A tear almost formed in his eyes when Draper opened his eyes.

"Are you going to kiss me now?" asked Draper in a soft voice.

Bourque's expression changed from fright to elation. He reached down and pulled apart Draper's coat. There was no blood. He felt Draper's chest and found he was wearing his Kevlar vest.

"Usually I require dinner before I let someone feel me up like that," spurted Draper as he began to laugh.

Bourque let out a loud laugh and then smacked Draper in the chest where the bullet dented the Kevlar. Draper let out a holler of pain. Bourque continued to laugh. "Quit crying like a baby," said Bourque as his laughter came to a end. "Better a couple broken ribs than a big old hole in your gut." He then slapped him in the chest again. Draper let out another holler of pain. Bourque stood up and dragged Draper up with him. The other men, running to their position, came to a halt as the two men stood up.

"Is he all right?" asked Bates. Draper was hunched over holding his chest. Bourque had his massive arm around him, holding him up.

"Yeah, he had his vest on," replied Bourque. "He's really lucky for that."

"Yeah," burst out Santana. "None of us would give you mouth-to-mouth, that's for sure." Everyone laughed out loud as they started to head back up the hill.

As the five men walked up the hill, they took time to look at the death that was spread over the hill. The bloodied gray bodies lay every which way for as far as they could see. In some places the bodies were stacked three high. It was obvious, to them, where they were positioned along the line. The bodies were stacked neatly in long lines in front of the four men. Bourque stopped his trek up the hill and rolled over one of the gray bodies.

"Hey guys, let's see what the C22 does to a real body." The other men headed to where Bourque was squatting over the body.

"Yeah, we never tested the gun on an actual human," replied Tompkins.

As the men gathered around Bourque, he tore the front of the shirt on the body that lay in front of him. Bourque pointed to a small hole in the mans chest, about the size of a pencil.

"Doesn't look that lethal, does it?" exclaimed Draper.

"No it looks like an actual 22 caliber hit him," replied Bates.

Bourque then rolled the lifeless body over onto its stomach. He quickly pulled the shirt over the body's head. Everyone's eyes widened as the gruesome picture of the man's back surprised them. The exit wound from the C22 was as big as a pie plate. The flesh around the exit hole was shredded and burned black. There wasn't much blood, as the bullet blew most of the blood from the upper body of the man. Internal organs were torn, but still visible. Any bones that were in the path of the bullet were shattered. Splinters of bone and flesh were stuck in bloody gobs on the dead man's shirt.

"Wow, what a mess," stated Draper in disbelief.

"I guess you wouldn't want to use that gun for squirrel hunting," added Bourque.

The men just stood over the body, taking in the carnage that the little gun delivered.

"We better get moving," commanded Tompkins as he looked at his watch.

The men once again started up the hill . They each went to the rock pile they defended. They collected all the weapons and ammunition they left behind, when they made their charge. Tompkins threw a plastic bag at Draper.

"We better pick up the spent casings laying around," commanded Tompkins. "We can't leave any trace of our intervention in the battle."

The men crawled around on their hands and knees picking up the brass casings.

Draper looked over at the ground where the Michigan line ended. In a blue heap lay the man he had contact with earlier in the battle. Draper froze as the reality hit him. He had never been in a battle where the man next to him was killed. His mind fell blank as he stared at the dead body. He just knelt there in a frozen state, until a rock hit him in the back. His head turned to where the rock came from.

"You O.K.?" asked Santana.

Draper shook off the new feeling and began collecting the brass from his weapons. "I'm good," was his only reply.

Once all the evidence was collected, the men headed up the hill to where Tompkins was walking. He jumped behind the rock and gathered his possessions. As he slung his M10 over his shoulder, he looked at the other men and smiled.

"Well, there's another chapter in this strange story." He reached out his hand and placed it on Bates' shoulder. "Let's get back to camp before someone spots us."

The five men walked into the thick forest and disappeared from one of America's greatest battles.

Chapter 24

Blood on their hands

The men pushed through the last bit of woods. They were elated to see the clearing where camp was located. They walked over to the fire pit, and let all their weapons and ammunition fall to the ground. Like their weapons, they too, fell to the ground. It was a few minutes before anything was said.

"That was unbelievable," murmured Draper. Blood was still on his hands as he rubbed his eyes. When he realized it was still there, he opened his eyes and held his hands out towards the sky. "I've got blood from a Civil War soldier on my hands. Bet no one I know can say that." He turned his hands around so he could see all sides of them. "Wait a minute," Draper burst out in a surprised voice. "I take that back. You were in the Civil War weren't you Bates?" Bellies shook at Drapers stupid remark.

"I was now," replied Bates.

Tompkins raised up and rested on his elbows. "I have an idea." Everyone rose up and looked at him with dull expressions.

"I think I've had enough for the day," replied Santana in a disgusted tone.

"No, listen to what my idea is," countered Tompkins. He turned his head to look at everyone as they reclined around the camp.

"All right," said Santana as he let out a long breath. "Let's hear this great idea." Everyone looked at Tompkins.

"During the battle," began Tompkins, "the wounded and near dead were taken to field hospitals around the town. We passed by one on our way out of town. Remember that big square, stone building just before Culp's Hill?" Tompkins looked around at everyone. They just shrugged their shoulders.

"Anyway, they had so many wounded and dead soldiers to take care of, they laid them out in the yards and roads, waiting to be seen by the field surgeons. As they moved the men into the building, others had to leave. If men were dead, they would just pile up the bodies in the basement or out on the lawn. As they amputated legs and arms, they would throw the limbs out the windows. There were so many amputations that the piles of arms and legs were stacked up as high as the windows." Tompkins stopped talking and stared into the woods.

"And your idea has to do with this, how?" asked Draper.

Tompkins looked at Draper and smiled. "I would like to see one of these hospitals." He then looked at his watch and tapped it with his forefinger. "It is only four o'clock. If we leave now, we can hoof it to town in about an hour." Tompkins looked at everyone again. They just rolled their eyes and lay back down. When his eyes met Bourque, to his surprise, Bourque nodded his head to say he would go.

The two men jumped to their feet and stood over the others.

"Are any of you going to go with us?" asked Bourque.

"No thanks," replied each of the three men in turn.

"All right then," countered Bourque. "Keep an eye on things around here. If you have any problems, just think them out. We should be back around nineteen hundred hours."

The two men holstered C22s and a couple clips each. They brushed off their blue coats and headed in the direction of town. A quick wave to the other men received no response.

They slowly made their way down the road as the dust from their boots filled the air behind them. They made small talk about the day's events and what they had seen on this strange journey. The sun filled the hot, hazy sky like the glow from a blast furnace. The sweat rings on their hats grew wider with every step they took. The wool uniforms offered insulation from the hot sun, but left them sweating like hogs on the inside. As they made their way down the two track road, they stopped only to point out things that were not seen in their usual world. Even though they had just been in the middle of a great battle, stopping to look at the rare vegetation and the lonely dirt trail relaxed their minds and bodies.

The sounds of gunfire still rang through the forests around them as the day's fighting was still occurring on distant battlefields. As the two men rounded a corner, the first buildings of the small hamlet became visible. The large square outline of the field hospital could be seen on the horizon. Tompkins pointed towards the building as they trudged on. Reaching the first building on the outskirts of town, the two men stopped talking. There was no sign of life around the building. The shutters were shut and no sounds could be heard from inside.

"The people in town must be scared out of their minds," murmured Tompkins. "I can picture them sitting in the corners of their houses, waiting for some sign of the outcome of the battle."

"Reminds you of the Middle East," commented Bourque. "It's funny how war has changed technologically, but how people react to it really hasn't changed."

Tompkins thought about it for a moment and then mumbled, "Yeah, it is funny."

The men made it through the outskirts of town without any problem. With all the fighting going on out in the farmlands and hills, town looked pretty much the way it was when they passed through it the previous day. As they neared the center of the town, people could be seen on their porches and moving around the town. They hurried from building to building or quickly ran to their barns to do chores. The streets were busy with horse-pulled wagons filled with the injured and the dead. They were moving in only one direction; towards the hospital.

As the two men came around the corner of a building, they were startled as a nurse rushed across their path towards the hospital. She was wearing a white dress and had her hair up in a bun. She looked up at the men with a startled look.

"Excuse me soldiers," she said as she scurried by them.

Bourque and Tompkins looked at each other with equally startled looks.

"Pardon us, Ma'am," replied Tompkins. He quickly tipped his hat to her.

"Excuse me, Ma'am," said Bourque, doing the same.

She stopped her trek to the hospital and turned towards the two men. They both took their hats off to show respect.

"Could you tell me how many men have come to the hospital today?" asked Bourque.

The woman had a look of dismay as she calmly answered, "We stopped counting yesterday, but I would guess near five thousand."

Tompkins looked at Bourque in astonishment. "How many doctors are there at the hospital?" asked Tompkins.

The woman fidgeted as she looked into the sky as if counting in her head. "I believe there to be around twenty." She gave the men a dismayed look. "I'm sorry, sirs, I must get to the hospital now."

The two men tipped their hats and thanked her as she sped towards the hospital and her horrible job.

Tompkins turned to Bourque and let out a deep breath. "Are you ready for this? It's going to be gut wrenching." Bourque just nodded his head and they began following the nurse down the road.

The closer they got to the hospital, the faster the nurse moved. The two men were amazed at her speed. Without missing a step, she moved through the door of the hospital and disappeared.

Bourque and Tompkins were still thirty yards from the hospital when they stopped cold in their tracks. From that distance, they could see men being taken into the hospital on gurneys. It looked like a hippie campout from the distance. Men were lying all around the hospital on the ground. The moans and screams of the men inside the hospital sent chills down Tompkins spine. He could picture men getting their legs cut off with hacksaws and no anesthesia. The smell of blood and death filled the air.

Bourque elbowed Tompkins and moved his head to the right, giving Tompkins the hint to move around the hospital to the right. The two men started to slowly move around the hospital grounds. Their eyes were glued on the men lying around the hospital. The looks on their faces told the entire story. Their eyes were filled with tears and their lips were hung in a frightful downward manner. They said nothing.

As they rounded the back of the hospital, they both stopped cold. The windows across the back of the hospital were wide open. Under each of the large windows was a bloody pile of body parts. The arms and legs were being thrown out the windows as they were being cut off the bodies of the injured men. The windows were at least seven feet above the ground. The bloody stumps of human limbs, piled under the windows, were at least five feet high. The men didn't know what to say. They just stood there in disbelief, staring at the most gruesome scene either of them had ever seen. They had witnessed the mass grave sites in Kosovo, but this was on a different level. No wonder the screams emanated from the hospital like calls from hell. Both men were brought back to reality when a leg was tossed out the window. The leg tumbled down the pile of torn flesh like a piece of maple, falling down a pile of split firewood. The flies and other insects fell upon the new dinner entrée before it hit the ground. Dogs were gathering around the area from the smell of blood and rotting flesh.

"This is not real," murmured Bourque as he wiped the tears from his eyes. "How could this be happening?" His eyes couldn't move from the gut wrenching site.

"This is the way it was done," responded Tompkins. "They had no idea there would be so many dead and wounded. They had no facilities to take care of that many men. They just did what they had to."

Tompkins felt a tear roll down his cheek. He quickly reached up and wiped it away before Bourque could spot it.

"The one thing that really gets to me is the way so many men died so impersonally. They had no family with them. They had no privacy. They just died and were discarded like old shoes."

Both men let out deep breaths as the reality of the scene began to harden their thoughts.

"Let's move around the other side of the building," said Bourque as he grabbed Tompkins' arm. Tompkins reluctantly followed Bourque as they moved away from the piles of discarded human tragedy. As they came to the next corner, Tompkins grabbed Bourque by the shoulder. "I have a feeling the scene around the next corner may be worse than the last one."

Bourque looked at him with surprise. "How could it be any worse than what we just seen?"

He turned and continued to walk around the corner of the two story, makeshift tomb. Tompkins reluctantly followed. Just before the two men came within sight of what was around the next corner, they both stopped. The looked at each other like scared boys who were doing something they shouldn't.

"Oh crap," burst out Bourque. "Let's buck up and do this."

He walked around the corner and stopped. Tompkins sheepishly came up behind him and stopped. Both men's eyes were as wide as they possibly could be. Bourque took a step back as if he were afraid of something. Tompkins stood glued to the spot.

In front of the men lay neatly stacked bodies of dead soldiers. Some were bloodied from surgery. Some had almost no sign of harm being done to them. The eyes of the dead seemed to stare at them as they stood frozen in horror.

Two men appeared from the back side of the stacks of dead soldiers. They had handkerchiefs wrapped around their faces to protect them from the rancid smell of rotting flesh. They wore long leather gloves and leather aprons. They grabbed a body like a sack of grain and carried it to a wagon, where they tossed the body haphazardly on the flatbed. They then returned to the pile of bodies and repeated the task.

Bourque and Tompkins stood only long enough to see the horrible task performed twice. They quickly backed around the corner and walked to a nearby grove of trees. They plopped down on the grass under a tree and sat in silence for a minute or two.

"So this is what you wanted to see so bad?" asked Bourque.

Tompkins looked at Bourque without expression. "I had no idea it was going to be like this. I had read about it and thought it would be something to see."

Tompkins looked up to the darkening sky and sighed. "No wonder Gettysburg is supposed to be one of the most haunted places on earth. So many men died so alone, so impersonally. They must be walking the earth, wondering what they did to deserve such a horrible death."

Neither men said anything for quite a while. Their minds were trying to absorb this horrible scene of death and destruction.

The sun was now sinking in the sky, causing long shadows to form around the grove of trees the two men sat in. Bourque slowly stood to his feet and stretched his arms. "We better get back to the camp now."

Tompkins turned over and pushed himself to his feet. "Yeah we better head back."

They took one last look at the stone tomb of a hospital. They then turned and walked back towards the outskirts of town. Their pace was quick, and they said nothing. They passed the last building in town and disappeared down the trail out of town.

Chapter 25

An omen

Back at camp, the men were busy cooking dinner and unrolling their bedrolls. The night was coming fast and they were worn out from the day's events. The smoke of the small fire slowly rose into the hot humid sky. When Bourque and Tompkins broke into sight of the other men, their spirits lifted at the sight of normality.

"I never thought I'd be so happy to see those guys again," said Tompkins with a sigh of relief. "I feel better already."

Bourque let out a chuckle and slapped Tompkins on the back. "It's amazing, but I feel the same way."

The two men lumbered up to the campsite and collapsed on their bedrolls. They both lay on their backs, staring up at the sky.

"Hey you two," burst out Draper. The sound of his voice brought smiles to their faces. "You guys look like you had quite a little trip."

"You have no idea," responded Tompkins.

"Did you run into anything interesting?" asked Bates in an excited tone.

Bourque lifted his head and looked at Tompkins. Tompkins lifted his head and looked at Bourque. They both started to laugh. The other men looked at each other and started to laugh.

"Let us in on the events," laughed Santana.

"Let's eat first, then I'll fill you in," responded Tompkins.

Draper handed out the dinner he had been fixing for the last hour. The men slowly savored the nourishment. The sound of spoons scraping metal plates filled the air. After the plates were scraped clean, the men reclined back on their bedrolls and relaxed. Bates lazily rose to his feet and tossed another log on the fire. He looked down at Tompkins and Bourque as he wiped his hands on his pants. Bates had spent enough time with both of them to know something had happened at the hospital. Something that left both of them in a somber mood.

"All right you two, fill us in on what you seen at the hospital. I've been around you enough to know something strange happened."

Tompkins looked up at Bates and then at Bourque.

"You can tell them," said Bourque.

"Gee thanks," replied Tompkins as he pulled himself to a sitting position on his bedroll.

"You've all been to military hospitals before," he began. "They are neat and clean. And although the atmosphere may be gloomy, it is generally a decent place to be." Bates, Draper and Santana raised up on their elbows, looked at each other and nodded their heads. They looked like they were getting ready for their dad to tell them a bedtime story. Bourque remained on his back. He lived the story . Tompkins was staring into the fire as he continued.

"When we got to the hospital, there were men laying all around the building." Tompkins swallowed hard. "You could hear the screams of the men from inside the building. The smell around the area was thick with blood, rotting flesh and death. Then we thought we would walk around the building. On one side of the building we saw..." Tompkins stopped talking, and his eyes never left the fire. The other men could see in his eyes that something he seen left an impression in his mind. From the look on his face and his lack of words, they knew it wasn't pleasant.

"Tompkins," called Draper. "You all right?"

Tompkins' eyes left the fire for the first time since he started telling the story. He shot Draper a grin and then returned his eyes to the fire. "As we were walking around the building, all I could think was that it looked like a giant tomb. It was square and made of large sandstone blocks. You know, like the ones you see in cemeteries."

He raised his eyes and looked at the other men. They were staring back at him with blank faces. "As we walked around the corner of the building," he continued. "What we saw was beyond explanation. Under each of the windows were piles of arms and legs. They had been cut off and just thrown out the window. The screams of the men inside could probably be heard all over town. The smell was horrible. The flies were all over the piles. Dogs were pulling at the bloody stumps. It was unbelievable."

Bourque now sat up on his bedroll and began to speak. "You guys remember the mass graves in Burma?"

"Of course we remember them," answered Santana. "How could we forget?" Bourque looked at him with a small grin. "This," he sneered, "was about ten thousand times worse. I actually felt sick to my stomach."

"I can't even imagine," interjected Draper with a look of horror.

"That wasn't even the worse part," interrupted Tompkins. "As we continued to walk around the building, we came to the back side." Tompkins gulped and took a deep breath. The kind that you take when you are trying to hold back some emotion. "Behind the building were piles of dead men. They were stacked like firewood. Men were taking the bodies and throwing them on wagons like grain bags. I can't even imagine where they were taking them." Tompkins was still staring into the fire. "Their eyes were looking right at us."

"Well, that's when we decided to get the hell out of there," shouted Bourque with a more lively tone. He reached over and slapped Tompkins on the back. The jolt pushed him forward, waking him from his trance. His eyes met Bourque's with contempt.

Bourque knew the hospital left a lasting impression on Tompkins. An impression that dug into his very soul. He might not be able to get over the gruesome scene, but he needed to get his head on straight for the next day's events.

"Listen Tompkins," whispered Bourque in a voice only Tompkins could hear. "I know that hospital was not what you expected, but you have to get over it. We need to focus on tomorrow and getting out of this whole mess."

Tompkins looked back at Bourque and nodded his head in agreement. "All right, I get it. I'll put it out of my mind." Tompkins lowered his head to the ground. "But it was so..."

Bourque cut Tompkins short. "I know it was, but you have to forget it. It's all in the past. Literally." The two men looked at each other and smiled.

"Yeah, I guess it is really is in the past," laughed Tompkins.

The air lightened around the camp as the men made small talk about the days' events. The sun was now set behind the trees and the silence of the forest overtook the men. Eyes became heavy as the fire crackled in the silence. It didn't last long as Draper rose up on his bedroll with sleepy eyes.

"Has anyone thought about how and when we will get out of here?" Everyone's eyes turned to Tompkins.

"I have no idea when this will end," Tompkins replied. "I definitely have no idea how we will get out of this. I thought about heading back to the mountain and going back through the tunnel. Maybe it was some type of time portal or something."

Everyone's eyes widened at the new idea of getting back to the present.

All of the men were now sitting up on their makeshift bed, waiting to hear more about Tompkins' epiphany.

"I don't know if it will work, but I seen it in enough movies to think it might be the way out."

Tompkins looked up to the dark purple and gray sky and thought for a moment. "I don't think we can make it back that way while this battle is going on though. I think we better wait until the battle is over before we attempt to make it back to the tunnel."

"Sounds good to me," replied Draper with new enthusiasm. "I've enjoyed this mission and learned a lot, but I'd really like to get back to normal stuff."

"I don't know," responded Bates. "This is kind of interesting."

Everyone turned to him with looks of disdain.

"What are you talking about?" replied Santana in a tone of amazement. Bates shrugged his shoulders and stared at the fire.

"I just think this is pretty cool. I don't have anything that important to get back to."

Santana shook his head in disbelief. "You're nuts."

Bourque thought it was time to interject some command to the campsite.

"Let's get through tomorrow and then decide what we will do next. I think we need to know what will happen tomorrow before we get some shuteye. Tompkins, why don't you fill us in on what will happen next."

Tompkins sat up on his bed and crossed his legs. He wiped some weeds and stones from a bare spot next to his bed. He reached behind him and grabbed a stick to write in the dirt with. He looked up at everyone to see if they were paying attention. With everyone's eyes glued on him, he began to explain the next day's events.

"The third day's battle takes place pretty much directly in front of us, about a half mile to the west. The Unions lines stretch across here." Tompkins drew a line parallel to the Chambersburg Pike. The Confederate forces are gathered along this wood line for about a mile or so." He drew a line in the dirt to show where the Confederates were camping that night. He then drew a wavy line through the dirt between them. "The terrain between the lines, consists of open fields for about a mile," he continued. "Being full of pride that his forces were superior to the Union's, General Lee made plans to attack the Union lines head on. He ordered more than fifteen-thousand men, to make a forced march across these fields, and hit the Union line at the center. He figured the Union had fortified the ends of their lines, since the Confederates had attacked them hard the last two days. He thought the Union lines would be most vulnerable in the center." Tompkins looked around to see if anyone was sleeping yet. To his surprise everyone was still wide-eyed and attentive.

"General Lee thought that if he spread his line out over the entire field and had them converge on the center of the Union line, he could split the Union Army and take the field. He would first unleash the largest artillery barrage ever enacted on American soil. His plans were to destroy the Union cannons and open the center of the line. Then as his men converged on the Union center, they would have no problem funneling into the Union line."

"That sounds like suicide," said Santana. "They had to march across the entire field in lines and then expected to have enough men left to win the battle. Only a moron would think that plan would work."

"Well, that's what Lee's commanders thought too," replied Tompkins. "They always followed orders though."

"I think that was one order I would be thrown in the brig for," interjected Draper. Everyone chuckled.

"The General that led the charge," began Tompkins again, "was General George Pickett. The entire charge was called Pickett's Charge. Perhaps you guys might have heard of it before?"

Everyone just looked at each other and shrugged their shoulders.

"Bates you should of," commented Draper.

"And why is that?" replied Bates, waiting for the punch line.

"Well, you were there, weren't you?" Once again the group had a quick laugh.

"O.K. you goofs," interrupted Tompkins with a roll of his eyes. "As the charge began, the artillery barrage began. However, the shells used by the Confederacy were not very accurate and they landed to the rear of the Union line, causing very little damage. The Union fired their cannons in retaliation. With the right aim and superior shells, they tore holes in the marching lines of the Rebels. They just kept coming anyway. Some fifteen thousand men marched across the mile long open field in long lines. Once they reached the Chambersburg Pike, they had to cross a fence. At the fence, they were in range of Union rifle fire. The cannons were loaded with canisters, filled with dozens of golf ball sized shot. The Union tore the Confederates apart at the fence. Those that did make it across the fence were then picked off by Union snipers. Just by pure mass, the Confederates did make it to the Union line and hand-to-hand fighting began. The Union then brought up reinforcements and squashed the Confederate charge."

Tompkins took a look around and saw the men's eyes getting heavy. He knew any further information would not be remembered anyway.

"Let's get some shuteye," commented Tompkins. "The battle starts at dawn tomorrow. I'll take first watch."

With that said, everyone laid their heads back and closed their eyes. As with every other night of this strange journey, snores were soon heard around the fire. Tompkins stared at the fire. He tried running through the events that might take place in the coming morning. It wasn't long before his mind became a tangle of the last two day's events and the scenarios of those to come. He shook his head and stood up.

"I have to keep a clear mind," he murmured to himself. He walked over to one of the Jeeps and pulled out another MRE. He sat on the hood of the Jeep and ate the meal. As he pushed another cracker into his mouth, he looked up into the hazy dark sky.

"What in the hell is going on?" he thought. "What are we doing here? How did we get here? What does this all mean? When and how are we going to get back?" Tompkins' mind raced with a million questions and no answers. He wasn't used to not knowing the answers.

A hole in the haze gave way to the dark sky, filled with stars above. As Tompkins took solace in the twinkling stars above, something caught his eye. The stars, that were twinkling so brightly above, hid a blinking light that seemed to be moving. He strained his eyes to see what it was. "It looks like a star, but why is it moving in a straight line?" he thought.

He ran around to the back of the trailer and threw off the Ghillie that concealed it. He opened the doors and grabbed a M10. He quickly shouldered the rifle and peered through the scope. With his free hand he adjusted the optics to its furthest setting. As the scope adjusted to the change, the object came into view. The blinking light brought a smile to his face.

"Finally, a normal sight," he murmured. "I gotta get Bourque to see this."

He ran over to the fire and kicked Bourque in the side. Bourque instinctively grabbed his foot.

He looked up at Tompkins with a disturbed look and asked, "What's up doc?" The look on Tompkins' face gave Bourque a hint that something weird was happening. He quietly rose to his feet and looked down at Tompkins.

"Bourque, you have to take a look at this," Tompkins excitedly spit out. "Come over here, away from the light of the fire." Tompkins grabbed Bourque by the arm and dragged him into the darkness of the meadow. "Look up at the stars, see anything odd?" Bourque rubbed his eyes and looked up into the sky. His head turned as he scanned the heavens above. His head suddenly stopped. He then rubbed his eyes again as if in disbelief.

"Use the M10," burst Tompkins. Bourque grabbed the M10 and pulled it to his shoulder. He stuck his face to the scope and peered into the sky.

"What the heck is going on?" He then dropped the rifle to his side and looked at Tompkins with a confused look. "Wake the others, they need to see this."

Tompkins ran over to the fire and hollered for the others to get up. The three men grabbed their M16s and jumped up.

They shouldered their rifles and scanned the dark surroundings.

"Easy guys," yelled Tompkins. "Everything is good."

The men dropped their rifles and turned to Tompkins.

"We have something you need to see." Tompkins turned and jogged into the darkness. The other men followed. They soon saw Bourque looking into space through the M10s scope.

"What's happening guys?" asked Bates.

"Look up at the stars and see if you see anything out of the ordinary," commanded Bourque.

The three men looked into the sky. Soon Bates' arm pointed to something in the sky. He grabbed Santana by the shoulder and told him to look where he was pointing. Draper twisted his head in that direction also.

"There's a blinking light up there," commented Draper.

"What is it?" asked Santana.

"Here, use the M10," said Bourque.

Bates grabbed the M10 and looked up into the sky through the scope. "Holy crap."

Draper then grabbed the M10 as Bates dropped it from his face. He quickly brought the rifle to his shoulder and stuck his eye to the scope. "I'll be dipped in," murmured Draper.

"Let me see," asked Santana, impatiently waiting for his turn. Draper handed him the rifle. Santana pulled it up and looked to the sky.

"I didn't realize they had jets during the Civil War," commented Santana. He lowered the rifle revealing a big smile. Everyone let out a laugh. They were true laughs. Laughs without hints of tension. The group, for the first time in several days, had hope they might be able to return to their time.

"How in the world could there be a jet during this time period?" asked Bates. Everyone turned his head to Tompkins.

"Don't look at me," laughed Tompkins. "I haven't got a clue."

Everyone looked back into the sky. They followed the blinking light with their bare eyes until it disappeared from view. After the blinking light was gone, they all dropped their heads back to earth. They looked at each other with bright eyes and grins. It was as if the sight of the jet gave them a burst of energy. They now knew they were somewhere in the real world. Where, they didn't know, but they now felt at ease, being closer to reality than they previously thought.

"I feel better about our situation," commented Draper. "We must be somewhere close to where we should be."

"That made a lot of sense," laughed Santana.

"But you know what I mean," replied Draper with a laugh.

"Let's get some sleep now," commanded Bourque. "I'm sure Tompkins will be thinking about this for the rest of the night."

Bourque reached out and punched Tompkins' shoulder.

"Anything we think will probably be dumb," Bourque added.

"Yeah, you guys get some sleep," responded Tompkins rubbing his shoulder. "I might as well keep the watch for a while. Maybe I can come up with a believable conclusion to this new piece to the puzzle."

The four men returned to their beds and quickly fell asleep. Instead of tension on their faces, they now had smiles. This new twist in their journey somehow gave them solace in their unusual situation. They felt closer to their world and it felt good to them. For the past few days, every situation they were thrust into was far from what they knew as normal.

Tompkins sat on the hood of the Jeep and once again stared into the sky. His brain was in full gear as the night slowly past by. His main concern was not keeping watch, but how this new piece to the puzzle was relevant.

Chapter 26

Day 3—Anything goes

Tompkins' head began to ache from his constant thinking. He glanced down at his watch. The date read July 4 and the time was 0400. The last day of the battle was upon them. In a few short hours the sounds of cannon fire would shatter the relative calm of the countryside. Tompkins glanced over to the dying fire of the campsite. His four compadres were peacefully sleeping, each in a different position.

"Today will hopefully be the key to this whole strange mission," Tompkins thought. "If only I had the answers they wanted. How are we going to get back to our world? When will we get back to our time? Why are we on this mission?" Tompkins closed his eyes trying clear his mind. It didn't work. There were too many variables to think about. When he opened his eyes, he was surprised to see Bourque standing in front of him. He instantly sat up straight and rubbed his eyes.

"Come to any conclusions yet?" whispered Bourque so he wouldn't wake the others.

"Not really," whispered Tompkins. "I can't seem to make any heads or tails of this whole deal." He raised his hands in an empty expression towards Bourque. The two men just stared at each other for a moment.

"Well, we just have to make it through this battle and then we can sort it out," comforted Bourque. "We all know you're doing your best to figure this out. Why don't you grab a few minutes of sleep. I'll take the watch." Tompkins looked up at Bourque and smiled.

"It sure has been good knowing you're here," commented Tompkins as he reached out and grabbed Bourque's shoulder. They smiled at each other as Tompkins headed for his bed.

Bourque turned and sat on the hood of the Jeep. He watched Tompkins plop on his bed and curl up into a ball. After a short while, Bourque could tell Tompkins was sleeping by his heavy breathing. Bourque sat in silence, listening for anything strange. There was nothing. He fell into a daze as the quiet night lulled him into a peaceful, calm feeling. He found himself fighting to stay awake, something that had never happened to him before. He always took guard duty very seriously and made sure his senses were at their very best. He slapped himself in the face to try and shake his sleepiness. His head cleared from the sting of the slap. He scanned the edge of the forest for movement. There was nothing.

As time passed, the sky was brightening from the approach of the rising sun. The sounds of the forest began to get louder as the birds and animals began to stir. Bourque strained his ears to hear anything new. His eyebrows raised as he heard the faint pounding of hoofs in the distance. He immediately jumped from the Jeep and ran to the four sleeping men.

"Time to rise," he commanded in a half shout.

The four men rolled over and looked at Bourque. The fire was almost out and the smoke rose slowly into the humid air.

"What's going on?" responded Draper.

"I hear horses coming this way," replied Bourque.

The four men jumped up from their beds and grabbed their rifles. Only seconds passed before they heard the sounds of horses.

"Maybe it's Buford," remarked Tompkins. "He knows where we're camped."

"You're probably right," answered Bourque. "But let's keep our butts puckered until we're sure."

The five men stood with their rifles shouldered as the pounding became louder. The sound of parting brush now filled the meadow. The men looked hard at the forest as the head of a horse broke through the underbrush. The five men placed their fingers on their triggers, ready for anything to happen. To their relief, a blue-clad man was perched on the horse as it cleared the brush and trotted towards the camp site. Suddenly, the brush erupted and a dozen more men in blue followed close behind him.

The man on the lead horse was not familiar to any of the men. He was much younger than Buford and very well dressed. His long blonde hair bounced under his wide brimmed hat as he galloped toward the men. He was not alarmed to see the men, which told Bourque he knew where they were camped.

"Lower your rifles," commanded Bourque. The four men immediately dropped their M16s to their sides.

As the young cavalryman approached, he raised his hand to show his peaceful intent. His horse came to a stop in front of the five men. The men following him formed a line behind him. They also showed no alarm at the presence of the men around the campsite. The lead man dismounted and walked up to Bourque. He saluted and then reached out a hand in Bourque's direction.

"Good morning, Sir," announced the man. "General Buford told us of your location and asked that we stop by to see how you were doing."

The four other men now moved closer to Bourque. Bourque raised his hand in a quick salute and then shook the man's hand.

"I'm sorry, you must excuse my brashness," said the blue-clad soldier. "I am General George Custer and these are my cavalry commanders."

The five men looked at each other with wide eyes. Except for Tompkins, they never heard of any of the men they had met during their journey. They stood in awe in the presence of one of history's most well-known generals.

"Good morning, General," replied Tompkins, stepping to the front of the group. "How can we be of service to you?"

General Custer took off his hat and smacked it on his knee. He smugly looked up at Tompkins.

"We were on patrol around the back side of these hills when General Buford came upon us. He told me of your situation and your unparalleled assistance in the battle yesterday. He asked that we make sure you are safe and ready for today's events."

Tompkins smiled and nodded his head. "Thank you for your concern, General. We had a restful night and seem to be prepared for any further orders."

"I have no orders for you," replied Custer. "General Buford wished me to inform you that two brigades from Pennsylvania had encountered several bands of violent Indians on their way to Gettysburg. The Indians caused quite a problem and ended up delaying about twenty cannons from the battlefield. He asked if you and your men would assist in any manner possible?"

Tompkins turned to the other four men and winked. He then turned back to Custer and asked, " Would you excuse us for a moment while we discuss these new orders."

Custer nodded his head. "Certainly, Sir. My men and I will await your return."

The five men moved about twenty yards away and stood in a circle. Draper had a big smile on his face.

"You guys all realize who we were just talking to, don't you?" His head moved back and forth looking to the other men.

"Of course we do," replied Bates in a condescending tone.

"All right," interrupted Tompkins. "Can we get past your starstruck meeting and get on to the meat of this meeting?"

Everyone laughed as Tompkins continued. "The odd thing about this whole meeting and the new orders is this. There was no interference by Indians that caused any delay in cannons getting to the battlefield. Everyone was at the battle yesterday, and the cannons should already be positioned." Tompkins stopped and looked at everyone. They just stood there with blank looks on their faces. He shook his head at their lack of response.

"What I'm telling you is that in the history books there is nothing about any Indians causing any delay in the Union movement." He stopped again and looked at the men.

Bourque let out an "Oh" and nodded his head in agreement. "What do you think this means?"

"I'm not sure," replied Tompkins. "I wonder what is causing these odd occurrences that are causing us to get involved in this battle? And I wonder what would have happened if we weren't here to help?"

Everyone looked at each other as if someone was going to spurt forth some great idea.

"I have no idea," replied Santana. "But what are we going to do about this new information? Does anyone have any good ideas?"

Finally Tompkins stepped up and offered some help to solve their new quandary.

"Let's get camp cleaned up, and then we can talk about our next move. I'll be thinking as you clean up. I'd better go tell Custer we'll be ready to go soon."

They all quickly turned and moved to their beds. They moved fast, getting their equipment packed and stowed in the Jeeps. Once everything was packed, they joined Bourque, who was leaning on the hood of the lead Jeep thinking.

"Everything's packed up and ready to go," said Bates. "Where do we go from here?"

"I'm not sure. We better wait for Tompkins to get back before we do too much thinking on our own."

Tompkins walked quickly towards Custer and his men. Custer seemed to be telling them a story, as they would all laugh and then look back to Custer.

"General Custer sir," interrupted Tompkins.

Custer and his men turned towards Tompkins and stood at attention.

"Yes Tompkins, did you men come to any conclusions?"

"We decided we will assist the Union Army in any way possible."

"Grand turn of affairs," replied Custer with a big smile. "We had better get back to our brigade now. We will convey your acceptance to General Buford when we see him."

Custer gave Tompkins a quick salute and pulled himself up on his horse. He lifted his gloved hand and tipped his hat to Tompkins. He pulled the reins of his horse and spun away from the campsite. His men followed behind him and they disappeared into the thick brush surrounding the clearing. Tompkins watched them disappear like the ghosts they were. He turned to return to his men.

Tompkins walked over to the Jeep and joined the other men. He looked at the men standing in a semicircle around himself and Bourque. He noticed the excited looks on their faces. The picture of three puppies, waiting to go for a ride in the car, came to his mind. He smiled then let out a little laugh.

"What's so funny?" asked Draper, waiting to be let in on the joke.   Tompkins looked at him and grinned. "Oh nothing."

Draper rolled his eyes in disgust, but stood ready for some new information.

"Here's what I think we should do," started Tompkins. "Bourque and I were talking, and we came up with a game plan for today's battle. We know the battle is going to take place at the Angle."

"What's the Angle?" asked Santana in a serious tone. All eyes turned to Santana and then back to Tompkins.

"I'm sorry," replied Tompkins. "The Angle is the little clump of trees that stand at the corner of two stone fences, right in the middle of the battlefield. Once we get into the open you will see where I mean. Anyways, the battle will be centered there. I think if we set up towards the left of the Union line, but towards the rear, we can be safe and still be effective."

Tompkins face changed from serious to unsure as he continued speaking. "I'm not sure what we will have to do, but I figure we can quickly react to whatever comes our way." He looked around at everyone and asked, "any questions?" Everyone looked at each other and shrugged their shoulders.

"We're right behind you," answered Draper in an excited voice. "Let's get this done so we can find our way home."

"Amen," answered Santana.

Bourque stepped to the center of the men and began giving commands.

"Make sure we have all the M10s, MR2PGs and C22s. Each of us needs to have an M16 and a full vest of grenades. Carry all the ammo you can for all the weapons. Oh and Draper, grab the extra Ghillie suits, I think we may have a use for them."

The men moved to the Jeeps and the trailer, gathering all the equipment they would need for the day. They stuffed ammo into any pocket they could and strapped on C22s. They swung M16s over one shoulder and M10s or MR-2PGs over the other. They all patted their sides and pockets to make sure they were all full. When they were sure they couldn't carry anything more, they all gathered together at the rear of the trailer.

Bourque glanced around at the group of men, making sure they were outfitted for the potential battle. He quickly noticed one man was absent.

"Where's Draper?"

The guys looked around the area and could not see any sign of Draper. The demeanor of Bourque changed from calm to tense. Just as he was ready to wring Draper's neck, Draper popped out from underneath the Ghillie suit, standing right next to Bourque.

"Here I is," he shouted as the Ghillie hit the ground. Bourque shook his head in disgust at the childish actions of Draper.

"O.K., Buckwheat is here," he countered. "Let's head to the battlefield. Keep a sharp eye out and call out anything odd."

Bourque looked around at the guys and then started his trek towards the battlefield. The other men followed behind with their loads of weapons and ammo.

As the five men made their way through the fairly clean forest, the shade of the forest soon gave way to the open fields, which would soon be a bloody mess. They broke through the last few trees, they suddenly stopped. Their jaws dropped at the scene before them.

In the distance, they could see the Union battle lines. The thousands of blue-clad men were lined up across the entire field, some one mile wide. Cannons were stationed across the line and to the rear. Men, horses and wagons were moving about the field in haste. The tension of the oncoming battle loomed heavy in the hot humid morning air.

"Wow, I've never seen this many troops in one area before," burst out Draper.

Everyone stood in silent awe at the overwhelming sight of the Union forces.

Tompkins swung an M10 off his shoulder and brought the scope up to his face. He slowly peered across the field at the Union line. The gun moved smoothly across the horizon and then suddenly stopped. It moved backwards for a moment and then stopped once again. Tompkins held the gun at that position for a minute and then dropped it to his waist. He lifted his arm and pointed to a spot right in the middle of the line.

"The only hole in the line I see is right there." He looked down his arm to show the others where the hole was. They quickly squinted their eyes in the direction of the boney finger.

"I think that is where the Pennsylvania Brigade is suppose to be. There is a break in the line, where at least ten cannons could be. There are no men there, almost like they are waiting for them to arrive."

He then swung the M10 back up and shouldered it. He peered through the scope in the direction of the rear cannons. Once again, he moved the gun along the line until he spotted something odd that caught his attention. Once again he noticed there was a hole in the Union line of cannons, where the missing brigade was supposed to be. He lifted his arm and pointed in the new direction.

"There is another hole that appears to me to be where the Pennsylvania Brigade is supposed to position their cannons."

Once again the other four men strained their eyes in the direction Tompkins was pointing. They stood in silence as they contemplated their next move.

Out of the blue, Bates broke the silence of the moment. "Hey guys, what if we set up right over there?" He pointed to a spot to the left, about three hundred yards to the rear of the Union line.

"From there we could cover the entire field with no problem," Bates exclaimed with a hint of pride. Tompkins turned to Bates and gave him a grin.

"That's a good idea," said Tompkins. "I couldn't have thought of a better spot myself."

The other men gave Bates a look of confidence and patted him on the arm as they walked by him, on the way to their new strategic location.

Their pace was fast as they homed in on the intended spot for their Union support. Once they reached the spot, they quickly unloaded their pockets and swung the rifles from their shoulders. They positioned themselves in a line, about twenty feet between them. As they laid their weapons on the ground around their positions, the sound of thundering horse hooves caught their attention. They all turned their heads towards the familiar sound and saw three men galloping towards them. They immediately stood to their feet and moved closer together.

The white flopping hat of General Buford brought a sigh of relief to the outsiders. As Buford came closer, he raised his hand in a friendly wave and brought his horse to a halt. The smile on his face was met by the five smiles of the men standing in front of him.

"How goes it men?" hollered Buford, above the snorting, prancing horses. "I see General Custer made contact with you this morning."

Tompkins approached Buford and saluted him. "Things seem to be going good," shouted Tompkins. "Yes, we met

General Custer earlier today. He filled us in on the new predicament."

Tompkins now was close enough to grab the bit of General Buford's horse. He reached out and steadied him.

"Do you have any new information or insights, General Buford?"

"Naw, nothing new. I see you have spotted our problem and are ready to assist."

"Yeah, I think we know what to do and how to do it. But to what extent we're needed is still a bit concerning," replied Tompkins.

Buford smiled and took off his hat. He slapped it on his leg and coughed as the dust filled his nostrils.

"You have done a exemplary job so far," called Buford. "Just keep the Confederates from coming through any holes, and you should be fine."

His eyes widened, and he crinkled his forehead. Tompkins could see something had come to his mind.

"What is it, General?" asked Tompkins.

Buford leaned down to get as close to Tompkins as possible. Tompkins moved as close to Buford as the horse would allow him.

"There is one odd thing that you may be able to help us with," whispered Buford. "What is it, sir?"

Buford turned to see how close the other men were. He then brought his attention back to Tompkins.

"I have reports of some sort of rapid firing gun the Confederates are planning to bring into today's battle. I believe it's called a Gatling Gun."

Tompkins' eyes widened at this new information. His mind raced to grab all he knew about the long extinct gun. He looked up to Buford with a confounded look.

"The Gatling Gun is not supposed to be introduced into warfare for quite a few years," informed Tompkins. "I wonder how and why it has showed up well before its time and at this battle?"

The two men stared at each other for a moment as they pushed their brains to the limit, thinking about this new problem.

"I don't know much about it," answered Buford. "But if it ain't supposed to be here, we need to get rid of it." Buford reached up and patted his horse's neck. "I was thinking, if you could use one of those suits to get close enough to it, maybe you could take it out. Blow it up. Keep it from changing the battle scene."

Tompkins rubbed his chin and thought for a second. He calmly looked up at Buford and smiled.

"I think I know how to keep the balance. Don't think about it for another second, General. We will take care of the problem."

Buford smiled and sat up straight in his saddle. He threw his hat back on his head and smiled.

"I knew you would," he said in a relieved tone. "God be with you and your men. The Union Army thanks you for your assistance."

With that said, Buford spun his horse around with a loud "Ya," and raced past his men towards the rear of the Union Army. The men who arrived with him tipped their hats to Tompkins and raced after him. Tompkins lifted his hand to his hat in a quick salute and then stood there, watching them speed away. As he stood there with his arms crossed across his chest, the other four men came up and stood next to him.

"What's the skinny?" asked Draper. Tompkins turned his head towards him and laughed.

"You're such a dork," was his only reply.

"What are our orders now?" asked Bourque in a stern voice. He reached out and smacked Draper in the back of the head.

"Let's get back to our positions and I'll fill you in," replied Tompkins.

Chapter 27

Tompkins to the rescue

The four men followed him back to their weapons and gear and sat down. Tompkins looked at his watch and shook his head. He lifted his head and in a serious voice began his explanation of the next step in their strange journey.

"General Buford has told me, his intel has informed him, the Confederacy has a Gatling Gun and plan to introduce it in this battle."

"OK," interrupted Bates. "Is that something odd?"

"Well I'm not real sure about the details of the gun, but I am pretty sure it shouldn't be at this battle and that it hasn't even been invented yet. I wonder how and why it's here now?"

"What did Buford want us to do about it?" asked Santana.

Tompkins took a deep breath and let it out. "He asked us to make sure it didn't change the outcome of the battle."

"And what did you tell him?" calmly asked Bourque.

The two men's eyes met for a second and Tompkins replied, "I told him we would take care of it."

The other men looked at each other and nodded their heads in agreement.

"What's the plan?" asked Bourque.

As usual, Tompkins swept away the grass from the ground in front of him and leaned back to grab a stick. He quickly started to draw in the dirt.

"You really like this classroom stuff, don't you?" asked Draper.

Tompkins just looked up at him and smiled. "We have about an hour and a half before the Confederacy starts the battle. We need to get to the Rebel line, destroy the gun and get back here before the battle begins."

He took a quick look around at the guys and then began drawing again. "It's about one mile from here to the Confederate line. I figure one of us can make it to the Confederate line and locate the gun. We can then take a few grenades and destroy the gun and hightail it back here." Tompkins sat up and looked at the other men.

"Wait a minute," chimed in Santana. "How are we going to move around the Confederate troops without being spotted?"

Tompkins smiled and leaned back towards his duffle bag. He never stopped smiling as he pulled the Ghillie suit out of the bag.

"This is how," burst out Tompkins as if he had just discovered the cure for cancer. "Good thinking," said Bates as he nodded his head in agreement.

"Who's up for the challenge?" asked Bourque.

The men looked at each other and then settled their eyes on Tompkins.

"I figured you would want me to do it. Bourque, you keep these guys in line while I'm gone."

Tompkins jumped up and began clipping grenades to his vest under his Union coat. He pulled out his C22 and checked the clip. He then pushed two more clips into his vest pocket. He patted his sides and looked at the other men.

"I'm ready I think," he said in an unsure tone.

"You might as well leave that heavy old coat here," added Draper. "No one will see you anyways, and you'll be able to move faster without it."

"Good thinking," answered Tompkins. He slid the heavy wool coat off his shoulders and let it drop to the ground. He then took off his hat and threw it on the coat. "Ah, that feels better already."

He quickly grabbed some grenades, clipped them to his vest and gave them a tug. Certain that they were secure, he grabbed the Ghillie suit and started to walk towards the Confederate line. Walking away, he turned his head back towards the men and said, "I'll be back." The men chuckled and waved their hands. Tompkins continued on his trek.

"Boy I hope he has his "A" game on," said Santana. "I don't like sending him alone on the eve of this battle."

"If anyone can do it, he can," answered Draper in a serious tone.

Bourque then added, "I can't think of a better person to do it. Well, maybe me." They watched him walk across the open field and then disappear as he threw the Ghillie suit over himself.

Tompkins made his way across the mile of open fields in good time. As he neared the Confederate line, he could see the gray troops busying themselves getting cannons in position and cleaning their muskets. He scanned the line looking for any holes that would grant him access to their interior. He saw a spot that looked good and headed for it.

He slowly made his way across the face of their busy line. He was impressed at their determination to make sure they were ready for the attack. Every man was attending to his job as if God himself had directed them. As he approached the spot where he would penetrate the line, a group of shabby gray-clad, barefoot men gathered at the spot. He stopped and crouched down. They were impervious to his position and continued to ready themselves for the attack. Tompkins kept still, waiting for the right moment to make his move to their interior lines.

Bourque was carefully watching the Confederate line through the scope of one of the M10s. He was scanning the line, looking for any indication of Tompkins' location. The Ghillie Suit made it almost impossible for him to locate his position.

"If I were Tompkins, where would I enter the line?" he mumbled to himself.

As he scanned the line once more, he spotted a small hole in the gray line and studied it carefully. He reached up and tuned the scope to one of its highest settings. With the power of the scope, he could make out the scared faces of the Confederate troops. He peered hard through the scope, watching for any odd movement. Something caught his attention. It wasn't the movement of a person, but more of a blur of grass that moved across the bottom of his scope. He brought the area into his line of vision and stopped. If he starred at the spot long enough, he could make out the optical illusion the Ghillie suit was emanating.

"Hey guys," he shouted. "Grab a M10 and look towards the left center of the southern Confederate line."

The men each grabbed their M10s and shouldered them. They began scanning the line in the direction Bourque had ordered.

"Tune the scope to two-thousand power," Bourque ordered as he held steady on the spot. "Thirty feet in front of the fourth cannon on the left. See the blur of weeds. That's Tompkins."

"Yeah, I see it now," yelled Draper. "I'm really surprised we can see him at all."

"I see him too," shouted Santana.

"I see him now," chimed in Bates.

The four men watched Tompkins intently as he slowly made his way towards the small gap in the Confederate line.

"I'm switching on the targeting system, just in case he needs assistance," shouted Bourque. "If someone makes him, he might appreciate some help."

The other men also switched their systems on, just in case. All four men followed Tompkins now, ready to assist in any way possible.

The grass was long and the grasshoppers chirped loudly as Tompkins carefully and slowly crept towards the fifteen foot hole between the gray soldiers. He made sure not to make any sudden movements that might give his position away. The Ghillie suit concealed him perfectly. To the human eyes of the Confederate troops, he was just another clump of grass in the field.

He cautiously closed the gap between himself and the line. Everything seemed perfect. He was now directly between the men on either side of him. They busied themselves without any indication of his presence.

Tompkins' attention was brought to his left and he froze. One of the soldiers rose to his feet and walked in front of Tompkins. The breeze of the man's legs pushed some field chaff into Tompkins' nose. He quickly brought his hand to his nose and squeezed it shut. The sneeze, that had just about given away his position, was quelled. He let out a breath of relief and continued to move forward. Just as he made it past the men on the front line, a loose horse wandered his way.

The horse walked right up to him and started to sniff around his position. It was startled at the new smell. The horse started bucking and prancing around Tompkins. Men from the front line ran to see what the fuss was all about. Just as the horse raised up on its back legs, ready to stomp down on Tompkins, a loud thud brought Tompkins eyes toward the horse. Hair, bone and flesh exploded as the horse was pushed over on its back by some unknown force.

The horse lay on its side and shook fiercely from the massive blast. Men were moving towards the horse as it let out its last breath. Tompkins now was in the middle of this unplanned event. He knew he had to move fast to stay concealed. He quickly crawled next to a tree and waited for the men to rush by. He then ran behind a wagon of supplies and jumped underneath it. He turned his attention towards the men gathered around the horse.

"What in the heck just happened?" shouted one of the Confederate Soldiers. His arms were held out straight from his side.

"Don't know for sure," answered one of the men. "The horse walked over to this spot and started goin' wild. Just like it smelt a coyote or something."

"Yeah, that's just what it was like," interrupted another soldier. "And then just as the horse was bucking up in the air, something hit it and flopped it over on his back." The man rubbed the fuzz on his chin in amazement. "Ain't never seen nothing like it before."

"Well what hit it?" asked the first man on the scene.

"Don't know," rang from the crowd gathered around the dead horse.

"Let's take a look and see," ordered the man as he bent down over the horse.

All the men moved in close to see what brought the horse down so completely. Noise rose from the group as they stared at the large hole torn into the horse's mid section.

"Holy cow, it looks like a cannon tore that hole," suggested one man.

"Naw, if it was a cannon, the hole would be a lot bigger," answered another man. The men stood there with puzzled looks on their faces. They whispered among themselves as to what could have caused this grizzly scene.

"Wonder if them blue bellies have some sort of new gun?" yelled one man.

"Why would they shoot one of our horses?" questioned another man. The scene became quiet now as the men thought.

"If the Union did have such a gun," said one man. "It would have to have a range of well over a mile. The closest Union soldier is out there on that ridge, well over a mile away."

Tompkins lay under the wagon, listening to the Confederate soldiers try to figure out what just happened. Suddenly it dawned on him. The shot could have only come from the M10. The precise hit and the power of the projectile was not of this era. He smiled knowing the other four men had his back. But the reality of the situation erased his smile. With the confusion around the horse, he thought it would be a good time to move further into the Confederate lines.

Tompkins began his search and destroy mission once again. He moved quickly from wagon to wagon and tent to tent. With the soldiers concentrating on the looming battle, he made his way around fairly easily. As he eliminated wagon after wagon, he soon found himself running out of options.

The last few wagons were stationed behind the largest tent in the area. There were guards posted outside the tent and important looking soldiers constantly made their way in and out of the canvas shelter. Tompkins approached the tent cautiously. As he neared it, he could hear battle plans being explained in detail. Tompkins stood next to the tent and listened. One voice seemed to do most of the talking. The voice was almost hypnotic. The battle plans he was explaining were completely insane to Tompkins, but he found himself believing it could be done.

"This must be General Robert E. Lee's tent," Tompkins whispered to himself. "I gotta hear more of this." Tompkins took a quick look around to make sure the coast was clear and then continued to listen.

"General Pickett," said General Lee, "are your men ready for this charge?" "Yes, General," answered Pickett. "My men are ready to end this war today."

"But General," said another man in an irritated tone. "There is no amount of men that can make that charge and survive. It is a march across open fields for more than a mile. We will be wiped out by Union cannon fire. And if we do make it to that fence along the road, we will be torn apart by Union sharpshooters and canister fire. This is ludicrous."

Tompkins became entranced by this conversation. He had read about this meeting a thousand times in history books. Now he was hearing it firsthand. The greatest military minds from the Confederacy were standing less than ten feet from him. He brought his attention back to the conversation as General Lee began to speak again.

"General, I have the greatest respect for our soldiers and would never put them in a situation such as that. Our cannons will destroy the center of the Union Army in part. Once the cannons have done their job, we will begin our march." There was a long pause before General Lee continued. "I have seen enough of this war. We have the opportunity to end it today and by the grace of God we will end it today. Our troops have always prevailed. Even under greater odds than this, our men have prevailed. We must seize this opportunity and make them pay."

Tompkins had heard enough. He now understood how so many men, under the charge of one General, could have lost their lives. General Lee was a great speaker and motivator. He made his generals, except for General Longstreet, believe they could take the field under any circumstance. He could make men believe their destiny might be death, for the cause of the Confederacy. He had heard General Patton speak before and felt the same way about him.

Tompkins glanced down at his watch. "Crap," he murmured. Time had passed by so quickly. He had only a short time to destroy the Gatling Gun and get back to his post.

He moved quickly to the wagons located behind the tent. He cautiously lifted up the canvas covering on the first wagon he came to. Underneath lay hundreds of cannonballs. He replaced the canvas and moved to the next. As he lifted the canvas, his eyes widened at what he saw underneath. Beneath the canvas, lay neatly stacked rows of ammunition cylinders, used with the Gatling Gun. He quickly threw the canvas back over the wagon bed and moved to the last wagon. He pealed back the canvas and peered inside. To his surprise three Gatling Guns lay on their sides.

Without thought, he quickly grabbed three grenades from his vest and removed the pin on each of them. He softly laid one grenade under each of the guns and replaced the canvas. He moved back to the ammunition trailer and placed one grenade in the middle of the pile of cylinders.

He moved back to the side of the tent and glanced around to make sure he was alone. When he was sure no one was near, he removed the Ghillie suit from his head and grabbed his last two grenades. He looked down at them and removed the pins. He glanced around once more and then fixed his eyes on the two wagons in front of him. He raised the grenades in front of him and depressed the levers. Without thought, he tossed one of the grenades on the wagon holding the Gatling Guns and then tossed the other on the wagon with the ammunition. He spun around and sprinted as fast as he could back in the direction he came from.

As he ran, he reached back and grabbed the Ghillie hood and pulled it back over his head. Just as he pulled the hood over his head, loud simultaneous explosions began from the wagons. Tompkins ducked behind a tree and looked back at the wagons.

Fire and smoke filled the air. Branches from nearby trees began falling all around the area. The sound of firing bullets began to fill the air. In all this confusion, the men meeting in the tent ran for their lives.

After a few minutes, the noise began to subside. Men ran from all directions to see what was going on. They grabbed pieces of the blown away canvas and began swatting at the fire-filled wagons. They worked feverously trying to put out the fires around their secret weapons. To no avail, the wagons burned. Defeated, the men backed away.

Tompkins noticed the men from the front lines were running towards the tent. He saw a hole in the line and, even though he would have liked to stay back to see what happened, he thought it best to get out of the area. He took off running as fast as he could, dodging men as they ran towards the commotion. He quickly broke through the edge of the forest and sprinted across the open field.

After about a half mile, Tompkins stopped to catch his breath. He turned towards the Confederate line. With his hands on his knees, he lifted his eyes to the woods. A thick column of black smoke rose from the tops of the trees. He stood up straight and pulled the hood off his head. He turned towards the Union line and his four men. At a fast jog, he headed for his post and the security of his four amigos.

Approaching the location of his men, he stopped and pulled off the Ghillie suit. He slung it over his shoulder and continued the short walk to his post. It was a relief to see the familiar faces of his four friends, racing out to meet him.

Chapter 28

Pickett's Charge

"Did you get the job done?" asked Draper in an excited tone. "We seen the smoke and heard the explosions. Then we seen everyone on the front line run into the forest. We figured you must have done it."

"Slow down, Draper," commanded Bourque. "Let Tompkins catch his breath, then he'll tell us all about it." Bourque reached out and grabbed Draper around the base of his neck and shook him.

"Yes I got the job done," answered Tompkins in a light hearted tone. "Did you have any doubts?"

"Of course we didn't," answered Santana. "We actually could watch you until you entered the woods."

"How could you see me? I thought the Ghillie couldn't be seen."

"I was trying to see your progress," explained Bourque. "I used the M10 scope and dialed it to two thousand power. We couldn't actually see you, but we could see a blurring of the area you were in."

"And you're the one that shot the horse then?" asked Tompkins.

"Yeah I figured I'd give you a hand in that situation." Tompkins' face lightened up and a smile broke across his face.

"Boy, I wish you guys could have seen the faces on those soldiers when they seen the hole in that horse," started Tompkins. "They were freaking out. One of them wondered if the Union had a secret weapon. It was pretty funny."

"How did you destroy the guns?" asked Bates.

"I just threw some hand grenades in the wagons. It was just that simple."

"Are you sure they were destroyed?" questioned Bourque.

Tompkins just smiled. "I'm sure they're destroyed."

Everyone seemed to be at ease now. There wasn't a lot of sharing of details about the whole incident, but they knew there would be time for that after they got out of this strange situation. They all returned to their posts and started the task of setting the rifles and ammunition in easily accessible positions. They were immersed in their jobs as the time flew by.

"Hey Tompkins," shouted Draper. "How long before the Confederates make this charge?"

Tompkins glanced down at his watch and then looked towards Draper.

"They should be starting any time now," he shouted back to Draper. "You'll know when they start, the cannon fire will precede the march. According to history books it's the largest artillery barrage ever on American soil."

"Sounds like it should be a really interesting show," replied Bates.

Tompkins stared off into the sky as he replied, "I'm sure it will be."

"Make sure your weapons are ready and your minds are clear," commanded Bourque. "All we have to do is make it through this battle, and we can search for a way out of here."

"10-4 on that, big man," replied Santana. "10-4 on that."

Tompkins stoically watched the woods he had just run from. He knew something was going to happen soon. He wasn't happy to be in the middle of this great battle, but he kind of looked forward to seeing the historic charge of the Confederate Army.

As if cued from a movie director, thousands of men erupted from the edge of the woods. Tompkins' eyes widened and he gasped. For over a mile men began to line the woods. Most of the lines were at least ten men deep. He never dreamed he would see so many soldiers in one battle.

"Holy crap guys," Tompkins burst out. "Look at that."

His arm pointed across the open field towards the Confederate line. All heads turned and looked to the west. There were no words for several minutes. All of the men were in awe at the force that had emerged from the distant forest.

"That is unbelievable," shouted Bates. He stood there with his mouth open, staring at the mighty beast before them.

"How many soldiers are lined up over there?" asked Draper. "I've never seen that many soldiers in one spot before."

"Believe it or not," shouted Tompkins, "there are over thirty thousand men lined up along those woods."

As Tompkins ended his sentence, cannon fire began to erupt from the hundreds of Confederate cannons. The explosions, from one cannon after another, shook the ground under the five men. The constant whistling of artillery flying through the air filled their ears. The loud blasts of the shells exploding, mixed in with the cannon fire, created a constant rumble.

The five men turned their attention to the Union line. Men were running to their cannons and diving behind whatever they could. Wagons were exploding as the Confederate fire found its mark. You could see there was a sense of utter confusion among the Union troops. To the surprise of the five men, most of the Confederate cannon fire was landing well to the rear of the Union line, causing little damage. Many of the flying bombs exploded in the air on their way to Union targets.

"The Confederate cannon fire is not very effective," shouted Bourque over the deafening explosions. "Most of the shots are too long."

"The Confederates have poor at best ordinates," shouted Tompkins. "They are using older style cannonballs. Most of them were made in haste and with inferior materials. The good stuff was made in the North."

"Hey guys," shouted Santana. "Look at that." He was pointing towards the Confederate line.

Everyone turned their heads to see what Santana was talking about. As their eyes moved in that direction, all they saw was a dense cloud of smoke. As the Confederates continuously fired their cannons, the smoke from the old black powder hung in front of the line like a dark storm cloud. The entire dark green forest was now shrouded in thick dark smoke. No Confederate was visible through the cloud.

The men's attention was now drawn to the Union line. The thunderous sound of cannon fire doubled, as they started their counter barrage of cannon fire. The sound was deafening.

Both sides were now firing constantly, trying to gain an advantage in this long range battle. It wasn't long before the advantage was clear. Almost every shot fired by the Union line was followed by a explosion of wood and metal on the Confederate line.

With each blast from the precisely placed Union fire, the smoke cloud would clear a little.

The Confederate line was now becoming visible. Gray-clad men were running for whatever cover they could find. Horses were running along the line without riders on their backs. The tree line was transformed from a thick, dark, solid green curtain of trees to a line of twisted and splintered tree stumps. More than half of the Confederate cannons were rendered useless in the first five minutes of the Union barrage. Their once powerful weapons of destruction were now heaps of metal and wood.

Soon the lines of men who had taken refuge in the interior of the woods emerged from the broken tree line. They quickly formed into their regiments and battalions. Men with swords took the lead and waved them over their heads. Waves of "Hoorahs" rang from the thousands of soldiers across the field. Hats were waving in the air as the men began to move forward in unison. Soon the field was covered with marching gray men. The sounds of Rebel yells now took the place of the Confederate cannons as the charge was under way.

The battalions of Confederates swarmed the open field like ants. They moved in unison and kept in neat lines. It seemed as if the entire maneuver impressed even God as an eerie silence fell over the field of battle. The only sound was the Rebel yells and the shouts of reassurance from the battalion leaders.

As the gray wave moved slowly across the field, the silence was broken by the repeated cannon fire from the Union line. The once perfect lines of gray were now being torn apart by the precise cannon fire from the Union cannons. The explosions sent men, body parts and huge clods of dirt flying through the air. The ranks of the Confederates now began to hesitate in their forward movement. Men were seeing their friends and comrades disappear in blasts of dirt and steel. They wavered and began to move in all directions. They now looked like mice, trying to evade the dives of a hawk. The only thing that held them together was the reassurance and steadfastness of their leaders. Their shouts could be heard between the constant explosions of the Union cannon fire, urging their men to move forward to the Union line. As quickly as the line would separate, they would reform and continue marching.

"Now this is a lesson in determination and guts," yelled Bourque. "I can't believe they've held together in the face of the Union cannon fire."

"I'd been running for the woods long ago," said Bates. "The cause must have been embedded deep in their heads, to keep them moving forward like that."

Tompkins was now scanning the field, looking for anything that looked out of place. He didn't even hear the voices of the other men as they shouted across their positions. He carefully tried to put the pieces of this moving puzzle together, as the Union barrage kept changing the formations.

Suddenly something odd stuck out to him. One battalion, to the right of center, was moving faster than the others. They had yet to take a direct hit from the Union fire. He quickly looked back at the Union lines of cannons. The battalion that was moving so freely, was in the line of fire of... no one! The cannons that were supposed to be manned by the Pennsylvania Brigade were missing. Tompkins head moved back and forth like a man watching a tennis match. His strange behavior didn't escape the eye of Bourque.

"What's going on?" shouted Bourque.

Tompkins eyes turned to him, and he quickly shouted. "I've spotted our first problem."

"What is it?" replied Bourque. Tompkins moved closer to the center of their position so he could be heard by everyone.

"Listen up," announced Bourque. "And pay close attention. Tompkins has found a glitch in the charge."

Everyone gathered near the center of their position and all eyes focused on Tompkins. He lifted his arm and pointed to the lucky Confederate battalion that was marching ahead of the others.

"See that battalion marching ahead of the others, just right of center. If you look at the Union line of cannons, you can see a hole. That is where the Pennsylvania boys should be. I think they are moving so easily because the Pennsylvania Brigade is supposed to be taking them out."

Everyone strained their eyes and moved their heads back and forth to see the correlation.

"I think you're right," shouted Draper. "What should we do now?"

Tompkins stepped to his pile of weapons and grabbed his MR2PG. He racked a charge into it and gave them a serious look.

"Bourque, grab your MR2PG," he ordered. "Let's see if these things work in the field."

Bourque ran to his stash and grabbed his weapon. He then racked a charge into the rifle and ran next to Tompkins.

"The rest of you grab your M10s and get over here," ordered Tompkins.

The men raced to their weapons, grabbed them and returned to Tompkins and Bourque. The five men stood facing the moving Confederate Army.

"What now?" asked Draper.

Tompkins pulled his MR2PG to his shoulder and fired one round. The shot hit the front of the Rebel battalion and sent bodies flying.

"You see that everyone?" shouted Tompkins. "That's the target. Let's wipe 'em out."

The men with the M10s spread out and knelt on one knee. They pulled up the massive rifles and found their targets.

"Tell us when," shouted Bates as his finger began applying pressure to the hair trigger.

"Work your way from the left flank to the right," ordered Tompkins. "Bourque and I will concentrate on the rear."

There was a short pause and then Tompkins gave the order. "Do it," shouted Tompkins. The cross hairs of the three M10s steadied as the triggers released their hell. The first three shots blew the unlucky recipients off their feet. The faces of the men next to them paled. They hesitated for a second and then continued forward. Tompkins and Bourque then sent two more MR2PG rounds into the group. What was once a well-oiled marching machine was now a frightened and ragged mass of confusion.

Draper brought his cross hairs to the battalion leader. The man was waving his sword in the air, trying to urge his men forward. Draper depressed the trigger. The projectile only took a second to deliver its deadly message. The two hundred men marching across the field now stopped dead in their tracks. One man dropped down to his knees and tried to revive the leader. He quickly dropped the man's head and looked towards the Union line with a look of fury. He jumped up, grabbed the man's sword from his dead hand, and waved it in the direction of the Union line. The battalion quickly reformed and continued to move forward.

Three more shots from the M10s dropped three more men. The MR2PGs began to rain their death on the center of the formation. The guns of the five men ceased firing only when their clips were empty.

Bates kept an eye on the target as the last of the shots were fired. What once was a determined battalion of over three hundred men, was now a ravaged group of less than one hundred. The remaining men began to turn and run towards the other upcoming Confederate battalions. As the confused and demoralized men met the other troops, they hesitantly fell in line with them. Slowly the masses of gray moved towards the center of the Union line. The only obstacle left was a fence that ran parallel with the road that dissected the battle field.

The five men stood together and watched the battle unfold. The Union cannons continued to tear holes in the Confederate ranks as they helplessly moved toward sure death.

"See that fence out there along that road," shouted Tompkins, above the blasting cannons of the Union Army. "That is the hurdle that causes the Confederates to really stumble."

"What happens at the fence?" questioned Draper. "It's just a fence."

"That fence slows the advancement of the Confederates. It marks the point where Union sharpshooters take over. The Union cannons will be switched from conventional cannonballs to canister loads. The canisters are filled with large, marble sized balls that kind of resemble buckshot. As the Confederates gather at the fence and try to cross it, the Union cannons and the sharpshooters will literally mow them down."

The five men moved apart and returned to their positions. They quickly reloaded their weapons and turned their attention back to the battle raging before them. There were no words said as the five men watched the Confederates make their legendary death march. As the ranks of soldiers moved slowly across the field, the accurate Union cannons continued to wreak havoc on their movement. The exploding cannonballs sent large clods of dirt flying into the air. Men and human body parts mixed in with the dirt. The screams of the dying and wounded could be heard across the field. The explosions became more intense as what was left of the gray mass neared the fence.

"Hey Bourque," shouted Santana, "Let's move closer to the action."

Bourque looked at Santana and shrugged his shoulders. He turned to Tompkins and shouted, "Tompkins, what do you think about moving closer to the action?" Tompkins looked at him without expression. He turned his eyes to the field between them and the front line of the Union troops. He did some quick figuring. He thought they would be safe if they moved towards the left flank of the Union line. From there, they could assist the Union line just as efficiently as their current position. From the new position, they could see the action better. He turned back to Bourque and gave him a wink.

"All right," he shouted to the men. "Everyone grab your weapons and ammo and follow me."

Tompkins gathered up all his equipment and moved to Bourque's position. Bourque had gathered his equipment and was ready to move. One by one the men moved together, loaded with all the equipment. Tompkins pointed to a spot about two hundred yards to the northwest from their current position.

"Let's double-time it to that little grassy swale right over there. We will be in a good position to give support if needed, and we will be closer to the fighting."

Tompkins looked around at each of the men. "You know we don't have to get this close. It would probably be smart to stay right where we are."

"What fun would that be?" replied Draper. "We have been involved in this battle since the first day. We might as well have first row seats for the end."

Bourque shook his head and laughed. "Spoken like a real idiot. But it sounds good to me."

Everyone looked at each other and nodded their heads in agreement. Tompkins took a deep breath, and in a crouch, started to make the journey across the open field to their new destination. They made short work of the journey and fell into the tall grass of the swale, only one hundred yards from the Confederate right flank. They spread out through the tall grass and readied their weapons.

From their new vantage point, the battle became more personal. They now could hear the bullets whizzing around the battlefield and could feel the ground shake from the exploding cannon fire. The wails from the wounded and the shouts of encouragement from the battalion leaders echoed across the field.

Each of the men raised his head above the tall grass to watch the Union onslaught. The first group of Confederate soldiers was now at the fence. They tried to push the fence over, but found it too sturdy. They then began to climb the fence to continue their march.

"Fire," rang from the Union front line. A massive round of rifle fire sent lead whizzing through the air. The Confederate men, who were trying to climb the fence, fell limp over the rails. Every man that had made it across the fence, now fell to the ground in a gray heap. Wood, flesh and blood filled the air like a cloud along the fence. The men who were behind the fence, waiting their turn to climb it, took several steps back in retreat.

"Fire," was heard once again from the Union line and the deafening sound of dozens of cannons filled the air. The fence, and anyone standing behind it, exploded as the canister fire ripped wood and flesh to shreds. In a matter of a few seconds, the Confederates lost their entire front line. The men who did survive turned to run from the certain death that lay ahead.

The Union fire kept raining down on the Confederate troops. Just as it looked like the Confederates would retreat, one Confederate leader ran through one of the holes in the fence and turned to the retreating Rebel line.

"Join me, men, in our triumphant journey," he yelled with his sword waving above him, his hat stuck over the point. "Who will come with me? Who will come with me?" As he stood in the middle of the Union fire storm, the gray retreating mass turned and rushed towards him. The sounds of

Rebel yells filled the air once again. The Confederate soldiers funneled through the holes in the fence and made their way towards the Union front line. Some men climbed over the fence, stepping on the dead to assist them across. Others waited to make it through the holes in the fence.

The Union forces now unleashed everything they had. Every soldier fired his rifle and quickly reloaded. The gray mass was now gaining strength and momentum. Just as it looked like they might make it to the stone fence of the Union front line, the Union fire brought them to a halt. The Confederates only stopped to fire on the Union line. Blue soldiers began falling along the stone fence. The time it took to reload the cannons gave the Confederates the time they needed to advance on the Union line. As they made ten yards, the cannons would fire, and they would lose five. Slowly the thinning gray mass moved closer and closer.

"Wow this is really intense," shouted Bates. "These guys are all crazy as hell."

Tompkins' attention was turned to the extreme right flank of the Confederate line. They were moving to the left of the Union line without any conflict. Tompkins looked around to see if anyone had noticed their movement. He was surprised that no one was paying attention to them. Suddenly it dawned on him.

"Maybe this is where the Pennsylvania battalion is supposed to be. They should have had at least one hundred men with rifles somewhere near this point."

Tompkins gave a sharp short whistle and all heads turned to him. He pointed towards the one hundred men moving directly towards them uncontested. The men's eyes widened as they realized what was happening. Tompkins crawled through the tall grass and sat in the middle of the men.

"I think these men shouldn't be moving so easily this way. The Pennsylvania boys must have been stationed near here. They must have knocked down the entire battalion. I don't recall any flanking by the Confederates during this battle. They must have used cannon fire and rifle fire to stop them."

"What should we do about it?" asked Bates in an unsure voice.

Tompkins rolled his eyebrows. "I guess we need to take them out," he replied in the same unsure voice.

"Lets use our M16s and C22s," Bourque ordered in a commanding voice. "Use hand grenades once they get in range. If anyone makes it to our position, call them out and take action."

Chapter 29

Protecting the flank

Everyone looked at each other and took deep breaths. They then spread back out and popped their heads above the grass. The Confederate battalion was only fifty yards in front of them. The sound of metal clanking as the men racked bullets into the firearms brought them into ready mode. Bourque held his hand in a closed fist as the Confederates moved closer. He then dropped his fist and called out, "Fire."

The grassy swale erupted as the men fired their weapons on full automatic mode. The front line of the Rebels fell as the bullets ripped through them. Gray cloth and blood spattered the men in the second line. The looks on their faces showed they had no idea what was going on or where the shots were coming from. The tall grass concealed the five men perfectly.

As quickly as the first line fell to the ground, the second line followed. The rear of the battalion now flowed out to the sides, moving around the piles of dead men in their way. They moved quickly, firing at the unknown force as they ran.

Draper was at the end of the line, firing his M16 at anything gray. The brass of the fired bullets began to pile up at his side. He pulled the trigger one last time and the familiar click of a spent clip surprised him. He tossed the M16 down and reached for the grenades hanging on his vest. He grabbed a grenade in each hand and pulled them from the vest. He pulled the pins with the opposite hands and depressed the firing levers. He then tossed them towards the outside of the Confederate line. The blast of metal sent men flying through the air. The two blasts shortened the line by thirty feet, giving Draper time to grab his C22.

Next to Draper, Santana and Bates fired in controlled bursts. The barrels of their M16s were now smoking from the extended firing. Each burst from their guns dropped two or three men. They paid no attention to anything but the task of eliminating the gray intruders. The Confederates were now spread out and running in different directions, unsure of what was happening.

Bourque was firing his C22. The sound of the small caliber gun was muffled by Tompkins' M16 fire next to him. As he carefully fired the handgun at each individual target, the reality of the experimental bullet made him smile. Each man that was unlucky enough to be struck by the small projectile was lifted off his feet and slammed to the ground on his back. There were no wounded men getting up off the ground. They lay perfectly still, their lives completely blown from their bodies. Bourque continued to drop gray men as they moved across his sight plane.

Tompkins was containing the other end of the Confederate line. He would pick off the outermost man, working his way towards the center of the line. The pile of hot spent brass next to him caught the dry grass on fire. The smoke from the little fire rose up from the swale in a thin column. Tompkins didn't even notice the fire until the remaining Confederate soldiers turned their attention to it. As the fire began to grow larger, the Confederates started to run towards the smoke, as if they were moths drawn to a flame.

Tompkins glanced over and noticed the fire. He threw down his M16 and began to slap at the fire with his hat. As he finally put the small fire out, his eyes widened as he raised his head to the scene in front of him. The Confederate soldiers were running directly towards them with added verve. They were suddenly only twenty yards away from their position. Tompkins quickly grabbed his C22 from its holster and raised it to fire. Bourque, who was next to Tompkins, directed his fire towards the running men. Tompkins flipped the C22 to fully automatic and began to fire. The little gun began spitting out death at an unbelievable rate.

The oncoming soldiers began to fall like leaves from a tree. The remaining soldiers began to sprint. Closer and closer the Confederates converged on the men's position. The bullets from the five men continued to drop the men as they ran. Some of the gray-clad men tripped over the dead bodies, falling to the ground in front of them. Others jumped over their dead comrades, never breaking stride.

All five men concentrated on the remaining Confederates. The field of battle in front of them was now a thick carpet of gray and scarlet bodies. Only about fifteen gray men still stood, charging with a frightened fury. As the men continued to run towards the group, every stride brought death to one of them. Their faces paled as they realized there were only a few of the original one hundred left. Their resolve only intensified as the situation became more grave.

The sounds of steely clicks moved down the line of five men, as their clips emptied and their rain of bullets stopped. The lone man, who remained running towards Tompkins, realized his situation and covered the last five yards like a fullback moving to the goal line.

Tompkins put the sight of his C22 on the man and pulled the trigger. To his surprise his gun clicked from an empty chamber. His heart began to beat as if it were going to burst out of his chest. All he had time to do, was lie back on his back as the man made his leap to engage Tompkins, hand-to-hand.

As the man flew through the air, arms outstretched with open hands, his flight was diverted by a large mass. As a tiger leaps to defend its young, Bourque took one lunge from his knees and hit the man like a freight train. The two men landed next to Tompkins in a heap. Bourque instinctively put his hands around the man's head and gave a twist. The sound of snapping bone could only lead to one conclusion.

Bourque stood up and looked down at his prey. He wiped the saliva from the corner of his mouth and glanced at Tompkins. He lay on his back with his arms outstretched as if he still expected the man to land on him. He looked at Bourque and dropped his arms in relief, letting out a deep breath.

"Wholly crap," shouted Draper, his head sticking up above the grass. "That was awesome." His eyes were wide and his mouth wide open. Santana stood up and walked over to Tompkins. He stood over him, staring at Bourque.

"I've seen a lot of intense things in my life, but that takes them all," said Santana in a reverent voice. "I can't recall seeing anyone move like that before." Bourque looked at Santana and gave him a little smile. He then looked down at the dead man at his feet. He stood there for a moment with his head hanging down. He then lifted his arms as if he was unsure of what just happened.

"You ever just do something out of instinct?" Bourque asked. He looked around at the other men, whose faces showed him they were still in shock.

"I ain't never done nothing like that," replied Draper.

"I didn't even think about reacting, I just did," responded Bourque. "I don't even know why I killed the man like I did."

He remained standing over the dead body as he spoke. "I guess it would have been kind of interesting to talk to the man."

There was no sound from the grassy swale as the men digested the moment. The silence was finally broken by Bourque. "But I guess we won't be talking to this guy anytime soon," he said with a laugh. He lightly kicked the body with his boot, as if he was checking to see if he would move.

While the five men were having a battle of their own, they forgot about the main battle going on only a few hundred yards away.

"Hey guys," shouted Bates. "Look at that." Bates pointed to the little group of trees at the center of the Union line. The Union line was about to be breeched by the few remaining Confederate attackers.

Nearly two hundred Confederate soldiers had somehow made it through the Union hellfire and were now running towards the Union front line. They didn't stop to fire, but ran with their bayonets lowered.

The Blue front line fired, continuing to drop many of the attackers, but some of them made it through. The clank of steel rang across the battlefield as Confederate bayonets met the rifle barrels of the Union line defenders. Man against man was now the order of the day.

The Confederates fell on the Union line like hungry hyenas. They were able to push the Union line back and turn their own cannons against them. The front line of the Union defense was now retreating as fast as they could. Unbelievably, it looked like the Confederates might make a stand.

The five men stood in disbelief as the ragtag Confederate group tried to make a good fight of it.

"How in the heck could they make it that far, against such terrible odds?" said Bates. The five men just stood there in quiet amazement.

"I guess the reason they're fighting is worth any cost," replied Tompkins in a somber tone. "In our day, the reason for fighting is not as important as the outcome.

Heck, sometimes we wage war just for the sake of waging war." The men nodded their heads in agreement.

They each had been in situation that made them question why they were there. They carried out their orders because they were soldiers. Most times there was no great life-changing event they were trying to accomplish. At least for themselves. Most of their missions were to assist other people they didn't even know, or for that matter, care about. Each of them thought about how they would feel if they were fighting for a true cause. A cause that would affect their families and friends directly. Would they go to any length to defend their houses and property? Would they be willing to give their life for an ideal, like slavery or states' rights? None of them could give themselves a true answer. That kind of philosophical question could only be truly answered when a person is face-to-face with that situation.

"It looks like the Confederates may make a fight out of this, doesn't it?" asked Tompkins in a rhetorical voice. "Watch what happens now."

He pointed to the rear of the Union position. As the hand-to-hand combat continued at the front line, a huge wave of blue reserves was double-timing it to the battle.

"Wow, there must be thousands of them," burst out Draper. "The outcome's pretty obvious now."

"Yeah, the Union was ready for this to happen," answered Tompkins. "They knew the Rebel's resolve in this battle was too great to take them lightly."

"I can see why this battle is the changing point of the war," remarked Bourque.

"This must have crushed the South's spirit. And of course, losing most of your troops in one battle doesn't help either."

Tompkins turned to Bourque and smiled. "I see you've been paying attention to my little lessons after all." Bourque returned the smile and then returned his attention to the battle.

The blue wave was now entering into the battle at the front line. The once fierce fighting machine of the South now realized they were not going to win this battle. They quickly dropped their rifles and began to run back across the stone fence. The front line of the blue reserves knelt on one knee and brought their rifles up to their shoulders. "Fire," rang across the battlefield as the Union line fired their rifles. The running Rebels fell by the dozens as the Union lead balls found their targets. The Union soldiers reloaded their weapons and raised them once more to fire. They stood ready to fire, but no command came. After a minute they lowered their rifles and stared across the field.

What was left of the Confederate charge, now limped back towards the woods from which they had come. Some men stopped to pick up the dead or wounded. Others looked over their shoulders as they ran, to see if the Union Army was going to pursue them.

"That sure is a depressing sight," said Santana in a solemn tone. "They really got their butts kicked."

"Does the Union follow them?" asked Draper. "They probably could destroy the entire Virginia Army, if they attack now."

"No, they don't attack," answered Tompkins. "This was the Union's first real win in the war. I think they are a little shocked that they actually won. I think they realized what they just did to the Confederate Army and the morale of the South."

Shouts from the Union line brought the men's attention back to the union front line. The entire army was now grouped behind the stone fence they had just defended so gallantly. Men with American flags waved them wildly, standing on top of the stone fence. Shouts of "Hoorah" rang continuously from the Union ranks. Hats were flying in the air and men hugged each other. Men ran from all over the Union line to join the group at the stone fence. Other men attended to the wounded and dead. They carried the bodies to the rear of the line, loading them onto wagons.

Tompkins' mind flashed back to the military hospital he and Bourque visited yesterday. His eyes watered as he pictured the horrible scene. He knew the amount of men who would be brought there today, would make the scene ten times worse. He quickly wiped his eyes so no one would see his emotions.

"What should we do now?" asked Draper. The men looked at each other and then all heads turned to Tompkins. He looked down the line at each of the men.

"I know this may seem a little odd, but I think we should say a short prayer for the men that died or were wounded during this battle." He once again looked at each of the men.

"Good idea," responded Bourque in a commanding voice.

He then knelt down on one knee and bowed his head. The other men followed his lead and did the same. The five men knelt for some time. Each of them prayed with reverence. They knew the totality of war and the thoughtless death it brought to men. After about five minutes, the men raised their heads and stood to their feet.

"Great job men," commanded Bourque. He reached out and shook each of their hands. When he got to Draper he reached out his hand. Draper reached out to shake his hand and then pulled his hand back. Bourque's eyes got big at this show of rejection from Draper.

"Brothers don't shake hands," Draper announced. "Brothers gotta hug."

He then launched himself at Bourque and wrapped his arms around Bourque's large neck. The other men began to laugh at Draper's goofy display of affection. Bourque laughed and then threw Draper off him.

"Get outta here you doofus," laughed Bourque. Draper took another lunge at Bourque to give him another hug. Bourque grabbed Draper and adeptly spun him around, putting him in a full nelson.

"I appreciate the gesture," said Bourque. "But I don't swing that way."

He then released Draper giving him a push. The men laughed at the two of them. They had always enjoyed the banter between the two men. At this point in their journey, they were ready for some levity.

"Let's head back and pick up our equipment and brass," ordered Tompkins. "Then we can get back to camp and figure out what we should do next."

"Sounds like a plan to me," replied Santana as the men headed back to their last battle position.

CHAPTER 30

A glimpse of normality

The men busied themselves hunting through the tall grass, looking for their equipment and spent bullet casings. Draper sat down and looked up at the sky. The haze from the suffocating heat and the smoke from the past battle covered the sun like a piece of cheesecloth. His eyes focused hard on the haze as if he were looking for something.

"What ya looking at?" asked Santana. He slowly made his way over to where Draper was sitting, picking up what he could as he went.

"Nothing really. Just trying to take in what is really happening here. Every mission I go on, I try to find the difference between home and where I am. But everywhere I go, the sky seems different. Almost like the Earth has a different sky everywhere I go. Kind of dumb huh."

Santana looked at Draper with a new respect. Santana knew Draper as the funny, shallow, little impish man who only made fun of anything emotional or deep. For Draper to open up to him like this was rare, yet refreshing.

"I don't think it's dumb," answered Santana. "I sometimes do the exact same thing. Makes me feel like I'm soaking in the experience."

Draper looked at Santana and smiled. He appreciated the exchange between the two war hardened men. Usually they only talked about war or strategies. This was new to him. He would have liked to open up to Santana more. He would have liked to tell him that his levity in most situations was just a mask for his real feelings. How he usually felt the other men were his brothers, and he would do anything for them. But instead of telling him this, he just stared into the sky.

The haze cleared for a second and his eye caught a strange object. He squinted hard and stretched his neck to make out the object. Santana stared at Draper.

"What are you looking at now?" asked Santana in a bored tone of voice.

Draper said nothing but raised his hand and pointed to the sky. Santana craned his neck and looked to where Draper was pointing. A small object was moving across the sky leaving a white trail. He brought a hand up to his forehead to block out some of the dull sunlight.

"Hey guys," shouted Santana. "There's another jet flying over."

The other men dropped what was in their hands and ran to Santana and Draper. Santana lifted his hand and pointed straight up. All heads bent back and eyes strained to see the glimpse of familiarity.

"There it is," said Bates in a strained voice. His head bent in an unusual manner. "I feel better already."

"What do you think, Tompkins?" asked Bourque, keeping his eye on the jet.

"I'm not sure, but it looks real good to me."

The five men stood like cranes, staring up at the sky. The haze became thicker as the wind began to lightly blow towards them. As quickly as the object appeared, it disappeared. The five men dropped their heads and then looked directly towards Tompkins. He returned their stares.

"I don't have any idea what it means," was his reply to their concerted glares. Their eyes were still locked on him as if he were the Messiah. Tompkins looked at each man again and started to laugh.

"At ease guys. Let's get our stuff gathered up and we can talk about it as we walk back to camp."

To break their stares, Tompkins tossed an empty clip at Bourque. He instinctively caught it.

"Yeah," he hesitantly said. "Let's do that."

He looked at the other men, who were still staring at Tompkins. "Get moving," he shouted.

The other men broke their trance and began gathering their goods once again. Nothing was said by anyone as they went back to work. Bourque stood back and watched the other men. They seemed to have a new jump to their step. This new omen gave them a new hope for getting home. No one knew how or when, but once again they felt a renewed hope that they were moving in the right direction.

They quickly filled their pockets with empty brass bullet casings and slung their rifles over their shoulders. One by one they gathered around Bourque. Bates was the last to join the group. As he walked, he continued to pick up the brass that kept falling from a hole in his blue wool coat. Finally, all five men stood around Bourque and waited for his instructions.

"Well, our job here is done," Bourque said. "I think we did our jobs well and kept the balance the best we could." He glanced around the group with a half smile. The other men returned the smile.

"Let's head for camp and figure out our next move. Maybe we can come up with a good idea along the way."

The men nodded their heads in agreement and turned to head back to their camp. They walked in silence. The only sounds now came from the Union troops cleaning up their broken and shattered battlefield. Walking slowly across the open field, the men took time to look around the battlefield and the surrounding hills. The beauty of the terrain and the day almost made them forget about the battle they had just fought in. The noise from the Union Army, cleaning up their ranks, became less noticeable as their trek took them further from the battlefield.

As the five men made their way to the line of trees that led them to their camp, Bates stopped and bent over at the waist. The brass he had gathered from the grassy swale poured from his pockets as he bent over. The other men stopped and turned to him.

"What's the matter?" asked Tompkins in a concerned tone.

Bates was now heaving. Liquid began to spew from his mouth. After three or four heaves, Bates wiped his mouth and stood up straight. He looked at the other men with a pale face.

"I have that feeling again," Bates explained. "Feels the same as when we were on our way here, before we knew what we were getting into."

"Are you O.K.?" asked Draper.

"Yeah, I'm good now, but my stomach is still in knots."

Bates looked away from the men and bent down to pick up the spilled brass. Draper's eyes widened and a smile came to his face.

"I wonder?" murmured Draper.

"Wonder what?" asked Bourque.

Draper looked at Bourque with an excited look. "Remember when Bates first had this weird feeling? He got it when we were going into this whole mess."

He smiled now as this revelation hit him.

"Yeah and what does it mean now?" asked Bourque.

Draper stared him straight in the eyes with the big smile plastered on his face. "Maybe this feeling has come back because we are going to get out of this mess soon," shouted Draper. "Maybe we are closer to getting back home than we think."

Draper's head turned fast between the three men's faces. Bates finished picking up the brass and stood up once again.

"Does seem to make sense," Bates interjected as he threw Draper a puzzled look.

"Whatever it means," said Tompkins, "let's get back to the camp and get our stuff stowed. I have an idea, but we can't move on it until dark."

The men looked at each other and then double-timed it to the woods. They almost dove into the woods as they were almost at a run now. The once bloody battlefield that consumed their every thought now became the last thing on their minds. They dodged trees and logs as they traversed the terrain like bloodhounds after a coon. Within minutes they broke through the other side of the forest. They slowed their pace as the tall grass of the meadow came into view. At a fast walk, they approached their campsite.

Coming to their spots around the fire pit, each of the men pulled their heavy wool coats off and dropped them on the ground at their feet. They then fell on their bedrolls and sprawled out in exhaustion. Bourque began taking off his boots and the others followed suit. He then pulled off his sweat-stained wool pants and shirt. He sat in his underwear, enjoying the freedom from the sweaty, stinky Union uniform. He looked around the campsite. Everyone except for Tompkins was lying back in their skivvies.

Tompkins, who had taken off the Union uniform during his last mission, tried not to laugh at the others. They seemed like they were in heaven, not having those uniforms on.

"If you guys promise to put some clothes on," Tompkins laughed. "I promise not to let the world know you guys did this."

Everyone looked at each other and laughed. They quickly dug in their bags next to their bed rolls and pulled out their military issue uniforms. They pulled on the lightweight clothes and let out a deep breath of relief.

"I never thought I would enjoy putting this uniform on so much," exclaimed Draper. "Those old uniforms are nuts."

"It's amazing how something so simple could be so nice," added Santana. Everyone let out a laugh and lay back on their makeshift beds. Tompkins lay there for a second and then sat up as if he were possessed. His face glowed with excitement as a profound thought came to him. Bourque noticed his odd condition and sat up also.

"A spider crawl up your pants?" Bourque laughed. Tompkins looked at him and laughed.

"No, I just had a wild idea," crooned Tompkins.

The other men sat up now, ready to listen to anything he had to say.

"What if we wait until dark and start our way back towards the mountain. We can drive around the woods and go across the field we just fought in. Once we get to the road, we can take it back towards the mountain. With Bates' weird feeling, maybe we need to get back there as fast as possible."

Everyone agreed that was what they should do.

"We have about an hour before it gets dark, so if we get loaded up, we can get moving."

The four newly-clad men quickly put their boots on and laced them up tightly. Everyone then jumped up and began the task of packing their equipment into the Jeeps. They moved with renewed vigor with the prospect of a way home.

As they pulled the Ghillies off the Jeeps, they didn't even hear the pounding of horse hooves approaching. The whinny of one of the horses drew their attention away from their jobs at hand. Their heads spun around not knowing what they would see. They were met by the sight of several men on horses standing in a line. In the middle of the line was a familiar sight. The long blonde hair falling out the back of his hat and the neatness of his uniform told them it was General Custer. The five men approached the line of horsemen and stood at attention. General Custer shot them a long salute. They saluted him back with respect. His eyes moved from them to their Jeeps. He carefully studied the Jeeps before returning his attention back to the five men before him.

"I don't need to know what those contraptions are I guess." Custer spoke loudly. "I just wanted to come over and see how you fared during the battle."

"We fared well," replied Tompkins as he moved towards Custer.

"I am glad to see everyone is in one piece," answered Custer. "Both General Buford and myself were concerned for your welfare, but I see it was unwarranted. For that I am glad."

"Thank you for your concern, General," shouted Tompkins. "How did yourself and General Buford fare?"

General Custer smiled and tipped his hat to Tompkins. He had a sincere look of appreciation on his face.

"All went well. We won the day and the battle. I wonder though, if we would have, without your assistance." Custer looked up to the sky and wiped the sweat from his forehead. "I suppose, sometimes we all need a little outside assistance to win our battles."

Tompkins thought this was an odd thing for Custer to say. It almost seemed as if he knew they were not supposed to be there. Did Buford let him in on their predicament or was there more to General Custer than history let on?

"Thank God for that," replied Tompkins. "We are getting ready to move on now. Seems our mission here is complete."

"So it is," said Custer. "So it is."

Custer bent forward in his saddle and extended his hand towards Tompkins. Tompkins moved towards him and extended his hand. The two men shook hands and then saluted each other. Custer sat back in his saddle and spun his horse around. He turned his head back towards the men and took off his hat.

"Thank you men for your support in our cause," he shouted. "I am sure you will find your way home when the time presents itself." He then winked at them and placed his hat back on his head.

"God be with you men," he shouted as he gave the order to his men to leave. He lifted his arm in a wave and then rode away at a gallop into the dusk of the eve.

The five men stood silent in amazement. What Custer just said made them think hard about getting home.

Tompkins thought, "What did he mean, when the time presents itself?" Tompkins was brought back to the moment as someone hit his arm. He turned his head to see Draper standing next to him.

"You realize you just shook hands with General George Custer," he said in amazement. "I wouldn't wash that hand ever."

There was a burst of laughter at Draper's stupid comment.

"Draper, I sometimes wonder about you," laughed Tompkins, pushing him away from his side.

"Let's finish loading our equipment," commanded Bourque. "It's almost dark."

The five men went back to loading the vehicles. It wasn't long and they had them packed and ready to move. They jumped into their respective Jeeps and slammed the doors. The radio cracked as Tompkins voice filled the cabs.

"Let's take this slow and careful. Keep an eye out and follow our lead. Over." Bates grabbed the handset from its perch and put it to his mouth. "10-4, were right behind you."

Chapter 31

Draper's ghost

The two vehicles bucked forward and began their trek down the trail around the woods. They followed the two-track road as long as they could, but the half road, half trail soon began to veer the wrong way. They continued bumping along the edge of the woods, moving ever so slow in the direction they knew would lead them to the field they just left.

Tompkins and Bourque strained their eyes, searching for a way through the underbrush and forest. Bourque spotted a small thinning area in the forest ahead. He pointed a large finger towards the spot. Tompkins looked in the direction Bourque was pointing and headed for the area. Soon the two Jeeps found their way through the woods, sticking their hoods out of the forest edge like two giant beasts.

Tompkins looked at Bates, who was driving the other Jeep, and gave him the signal to turn off the engine. Bates flipped the key and the engine became quiet. Tompkins jumped out of his Jeep and looked across the open field in front of them. The rest of the men soon joined him, standing in a line to his left. He glanced down the line and then back at the field. The men stood in silent reverence.

"Hard to believe this big empty field was such a bloodbath only a few hours ago," mentioned Tompkins.

"Yeah, it seems so peaceful now," replied Bourque.

The only remnants of the battle visible to them were the Union troops still removing their equipment and dead from the far right of the field. All heads were turned towards the Union troops as they did their grisly duty.

"Boy, I wouldn't want that job," commented Draper. The other men quickly shot him a glance and then returned their eyes to the field.

"That's the hell of war we rarely see," answered Tompkins. "Back in the old times," Tompkins paused for a second, "I mean the present era, the battlefields were people's back yards and towns. We're fortunate, America has never had to deal with this type of war since, now."

The other men knew what he meant and let out a breath of relief to show their agreement. It wasn't long before Draper became antsy.

"What's our next move Tompkins?" asked Draper.

Tompkins looked up into the hazy darkening sky. He then turned to Draper and answered him. "Let's wait for a few more minutes until it's a little darker. We don't need to draw any attention right now."

"Sounds good to me," replied Draper. "Just let us know when you want to head out."

Tompkins pointed past the area they just fought in, towards the fence the Union used to destroy most of the Confederate Army.

"I think if we head across the field towards that fence, we can take the road away from this area and hopefully make it back to the mountain by tomorrow."

"Boy that sure would be nice," remarked Santana. He leaned back against the Jeep and cocked his head upward towards the sky. "It seems like it has been forever since we were back home."

"Well hopefully it won't be too much longer," replied Bourque. "Let's get back in the Jeeps and get ready to move out."

As usual, the men jumped at Bourque's command, and they once again entered their Jeeps. Tompkins and Bourque slowly entered their Jeep and relaxed in the soft seats.

"Think this whole plan will pan out?" asked Bourque.

Tompkins looked at him with an innocent smiling face.

"If it doesn't, I don't know what we'll do." Tompkins stared out the windshield of their Jeep. "I guess we'll just have to have faith that we will find our way outta here." He then looked at Bourque and shrugged his shoulders.

The sky darkened and the shadowy figures of the Union soldiers in the distance disappeared. Tompkins looked around the field and then at Bourque.

"Let's do this," he said, grabbing the shift lever and putting it in drive. Bourque grabbed the radio handset and put it to his lips.

"Let's take it slow and easy," cracked over the radio in the second Jeep. Bates reached for the radio handset and returned a "10-4."

The Jeeps slowly pulled away from the safety of their forest, beginning the slow trip across the open battlefield. Bumping across the field proved a simple task. It was dark enough, so they moved without detection across the open space. They soon made it to the grassy swale that was their personal battlefield earlier in the day. They slowly passed through the tall grass, almost at a reverent pace. The men looked out their windows with solemn faces. The one hundred or so gray soldiers lay in heaps where they had fallen to their deaths. A feeling of remorse ran through the men as they passed the dead bodies of the day's work. No words were spoken. Once they passed the deadly swale, Tompkins brought his Jeep to a stop.

"Let's get out and say a prayer over those gallant men," Tompkins requested to Bourque in a soft voice. Bourque nodded his agreement and they exited the Jeeps. The three men in the second Jeep jumped out and walked over to Tompkins and Bourque.

"What's up?" asked Draper.

"We thought it would appropriate to say a few words over these men, before we move on," answered Bourque in a commanding tone.

"Great idea," remarked Bates as he knelt down on one knee.

The rest of the men followed suit, except for Tompkins. He remained standing with his head bowed. He broke the silence as he began to speak. Tompkins wasn't sure what he should say, and he definitely wasn't used to speaking like this in front of other people. His faith was his own, and he didn't feel it was necessary to push it on others. The four men that knelt around him were his family. He was glad they seemed responsive to his request to say a prayer for these men. He took a deep breath and began to speak.

"Lord, thank you for helping us to remain safe through this terrible battle today. Forgive us for taking the lives of these men, though it was our duty. Help these brave men's souls to rest in peace in your presence."

Tompkins' voice stopped for a few seconds. He felt a wave of guilt run through his stomach. He fought hard to hold back the tears that were forming in his eyes.

"Please, Lord, be with these men's families. Help them to know they died with honor, defending what they thought was a great cause. Thank you, Lord, for your blessings on all of us. Help us to find our way home, as you help these men to find their way to your home. Amen."

"Amen," was whispered from the four men kneeling around Tompkins. They then stood to their feet, but their eyes remained on the ground.

"We better get moving," commanded Bourque, breaking the silence of the moment.

The men returned to the vehicles. They jumped in the Jeeps and started the engines. Like zombies, they continued their trek to the fence. They were all affected by the prayer Tompkins had requested. They all thought about the hundreds of men they had killed in the past. They thought about those men's families and the final resting place of their souls. They stared out the windshields of their vehicles, saying nothing.

Their attention was soon focused on the fence that appeared through the darkness. They could see piles of dead bodies and the destruction that lay before them. The Jeeps slowly approached the fence and then stopped. They stood still for a few seconds, then began to creep down the road through the death zone of the earlier battle.

Faces were pressed against the windows as they maneuvered through and around the dead bodies of the soldiers and horses. Muskets lay strewn around the road. Articles of clothing and personal effects of the soldiers covered the road like leaves . The men's minds raced as they witnessed the aftermath of devastation from the battle. After seeing enough death to last a lifetime, their attention soon turned from the windows, to the road before them. They slowly wound their way past the bloodiest part of the road and found open road ahead.

"I think this road is going to take us right where we need to go," commented Tompkins to Bourque. Bourque turned to Tompkins and spoke.

"That sure was an experience. We've seen a lot of stuff in our service, but never anything like that. Kinda glad it's almost over." Tompkins turned his attention to Bourque.

"Hopefully it's over. I see some horses coming our way across the field."

In the dark horizon, three horses could be seen galloping towards them. Tompkins brought the Jeep to a stop. The two men exited their vehicle and walked to the rear Jeep. Bates rolled down the window and asked, "What's up?"

Tompkins pointed out into the darkness at the men coming their way on horseback. The three men in the Jeep strained their eyes to see what Tompkins was pointing at. Their eyes widened as they caught sight of the horsemen. The doors flew open on the Jeep and the three men jumped out. They walked over and stood next to Tompkins and Bourque.

Draper moved next to Tompkins, elbowed him and asked, "Who are they?"

Tompkins' eyes never left the horsemen. "Hopefully friends."

The three men rode up and came to a stop. The horses bucked and snorted as they relaxed from their forced gallop. The three men dismounted and walked to up to the five men and their vehicles. Sighs of relief rolled from the men as the three men became visible in the darkness.

"Thank heavens it's you," said Tompkins as he shot a quick salute to the men.

The three men removed their hats and saluted back. General Buford, Newton and MacDonald smiled at the five men and then reached out to shake their hands. They all informally shook hands and shared relief at their present situation.

"Well, men," said Buford. "I am pleased you fared well in the battle."

"Yes, General, we came out unharmed and I think kept the balance pretty well," responded Tompkins. "We've been in many battles, but this has truly been a life changing experience. One I think none of us will ever forget."

Buford let out a small chuckle. "I would think not," he laughed. As usual, Buford slapped his hat on his thigh and a cloud of dust filled the air around his torso. He looked at the ground as the dust settled to the earth. He lifted his eyes and looked at each of the five men in turn. Newton and MacDonald stood behind him with slight smiles on their faces. The two men spoke no words, but the five men knew they were satisfied at the meeting.

"Men," Buford began, "I'm not a man of words. I'm not entirely sure why I was drawn here to this meeting. I guess to give you the thanks of the Union Army. You may well have saved the day and all of America's history." Buford smiled and laughed under his breath. "I gather that history will remain the same and you will somehow find your way home. It was an honor to meet and work with you on this project. If you can't find your way back home, I sure could use you in our brigade." Buford once again laughed, this time with feeling. All the men joined him in laughter at his offer.

"Thank you, General," interrupted Tompkins. I will remember your offer, if we can't find our way home. It would be an honor to serve with you."

All the men smiled and nodded in agreement. Buford stood in front of them now with a stern look.

"Seriously," he began, "it has been an honor to meet you men. I am relieved to know the future is safe with men such as yourselves in the service of our country. I truly hope you find your way home and live your lives in good health and as fully as possible. You five deserve all the blessings our Lord can grant."

Buford stepped forward and extended his hand to Tompkins. The two men shook hands and patted each other on the shoulder. Buford then moved down the line and did the same for each of the men. Newton and MacDonald moved in next to him and extended their hands in gratitude. After the men exchanged their sincere gratitude, Buford and his men started to walk back to their horses. Newton and MacDonald put their boots into their stirrups and hoisted themselves onto their horses. Buford started to do the same but paused. He turned his head back to the five men and smiled.

"I am sure you will find your way back to your homes soon," Buford spoke.

He then pointed to the rear of their vehicles. Back down the road stood a single man, his identity hid by the darkness.

"I think there is one thing left to do," continued Buford as he thrust himself onto the back of his steed. He grabbed the reins and pulled them back hard. "God bless you men. All of history is in your debt."

He then spun his horse around and the three men galloped away. As they disappeared into the darkness, the sounds of pounding hooves also disappeared. As if the meeting were with ghosts, they were gone. The five men looked at each other in disbelief. It was the first time any of them had opened up themselves enough to believe they had seen a ghost.

"Was that real or did they just disappear?" asked Santana. Everyone shrugged their shoulders as they didn't know what to make of it.

"I think we have to remember where we are and what were doing," answered Tompkins. "This whole mission we're on has been full of ghosts, if you think about it."

"Yeah, I guess you're right," commented Bourque. "We shouldn't be surprised by anything we see while we're still here."

The five men's attention suddenly turned to the lone person standing back down the road. No one knew what to do or say, as the person stood there in the darkness.

"Does anyone have any idea what is up with that?" asked Santana. Bourque took a step in the direction of the man, but an arm reached out and grabbed him.

"I get the feeling I'm supposed to take care of this," said Draper in a quiet solemn voice. "I'll be fine, just wait here."

Bourque took a step back and returned to his original position. Draper slowly began the walk to the mysterious figure. His mind was blank as he approached the man. As he came close enough to make out the face of the man, he stopped in disbelief. He squinted his eyes to see if they were lying to him. The face remained the same. He slowly approached the man as if he were in a trance. Coming face-to-face with the man, he stopped.

Draper's mind shot him back to the scene where he first met this man. The man was lying on the ground, bloody and near death. Draper reached into his pants pocket and grasped the small wooden cross he had carried since the meeting. He slowly pulled it out and looked down at it. He then looked at the man's face. He extended his hand to the man, the cross laid in his open hand. The man reached out and closed Draper's hand around the cross.

"You keep this to remember me and this place," the man said with a smile.

Draper stood as still as a statue, his eyes fixed on the man in disbelief. The two men stood face-to-face, neither sure of what to say. Draper finally came out and said what he was thinking.

"I thought you were dead," blurted Draper with a quake in his voice. The man smiled and released Draper's hand.

"I think I am dead."

"But how are you here now?" asked Draper. "Are you a ghost or something?"

The man let out a small laugh. He opened his coat and showed Draper his chest. Draper's eyes widened at what he saw. There was no blood or wound.

Draper's mind raced back to their first meeting. The man was laying on his back with a large hole in his chest. Blood was streaming from the wound as the man gasped for his last breath. Draper brought his gaze back to the man's face.

"Sir, I think I am dead," the ghostly figure spoke. "When a man dies on the battlefield, he is separated from the things he loves. His family, friends and home. His soul has a void that longs to be filled. When I was lying there on that hill, all I could think about was those things I would never see again. It was a bitter feeling. To die alone is a horrible thing."

The man cut off his explanation. A tear ran from his face and dripped on his jacket. Draper could see he was thinking of the things he would never see again. The things a man holds sacred. The man dropped his eyes to the ground, like he was ashamed of his emotions.

Draper thought about how he would feel in the same situation. His eyes teared up at the thought of being in this man's position.

"I guess as soldiers we try not to think about those things," consoled Draper. "I guess I never really thought about it too much before."

The man lifted his head and looked Draper right in the eyes. His face had a new expression. His face now had a glow to it. His lips curled into a smile as he began to speak.

"When I was lying there in my darkest hour, you came up. You tried to help me. I assumed you were the enemy, but you truly tried to save me. You showed me the kindness I thought I would never see again."

The man reached out and grasped Draper's hand again. "As the life slipped away from me, the last words I heard was the beginning of the prayer you said for me. When the darkness came, I was scared. But then a light showed, a light that almost blinded me. I felt at peace. I felt a higher power surround me. I didn't know what was going to happen next. So I asked if I could let you know that what you did for me meant a lot, I would appreciate it. The light faded and I found myself here, waiting for you to come to me."

The man's smile widened a bit and his grasp on Draper's hand tightened. His lips quivered a bit as he began to speak.

"Thank you for your kindness to me on that hill. Thank you for giving my soul the peace it needed to cross over to the other side. I know there are still thousands of souls, wandering around these fields, in search of what you gave me. I feel lucky that you were there. I am indebted to you forever."

The man's face now glowed with appreciation and love. Draper could tell the man was as sincere as he could be. Draper felt a tear run down his cheek. He just let it fall. A tear ran down the man's face and disappeared into the dust.

"I don't know how all this death stuff works," said the man. "But if I am ever able to repay you in any way, I will make sure I do."

He then released Draper's hand and smiled. He slowly turned and started to walk away. He looked over his shoulder at Draper and stopped.

"God bless you, Draper," whispered the man. "You will find your way home soon. I will make sure of that."

The man turned once more and continued to walk away. Draper stood there staring at the back of the gray-clad ghost. He blinked his eyes and to his surprise the man was gone. He strained his eyes to see where the man went, but there was nothing. Draper let out a deep breath and looked down at the hand-carved cross in his hand. He closed his grip around it and looked up at the darkness again. He thought about what the man said and how he said it. It choked him up when he thought about the man's death. Then it struck him. The man was going to be with his Lord. What better end to a soldier's life than that? He smiled at the thought of the man finding peace.

Draper turned and started to walk back to his friends. After a couple steps, he came to a complete stop. Something struck him funny as he thought about the words of the ghost.

"He called me Draper," he murmured under his breath. "How did he know my name, and how did he know I was going to find my way home soon?"

Draper shook off the whole thought. There were too many things running through his mind. He continued walking towards the other men. As he approached the men, Santana met him with a smile.

"What the heck was that all about?" asked Santana.

The other men gathered around Draper to find out more. Draper just held out his closed hand. He slowly opened it to show the cross the man had given him.

"Remember the man I tried to save on that hill the other day? Before he died, he gave me this little hand-carved cross. I just stuck it in my pocket and forgot about it."

"That was just before you were shot wasn't it?" asked Bates.

"Yeah, just before," answered Draper.

"What does that have to do with all this?" asked Santana. Tompkins and Bourque just stood behind the other men listening intently.

"That man I was talking to over there," began Draper. "That was him."

"Say what?" spurted Santana in disbelief. "How could that have been him? I thought you said he died."

Draper looked at him and laughed. "It was him," Draper said with a hint of disbelief himself. "He opened his coat and showed me his chest. It was completely normal. When I seen him on the hill, his chest was torn apart." Draper looked at Santana and Bates. He could see they were confused.

"The man told me he wanted to return and tell me thanks for my kindness before he died. That his soul was clear to go to the other side. He said there are thousands of souls around here that are still looking for that kindness I gave him."

"So you're saying he was a ghost?" asked Bates. Both he and Santana now had looks of interest on their faces.

"Yeah, that's what I'm telling you. And the thing that sealed it for me was when he called me by my name. I never told him my name. And then he told me something strange. He said that I would find my way home soon." Draper looked at Santana and smiled. "Kind of gives you the willies doesn't it?"

"Yeah it does," answered Santana. Santana's interest level was now peaked. Bates remained expressionless.

"He started to walk away," explained Draper. "I was watching him walk away, and he just disappeared into thin air."

Draper raised his arms in a gesture of disbelief. He knew what he saw and it meant a lot to him. It was a meeting that would stay with him for the rest of his life. He didn't want the other men to know how much it meant to him, so he acted like it was no big deal.

"Boy I guess that just falls into place with the rest of this whole mission," conferred Santana. "It seems weird, but I guess I believe it happened."

The three men turned and faced Tompkins and Bourque. They stood in silence for a moment before Bourque spoke.

"I guess we should be heading out," he said rubbing the top of his head. Tompkins slapped Draper on the shoulder and smiled.

"What an experience hey?" he asked Draper.

"Yeah, but I wish it were over," replied Draper.

Chapter 32

The road home

The five men stood in a line looking over the blackness of the battlefield. For the first time since they started this mission, they felt at ease. They relaxed and thought about what had happened the last three days. A feeling of reverence fell over them as they stood on the actual battlefield of the largest battle ever on American soil.

"Hey, you guys need to get out of here," shattered the peaceful silence. The men's heads jerked toward the announcement. A single light shone in their faces.

"The park closes at ten, you need to leave," shouted a man with a flashlight.

The man moved the light up and down the body of Bourque and then Tompkins. After seeing the military issue fatigues of the men, he dropped the light from their faces.

"Sorry men," the man apologized. "I thought you were just some sightseers trying to get a look at a ghost or something."

"Did you say the park was closed?" asked Tompkins in a quizzical tone.

"Yeah , this park closes at ten o'clock during the summer. The battle reenactment brings a lot of people to Gettysburg this time of year. I take it you men must have seen it."

Tompkins looked at Bourque and gave him an elbow in the ribs. They both smiled at each other.

"Does his voice sound familiar to you?" asked Tompkins to Bourque.

"Yeah, but I can't place it," replied Bourque.

"Can I see your flashlight for a second?" asked Tompkins.

"Sure," replied the guard as he tossed his Maglight to Tompkins.

Tompkins pointed the light at the other men and gave them a big smile. The looks on their faces told Tompkins they had not yet figured out what was happening. He then pointed the flashlight across the road behind them. The light from the flashlight shone on a monument of a man on a horse. He then moved it to the left and stopped it on a monument surrounded by several cannons. Then he shone the light back down the road from where they had just come. The fence that had just previously been a tangled mess of wood and dead bodies was now a clean erect fence, with no signs of the battle that had just ended. Tompkins tossed the light back to the park guard and started to laugh. The other men started laughing along with him. The punchline to this whole strange event hit them.

"I don't know what's so funny," laughed the park guard. "But I sure would appreciate it if you moved along as soon as you're done."

The men continued to hang on each other's shoulders laughing at the new twist to their journey. The park guard shrugged his shoulders and walked away. After a couple of steps the park guard turned back to the laughing men. He raised his hand.

"Thanks for your service to our country," he shouted.

The five men suddenly became quiet. They stared at the dark figure of the guard. "And thanks for keeping the balance." The guard gave his hand a wave, turned and walked away. The five men looked at each other with blank expressions. They then looked back down the dark road towards the guard. He was gone!

Bourque gave Tompkins an elbow to his side. "That voice sounded a lot like General..." Bourque's voice stopped for a second. "No it couldn't be."

Tompkins raised his shoulders to acknowledge the possibility, but then said, "At this point in time, anything is possible."

"Tompkins, are we back where we should be?" asked Draper in a confused tone.

Tompkins let out a long deep breath and replied. "Draper, I think we are right where we are supposed to be and right on schedule."

Draper let out a deep breath. "Boy it sure feels good knowing where and when we are," he replied. "But I sure wish we could have seen the reenactment."

Everyone started laughing once again as Bourque grabbed Draper around the neck. The two wrestled around for a moment, before Bourque released him. They all walked to their Jeeps, opened the doors and jumped into the safety and comfort of their vehicles. The lights of the Jeeps shone down the paved road as the vehicles began their trip to the East Coast and their next assignment. Tompkins and Bourque said nothing as they relaxed at the new normality of their trip. In the second Jeep, the three men talked wildly over each other about what they thought of the mission. Draper's head was between the seats and he was laughing and talking like a college kid on a road trip. Bates and Santana laughed and did the same.

The crack of the radio brought silence to the second Jeep. Everyone looked at the radio like it was a nuclear device with a blinking timer. Bates hesitantly reached for the handset and lifted it off its perch.

"Tiger one, this is Tiger two," chirped Bates. "Did you need something? Over." The radio cracked once again and the familiar voice of Tompkins rang through the cab of the Jeep.

"Tiger two, this is Tiger one. I think our next assignment takes us close to San Antonio. It would be pretty cool to see the Alamo, don't you think? Over."

The three men looked at each other with frightened expressions. They thought the same thing at the same time. Draper snatched the handset out of Bates' hand.

"Tiger one, this is Tiger two," shouted Draper. "Are you nuts? I ain't never going on a sight-seeing tour with you again. If I want to fight with Mexicans, I'll go to East L.A."

Draper threw the handset against the dashboard of the Jeep and sat back hard in his seat. Bates and Santana looked at each other and started to laugh uncontrollably. Draper looked at them with contempt and then burst out in laugher. Once again the radio cracked.

"Tiger two, this is Tiger one." Tompkins voice rang through their cab. "I'm sure our last mission was a once in a lifetime experience. I'm sure it can't happen again, over."

Tompkins looked at Bourque, who was giving him a mean stare. Tompkins' eyes met his. For a second they just glared at each other. As the tension reached its apex, the two men started laughing uncontrollably. Tompkins had to jerk the Jeep back on the road as his laughter brought tears to his eyes.

In the second Jeep, the three soldiers were not so enthused. They stewed at the thought of doing this again. Sitting back in his seat with his arms crossed, Draper broke the silence.

"I bet those two are just hoping something weird like this will happen again. The only thing at the Alamo I'm interested in, is to see if Pee Wee Herman's bicycle is really in the basement or not."

The other two men just looked at each other with confused looks, before they burst out in laughter.

The End

Breinigsville, PA USA
04 April 2011
259091BV00001B/1/P